Ruined in Blood

S.B. ELLIE

This is a work of fiction.

Names, characters, places, and events are products of the author's imagination. Any resemblance to real people, living or dead, is purely coincidental. Truth has no place here.

Ruined in Blood

Front Cover: AudiArt

Formatting: Refine and Format

There is no salvation here.

Only ruin dressed in devotion, blood binding bone, and Gods who do not forgive.
Step lightly, sinner.

And kneel before the altar.

You can pry the em dash from my cold, dead hands. *I regret nothing.*
(im_very_sorry — buffalo_farm)

<u>*For Brandon*</u> *– Thanks for chasing me through the woods... for research purposes, of course. This book belongs to you as much as it does me.*

For My Readers

This is a 'why choose' romance, where the female main character forms deep connections with more than one love interest.

Expect moments of intense emotional and physical connections between multiple partners, including M/M relationships.

Please read with an open mind, as this story embraces non-traditional relationships.

This book ends on a cliffhanger.

Brace yourself for what comes next.

Content Advisory:

Dub-Con/Manipulation
Birth Control Manipulation/Discussions of Pregnancy
Fated Mates (Non-Shifting) with Omegaverse dynamics
Dystopian Medical Practices
Graphic Violence/Gore
Substance/Drug Use
Cult Material/Religious Manipulation
Ritualistic Imagery (Animal Remains)
Death/Human Sacrifice

<u>Character Playlist</u>
<u>Sel</u>ene—Lovely (Lauren Babic, Seraphim)
<u>Luke</u>—Provider (Sleep Token)
<u>Jace</u>—Karma (AJR)
<u>Max</u>—The Death of Peace of Mind (Bad Omens)
<u>Eli</u>—Shadow (Livingston)
<u>Rhy</u>—Cult Leader (King Mala)

Prologue

The town circle has long since lost its luster. Weathered stone pillars stand off balance, as if they've surrendered to the weight of time. The wind carries the scent of smoke, rot, and old secrets, swirling around the gathering of women standing in quiet, nervous anticipation. The fire at the center flickers with an unnatural cold, casting sharp blue shadows against their still figures.

The High Priestess stands before them, a figure draped in flowing crimson robes. Her eyes are cold, her voice smooth like velvet, but with an edge sharp as a knife and as ancient as the bond curse itself. She raises her hand, and the murmurs of the male crowd fade into silence.

"This is the most sacred bond," she begins. "This is the law that has governed us since the world was torn apart. Tonight you will meet your fate, and your blood will unite with the one chosen for you."

Slowly, one by one, women come forward and drop their blood in the fire. Their mates advance, driven by the urge to claim now that they're revealed. The Ritual unfolds slowly, imminent and methodical. The High Priestess continues to chant, voice carrying across the night.

A young woman moves ahead, taking her place near the fire. With a resolute expression, she holds her hand out in front of her with her palm turned upward. With one quick motion, she cuts across the meaty part of her hand. Blood beads, dripping down her arm, and she holds it over the flames, dropping it in the fire.

It sizzles and cracks, hungry for the offerings being given freely.

The flames scream, dancing around the pit in wild, unpredictable shapes.

Nightmares in the night.

A tall figure moves from the crowd of men. He stands with his face hidden beneath his dark cloak, and when he reveals himself, his stare locks onto hers with the certainty of one who has been waiting for this moment his entire life.

He holds out his own bandaged hand and takes hers.

The bond is found and formed. There is no going back. The High Priestess continues steadily as the flame grows.

Another woman steps up, her face pale. She cuts her palm with shaking hands and her blood drips into the fire.

This time, however, it changes.

The fire erupts bright pink and, from the edge of the circle, three men emerge, drawn to her like moths to a flame. Their wild, unyielding eyes fix on hers. The crowd gasps, whispers filling the air.

The bond is meant for one. *Never* more.

But there they stand.

Three men.

The High Priestess's voice falters and she stops speaking, her focus on the fire. The flames shift again, wild and angry, and the air grows heavy with fear.

"This is *wrong*," she mutters, more to herself than anyone else. Her eyes harden and she raises her voice. "She is *supposed* to be sacred. She is *not* the one."

The woman, eyes wide with horror, backs away. Two of the men who have stepped forward hesitate but the last one moves in her direction. The guards are fast and forceful, pulling the trio back and yanking the woman away. The crowd parts, swallowing them up, murmuring as they're led off.

The flames flicker once again before dying back down to the soft, hazy blue glow.

The High Priestess clears her throat and eyes the gathering, speaking not of ceremony, but of something deeper, "*One will bear the mark of four, and she will tear the veil. One will call forth the dark, and so shall the world kneel.* The fire will choose her when it is *her* time."

The prophecy echoes in the silence.

"When she comes, we *will* know." Her voice drops so that only the priestesses around her can hear. "And *we* will own her soul until The Watcher comes for her."

The fire crackles, smoke rising in twisting patterns.

A woman steps into the empty spot, her hand quivering as she slashes her palm, letting the blood drip slowly into the flames.

1

I wake with a pounding headache, the remnants of the dream clinging to my mind. The vision had been strange and filled with the screams of a woman I've never met. It was unsettling to listen to her cry out for her mates, especially considering the laws of Middlesborough where people are only supposed to have *one* mate at a time. One *bond* that lasts a lifetime.

But in my dream, she'd had *three*. And they were all fighting to hold her, touch her, as she'd been pulled away from them. I shake my head, the dream fading as the morning light filters through the cracks in my small window. The unease lingers, gnawing at the edges of my mind. I can't shake the feeling that somehow, that woman... *those men...* have something to do with me.

But realistically, *nothing* like that has to do with me.

I glance around my bedroom as I sit up, taking it in for the last time. It's just big enough for my bed and a tiny dresser for my clothes. The walls are bare, my window is covered by a tattered scrap of fabric, and the floor is dusted with whatever I tracked in last night.

Like most of the families in Middlesborough, we don't have much, but we've got full bellies and a roof over our heads. The Master takes care of *all* of us who live in the commune. His family has been the one to guide us since the end of the old world for generations now. The collapse, so we've been told, happened because of the loss of faith. The big cities crumbled, the governments fell, and our ancestors were left with nothing but their survival instincts. That's when the sect communes rose, each one carving out a piece of the ruins for themselves, and Middlesborough was born from the ashes.

We've been taught that the bond–the one that ties you to your fated mate–has always existed, a force as old as time itself. Our ancestors had been bound, and we, their children, will be bound, too.

It chooses *you*. It chooses *them*.

And tonight, it will be chosen for me.

Isn't that just *wonderful*?

I run my fingers over the fabric of the thin blanket draped across my legs and let my thoughts drift to tonight. I'll step forward, just like every other girl who's turned twenty-two this year, cut my palm, and drop my blood into the fire. The same fire that'll awaken the bond that's laid dormant inside of me, marking the beginning of a life I *haven't* chosen.

The same fire from my dream.

The Elders have prepared for this day since we were *all* born. They've trained us to believe that it's a gift, that the bond is a blessing. But it's *hard* to see it as a blessing when you have no say in who your bond is with. I've seen women with bruises, broken bones, nearly beaten to death... all because of the men they've been bonded to.

The bond is inevitable, I know that much. It's *sacred*. It's chosen by God, and we have no choice but to follow. They say that it's the strongest force in the universe and, once it's formed, there's no breaking it.

It's why so many women die under the fists of their bonded mates.

I don't know who I'm meant to be bonded to. But, whoever it is... tonight, I'll be going home with them. And I'll never be the same again.

And *that*? That scares the shit out of me.

The morning passes in a blur of routine. My mother fusses over my dress, running her fingers over the carefully mended fabric as if she can smooth away my nerves. My father, ever quiet, gives me a small nod of approval before heading out to the fields with the other men. I help my mother with the washing, scrubbing clothes raw against the wooden washboard until my fingers ache. The scent of damp linen and sun-warmed earth fills the air and the sound of Middlesborough hums steadily around me–children's laughter, the rhythmic chopping of wood, the murmurs of prayer carried on the wind.

Everything feels normal. I don't know why it does.

It shouldn't.

Not today.

I spent the day in a fog, wishing I had paid more attention to the way my mother's voice lilts when she sings over the clatter of dishes and to my father's scent when he returns from a long day's work, of earthy, familiar *safety*.

But time moves forward, indifferent to my nostalgia.

I slip into the traditional ivory gown, soft and weightless against my skin. It clings to my hips, shifting like water with each step. Sleeveless, it bares my arms to the air around me, while the fabric pools at my feet, modest and elegant. Around my waist, a delicate woven belt of dried reed threaded with gold twine cinches the dress in places.

As the sun dips lower in the sky, the pressure in my chest grows heavier. My mother sets out a simple meal, but I barely eat, my stomach too tight with nerves. She knows–of *course* she does, she was once in my place–but she says nothing, only squeezes my hand in quiet reassurance. My father lingers by the door as the sky bleeds red and gold, his usual silence stretched thin between us. When I step toward him, he pulls me into a rare embrace, his grip firm but fleeting. I nearly burst into tears when my mother follows, pressing a kiss to my temple.

She whispers something soft that I don't catch.

Then it's time.

I fasten my crimson cloak at my collarbone and step out into the cool evening air. My pulse is hammering as I make my way toward the town center. The path is familiar–I've walked it a thousand times before. Tonight... it feels *ominous*. The streets are nearly empty, most of the commune already tucked away at home, leaving behind only the of-age un-bonded–those of us who still need our fates sealed.

I walk alone, as is tradition. After tonight, I'll no longer just be Selene.

The fire will take my blood. The bond will claim me, and by morning, I'll belong to someone else.

Oh, God.

As I get closer, I can see the flickering glow of torches illuminate the crowd gathered ahead. The hum of conversation drifts over the air, an undercurrent of excitement and tension buzzing around. My stomach clenches–I can't be the only one *not* excited for this, can I?

"Selene!"

Guess so.

I don't have time to brace myself when a whirlwind of energy slams into my side.

Lena, my slightly-insane, sort-of friend.

She clutches my hands, her eyes bright with anticipation. "I can't believe it's finally here," she whispers, pulling me towards the crowd of women. "Tonight, we'll see him. Our *mate*. Can you *imagine*?"

I force a smile, but it might be more of a grimace. "That's all I've been thinking about."

She shoves someone aside so that her and I are on the edge of the group. "Oh, I hope he's strong. A warrior, maybe. Or one of the junior advisors. I wouldn't mind being mated to power."

I don't answer. I don't know what I want. Maybe just someone who doesn't beat me would be nice.

Lena squeezes my hand. "You don't seem excited."

"I am," I lie. I'm really *not*.

She studies me for a moment before shrugging. "It doesn't really matter who they are. Once we see them, it's over. We'll belong to them, and they'll belong to us."

I look at her. "Yeah."

She doesn't notice my hesitation. "I hope he's strong," she continues, twisting a lock of her blonde hair around her finger. "And handsome. Oh, *God*, Selene, what if it's Jameson? Have you *seen* his arms?"

I snort. "You mean the ones he uses to carry sacks of grain? Yes, *very* impressive."

She giggles, but before she can say anything else, a hush spreads through the crowd. The High Priestess steps onto the raised stone dais with the younger priestesses and younglings standing around her feet in reverence.

She is breathtaking, especially as young as she is. I always expect someone older when I see her, someone with the burdens of wisdom etched into their features. She's smooth and porcelain, her golden hair folded into intricate braids. Her sapphire robes glitter under the fire-light, matching the crystalline clear of her eyes. She doesn't look entirely real standing there under the moonlight, holding a single scroll in her slender fingers.

When she raises her empty hand, the silence becomes absolute.

"The Joining Ceremony is more than tradition," she begins, her words deliberate, as if she's rehearsed it a thousand times. "It is a *privilege*, a gift from the ancient ones. For generations, we have upheld this ceremony. It's been a tradition passed down by our ancestors. The bond has always been a force of nature. It's always been wild and unpredictable," she pauses, letting the word sink in. "Through the powers blessed and bestowed onto Middlesborough, we've learned to control it. We discovered the secrets of the bond. Before then, it was chaos. There were mates discovered by fate, not by choice. People were often bound too early and too soon, before they could understand what it truly meant. But we, the chosen, the true stewards of this land, we have been given the knowledge to harness the bond."

She steps forward and lights the fire. As soon as it catches, she begins to chant, and it glows a soft blue hue that grows in intensity. It's *eerie*, a fire that glows entirely blue that stands taller than a fully grown man.

"And so," she steps back on her dais to stare at us women. "Through The Rituals, we now bind the bond until individuals reach the age of twenty-two, when they come of age for mating. Before then, the bond sleeps. It cannot awaken until the time is right. This is our most sacred of laws. You have waited and prepared. And now, it is your time. You will come forward and give your blood to the fire. Your bond will awaken, and there will be no turning back. You will become one with your mate."

For a moment, there is only the crackling of the fire, the soft rustling of the wind, the lingering sense of the ancient magic–something power-ful, *forbidden*–hanging in the air.

The High Priestess's lips curl into a knowing smile. "This is *our* way. And tonight, *you* are granted the knowledge. Tonight, *you* are awoken."

I try to focus as the first women start to step forward, but I'm trembling. I can't feel my fingers because of how tightly I'm gripping my cloak. I turn my face to look at the men and where they stand, wondering who I'm bonded to, my eyes skimming over them.

I land on Luke, our Master's son.

He's already looking at me, those green eyes locked onto mine and, for the briefest second, I forget how to breathe.

God, he's so handsome.

I wrench my gaze away.

The first girl is shaking as she extends her hand over the fire. She doesn't hesitate as she drags the knife over her palm. She squeezes her fist, forcing it to drip into the flame. It flares high, burning a vivid blue for a moment before settling back into its pale, mystic glow. The reaction is instant. She looks up as a man in the crowd steps forward. He walks towards her with certainty. His palm isn't wrapped at all which means he's older than her by at least a year. She doesn't look like she cares though.

He takes her hand and licks the blood away, and she gasps as he pulls her into his chest. *His mate.* They walk off together to who knows where to finalize the claim. Nobody stops them.

It's beautiful. It's *terrifying.*

It's kind of disgusting.

One by one, they step in line. Each un-bonded girl stepping forward, each offering her blood, each finding the man fate has chosen for her. The fire blazes, bonds awaken, The High Priestess hums in her low, rhythmic chant.

Unsettlingly like my dream.

This is real.

I can't *fucking* do this.

I can't.

The High Priestess looks at me, and I realize that it's my turn. I'm rooted to the spot, and the woman behind me nudges me forward. The crowd of men is still large, and there's a high chance my mate is standing there. I'm in front of the fire but there's no warmth pouring off it, just frigid air, like ice in the winter.

The High Priestess's voice is lost to me behind the steady rushing in my ears, the panic rising up in my throat. I reach for the knife. It's heavy in my palm, too heavy for something so small. I swallow and press the blade to my palm.

The cut is clean.

Stings.

It bleeds down my wrist in a single warm line, dripping onto a burning log. The fire pulses in response. The flames crackle as if they've been waiting for this moment.

For *me.*

I *feel* it before I see them. There's a tremor in my chest, *deep* inside of me, like a beast that's been trapped, pacing in its cage, finally being set free.

The bond.

It comes to life, a violent surge that shakes me to my core. It burns hotter than any fire, cold and molten all at once, a force that wraps itself around my soul, a chain that tightens itself around my lungs and heart, suffocating me, *claiming* me.

I gasp, pulling my hand to my chest as it *claws*, alive and angry. It's been waiting, hidden inside for this. For *tonight.* The raw power–*its hunger*–pulses in time with my racing heartbeat. But not *just* mine....

I can't breathe.

I look up.

I can feel him.

No. Oh, *hell* no.

Oh, God. It's worse.

Them.

Luke, his presence like a dark shadow falling over me, seeping into every inch of my skin. His eyes are on mine, fierce and expectant. His bond touches mine, reaching through my haze, plucking at it like a shiny new toy. And next to him, his best friend steps out–

Jace, the healer. His gaze is a mixture of gentle determination. He feels like the calm before a storm, but his bond is no less potent inside my soul. He's soothing me from the inside out, but then it's taken over by–

Across the group of men, Max, a well-known warrior, steps out. His presence is a force all on its own, fierce and commanding. He stands taller than the others, broader, *stronger*. And when I catch his dark brown eyes, it's like lightning sparking–*too much, too fast.*

And then Eli, an outsider. I know *nothing* about him and that scares me the most.

He lingers at the edge, almost unsure.... I can feel it across the bond, how much he wants to walk away, but it's undeniable–this pull.

They walk towards the fire, claiming their place across from me. I can feel them, distinct in my chest, bleeding over one another, each tightening in and locking into place. The fire roars as the bonds pulse between us. I don't know who owns me more.

It's. Too. Much.

And then, as I come down, I realize that we're standing in the town circle at the Joining Ceremony.

The silence is *deafening*.

Everyone stares at us. The fire is the only sound in the air. *I can't fucking breathe.* I can't think of anything other than the woman in my dream, dragged away from her mates.

The men across from me–*my bond mates*–are shaking themselves from the haze and looking between each other as if *they're* finally realizing that there's more than one of them. They look at The High Priestess, and back at me, confused, elated, *desperate*.

A woman bonded to four men.

I feel the tears in my eyes before they spill over. A sob breaks from me, and the bond panics as it feeds from my fear. Jace sees it and takes a step forward, raising his hand as if to comfort me, but I back away, clutching my bleeding hand to my chest.

It's too much like my dream.

It's instant, the pain on his face from my rejection. The ache in *my* chest from denying him. The bond begs me to accept this. Accept them. *Give in.*

I want to run. I *need* to run away.

I take another step back, but it's Max who stalks closer, his head tilted, pupils blown wide with a smirk on his face. It's menacing and terrifying, and I whimper. The crowd is murmuring, but it's not enough to drown out the roaring *horror* inside of me, or the second step forward Max takes.

And then, she *speaks*.

"Rejoice!" The High Priestess holds her hands up, voice ringing out like a bell, clear and commanding. "The Seraph has been chosen!" The words hang in the air for a moment before she continues. "She is the one spoken of in the prophecy! The woman who will bring about our rise, the very key to our survival! She will unite us with strength, with power, and we will outlast every other commune in the world! This bond between her, and her mates will solidify the foundation of our future!"

Seraph?

I didn't fucking ask for this.

'*RUNRUNmakethemchaseyouRUNRUNRUN*'

I turn on my heel and run without thinking, driven by the screaming in my head. My feet pound against the cracked pavement, my cloak flying behind me in a wave of red. I hear their calls behind me, the sound of my name on their lips. I hear the cheering of the crowd, their applause.

I feel the bond in my chest pulling taut.

'I hope they chase me.'

I hope they stay *right* where they are.

I don't know where I'm going, only that I need to get away. The cool night air stings my skin, but the heat in my chest burns, and all I can feel is the flame growing stronger with each step.

I watch as she runs away, and the bond in my chest flares with *refusal*. But deep down, I know it's not truly me she's rejecting–not yet. She's terrified.

I can't blame her for that.

Chase her.

Max takes another step forward, his expression bordering on unhinged, and I snap my head towards him. My patience is already thin, having to stand here for my sixth Joining Ceremony in a row with the potential for no results, and I don't want to deal with the thick-headed warrior tonight.

I don't even want to think about dealing with him for the rest of my life.

"Don't fucking take another step, Maximus," I warn, keeping my voice low. I'm aware that fighting in front of the others, especially now that The Priestess has told everyone that we're supposed to be a bonded group, would do us no favors.

He turns slowly, that cocky grin fading slightly.

"And what, you're the boss now?" He's challenging me. He must think because he's a year older that he can do that. Best to put a stop to that right now.

"Technically, yes." I cross my arms, a mixture of defiance and responsibility. "Seeing as how I'll be The Master of Middlesborough one day, that means I'll call the shots *now*."

Max doesn't look convinced, but before he can say anything else, Jace's hand is on my shoulder, pulling me back. The fire flickers lower as another woman steps up to take Selene's vacated place. I look back at Eli, who's avoiding us completely, and then up to The Priestess.

"What?" I snap at her. She's got that odd glint in her eye, her lips pressed into an amused smile. Her presence alone sends a strange chill down my spine, and I fight to roll my eyes. I wish she'd just tell me what the fuck she wants instead of staring at me like that. I walk over to her dais and she kneels down.

"When she runs, you *chase* her," she tells me before standing back up and beginning her bizarre chant again.

I'm about to retort but the words settle in my mind like a foreign language that I've somehow *always* known. My chest aches with the bond's insistence, and the pull becomes inescapable. I glance back at Max, who's standing rigid, hand tightening around the hilt of his sword. It's not just me who's been affected by the words.

The Priestess is murmuring her ritual words. It ghosts over us, curling over the bonds. I'm already moving, my feet taking me in Selene's direction. It's like a tether. I know *exactly* where she is.

Behind me, I can hear Jace's steady voice.

"Luke, wait. Let's think this through."

But the bond doesn't *want* to think.

The world is narrowing as I push forward. It's all-consuming. Every step, every *breath*.

It's a hunger that can't be sated.

I hear their footsteps behind me, and I glance over my shoulder. Max. Jace. Eli. My chest tightens at the thought of competition.

I spin on my heel, my voice low and dangerous, cutting through the air like a blade. "Stay. The. *Fuck*. Back."

They stop but the looks on their faces change from confusion to fear to compliance. Eli's eyes flicker with brief hesitation, but then he shrugs, his expression cold and distant. "Fine by me."

Jace, however, fights to take a step forward. "Luke, the hell? This *isn't* you. This–" He glances at the others. "–we need to stay together. This bond. We need to figure it out. We need to do right by Selene."

I want to rip into him, to tell him to *shut up*, which is strange, because he's been my best friend since we could crawl. I force myself to breathe.

Max, however, isn't as patient. He takes a single step forward and, for a brief moment, I wonder if we'll fight right here. But I hold my ground. He stops, face twisted with rage as he realizes he *can't* move any closer. Something inside me thrums with a firm satisfaction, telling me I'm doing the right thing, urging me to claim what's mine before anyone else can.

Not that they *can't*, only that I have to be first.

"I said **stay**," my voice warbles, *authoritative*, deep. I don't even sound like myself. "I'm not asking."

Max doesn't try to take another step, but the fury radiating off him is tangible. He glares at me, one hand wrapped around the handle of his sword, the other clenched at his side.

He's practically vibrating with anger. "You *don't* tell me what to do, Luke. *Never*. Not when it comes to my mate."

I meet his gaze, clenching my jaw. The primal need to chase, *to claim*, burns in my veins. Nothing will stop me from taking her. So I don't need to fight him. Not tonight.

But he and I haven't been friends in a long time. Sooner or later, it might come down to a fight.

"*Our* mate, Maximus," I remind him, my lips curling into a smirk. "Who I'm going to find. Right. Now."

I take a step closer, eyes wide.

"And claim. *Hard*."

I look over my shoulder, then back to Max.

"Against a tree."

And *trust me*, it's going to be one *hell* of a claim.

Max growls at me, eyes narrowing like a predator ready to strike. He doesn't need to speak. His anger is loud enough.

Jace looks between us, his face caught between concern and frustration.

"This doesn't feel right. We need to figure out how to handle this," he says, barely a whisper, like he's afraid I'm about to snap.

Maybe I am.

Eli stays quiet, his earlier indifference now replaced by something unreadable. As I glance back at him, he doesn't offer a word of protest. I don't know much about him other than he keeps to himself and does everything he's asked. He's never been one to argue with me—not in the way Jace does. I doubt this'll be the time he starts.

I turn away from them, my eyes scanning the path ahead, already feeling the bond guiding me towards her.

My mate, *Selene*.

It doesn't take long to find her in the wooded area. I hear her before I see her—the soft rustle of leaves, the quick, frantic rhythm of her footsteps, a heartbeat ahead of mine. The bond pulls me forward, so new it feels like a physical ache. I push through the underbrush, the cold night air biting at my skin, but I hardly feel it. All I can feel is her.

Why is she running from me? Doubt? Fear? Maybe her bond is telling her to run, just like mine says to chase. Maybe this is how I'll prove myself to her.

It doesn't matter. I'll come for her.

She's fast. I can hear her breathing—frantic, uneven—her desperation almost palpable. But *I'm* faster. Every step feels like slipping free of the chains that have bound me. Duty, responsibility, the voice of reason that's fighting to gain access at the front of my mind.

She's close.

I see her silhouette darting through the trees, weaving between trunks like a ghost and I push harder, my lungs burning with the effort. My feet move like they're being pulled by some force outside my control. The bond is loud now, roaring in my soul, overpowering everything else.

There she is.

I don't think, just react. My hand shoots out, grabbing a branch and swinging myself around, straight into her path. She stops just in time but her eyes, wide and panicked, meet mine.

"Stop running, Selene," I demand, low and urgent. She stumbles back, eyes darting around like she's looking for an escape. But there's nowhere left to go. I step closer and reach out, grasping her wrist. "I said **stop**."

She looks up at me, chest heaving. For a split second, I see the tiniest spark of defiance. *Good*. That's what I like. Her breath is ragged and I'm *feeding* off it. Now that we're close, the bond–it's suffocating, closing in around my heart.

This is inevitable. It always was. I know that now with the way I've been watching her the past few months. It had a purpose. Somehow, I knew she was the one even then.

I reach out with my free hand, fingers brushing against her jaw. It's enough to make her freeze.

"You think you can fight me, Selene?" The words come out like a growl. "You think you can win?" I step closer, our bodies pressing together. Her pulse beats wildly under my fingers wrapped around her wrist. It feels much like my own. "You're *mine*. It's in your blood. I can *feel* it."

She pulls away, but the bond flares in my chest violently, and my hand circles her neck, holding her in place. She's fighting, but I can see it–the moment she realizes she's already lost. I bend my head slightly, and the way she gasps against my lips only drives me crazier.

I know what I'm doing. I'm cementing the claim. It's permanent, irreplaceable.

This makes it *real*.

I press my lips against her ear, causing her to shiver. "Take it off," I breathe. The words are simple. A command. She doesn't hesitate. Her hands tremble as she releases the clasp of her cloak, and it slips away, revealing the soft curve of her shoulders, the delicate lines of her neck. I groan as the bond demands *more*. She slips her belt off and tosses it to the side as I start to work on my own clothes. It's surprising how fast we manage to disrobe, but I watch as she keeps her eyes lowered, her face blushing as she exposes herself to me.

But I'm looking at her and she's *stunning*.

The air crackles between us with desperate need. My fingers brush over her tawny skin, and she arches into it, pushing against me, and I can't hold back any longer. I press my body against hers, a shuddering sigh slipping from me as I feel every inch of her... warm and soft and *mine.* Her hands glide down my chest, down the trail of hair on my stomach, as if she's memorizing every muscle.

"Don't fight it," I rasp. "We won't have to fight it anymore."

It's effortless to push her onto her back, her cloak spreading out beneath us like a dark pool. Her thighs fall open instinctively, framing me as I settle between them, the heat of her body already burning into mine. I'm pressed against her, all hard lines and throbbing need, and I can taste it in the way our lips crash together–our tongues clash for dominance, how much it's meant to be.

I lean over, the full weight of my body on top of hers, relishing every inch of her skin pressed into mine. Her cloak bunches beneath her against the unforgiving ground, but we're both too lost to the feeling to adjust it. All I can focus on is the frantic pulse of the bond, coaxing us closer, until the space between us is nonexistent. Her breath hitches in my ear as I nip at her neck, shaky with anticipation. It's intoxicating, the way she quivers beneath me.

My hands roam–gripping, tugging, *desperate* to feel every part of her. Her legs shift, wrapping around my thighs, urging me closer. I get my hand between us to press against her clit, rubbing small, deliberate circles against her wet flesh, and she moans against my throat. I don't know if she's innocent or not. I don't particularly *care*–it's not like I waited for her, either.

She rolls her hips against my hand as she chases her pleasure, whispering my name against my collarbone with her nails digging grooves into my shoulder. My mind spins with the knowledge that I've got her here with *me*, that she's mine. I slip a finger inside her, using my thumb to keep a punishing pace.

"Selene," I whisper into her hair, moving my fingers against her. "Let go, *let go.*" Her body tenses, eyes squeezing shut, as I feel her body tightening around me. The way she moves drives me mad. With a throaty whine, her back arches and she climaxes, her body shuddering violently beneath mine. I hold her as she falls apart, feeling the tremors as she succumbs to her pleasure, the bond sings inside my chest.

I'm dangling by the thread of control as I move, my lips trailing over her jawline, down her throat, feeling every inch of her skin beneath me. Her scent fills my senses, pushing me to the edge. I pull away just enough to look at her–brown curls fanned out around her, face flushed, body a *perfect*, vibrating mess.

She's *everything* I've ever wanted, everything I *desire*. I can feel the straining need in my cock, the bond demanding I satiate the claim, to mark her as mine.

Her eyes flutter open, her gaze hazy, but there's a hunger in it that matches the fire that burns inside me. I suck my finger in my mouth, cleaning it off, savoring the essence.

"**Now**," I growl. Her hands glide over my chest, tracing the firm lines of muscle before slipping lower, fingers wrapping around my cock. Her breath catches and the sight of her like this, undone, stroking me slowly, sends a jolt of need down my spine. I moan despite myself.

I *can't* wait any longer.

Without giving her a moment to think, I grab her legs and spread them wide as I position myself between them. She whimpers at my sudden movements but her body knows where to go, following my cues. She's drenched and I–*fuck*. I rub the head of my cock against her pussy, coating myself in her arousal. I can *smell* how much she wants this, wants *me*. It's an intoxicating scent I want to smother myself in. I breathe it in like a dying man, as if it's the only thing keeping me alive.

I thrust into her hard, and the bond flares into life like an explosion between us. I hear her scream, but I don't stop. I *don't*. My hands find her hips, locking her in place as I move inside her, setting a brutal rhythm that has her crying out, nails biting into my back as if she's afraid to let go.

I'm not gentle. The need, the *want*, is too fierce. Her body moves with mine, her breath coming in throaty cries, each one pushing me to thrust deeper, *harder*, until I lose sense of time.

"Say my fucking name," I demand, my voice low as I increase my pace. She can barely catch her breath, tears streaming down her cheeks, but I see the way her lips part as she tries to speak.

Oh, little lamb.

"Lu-Luke," she breathes.

That's all it takes. Her body tightens around mine as our new bond hums with satisfaction. I lean down, my mouth finding hers, swallowing her cries. I reach down between us, my fingers desperate to find that small spot again. I want her to come with me inside her. I want to *feel* her clenching around my cock. She's soaked, the entire front of her mound damp with her slick, making it easy to locate her clit. I lean back up, keeping my eyes locked to hers, as I press down on it and set a rhythm. I can tell it's the *right* one when her mouth falls open and she cries out, throwing her head back against the leaves.

"Let me feel you come, little lamb. I want every last drop of you on this cock."

I slam inside her hard until she's coming undone beneath me once again, my thumb pressed tightly to her clit. Her body shakes violently, calves wrapped tightly to my thighs, as her second climax crashes through her.

I keep moving, because I'm *there*, and I *need* it–need her–just as much.

It builds low in my gut, the tingling that tells me I've reached my peak. I run my tongue along my lower lip, tasting what little taste of Selene is left there. I can't wait to bury my face between her thighs and worship her the way she deserves. Her hand comes up to my chest, nails raking over my nipple and I–

The world tilts, and I'm cresting with her. I collapse on top of her, rocking our hips together. I bury myself as deep as I can as my release catches. I jerk against her, my face pressed into her neck, whispering her name.

"*Fuck*, Selene...."

We're both panting, our bodies tangled together in the aftermath, bond sizzling but satisfied around us.

It locks together in a way that feels like I'll never be alone again.

I storm past them, rage simmering under my skin. The firelight from the ceremony is dying down but the town circle is vacant. The fire pit is dead, the blue flame extinguished, and I look around the empty space, feeling anything but calm. My vision is clouded with red. I shouldn't be walking away from her.

None of us should.

We *should* have chased her *together*.

No, *not* together.

First come, first serve.

No.

I fight the thoughts as they come, the bond warring with my feelings as though it doesn't care what I believe. I guess, in a way, it's true. I've always pictured myself with a meek woman, someone quiet and dainty. Someone who lets me use her after my battles. Someone I didn't have to *share*.

And *now*? Now all I can picture is Selene–and she's *all* I fucking want.

"And he thinks he can just do that!" I snarl, not for the first time, throwing a glare back at Jace. I've known him his whole damn life, being two years older than him and Luke, but even *that* didn't get me between her legs first. "He calls the shots like he owns us!"

He exhales like I've finally broken through his patience, rolling his shoulders as he passes me. "Max–"

"Don't *Max* me," I snap. "You think I don't have the same bond? You think I don't want to be the one chasing her down?"

He stops walking and turns to face me, keeping his voice steady. It's the one he uses to explain difficult medical proceedings to unwilling patients–I've seen him do it before in the infirmary. "I know you do."

My chest rises and falls in heavy, ragged breaths. I'm on edge, like the moment before a battle. "Then why the fuck are we standing here instead of running after her? Why can't we chase her, too?"

"Because Luke isn't thinking right now. He's acting on instinct," Jace says, but I can see it in the way his jaw clenches. He's feeling it, too. The bond, the *need*.

"You think we're not?" I scoff.

Jace sighs. "I didn't say that. I *do* think you're pissed because Luke gave you an order, and you don't like being told what to do."

My fists clench, my whole body thrumming with the undeniable rage of the bond not being satisfied. It *stings* deep inside where I can't reach it, like an itch I can't scratch. Her absence scrapes against my soul like a dull, serrated blade. I turn to face Eli, who's been trailing behind us, silent as a shadow.

"You got nothing to say, stray?" I bark at him.

Eli barely lifts his head in my direction. "You're *just* now realizing he's the one running the show? Figured you'd have caught on by now, Max," he deadpans. I huff, ready to tear into him, but Jace steps between us before I can snap back.

"We *all* feel the bond, Max," he says softly. "But we can't *all* lose our minds to it. Someone has to think. And Luke... he *is* going to be The Master. That's just something you're going to have to accept."

I let out a sharp breath, dragging a hand through my long, brown hair. The worst part? I know that Jace isn't wrong. I've taken orders from Luke before during battles. I've followed him into hell and back and never, *not once,* questioned him this severely.

Never *publicly.*

"This is bullshit," I say as I crack my neck. Jace seems to relax and gives me a weak smile.

"I know, man," he says. We start walking again with Eli trailing behind us, ever the ghost. I wouldn't even know he was back there if I didn't sneak a glance every so often. To be honest, I don't know why he hasn't split off already.

"You didn't seem too pissed off back there," I point out, but Jace doesn't rise to the bait. Typical, cool-headed prick. Maybe I should pick a fight with Eli instead....

"I get it, though. I've seen men driven by instincts."

"Then why aren't we? He's almost feral and here we are–" I gesture forward, "–walking home."

"I don't know." He looks thoughtful. "I wonder if it has to do with the multiple bonds."

"Fuckin' ridiculous," I spit as we pass by his house, but he makes no move to go inside. I look at the door curiously as we keep going.

"I've seen some of the girls he's been with. They're usually pretty bruised after."

Heat flares in my chest, my vision darkening at the edges. I stop walking, and Eli collides into my back with a curse. "*What?*"

Jace is quick to wave the comment off as if he's realizing his mistake. "He just likes it rough, Max. So do *you*. He wouldn't intentionally hurt her."

As if *that's* supposed to make me feel better. *It kind of does.* I wouldn't hurt her. Not the first time.

I shake him off, pacing two steps forward before whipping back around. "*Intentionally.*"

Jace's expression doesn't shift from that measured control he has, but at least Eli looks as shocked as I feel. As much as I don't like him, we're in agreement about our mate being returned in less-than-ideal conditions.

"He just likes it rough," Jace repeats, holding his hands up in mock surrender as he looks between me and Eli. "Not in a way that would–" He stops himself, grimacing, as he thinks back to the girls he's seen. "Fuck.... It's not... he's not gonna *hurt* her."

I *know* Luke. Raised in the same training grounds, I've fought beside him, stood at his fucking right hand during every battle the last six years. I know the cutting edge of his control, the way it balances on a blade's point.

I *know* how easily it slips.

My hands clench into fists at my sides, trembling.

"I'll check her over," Jace promises, his eyes filled with a worry I haven't seen yet. Eli lets out a sigh beside me. "If... she's okay, then you can have her tomorrow. Once she's rested."

"It would be better for her to choose," Eli mutters, voice laced with disdain.

I bark out a bitter laugh at that. "Yeah? She doesn't really have a choice in that, *stray*. I don't know where you came from, but here? This is how it works."

Eli tilts his head, sarcasm dripping from his words. "Oh, I don't make the rules, do I? So what... I'll do Tuesdays, then?"

Jace and I exchange a surprised glance, but it's him who laughs. He claps Eli on the back and throws an arm over his shoulder, chuckling. "Come on, man, let's go home."

I raise an eyebrow, crossing my arms over my chest. "Yeah? And where's home? We're a five-pack now, Jace."

Jace smirks, his tone light, and points towards the hill. "We're going straight to the top."

Eli goes pale, his eyes widening slightly as he follows Jace's hand. "W-we're going to live at Luke's?"

"Sure, why not? He's got the biggest house. Plus, The High Priestess says Selene's some kind of Seraph, whatever the hell that means. Either way, we're getting the nicest place."

I shrug. "Eh, I'm not complaining. Better than the barracks."

I'm not so sure what Selene being a 'Seraph' will mean for her, but as long as it doesn't interfere with her being in my bed, then I really don't give a shit.

Still, I drag my feet the entire way toward Luke's place. This isn't really where I was supposed to end up, but here we are, stepping into the lion's den. Jace is already ahead of us, grinning like an idiot. He's been here a hundred times, maybe more. He knows this house.

But I know this house, too.

I know its rooms–cold, stone walls. Concrete floors with thick, plush rugs to cover the icy chill that hovers. Luke's father–The Master keeps everything under lock and key. No surprises there, we're all 'precious' to him here in Middlesborough.

The door swings open before we reach it.

Standing there in the doorway, like he owns the entire world, is The Master. He's tall, broad-shouldered, and wears the same cold, calculating expression I've always seen on him. Luke looks just like him, a nearly-identical clone–it's almost terrifying.

I nod in acknowledgement. "Master."

"The High Priestess came and spoke to me," he says. His tone is low, but there's an unsettling gentleness to it, something I'm not used to from him. "I have your rooms ready for you."

I tilt my head to the side, unsure if I've heard him right. "Rooms?" I glance at Jace, then back at The Master.

He steps aside, and we follow him in. It feels like walking into a place that shouldn't be lived in–it always has. Tall, arching ceilings. Dark, dimly lit corners. Cracked, black-paned windows. The ghosts of the previous generations before us haunt these walls, and yet, here we are, still living in their bones.

We follow him down a poorly lit hallway, the silence suffocating. Eli's stiff, walking like he's ready to bolt at any second. I can practically feel the anxiety leaking off him in thick, seething waves. Jace and I exchange a nervous glance. The Master doesn't seem to notice–or care.

"As I understand it, you're bonded as one group now through Selene," he says, almost thoughtfully. "You'll be staying as one group. No splitting up. But you'll sleep separately."

I glance over at Jace, who's still in a relatively good mood. The look he gives me has an undercurrent of confusion, and I can read what his eyes say easily–*things are about to get complicated.*

Eli grows rigid, like he's trying to disappear into the walls, and slows down to fall behind us. Jace catches on, smirking, and wraps an arm around his shoulders, practically dragging him along. "Come on, brother. You're part of this." He pats Eli on the back like he's trying to ease some of the anxiety. Eli doesn't say anything, but he doesn't shrug

Jace off either. He just keeps walking, staring at The Master's back, looking like he wants to be anywhere else but here.

We reach one of the rooms, and The Master pushes the door open. I step inside first, Jace trailing behind me, still half-dragging Eli like he's forcing him to accept his new life. I absentmindedly wonder if he'll always be this dramatic.

The room is massive. The bed against the far wall looks like it could easily fit all five of us without any trouble, the frame imposing and regal. There's no real decor to speak of, just the bare essentials, making the space feel both sparse and practical. A long, worn out couch lines one side of the room, and two dressers stand untouched, their surfaces free of any clutter. A massive window stretches across the far side, with a built-in seat that invites someone to gaze out. Nearby, a half-stocked bookshelf leans against the wall. A desk is neatly arranged beside it, minimal clutter and a few sheets of paperwork scattered across the top, but nothing too chaotic.

Across the room, I take in the bathroom. Now, that's something else entirely. It's bigger than any room I had in the barracks, no question about it. A private toilet is tucked away behind a separate door, but the real marvel is the rest of it... a massive soaking tub that could easily fit two people comfortably. The walk-in shower is a statement in itself, with two shower heads, spacious enough to accommodate the entire group if we wanted.

It's an indulgence I can't help but appreciate, though I can't quite picture using it with the others.

As I take it all in, it hits me.

This is Luke's *personal* bedroom. The quiet signs of someone who prefers simplicity, perhaps even control, over excess.

I glance at Jace, then at Eli, after our brief tour. The Master stands by the door, hands on his hips, looking at us expectantly. We're barely settled in, on edge, and I realize that this–*this*–is going to be our new home permanently.

I start to understand Eli's apprehension.

"Where is my son and his mate?" The Master asks us.

His.

Jace bites his cheek and I can tell he's debating about how much to say. Is there a wrong answer here? "Well," he starts, "she kinda... ran off. So he chased after her."

The Master's face softens just a fraction, and his eyes flash with approval. "Good. That's as it should be," he says almost to himself before raising his voice. "Your rooms are next door. I'll have some more... fitting clothing delivered. You will take all your meals in the dining hall, and I expect decorum to be followed."

Not that I'm complaining about having my own private space, but why *are we being separated?*

"Master... Selene... will she be staying with–"

His focus hardens again as he fixes us with a firm look and my protest dies on my tongue. "Remember your place beneath my son. He is the head male in your *group*. Do *not* forget it."

The way he says it makes my stomach twist. No matter what happens, Luke's in charge.

"I expect the first child to be his or there will be consequences." He doesn't wait for a response, nodding at us in a clear dismissal. "Goodnight."

With that he's gone, slamming the door behind him. The three of us stand in Luke's room, rooted to the spot, with the implication of his words hanging in the air. Eli moves first, walking over to the couch and drops down onto it. He runs his hand over his face and sighs, long and heavy. Jace, still a *little* too comfortable in the chaos, walks over to the bed and flops down with his hands behind his head. He kicks his boots off and stretches his legs out, groaning as he does it.

"Luke has the best bed. I bet ours are shit," Jace grumbles as he settles against the pillows.

I stay standing, feeling like I need to do *something...* something other than relax and wait for them to return.

Because that's all we're doing, isn't it?

I unbuckle my sword and set it down carefully on top of the dresser closest to me, the click of the metal loud in the quiet of the room. I turn around and lean back against the hardwood, scanning the room without really seeing anything. I can't stand the silence, not after living with others for so long. Being picked up as a warrior at seventeen, I've been living in the barracks for eleven years now. It's always noisy–the sound of water running, men sparring for fun, idle chatter.

I can't stand it any longer. I need to speak, to stand guard, to pick a fight....

"So... he gets the first kid too?" I spit.

Jace leans his head up to look at me for a second before flopping back down. "I think that's a given."

It makes sense. He's The Master's son–the future Master himself–and his child will take his place. But his response grates on my nerves, no matter the logic behind it.

"Guess that's our life now, huh?" I ask. At my tone, Jace shifts on the bed, propping himself up on one elbow. "*Bowing* to Luke."

"I think you're being dramatic," Jace mutters with an eye roll. Eli hasn't moved from his position, his face buried in his hands, elbows on his knees.

"Am I? This is how it'll start, Jace. He wants a night with her, so we have to kneel. He wants a week with her, so we are pushed aside. What about when he wants a *year* with her... what do we do then?"

Eli looks up, as if he hadn't considered this. He looks wrecked and some twisted part inside of me is happy to see I'm not the only one torn up about it.

"Does it stop there?" I press on. "What if he forbids us from having *any* children with her?"

"He wouldn't do that," Jace says, but his expression is suddenly nervous. I press on, happy to pick at the wound.

"You'd know, right?" My voice is taunting, bordering cruel. "You're his best friend. Maybe he'll let you *share*."

"Lay off him, Max," Eli speaks up suddenly. I turn and look at him, happy for a new opponent.

"Yeah? What about *you*? Do you think *you* have any pull here? You, who we found *wandering* around and took in? A drain on our resources... that's all you've been."

"Max, stop being an asshole." Jace sits up fully now, holding up a hand. Eli closes his eyes, dropping his face back into his hands. I'm surprised at the drop of disappointment that runs through me. I was looking *forward* to a verbal sparring match with him. I was *finally* going to be able to test his mettle–Eli, known for his sarcasm and quick wit.

"It's true!" I throw my hands in the air. "Just walking around outside the gates and we take him in! He doesn't *do* anything!"

"That's not true and you *know* it. We take in those we conquer all the time. He's no different."

I look between Jace and Eli and roll my eyes. *What are they, secret besties now? Should I give them a minute to braid each other's hair and talk about their feelings? Luke will probably be jealous. He does adore Jace.*

"It *is* different. He's a *leech.*"

Jace looks at Eli. "Tell him."

"Why? So he can pick me apart?" Eli's voice is small.

"Tell him what you do for us," Jace presses, even as Eli shakes his head. There's something more, something I'm unaware of. Eli finally looks up at me, his brows pulled together.

"I'm... I scout. When I was found, I was only fourteen. The Master made me prove myself so that I could stay here. He'd send me into areas he doesn't want to send *your* warriors and I scout it out and report back."

Oh.

I feel my face falling as I process what he says. The threats he must have faced as a teenager, just to earn his bed. The things he *still* does.

Alone.

To keep me and my men safe. To keep Middlesborough protected.

Fuck.

As much as I hate to admit it, I can't help but respect him. The risks he takes, the things he's seen and done. He might be a sarcastic little shit, but that doesn't change the fact that scouting is a dangerous game.

He keeps talking, voice rising in intensity as he stands up. "I'm sent out when The Master needs someone to watch a rival sect. I watch them closely. I find out what makes them tick. I find their weaknesses. I report back, give that information to The Master and The Warden, and after that? I do *nothing*. I have no other purpose until my next mission."

He's on me now, only an inch shorter with his fists clenched at his sides. His entire body vibrates with barely contained rage. I've never seen him angry before, and it sends a chill down my spine. He would have made an *impressive* warrior, and I absentmindedly wonder if it's too late to train him in the way of the blade.

"I've *earned* my place here. Through *my* sweat. *My* blood. Through the lives *I've* taken. *I've* proven myself time and time again. And I'll be *damned* if I'm questioned by *you*, blade wielder."

The venom in his words makes my title sound like an insult as it leaves his mouth. I recoil as if he's physically struck me. His words sting more than I want to admit. It's a reminder of how easily power can be wielded in places like this, but also how *fast* my opinion of him shifted. Even as I try to not let the words affect me, I'm *bothered*.

He huffs, storming off to the bathroom and slamming the door behind him. Jace watches him go, eyes bright with amusement. He chuckles, rolling back onto the bed, and lets out a lazy sigh.

"Damn," he says. "You really get under his skin, don't you?" He looks at me as if he's just witnessed a magnificent show, but his tone drips with sarcasm. "This should be *fun*."

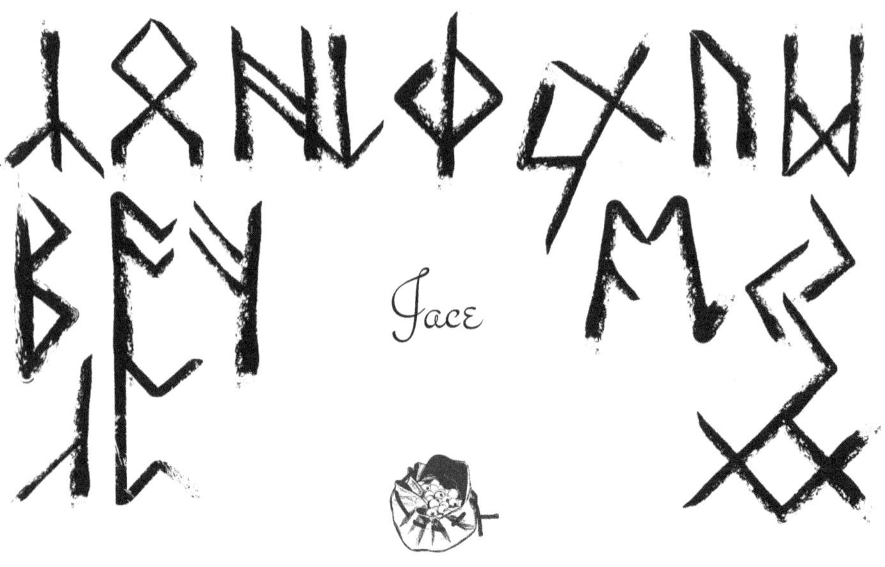

Jace

Eli's holed up in his room and Max has run off to find the kitchen, but here I am.

Wide awake, staring at the ceiling from my spot on the bed.

The bond in my chest aches intensely, reminding me that I have yet to stake my part of the claim. It's not painful, not quite. But it's *bordering*. It's made itself known behind my ribcage, a second heartbeat that pulses steadily with mine, reminding me that she's out there. She's mine. She's *real*.

Well, not just mine.

Ours.

I've spent so many years at the Joining Ceremony standing in the crowd with the other men, hoping for my mate to appear. Six long, *lonely* years. The only comfort was knowing Luke was right there with me, just as alone, year after year.

I never thought I'd have to *share* her.

But now that I am, it doesn't feel as strange as I imagined. It feels... *natural*... and I don't know how to take that.

I always imagined the bond would feel different. I've seen men driven borderline feral by it, consumed by the haze of some unconscious drive, unable to think beyond their own needs. I've treated their women, torn apart–utterly ruined–by mates who've lost themselves to jealousy and possession. I braced myself for that all-consuming, overwhelming desire, for something *dangerous*.

But all I've felt since I saw her standing behind that glowing blue flame, wrapped in a crimson cloak, is a relentless sense of *devotion*. Not obsession, not *totally*. Not hunger, not *exactly*. Just this deep, unshakable need to make sure she's safe. The kind of *protectiveness* that keeps me awake right now, waiting for them to return.

Even if that means facing Luke's wrath when he comes through that door.

I'm sure I could do what Eli did and sneak off to my own bed. I can force Max into his own room and let Luke have his time with Selene. It's not that I *don't* trust Luke. He's my best friend. It's not that I won't trust Max... well, Max is *Max*, he's reliable enough.

I keep staring at the ceiling, too wired to sleep, thoughts racing around the picture of bruised handprints on mocha skin.

I just need to check on her–that's all. Luke wouldn't hurt her.

Max wanders in eventually and, without a word to me, takes over the bathroom. I listen to the shower run for a while, wondering why he doesn't go to his *own* bathroom.

Probably the same reason I hold my lonely, pathetic vigil on Luke's comfortable bed.

It's late when they return.

The door swings open and Luke steps inside, carrying Selene in his arms like some kind of white knight. Her cloak is draped over her legs, her dress secured firmly over her body. I'm not fool enough to think they *weren't* intimate at some point tonight, but there's only a small amount of jealousy burning in my gut.

And not that he's had her, only that I didn't get to *share*. Strange.

She's completely out–fast asleep, her head tucked into his shoulder. I glance between them, taking in the picture they make. I can feel my bond with her, humming contently now that she's close, but beneath it, a new thread, something familiar and so *foreign*.

Luke?

I lean back against the headboard, arms crossed.

"So," I whisper, keeping my voice low to avoid waking her. "You back to normal or should I brace myself for more mate-crazed Luke?"

He glares at me as he kicks the door shut behind him. "Shut the fuck up, Jace."

I smirk. "That's a yes then."

He snorts quietly, pointedly ignoring me as he adjusts his grip on Selene. "You gonna help me, or are you just here to be an asshole?"

I climb off the bed, avoiding my boots as I slip off the side. "Why not both?"

Luke mutters something under his breath and I walk towards him. He stares down at her, jaw firm, and I give him a confused look.

Is he not going to hand her over after he demands my help?

After a second, he sighs and shoves her into my arms like he's glad to be rid of her. The moment she settles against me, the bond flares and I fight to keep myself rational. I tighten my hold without thinking as he shakes his arms out, most likely to get the blood flowing again. She's a full-grown woman, not exactly light, and if he carried her as far as I *think* he did, I can imagine the strain.

I *could* steal her away now. Luke couldn't stop me as fatigued as he is. I could slip out right now and hide her away from him. But I feel that string of him inside of me and I can't help but reach out to it, curious. My bond touches him, and it flares to life much like it did by the fire with Selene–a lifetime of friendship and love, built right there in my soul. His eyes fly to mine, wide and panicked.

"The *fuck* is that?" His hand flies to his chest.

"I don't know, man," I mutter honestly, looking down at her.

"Just...." He rubs a hand over his face. "She's exhausted. *I'm* exhausted. Put her to bed. We'll figure this shit out tomorrow."

I don't move. Instead, I shift my grip so that my fingers graze her wrist, and I press the delicate bones there with my index finger. I can feel her pulse and it's fast. Not enough to be concerned, not as a healer, but enough as her mate that my own heart rate jumps.

"I want to check her over," I say firmly.

Luke groans, rolling his head backwards. "Jace–"

"You've been out there for hours. You might not care, but I have to do this." I level him with a look that begs him to argue with me. He opens his mouth as if to retort, but snaps it shut and waves his hand off to the side dismissively.

"I *do* care, I just know she's fine. But whatever. Be a healer right now, if that's what helps you sleep tonight."

It *will* help me sleep. I carry her to the bed, easing her down carefully on her side. She hardly stirs when I push back her cloak, exposing the velvet fabric of her dress, the smooth lines of her throat. My fingers are delicate over her skin, checking for bruises, for anything out of place. She moans sleepily when my thumb runs over her bottom lip.

I ease up the hem of her dress, but she doesn't stir much other than to roll slightly on her back. Luke watches at the foot of the bed, arms crossed over his chest as I spread her thighs gently, just enough to check for signs of damage.

A frown tugs at my mouth. Her skin is flushed red in spots, irritation blooming across the soft skin of her inner thighs. My stomach clenches as I ghost over the beginning of a bruise, her fine hairs catching the dim light.

I glare up at him. "You could've been more careful."

Luke snorts, tapping his arm with his hand. "She's *fine*."

I lightly press my thumb down, hovering over one of the spots. She doesn't react, but I don't feel better. She's going to be tender tomorrow and *I'm* going to have to tell Max he can't take her until these bruises fade. I'm sure he'll take *that* well. "Still."

Luke rolls his eyes, exasperated. "Trust me, you'll figure it out soon enough." A slow, shit-eating grin spreads across his face. "Jace, finally getting his hands *dirty*."

I'm lifting her dress, just enough to check that he hasn't damaged her sensitive flesh, when he says it and my face grows hot. She's still a little swollen, her labia coated in a thin sheen of pink and clear fluids and a dark dusting of curly hair.

My mouth falls open as I stare at her, and I feel all the blood rushing south. I can't help running my thumb over her.

Oh. My. God.

"So original, Luke," I manage to choke out as I push inside her, just up to my first knuckle. It's so *warm* inside, still so *supple*–I withdraw. I hold it up as I lay her dress back down and show him the streaks.

"You either tore her enough that she bled or you were the first," I point out. He steps around the bed slowly, keeping his eyes on mine until he's right next to me. He grabs my hand and brings my thumb to his mouth.

"I aim to please," he says with a grin, sucking the digit in between his lips. I yank my hand free, wiping it against my shirt and look back down at her. I don't want him to see how my cheeks flare with heat, or how his words have affected me, but I think he does, because he chuckles behind me as he walks towards the bathroom.

I cover her with the blankets instead.

"She's not made of glass, Jace."

Maybe not. But that doesn't mean I'm going to stop taking care of her.

I climb into the bed, careful not to move her, and lean back against the headboard. She curls into my side, her face tucked into my hip, and I gently put an arm around her shoulder.

The bond curls contentedly in my chest. I sigh, letting my head fall back against the headboard and my eyes slip shut. I hear the shower start in the bathroom. I hear a door open and close and, for a second, I'm confused as to why Eli came back–

The movement on the bed startles me enough that I open my eyes again.

I blink the fog away and look around the room, trying to focus on what's causing the hairs on my arm to stand on end–until I see *him*.

Max is on the bed, crawling over her. He shoves my arm away.

The dusky light catches on the harsh angles of his face, his dark skin eerie in the shadows of the night, pupils blown wide with something darker than lust. His hands press into the mattress on either side of her hips, caging her in. Selene stirs beneath him, body tensing before she's even fully awake. Her breath hitches as she tries to push herself up, but Max doesn't back away.

"Max... *no*...." I warn, but he doesn't acknowledge me. His gaze stays locked on her, pressing down with his weight.

"Wake up, *wake up*, pretty prey," he mutters. "It's time."

She shrinks against me, her fingers curling into my shirt. "Time for what?" she asks in a small, shaking voice.

Max smirks, brushing a knuckle down her arm. "You *know* what."

That's *enough* of that.

"No," I say, louder this time. I adjust my body to try and shield her, wrapping my arm back around her shoulder and pulling her further against me. "She's exhausted. She's not doing this right now."

Max finally blinks, his sneer slipping as he drags his eyes from her to me as if he's just now realizing I'm here. "It's part of the bond, Jace. You feel it too! She's *ours*. I'll even let you have her *with* me if you just get *out* of my way."

I grit my teeth, my hands tightening on her elbow. "She's *not* ready. Not after what Luke did."

A tense silence stretches between us. Max's jaw tics, his body coiled over hers, unwilling to retreat. Here, in the shadow of Luke's bedroom, a battle of wills.

But I'm *just* a healer and he's the warrior. I've never been a fighter– but I'd do it for her.

Selene's heart races against my side. I can feel it through her ribs as her nails start to dig into my stomach.

"**Move**," I put everything I've got into the word. Warning. Rage. *Command*. Something deep, *guttural*, from my chest–*from my ancestors*–comes out and Selene whimpers.

Max holds my eyes for a second longer before huffing out a low, muffled curse. He pushes off the bed, going to his knees, mumbling under his breath. He doesn't *leave,* but he does back off, rolling on my other side away from her, running a hand through his hair as he does it. Selene is stiff against me, her chest rising and falling in small, shallow breaths as she struggles to calm herself. I glance down at her, lowering my voice.

"Are you okay?"

She doesn't answer. Just nods, small and stiff.

I level a glare at Max, my voice like steel. "Next time, *ask*."

He doesn't look at me. Doesn't apologize. Just falls to one of the open pillows, his back towards us.

I don't care. I keep my arms around Selene, holding her steady, because I won't let this happen again.

Not to her.

Not when I've seen so many other women torn apart by the men who were supposed to care for them.

She turns her face up to look at me, blue eyes shimmering with unshed tears, and she lets out a breath.

"Thank you."

I lean forward and press my lips to her forehead... because if I did anything else, I'd lose control.

I'm not the first one awake, which throws me off. My father drilled the 'rise before the sun' mindset into me since I could walk, and I've followed it religiously... until today. When my eyes open, I'm tangled up in the mess of my new reality.

Why the hell are we having a sleepover in my *room?*

Selene's body is pressed against mine, her back to my chest with her steady breath one of the only sounds in the quiet of the morning. What catches my attention is how Jace is positioned with his head resting against hers, his hand across her thigh. Max is sprawled out on the other side of my bed, his chest flat against the mattress, snoring like a damn bear. The sounds of him are oddly comforting, even though the air in the room is thicker than it should be.

It's *strange*, the feelings I have in my chest. The bonds existing there.

Bonds. I feel it now–the pull of Selene, that iron tether that connects me to her. But it's not *just* her. Right beside it is a smaller string, a quieter channel in my chest, pulling me to Jace. I don't know what it means but I *know* it wasn't there before. I could feel it last night when I was in the shower, the connection between us ever present in my mind like a distant whisper.

I should probably ask The High Priestess about it. She's the only one who might know why I've got two bonds now... but something holds me back. A deep gut instinct that says telling her would be the worst mistake I could make. Ignoring the nagging curiosity, I look around for the last member of our odd little group, because if everyone else is here, why *wouldn't* Eli be lurking nearby?

I sit up slowly, careful not to wake anyone else. The floor is cold beneath my feet, a reminder that nothing in this place has ever been warm enough to feel like a home. It's all cold stone and frail wooden beams, all jagged corners and cobwebs and dusty rugs. Tall bookshelves filled with texts I wasn't allowed to read for the longest time, rooms I couldn't visit, a basement I was forbidden from going down into....

As I step into the bathroom, I catch a glimpse of myself in the mirror. I'm not surprised by what I see–it's me, still Luke. But it's *not*, is it? Dirty blonde hair, green eyes, freckled skin–random muscles built through years of hard work and the occasional lean season. The man I've always been is still there but there's something new inside him. Something awake and restless. Someone who has a whole new meaning of responsibility.

I look away and see Eli.

He stands inside the shower with the water off and looks at me expectantly through the glass.

"*What*?" he asks me, already annoyed.

"Just... checking in on you, " I reply carefully, although I'm not sure why. He grabs a towel from the bar and wraps it around his waist with one fluid motion. His eyes don't leave mine, studying me as if I'm the one who needs to explain myself.

"Or checking me out?" His words drip with sarcasm, and *damn*, I had no idea he was this cocky.

"*Hardly*." I roll my eyes. "I thought you stayed in your own room last night?"

"And miss out on this shower?" He gestures around him and I consider the stall. I know it's a great shower, so I can't exactly fault him. The rooms given to them aren't the *worst*, but they aren't the greatest either. They've got beds, attached bathrooms that function, but they're bare minimum for guests that stay here. I turn my back on him and walk to the door.

"Hurry up," I throw over my shoulder. "I'm about to wake the others so we can head down for breakfast."

"In *what*?" he calls back, gesturing to the towel, and I pause.

He's not wrong. Bonded couples usually head back to the male's residence after the Joining Ceremony and that's where they'd stay from that point on.

But we'd all come to mine. All of us.

I hadn't evaluated it but when I think about it, I'm not entirely surprised either. It makes sense, considering everything. We're expected to stick together now and my house is the biggest. Hell, I don't even *know* where Eli lives and Max has been in the barracks for years. Jace's place is too small for all of us, and since I'm The Master's son—of course, I'm the one expected to host.

Jace is awake when I return and he's trying to wake Selene with a gentle kiss to her forehead. I watch for a moment, my stomach tightening at the sight. It's part jealousy, part adoration. It'll take some time to get used to this, but I can already see some silver linings to this whole multiple mate bond thing.

When Max and I are out on missions, she'll be well cared for at home by Eli and Jace. She'll always have someone here to protect her.

And I won't have to sacrifice any of my duties to keep her safe—not that I wouldn't in a heartbeat. Anything to be rid of my role in life would be a gift I'd happily accept.

I walk over to the bed and slap Max on the calf, hard enough to make him grunt. He stirs, but he doesn't wake so I do it again, this time with more force.

"Get up, warrior," I mumble, punching his foot. He grumbles under his breath and rolls to his back with a disgruntled sigh. His eyes flicker open, and he shoots me a half-hearted glare, holding a hand up to his eyes to block out the morning light.

"Fuck *off*, Lucas," he groans, but sits up anyway, rubbing his face.

"Breakfast," I say, turning towards the door. "We've got shit to do."

Namely, I've got to get Eli something to wear.

Max stretches, yawning like he's about to go back to sleep, but when he sees Selene tucked against Jace, hair messy and eyes still closed, he pauses. A look of regret crosses his face, and I briefly wonder what that's about before I refocus on the task at hand.

Right. Clothes. Selene will need them, too. Her dress is still smudged in dirt....

"Come on, Max," I urge, glancing at Jace while he runs his hand through Selene's hair. "We have *literally* no time for that. She can sleep later."

Jace sighs heavily, as if *I'm* the one inconveniencing him, but he doesn't move. He just stares at her like she's the only thing worth looking at in this damn room.

I can't blame him. I feel the same way. I'd let her sleep all day if she wanted.

Before I can say anything else, there's a knock at the door.

I freeze, turning slowly toward the sound. Eli emerges from the bathroom still in just a towel, his black hair damp and hanging in messy strands around his gray eyes. He leans against the doorframe casually, but I can read his cautious, guarded gaze.

"Now, *who* could that be?" he asks, raising a mocking brow at me. I don't answer, moving towards the door, and unlocking it.

When it swings open, a woman stands in the hallway, her head bowed, eyes trained carefully on the floor in a show of respect. She's holding a pile of freshly folded clothes, a set for each of us.

"Sir Luke," she says softly. "The Master has requested that you and your group join him for a late breakfast at your earliest convenience."

She doesn't wait for permission, stepping forward to hand me the clothes. I take them without a word, folding them over my arm and waiting for her to leave. But she remains in place, eyes down, every inch of her posture radiating the quiet obedience my father commands from his working girls.

"Is there a specific time for breakfast?" I ask.

"Whenever you are ready, Sir Luke," she answers. "The Master will be expecting you shortly."

With that, she bows her head, steps back, and walks away. I shut the door behind her and re-engage the lock.

"That solves that problem." I hold up my arms at Eli, who just scoffs as I toss the clothes on the bed. Jace and Max sit up to watch me pull the pile apart, sorting them into who they belong to.

Mine are easy—soft brown jacket, dark pants, and a black shirt, all obviously from my laundry. Jace's are a bit different, the green tunic of the Healers, black pants, and a white shirt. Max's are a size bigger than the rest, and I toss him the dark red fabric without looking. Eli walks over, holding the towel at his waist, and grabs his black pants and shirt. I hold Selene's dark blue dress in my hands a moment longer as she stirs.

A drop of guilt bleeds into the bond—*I must have really worn her down, damn*—and I toss the dress to Jace.

"Get her dressed," I say, turning away to pull last night's shirt off, tossing it to the floor. "We shouldn't keep my father waiting."

The walk to the dining hall is silent, save for the scuffing of our shoes against the stone floor. Selene stays between Jace and me with Max a step ahead and Eli trailing behind. She moves stiffly beside me, keeping her steps small. I don't have to ask why. I can feel her discomfort through our bond. She's sore. I fight the urge to slow my pace for her. We're already late and he's going to be pissed.

The hall is nearly empty when we step inside. A few attendants linger at the edges, eyes down, hands clasped at their waists. The table is already set with thick cuts of meat, slices of cheese, various vegetables and hard-boiled eggs, cracked just enough to peel. Efficient. Practical. No excess. At the head of the table sits my father.

The Master.

Can't read his damn face as we get closer... *typical.*

"You're late." His tone sets me on edge. Is he furious? Is he *fine*? I never know which it is with him, but I can take a wild guess. I'm almost *always* right.

I pull out a chair for Selene before taking my seat beside her. "My apologies, Master." *Never* father, not to his face. I meet his eyes, keeping my tone respectful. "It won't happen again."

He hums thoughtfully, nodding as he gestures to the food. "Eat."

Jace is the first to move, pouring a cup of water and pressing it into Selene's hand before filling his own. Max takes a seat, immediately reaching for the meat. Across from me, Eli sits and leans back in his chair, plucking a square of cheese from the platter like he'd rather be anywhere else.

To be honest, so would *I*.

Selene falters. When she reaches for the bread across the table, I see it–the slight wince, the way she shifts in her chair to ease the strain. The Master notices too. His gaze lingers on her a second too long before returning to me, a small smile tugging at the corner of his mouth.

"It seems your Joining Ceremony was thorough."

Heat rises to my neck and I force my face to stay blank. Jace knows what I have to do, but I can only *pray* the others pick up on it. "It was... as it should be."

He chuckles, waggling his eyebrows at me before taking a sip from his cup. "*Good*. Good."

Every conversation with him is a careful game. The Master doesn't just listen... he measures, he searches for cracks. Every word is a test. Every hesitation is a weakness to exploit. He's never been *just* a father, not even when my mother was still alive. He's always been this... and it's why I've always hated it here.

We eat in silence, only punctuated by the clinking of metal against the ceramic of our plates. Selene keeps fidgeting next to me, nibbling on her food. The bond aches with *shame*, with pain. Enough so that I want to wrap her in my arms and take her back to our room. I look over her head and catch Jace's eyes and see that he feels much the same as I do.

So these joint bonds have *several* uses it seems....

"Tell me, Seraph," The Master starts, and my head snaps up. "When did you last bleed?"

We all pause at the question. It's *personal*, to her and now to us as her mates. She swallows hard, looking at me first as if I can save her then back to her lap when she realizes that I *can't*.

I'm sorry, little lamb.

"A-a-a week ago," she stutters quietly. I want to *crawl* over the table and strangle my father. The only thing that stops me are the two guards posted in the doorway behind him.

With a pleased smile, my father raises his cup. "Then let us toast to a swift conception."

The blood in my veins turns to ice as her lip quivers with his words.

Next to Selene, Jace's fork slips from his fingers, clattering loudly against his plate. He doesn't move to pick it up. Max goes rigid, his knuckles white against the edge of the table. He stays silent, but I can practically hear his teeth grinding against one another with how tightly his jaw is clenching. Eli doesn't react at all outwardly. His eyes remain fixed on his plate, shoulders loose, posture indifferent. But I'm starting to read him, even with only a single day spent together. That stillness is defensive.

He takes his bottom lip between his teeth, rolling it slowly, biting down hard enough I see a bead of blood drip down his chin.

I inhale deeply, my hand finding hers under the table, squeezing it. She tightens her fingers in mine.

"It would be *wise*," he continues, "for you to forbid the others from touching her again until she carries your child."

He assumes that we *all* took her last night.

A bold assumption. Bastard.

Max makes a sudden, stilted move across the table like he's about to stand and throw his plate at my father's head, but he *barely* catches himself. His nostrils flare, and his grip tightens around the hilt of his sword. I wish he'd plunge it into my father's neck, honestly, and do us *all* a favor.

Eli *finally* moves, just the slightest tilt of his chin in my direction, eyes begging me for action. I ignore him as I force myself to meet my father's gaze.

"Of course," I say smoothly, lifting my own cup with my free hand. "What could be more important than securing our future?"

The Master smiles, pleased, and drinks deeply. Max's lower lip shakes as he looks down at his plate to hide the rage. Eli reaches forward and lifts his cup, but his eyes are narrowed on me. Selene stays very still, but her hand shakes in mine.

The Master sets his cup down and dabs his mouth with a napkin. "*Now*, this is the perfect opportunity to discuss your new roles in our society."

Selene subtly adjusts beside me. I want to put an arm around her, to shield her from this. She's still reeling from being humiliated by my father, but she says nothing, keeping herself invisible. *Smart girl.*

"My son," he gestures to me, "is already training to take my place when the time comes. The Seraph will train with The High Priestess for her new role starting tomorrow. It is vital that the other...." he pauses, and I see a flash of distaste cross his face, "bond's *mates*... prove just as valuable to our society."

I see Max's temper reach its end as Jace turns to face my father. Eli schools his face into a mask of neutrality while he licks his bottom lip every few moments, soothing away the bites.

"Max." The Master clears his throat. "You'll begin your training directly under The Warden today. When the time comes, you'll take his place and lead our armies."

Max meets his look head-on. He doesn't bow, doesn't nod, just stares with his jaw clenched so hard I can see the veins in his neck straining. The Master either doesn't notice or doesn't care. Probably the latter, knowing my father.

"Jace." His attention shifts. "You'll begin training under Vitalis to assume leadership of the Healers." Jace nods stiffly in return, and The Master leans back in his chair, pressing his fingers into an arch in front of his chest. "This is an honor. You should all be *grateful.*"

Max slams his fists down on the table before shoving himself away. My father watches him go, an amused gleam in his eyes.

"*Grateful,*" he repeats as Max storms out the door.

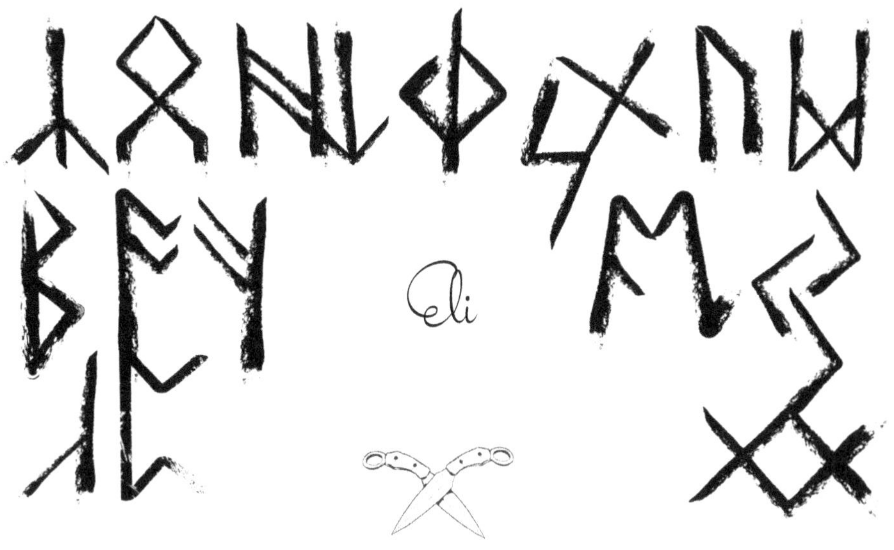

The scrape of Max's chair echoes long after he's gone. Selene's frozen between Luke and Jace, her food left untouched, chin tucked to her chest. Jace pokes at his food, but I can tell his appetite is long gone while Luke remains cold and composed, facing his father at the head of the table.

I can see his arm in Selene's lap, and I'm glad she has his support. I'm fighting against sending her comfort through our bond.

It's better if she doesn't get it from me, to be honest. The more distance from me she has, the better.

I keep my head down, focused on my plate even though I have no intention of finishing what's there. Drawing attention to myself is the last thing I want, but this breakfast has gone on too long already and I–

I can *feel* what's coming before The Master even speaks.

"Oh yes," he muses, dabbing at the corner of his mouth again with his napkin. He tosses it to his plate. "*Eli*. We can't forget about you, can we?"

We could... I wouldn't mind in the slightest.

I force my demeanor into something passive as I glance up. I've had years of practice looking this man in the face doing *just* this. His eyes are assessing me, just as they always do, like he's still deciding what I am, what I'm capable of.

They'll find nothing.

"You've proven yourself to be... useful." He pauses, tilting his head, "So why stop now? I'm creating a role for you. *Sentinel.* A silent watchman. You'll begin training new scouts that answer to you, ensuring we always have eyes where we need them most."

I nod once, the only acceptable response, even as my stomach threatens to expel the meager breakfast I've eaten.

"Understood, Master."

He smiles at me but there's no warmth in it. "Good. Lucas, our meeting?"

He stands, signaling the end of the meal. Just like that, we're done. The conversation is over. His decisions are made. And my status as an outsider is done, just like that. I'm now remade into something else entirely.

Fuck.

The Master turns without another word, his robes sweeping behind him as he strides out of the hall. The silence he leaves behind is dense, and I'm not sure there's anything left to say. The guards leave with him, as does most of the staff. Only two remain behind and begin to clean up the empty plates.

"This is a good thing." Luke's eyes are looking from me to the girls picking at the food left behind and, biting at my tender lower lip, I nod along. I can read his face easily enough to know *why* he said what he said, even though it grated my nerves.

"Of course, *sir.*" The word is bitter, but there are tattling tongues nearby. "Whatever you think is best for us."

Jace pushes his fork through the remnants of his meal, his lips curled. After a moment, he mutters, "I need air," and stands abruptly, his chair dragging against the floor as he moves it back to leave.

Max is long gone.

I should be next but my legs feel heavy.

Luke runs a hand through his hair before straightening, looking back at me. He's asking me to play along when he says, "Stay with Selene until I'm done this morning."

It's not a command, not *really*, but he knows I don't have anywhere else to be.

My stomach clenches in anxious knots but I nod as if I don't feel the blood draining from my face. "As you wish."

Selene looks up at him as he stands. She doesn't ask him where he's going. She knows he's got responsibilities, the same as Max and Jace do.

That leaves me on Selene babysitting duty.

Me. *Alone* with her.

He *knows* what he's setting up, right? Freshly bonded, with our claim still unsettled....

I force myself to breathe evenly as I watch him bend at the waist and press a kiss to her temple before he pulls back and winks at me.

Yeah... he does. He knows *exactly* what he's doing.

Mother*fucker*.

He's disobeying his father's commands almost directly by leaving her in my care. He knows what's going to happen....

He walks out.

My fingers twitch at my sides, gripping my pants to avoid climbing over the table and mounting her right here on the vegetable tray.

I can't have her.

I *won't*.

This version of the bond is a trick of the mind, *an instinct shaped into something unnatural*, I remind myself. My people's bonds–real, *true* bonds–are sacred. They come with time, with choice. They weren't yanked from our veins generations ago in some Ritual that stole our souls from one another before we even had a say. They weren't forged in fire and blood.

Real bonds? They're *ancient*. They mean everything to my people and they've been *bastardized* by The Master and his witches.

But this foreign bond doesn't care what I think or what I need to do. It prickles under my skin, stretching to her, testing the space between us. My pulse kicks up, heat curling in my gut and I have to force myself to look away before I do something stupid.

Like reach for her.

Like *beg* for her.

Let myself want her.

Look at her.

"Get. **Out**," I command. The two servants remaining in the room scatter and I lock eyes with her across the table. Something snaps inside me. Her breath catches, lips parted with her lower lip trembling like she's fighting tears. She looks wrecked–but I know, deep down, I *know* how to fix it. And damn it, I *have* to.

I just *do*.

I stand abruptly as if I've no longer got control over my own limbs, pulled like a puppet on warped strings. My chest constricts, pulse racing with the tug of the bond impossibly tight. Each step towards her is like I'm walking to my own death, but I can't stop. I can feel how bad she wants this–wants *me*.

When I finally reach her, I don't say anything. I don't need to. There's an electric need crackling between us whispering directly in my blood. I see the way her eyes darken, the subtle lift and fall of her chest matching each silent, tortured beat.

I'm *so* close to losing it.

I reach for her neck, my fingers brushing her skin, the beat beneath my touch like a drum. I don't even *try* to resist when my lips meet hers. It *sears* through me, making everything else blur until it's just the heat of her mouth, the way her body quivers beneath mine. I feel the raw, desperate need that's been clawing at me since last night since I first felt her bloom in my soul.

I can't think. *I can't fucking breathe.*

In one swift motion, I have her thrown over my shoulder. She gasps, her small fists beating at my back in shock when I start walking from the room.

"What the *hell*?!" she snaps, wiggling against my grip. She's *trying* to get away. That's *normal*, even expected in my people. It's refreshing to watch her squirm. The bond doesn't give me the choice to let her go for a chase, though, even though I think I'd like her to run.

It's consuming my senses and I can't escape my instincts.

"Eli! Put me down!" She's nearly shouting now, but I'm relishing in her resistance. Watching woman after woman cut their hand and drip blood into the fire last year and blindly accept fate had been terrifying. There's supposed to be a fight before the claim.

You're supposed to *earn* it.

"Not happening, princess," I mutter, fighting to control myself from taking her here in the hallway. My hands are gripping her thighs tightly. I can feel her confusion—her urge to resist—but there's something else there, too. The bond is *sick* with it, the desire for her to give in, to roll over and let me claim her. It's weaving its poison through our minds and begging me to claim her, to own her in ways I can't explain.

Fuck.

I make it to Luke's door.

Why Luke's door? Why am I here?

She squirms against my grip, trying to free herself again. I don't let her, shutting the door behind us.

Safety. Home. *Nest.*

"Stop fighting me," I growl, the command slipping out before I can stop it. She slows, relaxing at my order, her breath hot on my neck.

"Eli?" A mixture of fear, anger, and confusion. It burns between us. I'm lost, too.

I had no choice but to complete The Ritual when I arrived, The Master's demand before he'd let me stay. It was *days* of agony, terror and suffering and I was only fourteen at the time. My bond was deep inside me, burning and thrashing, begging to stay free. I had to force it down and, when I did, it grew *quiet*. It lived inside me in the cage, angry, but silent.

It's weak, and it's *furious* with me now that it's free.

I set her down but I don't let her go, holding her body to mine.

"I know you want to run," I whisper, watching her eyes flicker with panic. I can see it now, the instincts trying to kick in. "You're programmed to run, aren't you? My good girl. I shouldn't complete the bond." I run a hand across her cheek and grip the back of her hair. "But I think it's too late for that, princess."

Her eyes widen, and she tries to take a step back. My hand tightens in her hair and on her waist, pulling her back to me. She whimpers.

"Don't." My voice drops to a growl. "Don't back away from me."

She puts her hands on my chest, pushing at me, but I can't let her go. I walk us over to the bed, and she huffs, frustration and fear flashing in her eyes. She doesn't get to run, but I'll let her fight me.

That'll make it better.

I throw her on the bed, her body bouncing when she lands. She makes a quick, breathy sound, ready to crawl away, but I'm already on top of her, straddling her waist and pinning her in place. I don't give her a chance to pull away. I can feel how close our bond is now, how it vibrates with joy.

"Do you know what you're doing to me, princess?" I've lost it. I *know* I've lost it. "You're *mine* right now. And there's *nothing* you can do to change that."

She stops wiggling, her hair fanned out against the pillow, chest heaving, and tilts her head back to expose her throat to me.

"You'll complete the claim with me, Selene."

I drag a hand over her throat, down the curve of her chest, working loose the buttons one by one. Slow, *deliberate.*

I *could* tear it apart, rip it off her body like the animal that I am.

But I don't.

No, I want it to last. I want to feel every tremor of anticipation that wracks her body beneath my touch.

Her breath stutters as her dress parts, slipping from her shoulders, baring her inch by delicious inch. And then, *finally,* her breasts spill free, nipples tightening against the cold. She squeezes her eyes shut like she can pretend she isn't trembling with something that isn't fear.

I can tell. The bond doesn't lie. She wants this.

"You don't have to be scared, princess." I keep my voice soft but no less commanding. My thumb drags over her breast. "Tell me you want this."

Her lashes flutter. She's still fighting–herself, me, the inevitable pull that is *us.* But I see it falter. I see her let go enough to nod. Her lips part, and that's all the invitation I need. I crash my mouth down on hers. She tastes like my dreams, *intoxicating,* and, when I lick her lip, she lets out the neediest sound.

The claim is crafting the chain between us, link by link. It's too late to pull away.

It's *been* too late to pull away, since the fire ignited in pink flames last night.

"It's okay," I murmur, dragging my lips along her jaw, down her throat, tracing my tongue along her skin. "I know you have to fight. I know I have to *earn* this."

I pull back enough to catch her stare. She looks confused, as if she doesn't know *how* I know what she's thinking. But I understand this ancient dance far better than she ever could.

"Go on, then."

And she does.

She darts forward and bites down on my lower lip, hard enough to reopen the wounds.

A growl rumbles from my chest. I swipe my tongue across my lip, tasting copper and iron, and I'm done for.

Her bond wants her to run.

No.

Her body wants her to *obey,* and I bend down, dragging my tongue over her jaw, scraping the delicate skin of her throat enough to make her feel a fraction of what wars inside of me.

"It's there, isn't it?" I kiss her pulse point, coat it in my blood and she whines, arching into me. "The instincts buried inside you. You can feel them, can't you?"

Her hands are on my hips, tightening in my shirt.

"They hid the bonds. Made them tame. But that's not what you are, princess. You were meant to fight."

A ragged breath leaves her lips. "*Yes.*"

I slide my hand up to her neck and press down, just enough that she remembers I'm in charge and press another kiss to her mouth. Her legs are between mine, fighting to be freed.

"They don't want you to feel this way. But this is the way it's supposed to be. I want you to fight me. I want you to sink your teeth in and take what's yours."

Her eyes flash, and she *moves.*

I barely register her shoving my chest, flipping me to my back before she's on top of me. My breath comes out in a low, rough laugh.

"That's it, *that's* my mate," I say, voice thick with arousal.

She's panting, her eyes blown wide, fingers pressing to my shoulder like *I'm* the one that's going to bolt.

But I'm not. *Fuck.* I'm not going anywhere.

Her knees bracket my hips, weight sinking into mine like she's finally figuring out what she can do. She's claiming me as hers.

"Go on, Selene. Take it. Take what you want." It's a challenge. A dare.

She rocks her hips against mine, and I groan. I'm already hard–*fuck*–and a pulse of heat down my spine doesn't help.

I drag my hands up her thighs, fingers pressing in just to feel the way she reacts and say, "That's it, keep going."

Her hands move, sliding across my stomach, tracing the ridges of my abs like she's memorizing them, before she pushes my shirt up completely. Her pupils darken, and I just watch her *see* me.

She sees me.

I watch her come to terms with the thing inside her that takes over her mind.

Her fingers are at my waistband, working at the button, the zipper.

I groan the second her hand brushes against my cock–just a whisper of a touch–but I'm so fucking hard that it hurts. I'd rock up against her but I'm afraid that if I move at all, she'll run. After a second, she wraps her hand around me, and I can't stop myself from jerking up into the heat of her palm. She's sliding up and down, *up and down*, using the fluid beading at the crown to wet her palm, gliding down my shaft–

"*Fuck*," I grind out, head tipping back into the mattress. "*Fuck*, yes."

She's shifting above me. And then I feel it–the slick, unbearable warmth of her pussy pressing right against me. Her thighs tremble where they grip mine, and I feel how wet she is for me, how ready, how much she needs this just as much as I do. I grip her hips, holding her steady.

"Are you ready?" I ask. She looks at me, mouth parted, as she guides me inside.

"*Yes,*" she whispers, sinking down slowly, inch by inch. Tight. Hot. *Perfect.* My fingers dig into her hips as I fight my desire to buck up into her.

She's so fucking wet. So soft. *So slick.*

She lets out a half-gasp, half-moan, her hands braced on my chest, nails digging in, and–*fuck*–that only makes it worse.

Better.

"You feel so fucking good," I groan. I sound wrecked. *Needy*.

I don't even finish my thought before she's moving. Her thighs flex and she's lifting up, dragging that unbearable heat away before sinking back down again and I'm slipping deeper inside her.

A low, guttural sound rips from my throat. And she *moans*.

I don't know how I manage to hold it together. That sound will haunt every dream for the rest of my days. I'll carry it in my soul for the rest of time.

I look at the space where our bodies meet as my fingers stroke over her skin. Her head is tipped back, lips parted while her body sets a slow, tortured pace that makes my vision darken at the edges.

She needs to go *faster*. I growl and tighten my grip on her waist, fully intending on speeding her up. She moans again and–*fucking*–I snap.

I sit up, wrapping my arms around her back while my mouth finds her neck. I bite down hard on the spot where her neck meets her throat. I taste my blood on her skin mixing with her sweat. Heady, *euphoric*.

My favorite flavor.

She cries out, her hands slapping my shoulders, clutching me close, and I press my forehead to hers, forcing our eyes to meet. She's moving against me, more steady now that she's found her rhythm, but it's not *enough*. She doesn't know how to move like this. It's too clumsy for either of us to find release.

I flip her.

She yelps as her back hits the mattress, but I don't give her a second to think. I pin her wrists above her head and press back inside her. Her eyes go wide as she whines.

"*Fuck*, princess. Be a good girl now and take my cock," I say, dragging myself out before thrusting back in, filling her. She gasps, arching her back.

"Eli–"

"You feel so fucking good." I press our lips together in a bruising kiss, swallowing her cries as I set a brutal pace. The room echoes the sounds of our bodies slapping together. Her legs wrap around my thighs, her body rising to grind against me.

"Eli, *please*." She's right there. I reach up and grip her jaw, right at the edge of her throat, forcing her eyes to mine. I angle myself so that her clit is the focus of my thrusts, so that my cock is hitting that spot on the inside of her body. I feel her growing wetter with every thrust.

"Look at me." I keep grinding my hips against hers as she moans in my ear. I *know* what I'm doing, pressing my body down like that against hers, *right* there on her clit. Her eyes are wide, hips shaking. She shudders once, squeezing her eyes shut, and I know–

"**Come for me**."

She *shatters*.

And *fuck*, the way her body tightens around me, it sends me over the edge, too. I bury my face in her throat as I come, my breath ragged against her skin. For a long moment, neither of us move. Our sweat soaked bodies remain pressed together as we allow our hearts to catch up.

I can feel myself growing soft inside her, and I slip free after another moment.

Her fingers come to my hair, brushing through it softly, and she starts to hum a tune that I don't know.

Tears brim my eyes as I realize what I've done.

I've *lost*.

I've fucking lost.

I stand, leave her in the bed, and walk to the bathroom, shutting the door behind me.

What the *actual* hell was that?

My skin feels like it's been set on fire and my body aches in places I didn't know it could. I stare at the ceiling, mind numb, still processing the wave of heat that had coursed through me. I've been so sure that I could resist the bond when I ran–ignore it or at least fight it–especially when I had seen the *four* of them standing there last night... but the way it felt when Luke and Eli touched me... it was like nothing I've ever experienced.

I want to cry when I think about how easy I gave in. Twice. *Twice!*

My track record is garbage.

The bond... it doesn't feel like some natural thing. It's suffocating me. Like a leash around my throat, around my soul, pulling me in different directions. I don't know which way to go. The moment I picked Eli, I *felt* the urge to fight... but the instincts to give in had swallowed everything else. It overshadowed *me*.

I rub my hands over my face as I test my legs, stretching the aching muscles. I'm not sure how smart it is to be intimate so frequently, especially if it's going to make me hurt this much every time.

I do have four mates, so I need to be smarter about this....

Why does it feel so *right* to submit even though I had the desperate desire to fight him? I kept hearing the screaming in my head to run, to fight, to make him earn his way between my legs and into my soul. To prove his place in my bond. I don't even *know* what any of that means.

But his whispered words guided me. Convinced me that he was a safe choice.

And then he left me here. Just walked off like I didn't just... like we didn't just... you know *what*?

Fuck him.

So why does my bond sting at his rejection? Stupid. Absolutely stupid.

I sit up, grimacing at the way my skin sticks to the sheets. My dress is still bunched around my waist, half-on, half-off, and I feel the rush of Eli's release leaking out of me.

Ugh.

I wonder who will get the first child?

I rake a hand through my hair trying to ignore how my insides throb, and slide to the edge of the bed. My first instinct is to wipe between my legs, but the thought of redressing *now* while feeling like *this* makes me want to scream. I need a shower. *Now.*

But when I glance toward the bathroom door, I remember that Eli is there.

I consider waiting for him to come out. Maybe he'll come slinking back after finishing whatever moody, self-loathing ritual he's got going on in there. But the longer I wait, the more my skin crawls, and I'm not about to marinate in my own sweat and his semen just because he wants to be dramatic. I push to my feet and march to the bathroom door. I don't knock. He didn't ask *my* permission before throwing me on the bed, so why would I give him the courtesy of politeness?

The door swings open, and he's there, leaning against the sink, arms braced, his head bowed as he glares at his own reflection like it personally insulted him.

"Oh, good *God*," I mutter, rolling my eyes.

His eyes narrow when he sees me. "Do you need something?"

"A shower," I say flatly, stepping inside and shutting the door behind me. "But clearly, you're busy having some sort of existential crisis, so I figured I'd come join in."

He grinds his teeth, eyes flicking between my face and my still exposed breasts, but he doesn't say anything. He's detached, already checked out, like he's decided how this'll go.

And that *really* pisses me, and the bond, off.

"You're just gonna stand there and mope?" I snap, crossing my arms. I'm still sticky, leaking down my leg, bond burning with embarrassment about being left in the afterglow. "You didn't seem so detached when you were *inside* of me, Eli."

His fingers tighten on the edge of the counter, the only way I can tell my words affect him. Otherwise his face remains impassive, a strikingly different man than the one who whispered in my ear, pulled me underneath him, made me *want*.

"That was a mistake."

Excuse me?

I bark out a laugh but it's laced with poison. "Oh, a mistake? That's rich." I step forward, shoving his shoulder. He doesn't budge. "You were *so sure* of yourself a few minutes ago. Told me to *feel* it. To stop running from you. And now what? You regret it?"

"I don't regret it." He looks up at me. "But that doesn't mean it's going to happen again."

My breath catches and I despise the way my chest tightens at his words. I hate how I've become so dependent on him in a matter of minutes with just a handful of words.

"You don't get to make that decision."

"*Yes*, I do." He uses that gravelly, low tone on me, and I find my chin tucking to my chest unconsciously. The bond cries out, dejected at the idea of never lying beneath him again. My mind, however, is furious at how calm he is. How he won't give me something, *anything*, to hold onto while I tear into him.

"Fuck. You."

I don't wait for a response. I'm not going to get one from him–the stoic asshole that he is. Instead, I yank my dress over my head and throw it at him. It smacks him in the chest before dropping on the floor. His eyes stay locked on mine, not my bared body, not the bite mark he put on my bloody throat.

Fine.

I turn my back on him, step into the shower, and crank the water to scalding. Eli storms out, slamming the door behind him while I rinse off quickly. I feel him as he leaves, but as fast as he's gone, Luke's presence replaces his. I turn the water off and towel dry, grimacing when I realize that my dress is covered in sweat and Eli's release.

Well, *that's* not going back on.

I curse myself for not thinking properly as I clutch the towel to my chest and walk out of the bathroom. Hopefully Luke won't be too pissed at me. He *agreed* with his father at breakfast even if he did squeeze my hand like he had been trying to tell me something.

Thinking back to this morning, I'd never been so humiliated in my entire life.

'When did you last bleed?'

What a bastard The Master is.

Luke's sitting on the edge of the bed with his arms crossed when I walk in. He glances up, his eyes skimming over my wet hair and the towel clinging to me. A small smile tugs at his lips but it falters when he sees the bite mark on my throat. Beside him sits a neatly folded pile of clothes.

"What's that?" I ask, closing the bathroom door behind me.

"I figured you might like something other than those dresses for when you're in the room," he says, picking up the top article of clothing and holding it out. "My father might not approve of pants on a woman, but I don't care. Wear what's comfortable when you're here."

I blink, thrown off guard. "Oh... thanks."

"Of course. You're my mate," he says, voice firm. "It's my job to take care of you. I'm going to be busy as hell from now on, but I'll do my best to give you what you need."

I cross the room and grab a shirt from the pile. After a moment's hesitation, I drop the towel. He's already seen everything so there's no point in being bashful now. Still, the way his gaze lingers on me makes something in the bond flare up and demand my attention. I'm too sore to even entertain it right now but it's interesting that, even after Eli, it still wants Luke.

I wonder if the lust aspect of it will ever fade, or if I'm doomed to be a harlot for the rest of my days, passed around my group like a cheap toy.

"I'm assuming you and Eli completed your parts of the claim."

I freeze mid-motion, my shirt halfway over my head. My silence must be enough of an answer because he lets out a breath, dragging a hand through his already-messy hair.

"I don't agree with my father on a lot of things, Selene," he admits, his eyes never leaving mine. "That's one of them. Keeping you from your other mates... it isn't right."

I stare at him, pulling my shirt down as my heart races in my chest.

"You're allowed to *disagree* with The Master?" I tease, breaking through the awkwardness. His fingers twitch like he wants to reach for me but he holds back. As I pull my pants on he leans closer, speaking low.

"I can do what I want. Especially when it comes to *my* mate. And *my* mate's mates."

"Thank you." I bend down to press a soft kiss to his cheek.

I don't forget that he hunted me down after I'd run away from him. I don't forget that he claimed me on the forest floor like a desperate animal.

But then I *also* remember how he looked at me when he pulled out and saw the blood. The way he apologized profusely, gently redressed me, and carried me back to his house as if I was a delicate, precious thing.

The picture I have of him in my mind is a mess–half-formed, undecided. I wonder what it'll take to finally make up my mind about him.

"I wanted to ask... if you could feel other bonds. Between me and Jace, maybe," he asks.

I run my fingers through his hair and try to focus. I search my bond, pulling at the threads between us. Jace responds faintly, curiosity rippling through our connection, but there's nothing on my side between Luke and him. Nothing *distinct*, nothing attaching them.

"No," I reply, pulling away. "Do you?"

He nods, his fingers lightly brushing my lips. "Faintly. Last night, there was something there... it felt like a mate bond, but different somehow."

"Maybe it's because you're both bonded to me."

"If that's the case, wouldn't Eli and Max feel it too?" He frowns, his brows furrowing slightly.

"I don't know." I pause. "My bond... it's weird, too. It's not calm or quiet like they told us it would be. It's loud. It wanted me to run from you but at the same time, it demanded that I *submit*." My voice drops as I lean in, pressing our foreheads together. "I'm scared of it."

"And now?"

"It's satisfied," I reassure him.

He brings his hand up to cup my cheek. "I don't think we should mention this to anyone else," he says softly, "not until we're sure there isn't something wrong with us."

"You think there's something wrong with the bonds?" I ask, barely above a whisper.

"We don't know enough about bonds between multiple people. I'll try to see if I can find something else about it in our history, but I don't know what I'll be able to access." His voice is serious enough that I nod.

"Eli mentioned something.... He said they didn't want me to feel this, that they made it... tame."

Luke's brows furrow, his fingers tightening on my hips. "He said that?"

I shrug, trying not to let the heat creeping up my face show. "I was pretty... distracted, so I might not have heard it right...."

Luke's fingers play with the waistband on my pants but he's focused elsewhere. "I'll have to talk to him. Do you know where he went?"

"We... had an argument," I admit, biting my lip. "He left."

Luke smirks, shaking his head. "You're a troublemaker, you know that?"

I can't help the smile that crosses my lips. "I know."

I leave her in the room and return to my father even though I don't want to. She shouldn't be alone after being claimed but I have no choice, really. I'd only managed to sneak away, and I know I'm going to pay for it as soon as I'm back.

Eli shouldn't have left her... but maybe he just doesn't *know*.... He wasn't raised here. Maybe he doesn't know what he's supposed to do, and I shouldn't fault him for it. Wherever he came from, it sure as hell wasn't as refined as we are, that's for sure.

I *should* spend more time with him, seeing as how we're going to be around each other for the rest of our lives. Getting to know him isn't a bad idea. Jace already has a pretty good opinion on him, and Max....

Well, Max is *Max*.

He'll come around.

"Unless you were in there putting a child in her, then there's *no* reason for you to be running off in the middle of important matters," my father scolds me. He's leaning over a crudely drawn map that has all the other communes in the area surrounding ours with Middlesborough in the center. I keep my face neutral as I approach the plat and look down at the pieces he's set out. His finger keeps tapping on Sableford, the only sect that's close to our size in this region. Up to this point, they've been a neutral party.

"What are we doing with this?" I ask instead, trying to distract him. The look he gives says he doesn't buy it, but he doesn't press further.

"You've had a lifetime to prepare for your role." He smooths his hand out over the map as if it's some grand discovery and not something that's been in this room since *he* was a child. "But there's things I've kept from you. Things you weren't prepared for. I'll be honest with you, I didn't expect The Seraph to appear in our lifetime. I'd hoped, but...."

"If she hadn't, would you be telling me this?"

"One day. You'd have to know to pass it along to your children, and them to theirs." He levels me with a look. "I don't believe you to be ready *now*, but we're out of time. The High Priestess is going to start preparing The Seraph to fulfill the prophecy."

"Then is it wise for me to...." I don't even want to ask him, but the words are already out of my mouth. "Should I even be trying to get her pregnant?"

"There's nothing in the prophecy that says she *isn't*," he smirks, "and it's not like it would impede her severely at this point. They don't swell until the later months, anyway."

I have *zero* intentions of putting a baby inside of her if I can help it.

Not that the idea *doesn't* have appeal, but my father's been mumbling about some grand prophecy since I was a kid. If *this* is the one he's been talking about all this time, then there's no way in hell I'm bringing *my* child into that mess.

"What's she even *doing* as The Seraph?"

"That's not for us to discuss." He brushes me off. "We need to focus on this–" His hand lands on the center of the map, right on Middlesborough. "–and on victory."

"*Victory?*"

"Yes, Lucas, keep up." He's annoyed with me now. Nothing new, but no less dangerous. "A bit of pussy and you're *completely* fatuous. I thought we got rid of this infatuation *years* ago."

I can't help but grimace when he brings up my first experience with women, all carefully picked out by him. It still bothered me, knowing he was the one deciding who would 'teach me' all about intimacy. But like everything else, I had no control over it.

"I'm *listening*, I just don't know what victory you're talking about. We eliminated the last of the band that challenged us weeks ago and there haven't been any more. Is there a threat I'm not aware of?"

He sighs and falls back in his chair and I know that I've pushed him too far. I take a seat in the chair opposite his.

"This is *bigger* than little fights with others. This is the rest of our existence, Lucas. We're going to conquer all of them at once."

I stare at him in shock.

"How?"

"The Seraph, of course."

I think of Selene. Of soft, gentle, *sarcastic* Selene. She's not a warrior. She's not anything at all.

"Right." I hold the sarcasm back as best as I can. "And how is The Seraph going to conquer *all* of the world without *any* sort of abilities? I won't let her on the battlefield."

"Oh, you won't *let* her?" He looks amused at my refusal. "I think you'll find that once her training with The High Priestess is complete, you won't be in a position to tell her what to do anymore, Lucas. She'll be the one in charge of your little harem."

"Can you *stop* calling it that?" I snap. "That's the third time you've said that this morning since I've been here, and it's getting on my nerves."

He raises his eyebrow at me. "But that's what it is, isn't it?"

"You want The Seraph. You want this special ability she has to *apparently* take over the world. You're even thrilled I'm part of this... right up until you realize exactly what it means to be part of it."

"Sharing your mate makes you a lesser male."

I stand slowly, my blood boiling. I can feel Selene in my chest probing my rage, trying to calm me down. To a lesser extent, I can even feel Jace trying to pull his string away from mine.

"I'm not anything less, just because I have to share." I advance on him and he looks at me, confused at my sudden confidence. "My mate's *mates* aren't anything less either. You'll stop treating them as such. If you want us to help you do this, then you'll treat all of us with the respect that we deserve. I'm tired of being treated like an inconvenience."

He eyes me silently for a moment and, when he speaks, his low tone sends shivers down my spine. *Too far, too fucking far.* "You think just because you're my *son* that I won't have you killed in your sleep? You'll *all* stay in line. You'll do *exactly* as you're told, *when* you're told, *without* complaint. If I suspect *anything* going on behind my back, I won't *hesitate* to make you *suffer*. I've waited my entire life for this day. I've done *nothing* but pray for this moment and it's *finally* here."

He looks crazed—his eyes practically glowing with madness.

"*Nothing* will stand in my way. Not even my *own* blood."

I swallow down the hate, locking myself back into the composure that's kept me alive the last few years. I can't argue with him anymore. He's made himself clear, and I have *no* doubts he'll follow through on his threats if I step out of line.

He's done it before.

I think of my mother, her gentle face fleeting in my mind before I force it back into the box I've kept her in, locking it away to keep from breaking down in front of The Master.

I nod. "Understood, *sir*."

His smirk tells me he knows exactly how much effort it takes me to force those words out. He pushes back from the table, rolling his shoulders as if he's no longer stressed out about whatever I've done.

"Come. We've got to go speak to The Warden."

I stiffen. "About?"

"The *war*." He looks at me as if it's obvious, as if he's forgotten he *just* told me about his grand war plans this morning. I don't respond right away, focusing instead on steadying my breathing as he motions for me to follow him out of the room. I can feel Jace's anxiety *eating* at me. I try to reassure him that it's fine, but he pushes me out again. I turn back to Selene who seems to be taking advantage of her morning alone. She feels asleep, the bond dormant and settled, humming away happily.

The halls are quieter than normal, a side effect of the Joining Ceremony. Most people are tending to their new bonds or nursing celebratory hangovers, but my father doesn't acknowledge any of that. He walks with the same measured steps as always, expecting me two steps behind.

And I am. Because there's no choice.

The training ground is alive with movement. The sharp clatter of steel against steel ripples through the air, punctured by grunts of exertion and the occasional barked order. Dust kicks up beneath the boots of warriors locked in sparring matches, the ground beaten down from generations of relentless training.

The Warden stands at the center of it all, a mountain of a man watching his soldiers with a gaze like a blade honed for one purpose–to kill. He's built a living fortress with broad shoulders, thick arms criss-crossed with old scars, every inch of him carved by war. His deep, rich brown skin carries the marks of a lifetime spent on the battlefield—a history written in blood. A thick, graying beard frames a face, set in a permanent scowl, and a nose crooked from a long-healed break. If there's anyone who lives here that embodies war itself, it's *him*.

Standing just a few paces from him, arms crossed, is Max.

His eyes flicker to mine immediately, but he doesn't speak. He just tightens his stance, like he's not pleased to see me.

My father steps forward first. "Warden."

The massive man doesn't look away from the sparring match in front of him. One of the warriors stumbles, nearly eating shit before recovering with a vicious strike. Only then does The Warden grunt in approval and turn his attention to us.

"Master," he greets, voice rough as gravel. His gaze slides over me, lingering just a second too long before his eyes shift back to my father. "What can I do for you?"

I glance at Max again. His uniform is streaked with dirt, arms covered in fresh bruising. He looks at home here, far more than he ever might in our new 'shared' space.

I wonder if he'll ever use his new room, or if my bed is where he'll sleep every night?

I step up beside him, keeping my voice low. "So, is this what you do in your free time? Stare at sweating men all day?"

Max huffs out a breath. "Better than being The Master's *lapdog*."

I smirk. "You sound jealous."

He scoffs, shifting his weight. "Of what? The privilege of following orders like a well-trained hound?" His voice drips with sarcasm. "Yeah, I'm *really* missing out."

I roll my eyes but before I can respond, the Warden's voice cuts through the space between us.

"Save the lovers' spat for later."

I tense when my father chuckles, but Max just shakes his head, mumbling under his breath. The Warden turns back to my father.

"You said war. Is it finally time?"

My father gestures for him to walk away from the heart of the training grounds. The Warden falls into step behind him, his heavy boots crunching against the packed dirt. Max and I follow a few paces behind, just far enough to be ignored but close enough to hear.

Max grunts out, "This should be fun.

I shoot him a sideways glance. "You don't *have* to come."

"And leave you alone to bask in your birthright?" He scoffs, placing a hand on the handle of his sword. "I'd *never* forgive myself. I fucking *have to*, or did you forget our new jobs?" I grit my teeth. "So, what's this war *actually* about? Master finally getting bored of our 'long-lasting' peace?"

I snort, only because it's been about three weeks since our last scuffle, but I drop my voice down low as I stare at my father's back. "He threatened to kill us."

Max stops walking for a half a second before catching back up. "*What*?"

"He told me if we step out of line... if we don't agree to do what he says, *when* he says to, then he'll put us down." I glance at him. "*All* of us."

Max's jaw tightens, his fingers flexing on the hilt. "Right. Because nothing says devotion like a fucking death threat."

I hiss through my teeth. "Can you at least be a little more subtle about it?"

"Subtle?" He lets out a short, humorless laugh that earns us a backwards glance from my father. "You think I'm gonna stand here and nod along like a good little warrior while that bastard threatens my life? My *mate's* life?"

"No." I glare at him, slowing my steps. "I think you're going to be smart and not make a *scene*."

"Yeah, well, that's a big ask."

I internally sigh. My father slows, his attention fully on us. Max quickly schools his expression into disinterest and looks off into the distance, ignoring me. I try to replicate it but I'm hyper-aware of the look my father gives me.

Shit.

The Warden crosses his arm, looking between Max and I skeptically. "So, tell me. If war is around the corner, where are we finding warriors?" he asks my father.

The Master smiles. "The Seraph will provide."

Max tenses next to me, his breath catching, and I know he's caught on to the severity of our situation.

Good... thick-headed asshole.

"The Seraph may be powerful, Master, but I doubt she alone can provide an army the size we will need to convert every other sect. Warriors are not born from faith alone."

My father's smile deepens, though his eyes darken just enough to remind us *all* who has the power here. "And yet, The Seraph *will* provide. I have no doubt."

The Warden hesitates, brow furrowing as he considers the words. As war-torn as the man is, he's politically savvy too. He knows my father's games. "And if not? Then what?"

Without missing a beat, my father's voice turns cold. "Why do you suddenly doubt your faith, Warden?"

The Warden's eyes flick to the floor briefly before his lips part in soft prayer. He raises his index finger, presses it to his lips and then to his forehead. He straightens after, the fire in his eyes alight once more.

"I will *never* doubt that God provides," he says firmly, leaving no room for argument.

Max is rigid next to me, his fingers curling and uncurling into fists.

But what sends a shiver down my spine isn't the palpable anger rolling off him in tangible waves–it's the way his hand has suddenly wrapped around my wrist, gripping it tight enough to remind me that we're stuck in this *together*.

I've been alone in this mess for so long, to suddenly have an ally is–

The rage in my chest is so hot, it's like fire. When I feel Jace's bond, he shoves my anger back inside of me. He's getting better at it, even after just a few attempts.

I glance at Max, catching the fear and frustration in his eyes. His nod is almost too shallow to miss, but I see his chin dip, and I feel him squeeze my arm.

I can't answer, not yet. Instead, I glance back at my father, my throat tight. Max's arm falls from mine. "She'll do her part," I say, the words tasting like ash on my tongue.

The sudden scream rips through the air, cutting through the tension. My head snaps towards the noise, instincts flaring. It's the kind of scream that belongs on the battleground–painful and desperate– when my own sword strikes a man down.

Before I can react, a warrior comes rushing toward us, face pale with panic.

"Warden!" he calls out, breath coming in frantic gasps. "It's Hal. He's been cut. It's deep, on his thigh! He's down, barely conscious!"

The Warden doesn't waste a second. His expression hardens, his eyes narrowing with single-minded focus. "Max, stay here," he orders as he darts forward, following the soldier to where the injured warrior lies. It isn't far from us, and we watch as The Warden takes a knee. I look over at Max, who stares at the scene, mouth set in a thin line.

A moment later the Warden's voice rings out again, but this time, it's laced with urgency. "We're done for the day! Get back to the barracks, all of you! No more training until further notice!"

The warriors reluctantly disperse, but Max doesn't move from my side. His eyes are fixed on the Warden as hands work to assess the injury. It's a mess of torn flesh and blood, a nasty wound that's already spreading dark crimson across the ground. Hal is in and out of it, groaning as the Warden directs two others to remain behind and assist him.

"Stay back here, Max," The Warden tells him, lifting Hal into his arms. "Get everyone secured."

"Yes, Warden," Max mumbles, tilting his head in acknowledgement as the Warden passes by us, trailed by the two warriors.

My father's voice is behind us, cold and detached. "You'll both join me for dinner. We'll discuss matters there."

Max's eyes dart between The Warden and my father, his frustration visible but he nods stiffly. The Master doesn't wait for further confirmation from me. He simply turns on his heel and heads back to our home, leaving Max and I to stew in the stench of freshly-spilt blood.

Jace

It's strange, apprenticing under Vitalis.

All the knowledge in the world is at my fingertips and yet, I have no desire to know it.

I didn't earn this position.

It feels... *tainted*.

I follow Vitalis around in his flowing white robes, listening as he talks about the various supplies we have stored and what he does with them. I take detailed notes as best as I can while he walks and talks, waving his aged hand around wildly.

I should be grateful. *Honored*. But all I can feel is this gnawing sense of doubt crawling under my skin like an infection I can't treat.

This isn't *mine*. I didn't study for years even though I've dedicated my life to healing. I've *only* been bonded to The Seraph... and Vitalis has made it *well known* that I don't deserve this position.

I force myself to focus as Vitalis points to a row of dried herbs bundled and tied to a rack. "These, when crushed into a poultice, can draw out infection. *But—*" He turns, peering down his curved, freckled nose. "—too much, and it can burn the skin."

I nod, scribbling it down. This is all knowledge the higher level healers learn. Things I would have learned in ten years if I would have proven myself worthy.

A sudden surge of anger slams into my chest.

Fucking Luke.

I grip the edge of the counter, trying to breathe through it. Selene is there, soothing and serene, but it's not *enough*. The bonds are still new, still unpredictable, and I haven't sealed my part of the claim yet. It's going to continue to push the boundaries. I've been fighting it all morning, and I'm *exhausted*.

Unfiltered rage simmers beneath my ribs.

The kind that makes me want to drive my pencil into Vitalis' throat.

I give the energy a massive shove back towards Luke, forcing him to take his anger back. I breathe heavily, my eyes shut tight, as I try to come back to myself. As much as I believe settling the claim will fix this, I'm *not* forcing myself on Selene.

I want her to *ask* for it.

Besides... there's the *small* matter of my new bond with Luke. Will he and I have to complete our own claim because I am not–

I come back to myself after another deep breath and open my eyes.

Vitalis glares at me but before he can say anything, the stock room door bursts open.

"W-W-Warden needs y-y-you," a young healer stammers. He's breathless, eyes wide, and I see the streaks of blood across the front of his shirt.

I don't wait. I shove past him and rush into the infirmary, Vitalis on my heels, and find the Warden standing over a blood-soaked table. The warrior thrashes wildly, held down by two others. His leg is a mess of torn flesh across the meaty part of his upper thigh but I don't see bone. I grasp the Warrior's knee and pry the wound apart, just enough to try and see how deep it is.

"He took a blade to the thigh," The Warden says, matter-of-factly. "Cut clean through the skin. I don't think it got anything vital."

The other healers look to Vitalis for instruction, but I'm already stepping in and taking control.

"Get me the boiled water and fresh bandages," I bark. "I need the cauterizing iron! Now!"

A healer hesitates, looking from Vitalis to me.

"**NOW**!" I grasp the Warrior's thigh, trying to hold the gash together, but his leg is slick with blood and my fingers slip. The healer scrambles to obey as my voice warbles with a deep, harsh grumble. It burns in my chest but I'm too lost in the sight of the weeping wound to think about *why*.

My hands are sticky with his blood.

There's no time for herbs. No time for stitches and trying to heal the inside first.

I need to seal this *now*.

Vitalis watches over my shoulder, not saying anything, not *doing* anything.

Useless old bastard.

Water is splashed over his thigh washing away most of the blood, but it starts to flow instantly, and I know we're out of time. The bandages are on standby for me, and I request more water for the clean-up after. The iron is placed in my hand, already burning hot, and I look up.

"Hold him," I say. The Warden nods once, reaching for the thigh I'm holding to keep the skin together for me.

I press the flat side of the iron to his skin. The warrior screams, body seizing, but the bleeding stops immediately. The room smells like charred flesh, rotting and fetid, like blood that's been boiled mixed with copper that's been overcooked. It sticks to the inside of my throat, thick and sour. I swallow, forcing it down as I hand off the iron to the waiting hands and use the water and a fresh rag to wipe at the new, sensitive skin.

It's not pretty, but it'll work.

He's going to live. *That's* what matters the most to me. *Life.*

When the chaos settles, Vitalis faces me. "Return to the storeroom, and wait for me there."

I nod and step away, wiping my hands on the front of my smock. It'll stain, but I don't realize that until I'm already stepping through the door.

Standing in the quiet of the room, I glance around at the shelves. My eyes land on a small bundle of dried roots and something clicks in my mind—something I'd read a few months ago in a book I wasn't supposed to be reading.

A book that had been *burned* after it had been found... after *my* stupid ass had dropped it in the main area of the infirmary and Vitalis had picked it up.

An herb that, when prepared properly, can *prevent* pregnancy.

My fingers twitch. My body is moving before my mind catches up, and I'm reaching for it, tucking it into my pocket just as footsteps approach and throw the door open.

"Step away from those," Vitalis' voice cuts through the silence.

I slowly turn to face him.

"You have no reason to be touching any of those yet," he says, watching me closely. I nod, stepping back, my heart pounding. The weight of what I've done sits heavy in my pocket.

But Vitalis doesn't look at my pocket, he looks at *me*. Directly into my eyes, judgement sitting heavily in his ancient ones.

"You acted fast," he says finally, folding his hands in front of him. "The warrior would have bled out had you not intervened."

I don't relax. There's a 'but' coming. There always is.

"*But...* you could have saved him *without* branding him like livestock."

The words are like a slap, and I fight to keep my features from betraying me. "Th-there wasn't time to do it any other way. It was deep, and nothing else would have stopped the bleeding faster."

Vitalis hums, looking around the stockroom. "There is *always* time for precision, Jace. You cauterize the wound, but at what cost? The muscle damage is permanent. He won't be able to fight again."

I grit my teeth. "The Warden is more worried about *that*? He'll still be alive, at least."

Vitalis pinches the bridge of his nose, something between disappointment and reluctant approval. "*Yes.* But next time, I expect you to think before you act." He presses his lips into a thin line and steps towards me. I feel my breath hitch, and my stomach clench painfully. I can *feel* Luke inside of my chest, probing to make sure I'm okay but I shove him away again.

He's going to find out, he's going to find out, *he's going to fi—*

"A true healer does not rush to burn away what he does not understand."

My fists clench at the insult but I nod anyway. There's *nothing* I want to say. He can't strip me of my title or humiliate me in front of the others–

But somehow, this is *worse*.

He thinks I'm *incompetent*.

"Go," he says, waving his hand towards the door. "We'll resume tomorrow when you're ready to proceed."

I don't hesitate, pushing away from the counter. I keep my pace measured and my face neutral, even as I feel the sweat rolling down my spine. Only when I reach the front steps do I exhale, shoulders slumping forward.

The herbs are *still* in my pocket.

I make my way through the winding paths of the town, keeping my head down as I navigate the familiar streets to my old house. It's a quiet walk–nobody says anything to me now that I've been elevated.

Or tainted.

I should have expected it, but it still sucks when I see people darting out of my way.

My parents are hardly ever home. Duty has always called them elsewhere, leaving my old home feeling more abandoned than lived-in. I don't imagine today will be any different.

The door creaks as I step inside, the scent of dust and dried herbs filling my lungs. My feet carry me through the empty hall, past the small sitting room and up the staircase to my old bedroom. It's exactly as I left it–neat, sparse, hardly filled except with necessities.

I close the door behind me and move straight to my desk. Pulling out the small mortar and pestle I used for my early days as a junior healer, I retrieve the herb from my pocket and set it inside. My hands move automatically, grinding the dried leaves into a fine powder. The repetitive motion is calming and lets my mind wander as I work.

I don't know if it'll work. I only have what I read in that old book, and I don't even know how accurate *that* was.

But if it does....

I'll have to talk to Luke about it. See if he thinks it's worth giving to

Selene. As far as I can remember, this herb has no other purpose and *no reason* to be hanging in our surplus storage room. I start to grind the dark blue dried-out berries, watching as they turn from a green powder gradually shifting to an indigo.

My thoughts settle heavily in my chest. I don't *know* how he'll react. I know that, at breakfast, he was saying what he needed to. His relationship with his father isn't the best so there's a good chance he *doesn't* want her pregnant, but then again....

I don't really know *what* he wants when it comes to our mate.

Selene round with a child is such *a pretty picture....* I shake my head. I don't need to go down that path at all until Luke decides what he wants to do.

I'm debating if this is something we need to be doing without telling Selene. Maybe *she* wants a baby....

But the alternative....

I dump the powdered herbs back into their small pouch and tie it shut. For now, I'll keep it hidden from Selene until Luke and I know what to do next.

Until Luke and I can discuss it with *everyone*.

Blood drips down my arm in slow, lazy trails, soaking into the sleeve of my shirt. It isn't deep really, just enough to sting like hell and piss me off. I *should've* blocked that strike. *Should've* countered. *Should've* been paying attention.

But *no*, my dumbass is too busy thinking about the fact that I haven't gotten to fuck Selene yet. That I've slept next to her for three nights without touching her. That I have to sit at The Master's table and listen to him act like I should be *grateful* to be there.

Fucking ridiculous.

I rip my sleeve higher, scowling at the gash. It isn't even *impressive*, just a clean cut along the back part of my upper arm. I grind my teeth as it slowly leaks blood.

If it leaves a scar, at least it'll be a reminder not to let my focus slip again.

"Nice one, jackass," one of the other warriors teases as I pass by. I don't recognize him, which means he isn't worth knowing. I send him a look that promises him I'll remember his face, and his smirk vanishes. With a frustrated grunt, I stalk off toward the infirmary.

Fan-fucking-*tastic.*

More time wasted, more irritation simmering under my skin. Maybe if I'm lucky, Jace will be there and he'll stitch me up *without* giving me a lecture. Probably not. He'll fuss, tell me I need to be careful, and then look so genuinely disappointed I'll end up feeling guilty, which is *worse* than any scolding.

On second thought, I hope he chastises me.

By the time I push through the infirmary doors, I'm already over it. My arm throbs, my patience is shot, and all I want is a moment when I'm not being tested, talked down to, reminded of what I can't have.

But *sure*. Let's get this over with.

Jace looks up the moment I walk in, his expression shifting from calm to concerned in the blink of an eye. "What happened to you?" he asks, trying to keep his voice light. The teasing tone is there, of course. Caring and playful, like *I'm* the problem child he can't help but dote on.

I roll my eyes. "Oh, nothing," I mutter, laying the sarcasm on thick. "Just a little dance with a sword, no big deal."

Jace doesn't bite. Instead, he quirks a brow. "A sword, huh?" He steps closer, assessing the damage with a frown. "You sure you didn't *pick* a fight with this sword?" He walks to a table against the wall and grabs a yellow pouch sitting there. When he returns, he already has his fingers inside, pinching off a small amount of powder.

I watch him for a moment. "You've got the bedside manner of a rock."

He doesn't even flinch and instead gives me that patient smile of his while applying the powder inside my cut. I hiss as it stings but he clicks his tongue and continues to rub it in. "And *you're* not exactly the picture of an easy patient when you're leaking all over my floor."

I growl at him but it's mostly out of habit and only partly out of pain. The sting of the herbs is nothing compared to the irritation eating away at me. "Just *fix* it, Jace. Don't need your fucking commentary today."

"Alright, alright," he murmurs, working swiftly. "But *you're* going to have to stop getting hurt just to get me to take care of you." He's not even joking anymore, the focus of his movements is all business. The man's a perfectionist, and it's both annoying and impressive as hell.

As he prepares the needle and thread, I can't help the shiver that runs through me. I close my eyes when he brings them to my skin and gets to work.

Max. The Great Warrior of Middlesborough. Bringer of Death.

Future Warden.

Terrified of needles.

I can hear the teasing if it ever got out, which is why Jace is the *only* healer I've allowed to work on me for years. He's kept *this* a secret, and I have no doubt he'll keep more, especially now that we're basically brother-mates.

When he finishes stitching me up, he inspects the wound, then me, as if assessing whether I'll snap or thank him. "There. No more bleeding for you. Just try not to make me patch you up every damn day."

I grunt in response, glancing down at my now-bandaged arm. "Yeah, sure. No promises. What was that powder again?"

"Yarrow root. I'm half-debating keeping some at Luke's just for you."

"Huh." I lift my arm, grimacing at the pull in the stitch. I catch the jab, but I don't take the bait. I'm really not in the mood anymore. Jace watches me, debating about saying something else. I can see it in the way he presses his lips together, the way his fingers hover around the bag he's tying shut.

"Try not to rip those stitches open in the next hour, yeah? It needs time to set." There's genuine concern underneath the teasing. "I don't want to have to do this twice."

I snort. "I'll do my best." Not a lie... but it's not something I can promise. The Warden has been pushing me hard while he tests me for the new role I'm forced to fill.

The one that wasn't meant to be mine.

He sighs, moving away from me. "That's as good as I'm getting from you, huh?"

"Pretty much." I push myself away from the counter, testing my arm again. Still stings, but the bleeding has stopped and the stitches hold. "Besides, what would you do if I stopped showing up here all messed up? You'd be bored out of your damn mind."

Jace looks wholly unimpressed as he starts putting away the needle and thread. "Oh, *sure*. Because there's absolutely *nothing* else for me to do around here except fix *you* up when you're being too reckless."

"Exactly," I say, smirking.

He huffs a quiet laugh, shaking his head. "You're impossible."

"And yet, you keep putting me back together." I flash him a lazy grin as I step back toward the door. "Try not to miss me too much."

"Get out," he groans, but there's no real bite to it. "I'll see you tonight."

I chuckle, pushing through the doors and back outside, rolling my shoulder slightly just to feel the dull pull again.

The dining hall is too damn quiet.

Not *silent*, not with the clatter of plates and the low murmur of voices you'd expect from a family, but the kind of quiet that's unnaturally thick. The Master sits at the head, carving into his meat with precise, unhurried movements. Across from me, Luke mirrors him, shoulders squared, every motion controlled. Selene sits between Luke and Jace, as she does every meal, her presence like a flame in my vision, impossible to ignore.

And then there's Eli.

The poor bastard is on the receiving end of The Master's mood tonight. His plate sits untouched, his posture statuesque. I don't even think he's *blinked* in the last five minutes. The Master hasn't said much to him yet beyond the little comments about his work, a remark about his *loyalty*, an offhand observation that Eli seemed uncomfortable in his new role.

A death by a thousand little cuts.

I *should* enjoy it. The outsider, the one who doesn't belong at this table, getting picked apart. But it sits *heavy* in my gut, especially after learning what Eli *really* does for us.

I don't *like* it.

I cut a piece of food off my plate, chew it, swallow. Go through the motions. But my focus is distracted. *It's on her, always on her.* Every inhale drags in the scent of her lavender shampoo. The way the candle-light catches her hair, turning it into something almost auburn, makes my fingers clench my silverware. She lifts her glass to take a sip of water, and I have to bite my lip to swallow my moan at the delicate way her throat moves when she drinks.

I haven't *touched* her.

Haven't *had* her.

And every second sitting across from her, knowing I *could*, that I'm *supposed* to, only makes it worse.

My leg bounces under the table. I take a slow breath, trying to force my attention back to The Master's words before I do something stupid.

"...an outsider," The Master drones on. He isn't even *looking* at Eli as he speaks, slicing neatly through the ham. "Do you understand what a *privilege* it is to be here, Sentinel?"

Eli, to his credit, doesn't flinch. His fork hovers just above his plate, his expression carefully blank. "Yes, Master."

Always devoid of emotion. I'm starting to *envy* the guy, actually.

The Master hums, looking up as he spears the overcooked slice. "Good. I'd *hate* to think you might not appreciate what *I've* done for you."

Jace's gaze flickers between Eli and The Master cautiously, always concerned for his *friend*. The way The Master's lips curl, the way his soulless eyes linger a second too long on Eli, it doesn't sit right in my chest.

I do something even *I* don't expect.

"You gonna eat that?" I ask Eli, nodding at his plate.

It works, sort of. Jace puffs a quiet, awkward laugh while Selene lets out a soft snort. Eli blinks, shaking his head as he pushes his plate towards me.

The Master leans back in his chair. My stomach turns as his attention slides from Eli to me, and just like that, I *know* I've made a mistake.

Fuck.

"You seem comfortable, Warden," he says, amused. "A healthy appetite. Your training goes well, aside from your *many* slip-ups." He gestures towards my newly stitched arm. "You'll need your strength."

I finish the tasteless bite of green bean I've stolen from Eli. "Always, Master."

His smile stretches wider until we can see almost every one of his yellowing teeth. "And ready for the war, I trust."

I glance at Luke but he doesn't react. He's unreadable as ever, grip tightening on his knife. *Maybe I need to adopt Eli's tactic... wait... did he say–*

So soon?

We *just* crushed the last sect that came after us. Took their lands, took their resources, absorbed their people. It wasn't even a *battle*, more of a slaughter. There's been *nothing* from the others. No movement, no whispers of rebellion.

There's no *war* coming.

But The Master sits there, expectantly waiting for my answer.

I clear my throat. "A-always ready, Master," I say, carefully.

He grunts, seemingly pleased. "Good. Because it's coming sooner than you think."

A chill works down my spine, slow and unwelcome. I look at Luke again and this time, I *see* it. He's shocked. He schools his reaction quickly, but his brows had twitched and his mouth curled downward in a low frown.

He's just as confused as I am.

Selene looks between Luke and I, picking up on the tension, but she's keeping her mouth shut. Jace is back to looking at his plate, keeping himself as invisible as possible.

Eli? He's back to his statue form. *Smart.*

The Master picks up his goblet, swirling his wine. "It's *funny*," he says, almost to himself. His pupils are blown wide. "How they always think they have *time*. How they think they can *wait*. That we'll grow *soft*. We won't though, will we, Warden?"

I sit up straighter. I'm not the Warden, not yet, but he keeps addressing me as such. It's throwing me. "No, Master."

He nods approvingly, raising his glass in my direction. "Good." He takes a slow sip. "Because we'll be striking first."

I suffocate in the silence. I try to keep my face blank but my mind is *racing*. What the *fuck* is he talking about? *Striking first?* We've taken everything of worth. *Nobody* is moving against us. *Nobody* is challenging us. The Master sets his goblet down with a deliberate *clink*.

Luke finally speaks up, keeping his tone measured. "Do we have... reason to believe an attack is *coming*?"

But The Master is back to cutting up his flavorless meat. "We've discussed this, Lucas. If you aren't going to pay attention in our morning meetings, then what the hell am I *entertaining* you for?"

It hits me. His discussions with The Warden, while Luke and I trail behind and talk about his death threats....

He doesn't *care* if it's coming or not. He doesn't *need* a reason.

He *only* wants war.

He turns his cold gaze to Selene, and her entire body freezes.

The weight of that look is one of a thousand needles into your psyche. Her fingers curl into the cloth on the table, and her breath slows as she prepares for his next word.

She knows it'll be cruel, whatever he says.

"Selene," he flexes his jaw. "My son's *fated* mate."

Luke tightens his fist, cracking his knuckles next to his plate as he stares at his father.

"I trust you're... devoted to him."

Her face flushes red, throat bobbing as she swallows around the words. "O-of course, Master."

His gaze sharpens. "To him *alone?*"

The air in the room tastes stale, almost as much as the bread. She looks down to her plate, and Eli leans forward slightly. I watch red patches appear on his cheeks as he takes his lower lip between his teeth. His first show of emotion all evening and I think–

That mother fucker.... Did he and Selene....

I flick my eyes to Luke but he's focused entirely on his father. His grip on his knife is white-knuckled, trembling slightly, and I brush my own anger away. It's not important right now what Eli and Selene did... he's got as much right to her pussy as I do, realistically. If he got there first, then that's on me for not being quick enough.

"I... am bonded to all of them, sir," she says carefully, her eyes directly on her own soggy vegetables.

"Ah. Yes. The most... *unusual* arrangement indeed." The Master drums his fingers against the table, rhythmically, slow, methodical.

T-t-t-thrum, t-t-t-thrum, t-t-t-hrum.

"But this bond is one thing. Your *loyalty*, your *faithfulness*, is another."

T-t-t-thrum, t-t-t-thrum, t-t-t-hrum

The hairs on the back of my neck rise, and my nostrils flare at his implication.

Why is he bringing this up again?

"You belong to Luke as far as I'm concerned," he continues, waving his hand casually to the side.

T-t-t-thrum, t-t-t-thrum, t-t-t-hrum

My hand curls into a fist on my thigh. Eli bites down hard enough I see a line of blood drip out of the corner of his mouth.

"Father–" Luke sets his utensils down as Selene curls into herself, her head bowed as she absorbs The Master's words.

"Tell me, dear," The Master cuts Luke off, eyes still locked on Selene. "Have you honored that? Or are you *whoring* yourself out?"

T-t-t-thrum, t-t-t-thrum, t-t-t-hrum

"I-I-I–" Selene stutters, face bright red, but The Master doesn't allow her to go further.

"Jace."

"Yes, Master?" Jace looks up, his own face pale as he draws The Master's attention.

"You're the *healer*," he spits the word. "are you not?"

T-t-t-thrum, t-t-t-thrum, t-t-t-hrum

Jace sets his fork down. "I am, sir." The Master grabs a piece of bread and tears it apart absentmindedly.

"Then, from now on, you will monitor her cycles." He says it like it's *nothing*. Like he's asking Jace to keep track of the weather. "I want to know when it comes. When she's fertile. If I have to, I'll start monitoring the act myself."

T-t-t-thrum, t-t-t-thrum, t-t-t-hrum

Selene sucks in a breath as I go rigid with fury. Eli's bloodstained lip falls from his teeth, and I absentmindedly wonder if The Master will point that small flaw out, too.

Jace hesitates. *Too* long.

The Master's eyes narrow. "Is there a problem with this, *Vitalis*?"

His fingers stop.

Jace's lips press into a thin line as he rolls them back between his teeth. Slowly, he turns his head towards Luke, eyes wide in confusion. Luke inhales through his nose and nods once stiffly, as if his hands are tied and he *knows* it's the only answer he can give.

Fuck, it really *is* the only right answer here. Even *I* can see that.

Jace stares a second longer, brows drawn together, before facing The Master again. "Yes, sir."

The Master licks his chapped lips. "*Good* boy."

My chest *burns* with rage. *How fucking* dare *he....*

Selene stays silent but I can see the fury in her eyes as her lower lip quivers. She's *just* as pissed as we are, but she knows speaking out of turn will get her nowhere. The Master picks his goblet up again as if he's finally said all he wanted to. As if we aren't sitting here, our stomachs twisted into knots, our mate reduced to *chattel*, our lives at *his* will.

"*Now*," he says, gesturing to Selene's plate. "Eat up, my dear. You need to keep up your strength. Lucas nearly killed his mother during childbirth. It would be a... *shame* to repeat that, wouldn't it?"

My jaw is so tight it's a miracle my teeth don't shatter.

Monitor her cycles? Like she's a fucking broodmare. *Keep up her strength?* As if she isn't strong enough to birth a baby? I flick my gaze to Eli, who's got his eyes locked on Selene.

He's *furious.*

I can tell in the way his shoulders are stiffened, in the way his hands curl in the material of his pants, just how deep the anger goes. He stares at The Master, and I can tell he's imagining gutting him right here, *right now.*

I blink.

It's... *unexpectedly relieving.*

Eli, who keeps his distance as best as he can. Separates himself from us. Sneaks in and sleeps on our couch instead of the bed, who prefers to shower in the morning, who will do everything he can to be up and dressed for the day long before we're awake. Almost as if he's pretending he isn't in our circle *at all....*

He and I are *completely* on the same page right now.

I might not like the guy, but I *really* like this.

At least I'm not sitting here in this pit of fury alone. Jace and Luke make *eyes* at each other but they never look at me, and I can't help the jealousy that curls in my chest at *their* friendship.

That I don't have.

Eli's eyes shift slightly, catching mine.

For a single, brief second, we *understand* each other.

Then he looks away, reaching for his goblet. He forces a slow sip of his drink.

I turn back to my plate, but my appetite is completely gone.

"Let us pray," The Master says, voice flat, as done with this dinner as the rest of us. We bow our heads and lay our hands, palms upward, on the cold, worn tablecloth. As he's done with every evening prayer, he leads, his voice steady and practiced as though the chant is burned into his bones. "We take this meal in reverence, a gift of blood and bone. May our bodies be instrumental, our faith unyielding, and our purpose be one of your will."

The words flow from his mouth like an ancient mantra, and we repeat, a low, collective murmur. "For the Watcher, we are Chosen."

I keep my eyes open, staring down at my lap, trying to fight the suffocating dread creeping through my veins. For the first time in my life, the words don't sit *right* on my tongue. They feel *hollow,* and the prayer no longer holds any comfort.

There's a coldness to the words, like they've lost their meaning.

But maybe they've only lost their meaning to me....

"In his name, we are *Chosen.*"

"We are Chosen," we repeat, echoing in the silence, a chorus of obedience. I feel sick to my stomach. It doesn't feel like a prayer anymore.

It feels like a *curse*.

"And should we *falter*?" The Master asks us. My skin crawls.

"We shall be eviscerated," I whisper, words thick in my throat. The finality of it hangs in the air. My eyes flicker to Luke, and I catch his dead, empty stare.

He looks as if he believes *nothing* anymore and I'm struck–the terrible realization of how he's probably *never* believed it a day in his life.

Selene

I push open the door to Luke's bedroom, barely paying attention as I step inside. Mornings are *too* early, The Temple is *too* far away, and my bladder is *too* full for me to function properly.

My mates are already off doing whatever it is they do all day–*not that anyone bothers to tell me*–which means I have a few blessed minutes to myself before I have to pretend to be The Seraph.

Sacred Woman Extraordinaire.

I make a beeline for the bathroom, yawning as I shove the door open.

And *immediately* stop short.

Max is standing at the sink shirtless, arm awkwardly twisted as he tries–*and fails*–to clean his stitches. Water drips down his skin, catching the morning light in a way that is, frankly, *unnecessarily* attractive. His jaw is tight, face locked somewhere between frustration and mild murder, and when he notices me in the mirror, his scowl only deepens.

I raise an eyebrow. "Well, good morning to *you*."

He flicks water off his fingers. "What do you want?"

"To pee."

He blinks. I blink back. A drop of water slides down his shoulder.

"Then *pee*."

"Yeah, *no*, I don't need an audience, thanks."

He rolls his eyes but doesn't argue, which feels like a first. Instead, he goes back to trying to wipe the cut, lips twitching with irritation. It's not going well, and I feel bad for him. I lean against the doorframe, crossing my arms.

"Can I help, or are you going to just drip all over the floor?"

Max stops and looks at me. He hesitates *just* long enough for me to know he *wants* to say no just because he's stubborn, but he grunts and shoves the cloth at me after another long silence.

I smirk, stepping forward. "*See*? That wasn't so hard, was it?"

He mutters something under his breath but doesn't pull away when I take his arm, angling it to get a better look at the cut. I can immediately tell Jace stitched it because it's a damn good job. The skin is red and angry around the edges, so Max must have pulled at it. There's the faintest smudge of blood seeping through the top and I can see spots he can't reach. I press the cloth against it, dabbing gently, and he watches me with that dark, intense scrutiny I've come to expect from him.

For a guy who acts like he's untouchable, he sure gets hurt *a lot*.

"You know," I say casually as I wipe more blood away. "For the future Warden or whatever, you kind of suck at dodging."

His nostrils flare. "For The Seraph, you sass back *way* too much."

"Blasphemy." I shake my head, mock scandalized. "Hope *God* doesn't smite you for that."

"If he was gonna smite me, he'd have done it by now. I've got so much blood on my hands, babe...."

He's probably right.

I finish wiping the wound and drop the cloth in the sink, then reach for the small jar of salve sitting on the counter. It's some herbal healing mix Jace must've brought for him, I realize, and I scoop out a little on my index finger before smoothing it over the stitches. Once I've finished that, I start wrapping the fresh bandage around his bicep, trying to ignore how his muscle feels under my hand.

Aside from a slight twitch of his eyebrow, he doesn't even *acknowledge* that I'm touching him.

I glance up, my lips quivering with a small smile. Our faces are close enough that I can feel his breath on my lips. "You're welcome, by the way."

"Yeah?" He scans my face. "For what?"

I snort, releasing his arm as I step back. "You're a *real joy*, you know that?"

"For you? I try."

I tug the last strip of gauze into place, smoothing it over his arm with more care than I probably need to. "There," I say, rocking back on my heels. "Try not to be dumb and rip this one open, okay?"

Max doesn't look at the fresh bandage. His eyes are dark with something simmering under the surface, something borderline *feral*.

I shift, suddenly *very* aware of how close we are, and how full my bladder is.

I clear my throat. "Okay, well, I still need to–"

Before I can finish, his fingers wrap around my wrist, holding me in place.

"Do you?" he murmurs, amusement coating the word. I blink up at him, about to ask what the *hell* his problem is, when he tugs on me.

One quick jerk.

One step forward.

Suddenly, *I'm* the one backed up against the counter with my lower back pressed into the sink. I have no time to process what's happening before he's crowding me, the heat of him wrapping *around* me.

"What are you *doing*?" I ask, my voice shaking. Max lowers his head and drags his nose up the curve of my neck, inhaling my skin, his breath warm and unsteady against my pulse.

My heart *jumps*.

Our bond is *clawing* inside of me at our proximity, with how mere inches separates us from completing the claim. I can *feel* the unease rolling inside him, the restrained hunger in the way his hands flex on my hips. The air around us feels heavy with things unsaid.

I swallow hard. "Max–"

"I *want* you," he rasps against my throat, voice ruined with need. "You have no idea how bad I *need* you, my pretty prey."

A shiver rolls through me. His words settle low in my stomach, hot and aching as my body *pulses* with desire. I should push him away, *should* remind him that we're still figuring out our whole dynamic and that Eli was a mistake and that Luke was doing what he needed to do... and....

I *don't.*

I stand there, breath shallow, body *trembling* under his massive frame as his hand slides down the outside of my hip. His thumb teases slow circles, tracing the fabric of my dress like he's memorizing the shape of my body beneath it.

I bite my lip, fighting the urge to press myself closer.

He drags his nose up the side of my neck again followed by his lips. So wet, plush, *hot....*

He presses *himself* against me.

Solid. *Unmistakable.*

My breath catches, the air between us crackling with a nearly tangible hum. I grip the edge of the counter, desperate to hold onto *something* but I refuse to let myself give in.

His breath ghosts over my jaw, his teeth nipping at my chin. "You feel that?" he growls, rocking into me. "That's how bad I fucking *need* you."

A small, helpless whimper escapes me.

"You keep acting like prey, and I promise I'll show you what it's like to be hunted."

My mouth falls open at the declaration, and though my heart races, I manage to gasp out, "How *dare* you?"

His answer is a devastating smirk, tongue darting out over his lower lips with his hand gripping my hips as if he'll never be able to touch me again. I have half a mind–

His mouth moves to hover just over mine, letting me *feel* the shape of his lips, the absolute *imprint* of his restraint. And then, instead of *devouring* me like I half-expect him to, he *merely* kisses me.

A soft press of lips.

Nothing more.

It's *worse* than if he'd taken the kiss.

I make a strangled noise as he pulls back, hands sliding off my hips as if he hasn't just *ruined* me. He heads for the door but, as he crosses the threshold, he pauses and glances over his shoulder.

"Go ahead and pee, Selene. Unless you *want* me to stay and watch."

I glare, cheeks burning with humiliation, but he laughs and disappears.

I stand there a moment longer, heart racing, bond singing, *aching* desperately for relief.

What the hell?

I shake myself, trying to shove down the lingering heat curling between my thighs and finally do what I came in here for. When I'm done washing my hands, I step back out of the bathroom, still fighting through the haze he left me in.

Luke's sitting on the arm of the couch, arms crossed. His eyes are clouded over with lust and I know immediately that he saw. He doesn't say anything at first, just watches me shut the door and wipe my still damp hands on my skirt nervously.

"Come here, lamb," he says finally, standing up. I hesitate, not because I don't *want* to, but because I don't know what he's thinking or what he wants from *me*.

"***Now***," he adds in that low, *do-not-disobey-me* tone, and my feet move. He reaches for me as soon as I'm close enough, his grip tight as he pulls me into his chest "Let me take care of you."

He guides me to our bed.

I should say something.

We're both going to be late.

I'm expected at The Temple.

Isn't The Master waiting for you?

My heart hammers against my ribs and the bond pulses happily at the idea of being sated as he lays me down, warm palms smooth on my still quivering thighs. His fingers hook my underwear, and he slides them down my legs, taking the time to set them at the foot of bed. He's back not a moment later, raising my dress with agonizing slowness, eyes locked on mine, watching every emotion cross my face.

"Trust me, lamb," he murmurs, leaning forward to press our lips together.

I do.

God, help me, *I do.*

A single fingertip drags up the inside of my thigh, so light it's taunting. My thighs shake as his lips curl into a sly, satisfied grin, tracing lazy circles as he reaches my pussy, never quite landing on my clit, never *quite* giving me what I need. I rock my hips in a silent plea and he chuckles, sealing our lips together in a shallow kiss.

"Impatient?"

I glare at him... or I *try* to. It's hard to look intimidating when I'm trembling beneath him. "You're *cruel*."

"And you're *soaked*."

I make a strangled sound, *mortified*, but any retort dies on my tongue as he finally, *finally*, slides two fingers inside of me.

My back arches off the bed, hands flying to his shoulders to wrap around his neck. His name slips from my lips, barely a whisper but he hears it anyway because I've brought our lips together again. His movements are precise as he strokes me, his thumb tight on my clit as he plays me like a well-loved instrument. I moan into his mouth as his tongue strokes mine, fingers circling against that sweet spot inside of me, stroking them *just* right, as the pleasure curls low in my belly, burning, tightening, *climbing*–

"Luke," I gasp, holding myself together by a thread.

"I've got you," he breathes into my mouth. "Let *go*, Selene."

I do.

Pleasure rips me apart at the seams. I clutch at him, nails digging into his neck as I shatter. He works me through every last aftershock until I can't take any more, until I'm pulling back when the tingling turns *painful*.

When I finally go boneless against him, he kisses my temple reverently. I feel him crawling in the bed next to me, rock hard against my thigh, but he makes no movements to relieve himself. I don't grab at him either. I roll to the side, pressing my face into his chest, letting the quiet linger between us.

"We both have to leave," I say even as I make no motion to do so.

Luke's hand drags lazily down my spine. "We can stay a moment longer."

I don't argue as I let my eyes slip closed, listening to the steady rhythm of his breathing. The warmth of his body, the way he holds me like I'm treasured, the way he sits heavy in my soul–

It threatens to undo me.

"I'm sorry about my father. The way he's been treating you at dinner, especially."

I open my eyes and lift my head to look at him. "You're not responsible for your father."

"I still *hate* it." His jaw clenches. "I hate that I have to sit there and act like it's fine."

"I understand we all have roles to play," I tell him softly, running my hand across his chest. "You're protecting me as best as you can. Protecting *us*. That requires some sacrifice on all our parts."

Luke doesn't seem comforted but he nods, running his free hand down his cheek. "It doesn't make it right."

"No," I agree, laying back down. "But you aren't your father. I *know* that." His breath hitches like I've caught him off guard, and he tightens his arm around me, pressing a kiss to my hairline.

We stay longer than a moment.

The room is warm. The kind of warmth that settles into your bones, makes you lazy, makes it hard to move. Luke's arm is heavy over my waist, his hand resting just beneath my ribs, breath slow and steady against the back of my neck. Max is sprawled on the other side, broad and solid, one arm stretched across the bed, finger an inch shy of brushing my shoulder.

Outside the thunder rolls deep and low like a giant stretching its limbs. The rain follows in a steady rhythm, tapping against the window and filling the silence with that of a good, needed storm.

I roll slightly to test if my movement will wake them, but neither of them react.

Carefully, I peel myself away from Luke's hold. He makes a small noise in his sleep, his brow twitching, but his grip loosens. I slip free, easing myself off the bed, my feet meeting the cool floor with a quiet press of skin against stone.

Across the room, Eli is a dark shape stretched along the couch. A shirt is draped over his face, shielding his eyes from the dim light filtering in through the windows, his chest rising and falling in deep, even breaths. One of his arms is flung over his stomach, fingers twitching slightly, like he's caught in some half-formed dream.

To be honest, I'm not entirely sure *why* he doesn't go ahead and join us. We all already pretend to not notice him sneaking in late at night after we've gone to bed. It wouldn't be that far of a stretch for him to crawl in on the other side of Max where it's more comfortable than that small couch. We could still pretend he's not there if it made him feel better....

The rain is louder near the window. The steady *tap-tap-tap* against the glass draws me toward the small seat.

Jace is already there.

He doesn't move when I approach.

He's curled into the window seat, knees drawn up, arms resting loosely atop them. The flashing light catches in his hair and softens the curve of his jaw, keeping his expression passive.

His gaze is fixed on the storm beyond the glass.

Not simply watching it.

Lost in it.

There's something about the way he's sitting that makes my heart skip. Like if I weren't here, if the others weren't sleeping just a few feet away, he would let himself disappear into it.

I don't say anything yet.

I move closer, unhurried, watching for any sign that he's noticed me.

His fingers twitch slightly against his knee, but he doesn't look over when I lower myself on the seat beside him.

The window is cracked open, just enough so that a thin sliver of space lets in the scent of rain and earth, the charged, electric sharpness of a good storm. A gust of wind slips through, cool against my skin, lifting the fine hairs on my arm.

I pull my legs up, mimicking his posture. I wonder if he'll ignore me completely.

"Can't sleep?" I murmur softly.

His throat bobs as he swallows. "No," he admits reluctantly.

Another rumble of thunder rolls overhead, and I can feel the way his muscles tighten beside me. Jace exhales slowly, his head tipping just a fraction like he's listening for something I can't hear. When he finally speaks, his voice is quieter than I've ever heard it, and I'm not sure if it's because everyone else is still asleep or because the past still haunts him.

"I used to hate storms."

I hold my breath, afraid to shatter whatever delicate thing has opened up between us.

What I've *allowed* to open between us.

He keeps his eyes on the storm. His fingers are tense where they're tangled in his sleep pants.

"When I was little," he starts, slow and even, like he's picking each word out carefully, "the thunder would scare the hell out of me. The lightning, too. It wasn't just the sound. It was the way it shook the walls, the way it felt like something *alive*, something that would swallow me up."

His lips press together briefly, jaw clenching before he exhales again.

"I used to cry out for her. My mother." His voice drops lower, like he's speaking to the rain itself. "Every time. Every single storm. I'd scream for her, beg her to come to me. But she never did."

The drops splash on the open window. The next roll of thunder is softer, *distant*, but he flinches away anyway.

"She'd tell me to grow up," he continues, his tone flat. I can hear the pain underneath. "Told me to *be a man*. She'd shout it through the door. 'Stop being such a baby, Jace. Let me sleep.'"

I don't expect him to keep going but he does.

"Eventually, I stopped going to her." He swallows again. "Stopped crying. Stopped screaming. But I could never sleep."

He shifts slightly and drops one leg off the side of the seat, finally dragging his eyes away from the window to look down at his hands instead.

"I started listening instead. To the rain. To the wind. The way the thunder came in waves." A small breath of something not quite a laugh escapes him. "Eventually I learned to find comfort in it."

He glances up, looking at me for the first time since I joined him. His mouth curves at the corners but there's no humor in it. A deep, twisting pain bites at my heart. How a mother could be so cruel to her child....

I can picture it clearly–Jace as a little boy, tiny and afraid, sitting in the dark outside his parent's door, crying out for his mother, begging for comfort that never came. I see his small hands pressed against their cold floor, his tears soaking into the fabric of his shirt as he muffles his sobs because she doesn't want to hear them. I *feel* the way his tiny shoulders shake, the way the thunder rattles the windows around him, how he flinches at every flash of lightning–

Alone.

A child shouldn't ever feel so alone.

My stomach turns, my body almost recoiling at the thought of doing that to my own child.

Our child. Jace and I.

The image forms in my mind so easily. A boy with dark hair like his but with *my* eyes. He'd be small, *soft*, the kind of child that clings to warmth, that buries himself into his parents' arms like it's the safest place in the world. A kind soul that knows no cruelty because we've shielded him so well–

And I would never... *never*... let him sit alone in the dark, terrified, begging for me....

Jace sits so still beside me. The storm flickers through the window, casting shadows across his face, illuminating the tension in his shoulders, the way he bites at his cheek....

I move before I think.

I tuck myself into him, pressing my cheek against his chest, curling my fingers into the fabric of his shirt. He stiffens and inhales–a rapid pull through his nose–and then I *feel* it. The slow, careful way the stress leaves his body, how the breath he releases shakes slightly.

His arms come around me.

I let out a soft sigh as he holds me. He's solid, *steady*, not like Luke but like *Jace*–the kind of touch that speaks without words, that *heals*, that *grounds* me even though *I'm* the one trying to ground him.

A hand brushes my jaw, coaxing me to tilt my face up. He looks down, eyes shimmering and stormy in a way that has nothing to do with the weather outside. He strokes his thumb over my chin, over my lower lip, fingers curling lightly at the edge of my jaw and–

He *kisses* me.

Soft. *So soft. Slow.* The press of his lips against mine, a fleeting touch that awakens the bond, making it throb in a whole new way. When he pulls back, he presses the tips of our noses together.

"Thank you," he whispers, closing his eyes.

I smile, sinking back into him and letting the bond settle with anticipation inside of me. I nestle into his chest, pressing my ear against him and let the steady rhythm of his heartbeat *anchor* me. I breathe in slowly, body rising and falling with each steady beat of his heart. The rain is softer now, a slow pitter-patter against the frame, an occasional rumble of thunder rolling through the dark. Jace keeps his arms wrapped around me, staring out the window, lost again to the sounds.

I let him wander as I do what I intend–I ground his body to free his mind.

Something shifts in the room. The rustle of fabric, a flicker of movement.

I glance over.

Eli's watching us.

He's lying on the couch with his shirt draped over his face, but now it's pulled down enough to reveal the gleam of his eyes. Lightning flashes again, carving his face out of the darkness for a split second.

But I don't need it to see what's there.

The bond between us tremors with a deep vibration of something I can't *quite* grasp.

Want. Longing. *Restraint.*

He *feels* confused. Like he doesn't know what to do with *this*. With *me*.

Even though he's been *inside* me.

I watch him watching me with Jace and let the rain fill the space between us. Carefully, I let the edges of my lips lift into a subtle smile.

Small. Gentle. *Real.*

Our bond shivers in pleasure and I send something back his way. Not demands. Just warmth. *Comfort.*

His fingers flex against his bare chest, which rises on a slow inhale, then lowers again as the moment bleeds away. He holds my eyes as he contemplates what I'm doing before exhaustion overtakes him and he's pulling the shirt back over his face–

He's asleep again in seconds.

I keep watching him a moment longer as lightning flickers again, dancing across his skin. I turn back to the window, pressing my face into the safe, secure warmth of Jace.

Together, we listen to the rain.

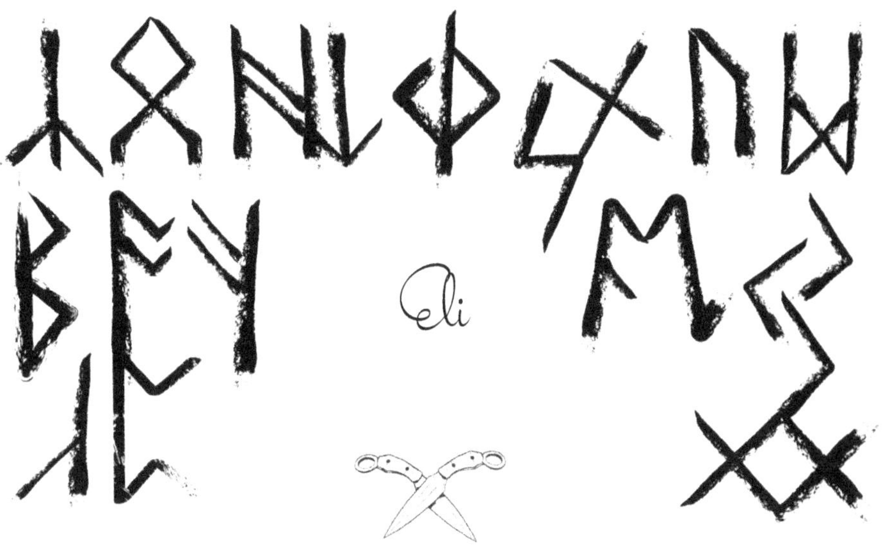

I'm *late.*

I shouldn't have touched her, because it's all I can think about now. Her body, pulling me in, that *perfect* heat that made every inch of me *feel.* The way she responded to me, so fucking eager, like I was something she *needed* as much as I *needed* her. I can still feel her around me, tight and slippery like she was *made* for me. It's twisted and fucked-up how I fist my cock to the thought of it *every single night,* to the thought of her soft, desperate moans, like she couldn't get enough and... *God, how I want more.*

But I can't have more.

Not when I'm *this* close to my goal. Not when every single second I spend with her chips away at my plans. I've got this fucking mission, the one she isn't part of. She's the *one* thing in this world I'd risk it all for and yet... *I can't.* She's tied to it. To Middlesborough.

To everything I've pledged to destroy.

To the things I can't let myself want.

But I *do.* I do want.

I want her more than I've ever wanted anything. Her eyes, the way they look at me like I'm something precious. Like during the rain storm when Jace had held her, and she'd seen me watching. Her laugh, so vulnerable and feminine that it makes my teeth *ache*, like she's not built for this world, like if I don't shield her, it'll swallow her *whole*.

The curve of her neck, the way she looks when her hair tangles around it when she's on top of me... hell, even the way she looks when she's lost in thought. *Fuck, I'm obsessed.* Every damn part of her calls me, *screams* my name even when I'm not with her. But I can't get too close. I can't let *her* get too close, because if she does, I'll risk everything.

And I can't do that. Not now. Not when I'm this deep in. Not when every part of me wars for her and *knows* how fucking stupid this is.

The worst part? I'm not even sure what *she* wants. Not when she has *them*. The others.

But still... there's *our* pull. The constant ache in my soul that makes it impossible to think straight when she's near.

I can't be the one who fucks this up.

But God, if I didn't want to *taste* her... just *once*....

I shake my head violently, shoving the thoughts down as I slip past the gate and nod at the guards. They *barely* glance at me. At this point, me fucking off into the woods is routine. One of them even waves as I pass.

I don't wave back.

The moment I'm out of view, I pick up the pace, jogging through the thick underbrush. I know all the tree roots on this route, every hidden dip in the wood line. Eight years of sneaking along this path will do that.

And in eight years, I've never been late for a meeting. Not *once*.

Until now.

Being bonded wasn't part of my plan.

It *shouldn't* have happened. I'm not from here. These aren't *my* people. This isn't *my* destiny. And yet....

It feels wrong. It feels *right*.

Not just because it's a bond I never wanted, but because something about it is *off*. Different. I can feel the magic there, coiled tight like a noose around my ribs but it holds back. Doesn't allow my bond the freedom it deserves. It's quiet, somehow contained. I *should* be grateful but all it does is make my skin itch with suspicion.

After having The Ritual done on me, I studied what I could on Middlesborough's bonds. Learned how they were supposed to feel from Malachi, the way they ripped through you like wildfire. This isn't that, not entirely. This is something else–unnatural, restrained in a way that I don't *understand.*

And that's a problem. I don't know *how* they did it. I can barely remember anything but pain from my Ritual and that *really* bothers me.

By the time I reach the meeting point, my lungs are on fire and my shirt is sticking uncomfortably to my back with sweat. Malachi is already there, leaning against a tree like he's got all the time in the world. Arms crossed, posture relaxed, but those sharp blue eyes don't miss a thing. He gives me an annoyed once-over, irritation flickering across his face, then it's gone, smoothed into something dangerously close to concern the second he gets a good look at me.

"What's wrong?"

"Everything," I pant, bending over, hands braced against my knees as I try to catch my breath. My head feels light from the sprint, vision swimming. "Fuck, Malachi. *Everything.*"

He straightens, uncrossing his arms, mouth pulling into a tight line and that *look*–the one that says he's done with me–settles on his face.

"Are you in trouble?"

"I've been bonded."

"Well, shit," he says, placing his hands on his hips, clicking his tongue. He exhales, eyes flickering over me like I might be joking. "That's no good."

"No, Malachi, it's *not* fucking good," I snap, straightening despite the way my ribs protest. "I was supposed to be undercover, not *bonding.* I didn't think I could even bond with anyone in this sect."

He tilts his head, considering my attitude. "I take it this wasn't something you could walk away from."

I let out a humorless laugh, rubbing a hand over my sternum. I can *feel* her plucking at the bond again. She likes to do that every so often to remind me that she's still there.

As if I could forget it.

"Oh, *sure*. I'll just tell The Master I'd rather not participate in his sacred Joining Ceremony and see how *that* goes for me."

Malachi grimaces. "Point taken."

I press my fingers against my temples, willing my pounding headache away. "And it's not just that. Something is *wrong* with this bond. It's not how you described it to me."

His brow lifts slightly. "Wrong how?"

I shake my head. "I don't fucking *know*. It's there but it's mostly quiet. Like it's been leashed? It takes control sometimes but... it's limited in its power." I pause. "Contained, since The Ritual."

Malachi's expression darkens. He's never liked Middlesborough but after I'd gone.... He didn't like the idea of sending a fourteen-year-old into the fight but when my blood father had offered me up, not enough voices had spoken against it.

Malachi was the only person from my sect that I'd seen in eight years. He's practically raised me behind enemy lines, guiding me through puberty, through my questions about the bond when I got closer to the Joining Ceremony last year and about what I might experience.

It's how I *know* this bond is warped.

"That's concerning," he mutters, rubbing a hand over his scruffy jaw. "And it doesn't resemble anything that I described to you?"

"If it did, I wouldn't be standing here bitching about it."

He lets out a low hum, the kind that usually means, '*this is bad, but I don't want to say it yet*'. Then, finally, "It'll all be okay. We can figure this out."

"I haven't told you the next part. They named my mate The Seraph... some kind of mystic. Do you know anything about that?"

Malachi's entire body goes still. Then, he *inhales* an actual, audible gasp. His eyes grow wide and, for the first time since I've known him, he looks genuinely scared.

"They named her Seraph?" His voice is barely above a whisper.

I blink. "Yeah. Why?"

He doesn't answer me right away, just presses his lips together, glancing away to look at the trees.

"Malachi."

Nothing. I step closer, lowering my voice. Rage burns in my chest. He has information about *my* mate.

"What does it mean? I've never heard *anything* about The Seraph. It's all gotta be under lock and key, so if you know something, then you need to tell me."

His jaw works like he's debating whether or not to say anything. And that? That *pisses me off*.

After I've spent eight years of my life here. After I've given *everything* in exchange for Sableford–fed them information to take Middlesborough down, sabotaged from within, laid my life on the line for them.

At *fourteen*.

Offered up by my father, who was distraught over the death of my mother and none of the other bond mates refused.

None of my siblings *cared* enough to speak out.

"You *clearly* know what it means. So unless you want me to storm back in there and start asking them as their new Sentinel–"

His head snaps back around. "Don't."

"**Then *tell* me.**" The command comes from deep inside my chest, surprising even me. I have no control over it yet, and Malachi takes a step back, his lips parted in shock.

His eyes are full of sympathy. "It's... there are five of you, aren't there?"

I frown. "Yes."

Malachi walks back to his tree and leans against it again. He looks around like he's making sure no one is listening in on us before continuing.

"You've done your job well, Elijah. Better than anyone expected a child to do," he starts, sinking down to sit against the forest floor. "But there's things I haven't told you. Things I never expected you to be able to find out." He looks up at me and I crouch down to keep our eyes level. "You are like a son to me, you know. It *broke* me to hear they performed that Ritual on you and chained your bond. That you'd never experience that connection in your life with your mates."

"Well, I'm bonded *now*," I remind him.

"Middlesborough being able to harness this bond is generations old through some sort of ancient magic. We've heard rumors but could find nothing other than half of a prophecy that we didn't believe. Nobody could tell if it was real or part of their twisted doctrine–"

"What did it say?"

"–and now there's four of you," he continues on, his eyes filling with tears, "and The Seraph at the center. Whatever they're planning, it's big."

"What did the prophecy say!" I shout, my heart racing in my chest as my patience snaps. **"Tell me now!"**

"'*One will bear the mark of four, and she will tear the veil.*' That's the only piece we have. We don't know *what* veil, but whatever they're planning... it's already in motion."

My breath hitches and I sit down, running a hand through my hair. *Tear the veil?* That sounded like some *apocalyptic* bullshit. Knowing what little I've been able to find out about The High Priestess and The Master, it probably is.

I stare at Malachi waiting for him to say more, but he doesn't. He just sits there, looking like he already knows I'm spiraling.

"That's *it*? That's *all* you have?"

"It's all anyone has," he says quietly. "That's why we sent *you* to find more. We never expected the records to be so well guarded and, when that Ritual was performed, I knew you'd never be able to return home."

My hands curl into fists as my heart shatters in my chest. "You've *known* that this entire time and *never* thought to tell me?"

His expression hardens. "And what would you have done with it, Elijah? You were a *child* when I met you. You had your mission. Gather information. Survive. I didn't tell you because I didn't think it would *matter*." He slaps a hand to his thigh. "You couldn't come home. What would telling you do other than hurt you? And I didn't think you'd be *in* the prophecy mess!"

"Well, I *am* in it," I snap at him, "and now you're telling me I might be wrapped in some end-of-the-world bullshit? That *my* Selene is the bringer of doom?" I pull my hair, fighting the tears that are starting to sting. "What the *fuck* am I supposed to do with that?"

"I don't know."

I don't have the patience for his hesitation anymore.

I surge forward and grip his wrist, my fingers digging into his skin.

"Don't you *dare* hold out on me, Malachi. Not anymore. If you know anything else–"

"I don't," he cuts in, "not for certain."

I narrow my eyes. "Not for *certain*," I echo. "Which means you suspect something. Close enough."

Malachi swallows, gaze dropping to my hold on his arm. "I suspect… that by the time we figure out *exactly* what's happening, it'll be too late to stop it. We've lost Elijah. We've lost it all."

My blood turns to ice.

I release his wrist and stand so fast my head spins. The weight of it presses against my ribs, making it hard to think, hard to *breathe*. The bond burns inside of me, desperate to run to her and hold her tight. *My poor princess.*

"Elijah," Malachi warns, watching me like he knows what I'm thinking. Like he knows I'm about two seconds away from sprinting home and finding Selene, shaking her by her slender shoulders and demanding she tell me what the *actual* fuck is going on.

Except she doesn't know. She doesn't know any more than I do.

Neither does Luke, or Jace, or Max.

We're all bound to this fate. And to each other.

"Tell me about her."

I turn, looking down at him. "What?"

"The Seraph," he says. "*Selene.*"

I don't like her name in his mouth, like it's toxic, like she's already done something *horrible* to him. Not just a woman. Not just a victim.

"She's…." I trail off, putting my hand on the back of my neck and squeezing the muscles there. *How do I describe her?*

Malachi waits while I think, his eerie blue eyes locked onto me.

"She's… weak. Innocent," I say finally, because that's the *truth*. "Sarcastic. And a little bit of a pain in my ass right now."

Something flickers in Malachi's gaze, but I don't let him interrupt.

"She's not really like the other women in Middlesborough. They bend to their mates. She *fought* me. Her bond is just as fucked as mine, and I'm willing to bet the others are, too." I sigh, pinching the back of my neck. "She didn't ask for this. She didn't want this. She's bonded to *four* of us, Malachi. *Four*. And now all of Middlesborough will be calling her the fucking Seraph. She's terrified."

Malachi hums. "And you?"

I freeze mid-step. "What about me?"

His head tilts. "You say she's scared, but what about you?"

My mouth opens and then snaps shut.

Because–*fuck*–I *am* scared.

I'm scared of what this means. The burden of the prophecy, the bond rolling around angrily inside of me, the knowledge that sits heavy in my mind. I'm horrified by what Middlesborough has done, *how* they've done it and that I don't know how to undo it.

And I'm terrified *of* Selene.

Not because she's strong. Not because she's powerful. But because she's *not*. Because she's a *nobody* and yet, she's the center of all of this. A spark for something I don't *understand*.

"I don't know," I say instead, looking away.

I know Malachi can hear the lie but he doesn't call me on it.

My father's office always smells like old paper and candle wax, the kind of scent that clings to your clothes long after you've left. I stand across from him, my hands braced on the edge of his desk, eyes scanning the ancient map spread between us. Middlesborough sits at the center, thick black lines drawn around its borders. Beyond that, the other sects with several already blacked out from wars of generations past.

All I see are potential allies.

All he sees are potential *threats*.

"They're circling," he mutters, tapping a finger against one of the smaller towns on the eastern edge. "Watching. *Waiting* for a weakness to appear."

"Hollowden has kept to themselves for years," The Warden replies evenly, arms crossed over his chest. "There's no indication they're planning anything."

The Master sighs, shaking his head. "That's *exactly* what they want us to think."

I glance at Max while my father and The Warden go back and forth. He's standing just to my right, weight shifting onto one foot, the same way he always stands when he forces himself to stay quiet. He's watching my father, and I can tell frustrated by this pointless meeting.

He's not the only one.

I turn back to the map, keeping my voice level. "What do you suggest we do?"

It's an easy way to redirect him. Give him control of the conversation, let him work through whatever paranoia is starting to eat at him *without* pushing him too hard.

The Master narrows his eyes at the map, flicking his fingers against the desk. He's always been cautious and *calculating* but lately, it's *different*. His concern isn't about protecting Middlesborough.

It's suddenly about control. About seeing enemies that aren't there.

And it's getting *worse*.

My father presses his fingers into the chart, right against their small dot. "That eastern *sect*!" He spits the words out as if they leave a bad taste in his mouth. "They refuse to acknowledge me as their Master. They act as if they are above our laws, as if I am not the rightful ruler of this land."

His hand tightens into a fist, knuckles pressing into the worn parchment. "They don't tithe what I request. They withhold resources. They disrespect *me*. And that *cannot* be allowed."

The Warden rocks side-to-side, as if he's trying to think of an answer that won't set off my father. "That's not a reason for war, sir. They aren't mandated to tithe or trade with us."

The Master turns to me expectantly and cocks his head to the side. "What do you think, Lucas?"

Max moves beside me, stepping a little closer. Maybe he doesn't realize, but it firms my resolve. I keep my eyes on the map, scanning the sects, looking for a way out of this conversation. That eastern sect is *small*. Weak. Clinging to life.

A war with them wouldn't be a victory.

It would be a *massacre*.

I know what he *expects* me to say, but I can't form the words. I can't force them from my throat, no matter how many times I swallow around them.

"If they aren't a threat, then they aren't a priority," I manage to get out, rough over my dry tongue.

The silence that follows is louder than the ringing in my ears. I don't raise my head, even though I know my father is glaring daggers directly at me. Max takes another step forward and I see his sword glittering against his broad thigh in my peripheral vision.

I *know* he has my back. I just *know* that he wouldn't let my father hurt me.

"For now," he says slowly. He clicks his tongue a few times, rolling his shoulders back. His fingers drag over the map, tapping against the Middlesborough border, against the single gate to the outside before shifting to the western border. "And the Sentinel, he'll pull his new scouts from the most recent recruits."

The Warden frowns at that, the first show of emotion I've seen all day. "The new warriors are still green. They just need more training. They'll adapt."

The Master waves a dismissive hand. "Not all of them are worth the effort. They'll struggle in combat, making us weaker. They might prove useful elsewhere." He looks up at The Warden with a devious smirk. "Eli needs bodies for scouting. He should take the ones who can't hold their own in a fight. Train them for something else. We don't need dead weight. This way, if they perish, we aren't losing important numbers."

The Warden rocks back on his heels, the veins in his neck popping out as he bites back whatever he really wants to say, and glances towards Max. "What do you think? Anyone come to mind?"

Max runs a hand through his hair, looking once in my direction before answering. "I have *some* in mind, but not many."

The Master grunts, "Good, good." He presses his fingers into the map again. "I expect results from everyone. They're coming for us."

I feel the anxiety building in my stomach as The Warden looks directly at me, his brows drawn in the middle. He believes my father, but he's always been a reasonable man... and he's asking if there's anything solid to this claim. I shrug my shoulders as a sign that I have no idea what he's talking about.

The Warden leans over and slaps his palm to the map, covering Hollowden. They talk in low tones about the potential uprisings coming our way; my father pressing that Brackmere is next, following Hollowden's example, while The Warden attempts to soothe his worries. It's a pointless endeavor, but I mentally applaud him for the effort.

Max's shoulder rubs up against mine as I let out a slow breath.

"The Sentinel...." The Master says, looking back up at me suddenly. The breath leaves my lungs as I drag my eyes up to meet his. "You trust him, don't you, Lucas?"

Max freezes beside me.

"He's done everything you've asked of him," I say neutrally, avoiding the question. It's not that I *don't* trust Eli, but that's not what he's asking me. "For years now."

My father pushes up, standing to his full height, and looks between Max and I as if he's just now realizing how close we're standing, how similar we are in height. I wonder absentmindedly if it scares him, the protection I now have in Max.

"And yet, now I wonder about him.... A boy from nowhere, bonded to The Seraph," he scoffs. "Standing in a position of power after a single night. Convenient, isn't it?"

Max's fingers curl on the hilt of his sword but he makes no other move. Neither do I.

"A position you gave him, Master," I remind him. "*After* the fire bonded him to The Seraph. If he were a threat, we'd have known it years ago."

"Would we?" My father's grin is wild. "Loyalty is a fragile thing, Lucas. A man could smile in your face and bury a knife in your spine just the same." He taps his temple. "I expect you to watch him. *Closely.*"

I nod at him even though I *know* there's nothing Eli could do that would make me give him up to my father.

But the words make me pause. It's only a matter of time before he decides to act on this insanity.

"Go find Eli," The Master says, tapping his fingers on the map. "Bring him here."

"For what?" I ask, stepping away from the desk.

My father's lips press into a thin line as he glares daggers at me. "A *conversation.*"

I don't ask any more questions. I don't *need* to. I nod once, turn on my heel and leave the room in a hurry.

I find Eli wandering where he *shouldn't* be. He's in the farthest part of the house, where people don't normally go. He's not lingering near anything weird. There's no doors opened, no obvious snooping, but here's here–*alone*–moving with a kind of aimlessness that doesn't suit him.

Not that he isn't *allowed* to explore, but any excuse to find him suspicious is all my father will need.

He notices me before I can say anything about it.

"Looking for me?"

I stop a few paces away. "My father wants to see you."

"Awe, he does? I didn't get him anything." Eli exhales through his nose, a quiet huff of air, while rolling his eyes. "No wait, let me guess," he says, biting his lower lip. I crack a smile. "I trailed dirt through the house again? Oh, I've got it.... I looked at Selene too long and now she's *impure.*"

I let out a chuckle, shaking my head. "You won't like it." I hesitate, looking him up and down. He's freshly showered and in casual clothing–fitted dark pants and a black shirt that's somehow more *him* than his usual scout uniform of torn-up pants and a worn brown shirt. "He's got you a brand-new headache. You're pulling your new scouts from the rejected warriors."

"*Fantastic.* Love a challenge." He looks absolutely exhausted already even though it's not even late afternoon. "Those who are *disposable,* you mean."

"Something like that." I pause. "He also thinks you're suspicious."

If the statement bothers him, he doesn't show it. "Only took him this long? I'm honestly offended."

I shove my hands in my pockets and shrug as he glares out the nearest window, seemingly lost in thought, before slowly turning to face me.

"And what do *you* think?"

"About what?" I ask him.

He takes his lower lip between his teeth and I find myself drawn to the way his mouth moves.

Fuck, that looks good. Wait, what—

"You know what." He interrupts my thoughts and I look away, heat crawling up my cheeks. I rub a hand over the back of my neck as I take a few steps back the way I came.

"Well, I *did* leave you and Selene alone to complete your part of the claim, so that should tell you how much I trust you, brother."

A breath leaves him, long and slow. He drags a hand down his face, mumbling out, "Well, shit," before rolling his neck.

"You weren't trying to hide it, I hope," I shrug. "Because that's *why* I left her with you. I don't have some sort of fucked-up overlord claim to her just because of what my father says. You and the others have *just* as much right to her as I do."

"Tell that to Max," Eli grumbles out. I jerk my chin over my shoulder towards my father's office, fighting the grin threatening to take hold.

"He'll come around, you'll see. Come on, let's not keep the old man waiting."

The families start to file out, children clinging to their parents' hands, small feet shuffling quietly across the grass. They all look at me as they pass, their eyes wide with curiosity. I try to avoid looking at them, even though I know *why* they're staring at me.

The Seraph.

A name I didn't ask for, a title that doesn't *fit*.

Yet here I am.

I catch one little girl, maybe five or six, with her wide, innocent eyes locked onto me. She's too young to understand what's really going on, what it means to *belong*, what it means to be *chosen*. I wonder if she ever will.

I remember being like that, so tiny and naive, sitting in the back of The Gatherings with my parents, clutching pieces of bread, listening to the old priestess drone on and on. Back when my biggest decision was what game to play after the prayers or which offering to leave on the fire. Back when everything was *so* simple.

A slice of life you could eat without thinking about what it costs.

Now, everything is different.

Even my parents don't speak to me. Either because of my four mates or because of my title, I'll never know. The world is heavy on my shoulders even though I've never asked for it. I glance at the group of children still gathered by the back door of The Temple. They don't know it yet, but they'll soon grow up and feel a similar weight, that same suffocating feeling that their place in the world is sealed.

Without having any hand in it.

I can feel Luke's warmth against my back as his hand rests on my sweaty skin, fingers rubbing small, steady circles between my shoulder blades. It's a comforting gesture, but even that does little to calm the anxiety in my chest. He's always so *sure* of himself, and I feel like I'm constantly untethered to anything solid these days.

His thumb brushes a little harder against the curve of my spine, pulling me from my thoughts. "You okay?" he murmurs softly, just loud enough for me to hear.

I don't answer right away. I'm not sure what words I could string together to explain how I feel.

I nod instead and watch the children. The group has all but disappeared leaving a few stragglers, their eyes darting between their parents and me. They linger, not *quite* ready to leave the safe familiarity of the service.

It's *almost* too much to bear. I've spent too many years attending these rites, just a child - *one of them* - and now I'm standing here, caught between their world and the one I'm about to be thrust into. The Master is somewhere near the front talking with The High Priestess, and Eli knows better than anyone that eyes are *always* watching. He keeps his distance, cautious and silent, as usual. He's not one for sentimentality but I know that he understands.

He's still close enough that I can feel the quiet intensity that radiates from him.

It's a comfort to me, just as Luke is.

Max and Jace are over by the food spread, picking at the desserts. Jace has a piece of something sweet in his hand and I can just tell by the way he's eating it that he's doing it more out of habit than enjoyment. There's something *hollow* in the way he chews. It makes me wonder if he's even mentally here at *all* or if he's still lost in the storm from a few nights ago. Max, on the other hand, is standing at the edge of the table with his arms crossed over his chest looking out at the crowd with a certain kind of distaste, as if none of this has *anything* to do with him.

Eli adjusts next to me, not enough to close the gap, but enough that I catch the movement out of the corner of my eye. I wonder what he thinks of all of this since he didn't grow up here. Did his old home worship God, too? When he converted, did he find our customs strange, or has he come to enjoy them?

"Ready for your first *true* Gathering?" Luke asks, a soft hint of disgust in his voice. I turn to face him and swallow the question I'd like to ask. Although the children and the parents are gone, there's still plenty of adults around that are eager to get into The Master's favor that wouldn't hesitate to sell us out.

It's not hard to tell he doesn't want to be here. The looks Max and Eli keep shooting people don't help. And asking the questions I want to ask would only make things worse.

Does he not *enjoy The Gathering? Does he* not *believe in God? What's about to happen that he's so worried about?*

"Do I have a choice?" I whisper over my shoulder.

He laughs quietly. "Not really." I can see him smile, sly and knowing. "But don't worry, it's not so bad after a few months. Who knows, you *might* even feel closer to God...."

The words hang in the air, bitter with sarcasm, and I can't help but roll my eyes.

"Right," I mutter, "because nothing says 'closeness to God' like nighttime prayers."

Luke steps closer, pressing his chest to my back as he wraps his arms around my waist. "We'll be here with you."

I stare ahead, fighting against the unease rising inside of me. "Sure."

He seems to sense my snark and his arms tighten around me as a couple of people edge closer to us, listening in. "It's intense, I won't lie."

Max and Jace make their way back from the buffet, neither of them looking particularly pleased. Max's brow is tight, mood heavy with brooding while Jace picks at the apple in his hand, eyes darting around the field like he'd rather be anywhere else.

"Ready for this?" Max's arms are still crossed over his chest as he echoes Luke's earlier question.

Jace looks past me, then the others, as his mouth quirks up in that familiar, tight smile that I've started to recognize as his uncomfortable look. "Does anyone *really* ever get ready for this kind of thing?" he says a little too lightly.

What is about to happen that has all of them in this type of mood?

The cool evening air is settling over the field now that the youngest have been swept away and only those of us who have attended a Joining Ceremony remain. It's Middlesborough law–at twenty-two, you become an adult, are ready for a mate, and you're ready for The Gatherings where we honor God.

But **not** until then.

I don't know *why*, but I guess I'm about to find out.

My mates have already been through these monthly ceremonies since they're all older than I am. There's no discussion about this ceremony prior to attendance and I'm wondering how different it must be to the afternoon feast we've just been at where families attend, where we preach the word of God and where children make small offerings to the fire.

Where I tried to visit with my parents, and they turned away from me in *shame*. Where I'd cried into Luke's shoulder behind The Temple before we'd been forced to return to our spot and pretend everything was fine, because The Master willed it so.

Don't think about it. Don't think about it. Don'tthinkaboutit–

The High Priestess approaches, her long, flowing robes sweeping the grass beneath her bare feet. There's no mistaking it now–we're about to begin. Her voice cuts over the chatter as she tells everyone to gather around. It's a command, not a request, and I follow my mates to the dais where her precious younglings already circle the stone square.

Luke leads us to the front with Max and Jace at his heels. I follow them, my heart hammering against my ribcage. The crowd parts around us as we move. Seraph or not, we're now pariahs to the town, still *freaks*.

There's reverence. There's expectation. There's *horror*.

Four males.

Disgust.

To me.

Worship.

I feel the eyes on me as I walk, like I'm now this grand mystery and not *Selene*. Not the young woman who apprenticed in the seamstress' shop for two years. No, she's *dead*.

Burned alive in the blue flame on the night I split my hand and *gave* myself to four men.

This is it though. My first all-adult Gathering.

The High Priestess has already ascended the dais when we reach our place at the front. Without a word, Luke kneels. Eli follows a breath later, sinking down on my right. Max and Jace follow, lowering themselves with a kind of reverence that doesn't match the tension still clinging to their shoulders.

I hesitate.

It feels like everyone, including The High Priestess, watches me slowly bend over until I'm seated on my own knees. Luke's fingers brush against mine for the briefest second. He doesn't look at me, but knowing he's there helps somehow. The bond is my tether.

The entire field is dead silent.

The trees whisper as the wind carries song between them. Not even the birds chirp, leaving us to drown in our own thoughts as we wait. The High Priestess is bathed in the soft glow of the evening light, pale hair gleaming like a halo. Her lips are slightly parted, head tilted back, eyes closed as she holds her arms out to either side–

I look around and notice everyone has their faces down, chins tucked to their chests, and see Luke looking worriedly at me from the corner of his eyes.

I drop my face to stare at my knees.

Boom–Boom.

Boom–Boom.

A deep drumbeat cuts through the silence, making me jump. Slow, steady, resounding–the beat mimics the rhythm of a heart, each thud vibrating in my chest. I sneak a peek upward just to see what's happening.

Boom–Boom.

Boom–Boom.

The High Priestess remains still, her palms facing the sky. The drum continues, unrelenting in its slow, deliberate cadence.

Boom–Boom.
Boom–Boom.

"We bow before the Watcher, He who waits in the Dark." Her voice echoes over the crowd. Most of Middlesborough is here and yet, she is able to carry her voice over everyone. I blink up at her, even though everyone else has their head tucked down.

The words rise from the crowd in unison, a single tone of devotion.

Boom–Boom.
Boom–Boom.

"We bow. We serve. We are chosen."

It presses against me, the response, utterly *absolute*. I hear it from every direction around me. Luke's steady voice beside. Eli's gentler, more measured tone. Even Jace and Max on the other side of Eli are repeating it, too. The entire mass of kneeling figures are echoing the prayer like it's been ingrained into their bones.

I don't know the words, but they taste like ash on my tongue.

Boom–Boom.
Boom–Boom.

"What is the price of faith?" The High Priestess asks.

A pause, then–

Boom–Boom.
Boom–Boom.

"Blood."

I flinch. Not outwardly, not enough for anyone to see *if* they're looking at me. But I feel it, *deep inside*, a slow strike of unease that tightens with every beat of that drum.

The answer feels like too much.

Not because it's unfamiliar. I've heard it before, countless times at the afternoon gathering, wrapped in warmth.

What is the price of faith, little ones?

"A world made safe."

It's *always* been simple. Faith is supposed to *guide* us, to make sense of the world's cruelty, to *prevent* another collapse. It's supposed to be *good*.

But this?

Boom–Boom.

Boom–Boom.

"What is the reward of our faith?"

Another pause–

Boom–Boom.

Boom–Boom.

"A world remade."

I stare ahead, my hands curled into fists against my thighs. I feel *sick*. I *know* what I'm hearing. I *know* what I've been taught. What I *believe*.

This doesn't feel the same.

"Faith is not for the faint of heart." The drum carries on, a slow, pulsing heartbeat. "To serve is to *bleed*. To be chosen is to be *remade*. We do not flinch from pain, nor do we fear sacrifice. The Watcher does not *ask* for blind obedience. He does not *demand* from the unwilling. He waits. He watches. And when we offer, He *takes*."

She takes a measured step forward and the torches surrounding the dais flicker as though they, too, are listening.

Boom–Boom.

Boom–Boom.

"We are the vessel," she continues. "We are the hands that shape the world. And through our faith, the old wounds of the world will close. Through our offerings, the new dawn will rise."

The crowd keeps their heads down, aside from a select few that are new to the ceremony. The High Priestess looks directly at me and my heart pounds in my throat. She lifts her hands, pale against the firelight.

Boom–Boom.

Boom–Boom.

"So we give."

From the sleeve of her robe she produces a small, curved blade, gleaming off the torchlight as she turns it in her fingers. There is no hesitation, no ceremony in the act–just a single, fluid slice across her palm. The blood wells instantly, dark and thick, spilling over her fingers as she clenches her fist. It drops over the dais, splattering against the stone, seeping into the grooves carved along the top and sides.

"Now, my faithful," she grins at me but I feel no solace in the act, "you must *touch* the earth beneath you. Let it *know* you. Let it *feel* your devotion."

Without hesitation, I hear everyone scraping at the ground around us. Luke sets his hand down, and even Eli places his palm on a patch of grass. I slowly do the same, the dirt cool beneath my palm.

"Close your eyes," The High Priestess commands.

Boom–Boom.

Boom–Boom.

And I do. I close my eyes.

"*Listen.*"

For a moment, there is nothing.

Nothing but the silence.

The slow, steady pull of my bonds, *yes*, but something else deep inside of me. *Unseen. Reaching. Wanting.*

I'm trembling.

Boom–Boom.

Boom–Boom.

"Look at me, my faithful." As one, the mass obeys.

The High Priestess is stepping down from the dais with controlled poise, the blood from her palm still dripping down her fingers. The crowd remains on their knees, waiting for her guidance.

She moves through them.

The slow, deliberate steps of someone who holds all the control.

My breath catches when she stops, scanning the gathered bodies with narrowed eyes. She lands on a man a few rows back, a laborer from the looks of him. Broad shoulders, calloused hands, tanned skin.

I don't think there's a reason *why* she picks him.

She extends a single, blood-soaked finger and points. "*You.*"

The man doesn't hesitate. He rises, leaving behind a woman who watches him with a tear-soaked face, and blindly follows as The High Priestess leads him towards the front.

Luke's hand slides along the ground until his pinky is next to mine. Eli slowly moves so that our legs are touching.

What are they so afraid of? What's about to happen?

The man and The High Priestess reach the dais and she faces him.

Boom–Boom.

Boom–Boom.

"Your faith is strong," she tells him, running a hand over the man's torso. "Let us see the body that serves Him. Kneel at His altar."

The man pulls his tunic over his head, baring his chest to the firelight. The muscles of his back ripple as he bends down obediently and faces the dais.

"Both hands," she instructs, gesturing to the stone. "Hold the altar."

The fire crackles.

"Faith is not without sacrifice," she says, voice ringing clear. "To follow the Watcher, we must offer not only our world, but our bodies. Our pain is proof of our devotion. To suffer in His name is to be made holy."

A wave of agreement passes through the mass. A prayer, maybe but I can't hear anything over the pulse in my ears. Luke's fingers cover mine but he says nothing.

The High Priestess steps behind the kneeling man, her hands hovering just above his shoulders. "*Prove* your faith," she commands.

And then—

Boom—Boom.

Boom—Boom.

His fingers tighten into fists, then splay wide against the stone. He takes a loud breath. Deep. Shaking.

He slams his right hand against the stone.

Again.

Again.

My eyes go wide in horror as I hear the bone crack.

Eli's hand flies to my lower back, holding me in place. I can tell my face says it all, how disgusted I am, how badly I want to run, but I stay on my knees as the man beats his palm against the pulpit.

His pinky bends wrong, jagged and broken. He slams his hand down again and another low sound splits the nights.

Another.

Boom—Boom.

Boom—Boom.

Another.

Boom—Boom.

Boom—Boom.

Another.

Boom—Boom.

Boom—Boom.

It takes four more breaks before his hand lies limp, fingers mangled and useless.

My breath is stuck in my throat. The drum plays, beating heartless heartbeats into the night.

The man lifts his left hand and begins again.

I can hear the bones breaking, can see the ruin of his hands, and yet... *no one*... stops him. No one gasps, or whispers, or turns away.

This isn't *horror* to them.

Only to those of us that are new.

This isn't *abhorrent.*

This is the price of *faith.*

When it's over, when his hands are nothing but broken things attached to trembling, sweat-soaked arms, The High Priestess finally bends beside him. She lifts the ruined hands, cradles them with the same tenderness I've seen a mother give her precious newborn—

And presses her bloodied palm to his forehead, letting it drip down his leaking nose and tear-soaked cheeks.

"You are *blessed*, Josef."

The mass bows their heads and I follow, if only to look away.

Luke's jaw is locked tight, his fingers clenched around mine, holding me still. Eli's hand on my back is fisted in my dress, as if *I'm* the one grounding him.

A mockery.

I try to pretend I don't feel sick.

The High Priestess' voice rings out in the silence.

"The weak will fall."

The crowd echoes as one, but I can't find the words.

"The weak will fall."

"The faithless will burn!" she screams into the air.

"The faithless will burn."

"The chosen... will rise!"

"The chosen will rise!" The words wrap around my mind. They feel final. A *promise* I don't want to keep.

As quickly as it began, it's over. We press our index finger to our lips, then to our foreheads, and we're free to leave.

The mass moves as one, standing and murmuring amongst themselves . I should stand, too. I should follow Luke and Eli as they start to get up, but I don't get the chance.

The High Priestess is suddenly there right in front of me. She's grinning as if we're old friends, as if her gaze doesn't pin me to the spot with fear. I barely have time to react before she lifts her hand and presses her palm to my forehead.

Her *blood-soaked* palm.

The warmth is startling. The stickiness of it, the metallic scent that floods my nose.

I'm going to vomit.

She leans in close enough that I know the words are *just* for me.

"One day," she says, thick with certainty "As The Seraph, you will help me with these."

My stomach violently protests as she smiles down at me and lowers her hand to my cheek. She places a delicate kiss on my blood-stained forehead.

"One day *soon*," she breathes against my skin.

And then she's gone, moving past us as though she never stopped at all, her presence vanishing into the crowd of believers and into the night.

Eli wraps his arms around me. "Well, that was sufficiently *fucked*."

Luke reaches forward and wipes his palm against my face, ignoring the way Eli seethes. "Let's go."

I should *run*. I should scream, shove them both away. Rip off the dress I put on and tear through the woods until my legs give out, until my lungs burn and my mind is blank and my body is my own again.

But my feet won't move. My mouth won't open.

I nod, because there's nothing else to do.

Because this is my life now.

Because I don't have a choice. I've *never* had a choice.

I'm pulled to my feet and we step through the mass. Hands reach out, grasping at Luke's.

"A powerful gathering, Sir Luke," someone says, clasping him on the shoulder. "The Master must be proud."

Luke forces a tight smile, his grip firm as he shakes the offered hands, nodding like the perfect son he has to be. Max and Jace aren't spared, either. People murmur praises, clapping them on the back. Jace agrees, forced and hollow, while Max's jaw ticks, his smile more of a grimace.

Do the onlookers notice? Do they care?

Eli doesn't bother. His hand clamps around my wrist, pulling me tight against him, his other arm wrapping around my shoulders. A shield. A *warning*.

Do the eyes that rake over us immediately run to tell The Master?

His disgust is barely masked, body tense as he glares at every person who dares to look at me too long. I hardly register any of it. The congratulations. The murmurs of *'a blessed night'* and *'we are all closer to Him'*. It all blurs together as we try to escape.

By the time we clear the side of The Temple, I can't take another step.

I rip free of Eli's grip, stumble to the wall, and heave violently. The force of it wracks my entire body, and I brace my hands against the crumbling stone as my knees attempt to buckle from under me. My stomach clenches, clenches, *clenches*, as if it's trying to purge more than just my early dinner.

There's a muffled, "*Shit*," from Max.

Jace is at my side in an instant, one hand on the back of my neck, the other holding my hair away from my face. "Breath through it, Selene," he instructs. "Just try to breathe."

Eli doesn't say anything, but I can *tell* how frustrated he is by his uneven breathing. "She wasn't ready for that." He's furious, pacing back and forth, pulling at his hair.

Luke stands away from us, arms crossed. "No one's ever ready for their first time."

Eli's head snaps toward him. "*That's* your answer?" His voice drops even lower, a *barely* restrained snarl. "She just fucking threw up and you're saying–"

"It's the truth," Luke cuts in, calm but unyielding.

"Fucking cunt *coated* her in blood–" Eli trails off, rubbing his mouth.

Jace rubs slow, steady circles on my back. "She just needs a second."

"We should've prepared her...." Max mutters, shaking his head. He gestures to my face. "Can you get that off of her?"

"You know we couldn't," Luke tells him, stepping forward while digging in his pockets. I push away from the wall, wiping the back of my hand across my mouth. My limbs feel weak and my throat burns, but I try to straighten up anyway. Jace keeps his hands on my waist, steadying me.

Eli sends a seething look in Luke's direction. "You *wanted* her to see that?"

Luke lets out a breath when he pulls a small cloth from his pocket and hands it to Jace. "That's what she *is* now. That's what we *all* are, Eli."

Jace takes the rag and wipes at my face carefully while Eli bites his lower lip hard enough that a bead of blood drips down his chin. Max takes a step toward him while Jace turns my face so that he can wipe at my cheek.

"Are you okay?" Luke watches me carefully.

I want to laugh at the absurdity of it all. *No, I'm not okay.* But I nod, voice hoarse. "Fine."

None of them look convinced.

Eli lets out a slow, humorless chuckle and walks away with Max. I watch them go, feeling a strange numbness overtaking my chest. Luke glances at them but doesn't comment. He turns back to me, voice quieter. "We should go."

I close my eyes, the lingering taste of bile on my tongue.

This isn't a one-time ordeal. This is every month.

Every.

Single.

Month.

The thought churns my gut, threatening to drag me right back down as I take Jace's hand and let him lead me home.

Two weeks have passed. Two weeks of waking up in the same massive, unfamiliar room, tangled in sheets that still don't smell like home. Two weeks of dragging myself out of bed, sitting through stiff, silent breakfasts where everyone pretends that *Gathering* didn't crack me wide open and make me want to throw my faith off a cliff to watch it crumble.

We've all been shuffled into our new roles—Luke's buried in his leadership training like he's preparing for war. Max is breaking his body under The Warden's watchful eye. Jace is drowning in patients and pressure at the infirmary. Eli... he's vanishing into whatever vague tasks The Master dreamed a Sentinel should do.

And me? I'm the *mystical Seraph*. Which apparently means I get to smile while being paraded around like a living prophecy I don't want.

A symbol of divine fate everyone is *afraid* of.

Well, *that* and sitting through the most boring history lessons I can think of.

Dinner's the worst, though. Every night, we sit in The Master's dining hall, listening to him as he picks apart our failures. He speaks of strength, of duty, of *expectations*. How we're failing him. How Luke needs to be more commanding. How Max needs to fight harder.

How Jace needs to balance care efficiently. How Eli needs to choose *more* scouts and start training them. How I need to be worthy of my bond.

And fill my womb.

As if that's *all* I'm made for. As if blood and obedience and an empty smile will make me the holy relic they desire....

Fuck.

By the time we return to the room we all now share, exhaustion clings to us like a second skin. My bond burns, raw and wanting, but I don't act on it. I can feel it humming beneath my skin like an unanswered call as it echoes off theirs. They don't answer it either. Not because they don't want to, but because they're just too *tired*.

Or maybe... we've all learned how to ignore the parts of ourselves that scream about how wrong *this is....*

Every night I crawl into bed, waiting for the advance that never comes. My bond screams for more. For connection. For *closeness*. But all I get is silence and the steady, distant breathing filling the space between us.

Luke's arm around my waist and my face pressed into Jace's chest.

The memory lingers as I sit on The Temple's stone bench and I force my focus back to the present. The youngling drones on about the glory of Middlesborough, the divine will of our God, how we were blessed with the knowledge of binding our bonds, and the sacred duty of The Seraph. It's all the same history—sans sacred duties and mystic being–that I learned growing up, but the wording is *different*. More grandiose.

Ominous.

Much like the Gathering.

Like she's setting the stage for something else. *Preparing me.*

I shift uncomfortably, my back aching from hours of sitting still in my heavy velvet dress while The High Priestess watches me from her gilded throne. She hasn't spoken much yet–hardly at all in the last week–just observes me with her cool, knowing gaze.

The youngling continues, her tone full of rehearsed reverence. "And so, The Seraph stands at the heart of the covenant, her bond as the guiding light–"

"Okay," I interrupt, shifting again. I'm just happy I'm not sore between my legs anymore. "But *why?*"

The girl blinks, her arms falling to her side. "What do you mean, Sacred One?"

I grimace. *Hate that–Sacred One.* Only mildly better than Seraph, but not by much.

"I mean, why does any of this matter? I get that the bond is important, but why am I sitting here listening to you recite a bunch of things I already know?" I wave my hand vaguely. "I could just read it myself."

The High Priestess finally speaks and a chill moves down my arms. "Understanding comes not from words but from *devotion*, Selene."

I swallow as she pins me down with her gaze. Something about how she looks at me sends my attitude reeling. "Right. Devotion. Got it." I nod. "Sorry."

Her lips curve slightly, though I don't know her well enough yet to gauge if it's in amusement or warning. "Patience. There is much yet for you to learn. Please continue, Mercy."

I *really* don't like the way she says that. I don't like any of this.

I'm reminded of my dreams, of the screaming woman ripped from her bond mates, and my own bond clenches at the thought.

I'm starting to think there's a whole lot more to Middlesborough that I don't know about but I'm not stupid enough to start questioning it now.

The youngling, Mercy, is a girl barely past sixteen. She's *breathless* in her devotion, lined up to be the next High Priestess from what I understand. She's been at The Temple since she was *four*.

"The Seraph is a blessed being," Mercy tells me, hands clasped daintily in front of her. "She alone has the power to reach beyond the veil and speak to God. Through her, divinity touches our world."

I fight the urge to roll my eyes. I've never spoken to God a day in my life–I'm pretty sure that's why we've got a High Priestess.

But the way she says it bothers me.

"Beyond the veil?" I echo, cocking my head to the side. "What does that mean?"

Mercy beams, elated that I'm apparently taking an interest. "The veil that separates us from the higher realm. The Seraph is the only one who can glimpse beyond it. She is the bridge between the mortal and the divine."

Bull. Shit.

I open my mouth and shut it twice. I want to argue, to call this what I *think* it is, but I don't.

"So... you think I can just... have a *conversation* with God?"

"If you are worthy, he will answer," Mercy says solemnly. "And if you listen, he will show you the path."

I stare at her.

"*If* I'm worthy?" I echo. The High Priestess leans forward again, eyes shimmering with hunger.

"You were chosen by the fire. You *are* worthy. We just have to prepare you," she says with a menacing grin.

I nod along and Mercy continues, but as she drones on about destiny, about divine purpose, about being *chosen*–I'm absolutely positive that I am *not* the one.

As much as it kills me to admit it, because I care deeply for my mates, the fire chose *wrong*.

It's three days later when my history lessons change. The High Priestess, as always, greets me from her throne with her cryptic smile while Mercy stands at the bottom of the throne, hands clasped together with her head lowered. I approach and bow my head in reverence even though I'm starting to think they know I'm a fraud.

"We're going to deepen your connection, Seraph," The High Priestess says, honeyed voice filled with authority. "You need to understand the full power in your blood. To *feel* it, not just know it's there."

"What does that mean?" I ask, narrowing my eyes.

The High Priestess smiles at me. It's starting to become something I really, *really* hate. When she smiles like that, we're about to do something I don't want to do.

"We will help you reach a higher state. It's necessary for your training. You must *feel* your power to unlock its true potential."

"Feel it." I repeat the words back to her, as if by saying them aloud she'll hear how stupid it sounds.

But I'm led off to a small, secluded chamber deep in The Temple, its walls lined with thick tapestries and ancient, runic carvings. It's murky and musty, the air thick with incense already swirling around the room. The High Priestess gestures for me to join her on a pillow across from her, and I sit down cross-legged.

"Just relax," she says softly. "Let your senses guide you."

In the gloominess of the room, I get my first close up look at her. She's got her hair down today, golden waves hanging past her waist in loose ringlets. Her skin is smooth with a soft, almost unnatural glow. Her eyes are a piercing shade of blue, nearly white–she is ethereal personified.

I can tell why she became The High Priestess, if looks played any part in the selection of the role.

I don't trust her, but I can't refuse her either. Not if this is *really* part of my training.

The High Priestess reaches for a small pouch, smiling slyly.

"Here, Seraph. *Inhale.* It will send you to the deeper levels."

I pause before taking the sweet-smelling herbs from her. They're unlike anything I've ever come across before, vanilla and apple spice, yes, but something metallic underneath. Rust maybe, just a whisper of it.

Surely if she was going to kill me, it wouldn't reek of *dessert.*
Right?

"What is it?" I ask, looking back up at her. Her smile doesn't falter, but it doesn't quite reach her eyes either.

"A gift to help you focus. Something to... aid the process. It will open your mind–"

"–to the powers, right." I repeat my lessons back to her and she nods happily.

"Yes, that's right." She gestures for me to proceed. "Go on."

The smoke in the room is cloying and thick, clouding my head already. I open the bag and take a deep breath. The taste is both bitter and sweet, almost like burnt apple spice that sticks to the back of my tongue, immediately doused in too many vanilla sticks.

Almost instantly, the room pulses around me. The runes on the walls are shifting and alive. They writhe and flash with color, too bright, *too fast.* I blink, but the dizziness only drags me deeper into the strange haze that overtakes my sight. I think I'm about to speak, but the words don't make it out. Or maybe I said them. I can't remember.

Am I moaning?

I don't know.

My vision blurs and suddenly, I'm falling into a strange, trance-like state. It's too much–the incense, the spices. My breath becomes shallow, my heart racing in my ears.

The High Priestess takes my hand gently, like she's afraid I'll break.

My *mates*.

My *bond*. There's something there–it's not one of *mine*, it's something *new*... dark and powerful–

It's alive and it *doesn't like her touching me*. It snaps awake like a beast clawing at the walls of my chest. It screams for attention, panicked and painful.

Max's protective instincts surge first, his energy swirling around me like a cocoon, pulsing at the edge of my mind. Luke is next, his command crashing against me like a tidal wave. Then Jace, a steady warmth and gentleness that fights to ground me. And... Eli. It's cold, *unpredictable*, and I can't grasp it firmly enough to hold it close.

I'm *feral* with desire. It's not just physical anymore–it's deeper... primal and needy.

"*Focus*, Seraph." The High Priestess' voice cuts through the fog, her hand tightening on mine. "Let it guide you. Where are you?"

I'm losing myself. My need for them is too great. I can't escape it. I struggle to remain seated, to not give in to the chaotic pull of my bond. I ache with a longing I have no control over.

It swims within me–strength I didn't know I possessed until right now.

Power. Pain. The... veil... I can feel him in the shadows. Red eyes. He wants me. I can feel it. Teeth dragging across my soul. I blink and–

He's gone.

But I think I liked it.

It *scares* me.

My head swims, body tingling, and for a moment, I think I might lose my mind completely.

"I wa-want to g-go home!" I can hear myself screaming. It's echoing off the walls of the small room as I hide in the corner.

When did I get here?

The High Priestess and Mercy stand in front of me, both looking more annoyed than concerned.

"*Foolish* child, that was much too high a dose." The High Priestess scolds Mercy, who ducks her head in shame. There's something else flickering there, eyes locked on me with a hunger that I've not seen before.

"I-I-I'm sorry... I didn't mean... it was su-supposed to be...."

"Bend her, not break her!" The High Priestess is scolding Mercy now, who falls to her knees next to me.

"She'll be okay, right?" Mercy sounds more curious than anxious. The High Priestess sighs, rubbing her fingers along the bridge of her nose.

"She'll be more willing and the bond should build with time."

What?

"She won't remember, though," Mercy whispers.

"She won't question," The High Priestess says.

I want to remember, I want to ask questions. I want to ask what all of this *means*, because it doesn't feel *normal*. My teeth are buzzing, my tongue thick on the roof of my mouth.

Don'ttrustherdon'trustherdon'ttrusther–

Thick with sugar and ash, the smoke is everywhere around me. It's like moving through syrup, and I give up instantly. My limbs aren't mine anymore. My skin feels inside-out. They think I can't hear them, but I can. Am I crying? My face feels wet and slimy.

I *can*.

"She shouldn't fight the next one, and it'll get easier as time goes on. The bond will form, and her others...."

"So... a month, Priestess?" Mercy asks.

"I'd say less," The High Priestess looks elated and Mercy grins up at her.

I wrap my arms over the top of my head as the runes around me threaten to devour me. They're *coming* for me. I have to *flee*. I sob into my elbow.

It's coming for me. *He's* coming.

The bonds coil deep within me, suffocating.

I'm going to *die* here in The Temple.

Please, come save me. Please, please, pleasepleasepleaseplease–

"It won't be much longer now, Priestess," Mercy tells her, but The High Priestess is already leaving the room and I scream out again as the bond surges–it's going to *tear* out of me.

"You'll be okay, Seraph," she whispers as she rubs my overly sensitive arm.

Liarliarliarliarliar.

"He'll come for you soon."

Max

I arrive at The Temple, already exhausted from my training.

But I'm on alert. I can feel her in my chest–frantic, *panicked*. She's screaming for help and I can't just *leave* her here.

I had dropped everything and ran, even as The Warden screamed at me to come back.

I ran into Luke. He told me to find Selene, then stormed off after his father, pissed he couldn't come with me. No clue where Eli is–he's been gone for a week. And Jace? He's probably buried so deep in training he wouldn't notice if the altar itself started to bleed.

I cross the threshold of The Temple and am met by The High Priestess herself.

She *could* be beautiful, if you're into golden hair and white eyes.

But I'm much more partial to brown hair and deep blue myself these days.

"Where the *fuck* is she?" I demand, shoving past her. She holds her hands up as if to pacify me, but the rage in my chest is boiling over. I can hear someone screaming inside.

Selene.

"She's fine," The High Priestess tells me calmly. I'd love nothing more than to rip that smile off her face. "We *were* elevating and I believe

136

she was overexposed due to an error on a younglings' part. She will recover just fine."

"Is that her?" I try to walk past again, but she steps in my way. I huff, turning my gaze to her. She's not affected by my stare which infuriates me more.

"She needs to remain here until her elevation wears off, and then I will return her to you. She is safe, Maximus, I guarantee it–"

"You guarantee *nothing*," I spit at her, shoving past. The Temple is sacred, and by entering, I know I'm desecrating it. Younglings rush to stop me, but I push them aside, trying to find Selene. The High Priestess runs behind, gathering her skirts in her hands.

"She is safer here with me than in that house where the four of you will tear her apart! We *need* her!"

"For fucking what?" I spin around, stopping so fast she nearly slams into me. "What could you need her so bad she's being tortured for?"

She just stares at me, a shocked expression on her face.

"You are *not* worthy enough to know. You are merely a *vessel*."

I am *so* sick of being told I'm not good enough.

Every single night at The Master's table, he rips into each of us. As he demands perfection and the threats he fed Luke hang above my head. As I stare across the table into Luke and Jace's face, and know the three of us are on the same page–keeping Selene safe–and we take the brunt of the abuse.

As Eli disappeared without a trace, and when we asked about him, The Master finds new ways to bite into us.

As he tears into Selene's *'useless'* womb, which didn't take after Luke's—*or Eli's*—single attempt.

As The Master breaks us apart, I find myself less and less eager to finish the claim myself–less desperate to rut into her, less willing to crawl over her at night and take what's owed to me–because I can't imagine what he'll say to her once she *is* carrying one of our children.

If that child were to come out looking like any of *us* and not Luke.

I don't really care that Luke's given us his blessing to claim her–I really have no desire anymore.

But she isn't going to suffer under this absolute *cunt* today. Not if I can help it.

"Fuck this." I walk off, shoving the girls in front of me aside as I follow the sounds of Selene's screams. It drives me towards smaller rooms near the back, and I find her tucked away in a hidden room, sobbing in the corner, her head tucked between her knees.

The sight of her trembling, being comforted by another, is sickening. The youngling rubs her back, whispers sweet nothing in her ear, as Selene trembles against the wall.

I step into the cloudy room and her head snaps up.

Her eyes are wide, pupils blown out, lips swollen and red as if she's been biting at them, cheeks flushed as if she's warm.

Behind me, The High Priestess touches my neck. I want to turn around and ask her what the *fuck* makes her think she can just *touch* me when I see the top of Selene's dress where she's been pulling at the collar. It's as if she's trying to rip it from her body. It's stretched apart, exposing her collarbones. I want to put my lips on them. *Do they taste as soft as she looks?*

What the fuck?

I blink as she stands, using the wall to brace her trembling legs. She looks so fragile, so broken.

So innocent.

Delicious.

Her eyes lock with mine, breathing deep like she can *taste* the air between us. She steps closer and I can *hear* the pulse of my own heartbeat. It's *deafening*... like the steady steps of the impending hoard.

"*Maaaaaax.*" Her voice, *haunting*, curls around my name. Why does it sound so *damn* good? Why do I want her to say it again?

My hands move towards her instinctively, the pull so strong I can feel it overtake every other thought I've had this past week, calling me to complete the claim. The moment our fingers meet, it snaps through me, tugging tightly every fiber of my being.

And then it's all too clear *exactly* what I'm going to do.

"No!" The youngling's scream pierces the space between us, nails raking across my back. I barely feel them. Her presence here means nothing to me.

Nothing matters but Selene.

"You'll ruin it! You'll ruin *her*!"

"He won't." The Priestess' voice cuts through the chaos. All I can focus on is Selene. The way she moves, the curve of her lower lip, swollen and pink, begging to be kissed. She looks like she's glowing, even in the low light. I'm helpless to resist. She reaches up, tentative at first, her hands brushing my face, then pulls me lower. When our mouths meet, everything else falls away.

"Good." When she breathes to the youngling, I barely register it. I try to turn my head to face her, but Selene's hand catches my chin. "The bond will root deeper this way."

There is nothing but the intoxicating *taste* of her.

Fuck yes.

"Let's leave them be." The High Priestess is *still* here, pulling the youngling away.

The youngling is mad, though, her voice dripping with venom. "You'll *allow* them to *desecrate* The Temple with this behavior? He *corrupts* her!"

I don't spare them a glance. They don't matter. Not when Selene's breath is hot on my skin, when her fingers are pulling my shirt free from my pants, touching the hard lines of my stomach as though she can't wait for me any longer.

But the Priestess–the absolute *cunt*–speaks in a way that curdles my soul. She dismisses her youngling with a flick of the hand.

"The Seraph does what she must to fulfill her potential," she says softly. It's as if she's observing Selene with reverence, her voice a tad breathless and euphoric. "*Whatever* is necessary for her strength, for her elevation. The Temple will not break from this. This space serves The Seraph now."

I tilt my head back as Selene's mouth finds my neck and she starts to lick at the dried sweat on my skin. She sounds so *sure* of herself, of *Selene* and this grand power that she possesses. But I've seen Selene in the night, when she sleeps so soundly that she snores. I've watched her grow bashful when I've walked in on her showering to piss.

"And he'll serve her too," she adds in a near whisper, "especially when he's had his taste."

Selene, an all-powerful being? Still feels like a reach.

The High Priestess shoves the youngling from the room, and then turns back to me.

"You serve The Seraph, Maximus." Her voice warbles and I blink, trying to latch onto something solid. "*Remember* that. Her will is sacred and all that matters. You do what she wants."

I snarl at her, my patience thin. The incense in the air is curling around my mind, dulling my senses enough to make everything feel just out of reach.

Not enough to stop me from being fucking pissed that she's still here.

"Yeah, yeah, The Seraph's will, blah, fucking blah." I flick my wrist in her direction. "Just... get the fuck out of here before I *stab* you."

Her smile falters for a split second, but she's quick to mask it, nodding once, whispering, "Dominus," to the corner of the room before slipping away.

I don't care. Selene's *here*. She's touching *me*, kissing *my* neck. Her heat, the softness of her body, the way she's looking at me.

There's *nothing* else.

The bond sings between us, pulsing low that matches the throbbing of my cock. My hand traces her jaw–everything else is just pointless. The rest of the world? It's empty without her. I lay her back on the pillows, but she's quivering. I've had enough women under me to know the difference. It's not from desire, it's from *fear*.

I can feel the way her muscles twitch, like she's fighting running away.

I don't like that.

Her eyes are wide and unfocused. I don't even know if *she* knows where she is. Whatever they gave her, it's more than whatever is floating around the room. If I'm drifting on a nice cloud of sensation, she's *suffocating* in it.

She gasps, pulling away from me, but her feverishly hot body arches into mine. "No, *please....*" She's talking to someone who isn't me. I stare up at the corner of the room where she's looking, but it's just shadows.

I feel it–something thick, breathing in the darkness. The heat isn't from her, I swear, *it's commanding me.* I swallow hard, trying to find the words that I know are there somewhere.

"Selene." I try to ground her, holding her shoulder to the floor. As she wiggles against me, I rock onto her, moaning into her neck. She doesn't realize what she's doing to me when she moves–a seductress, albeit an *unwilling* one.

My blood boils but I don't want to rush her. I want to *savor* this.

She looks back at me, refocused, and tugs my shirt over my head. She wants me, but she doesn't. She's trying to push me away even as her nails dig into my back when I kiss her with bruising force.

Her eyes flicker back to the corner. *Something's wrong. There's an itch inside my chest. I feel* sick, *as if there's something else living inside me, taking control.*

"*Please....*" She's crying now, tears streaming down her temples into her braided hair. "*Please,* leave me...."

"I'd never leave you, sweetness." I move one hand to her waist, holding her trembling body to mine. "Listen to me," I whisper, my voice hoarse, "I'm not gonna hurt you." Her eyes darted between mine and that damned shadowed corner. "Trust me, *please.*"

A hunger, stronger than I've ever had. I'm ravenous *for her.*

She bucks beneath me and scrapes her nails across my chest. I suck air between my teeth. It's not gentle, her fear. She leans up, sinking her teeth into my collarbone, and the sharp stinging of pain makes it *worse.*

"Goddamn it." I clench my teeth, holding her hips down with mine. She's small, trying to fight me.

I hear it then, faint but unmistakable. A voice in the fog, drifting across the shadows of the room.

"*Little fire,*" it whispers, searing into my mind. It doesn't feel like mine, even as my mouth moves. The pressure in my skull mounts.

I'm not sure what changed. She'd approached *me.* She'd kissed *me.* I breathe through the rage building inside of me, my hand sliding to her wrist to pin her down.

I *need* to be gentle. Her fear is driving me wild, but I can't hurt her.

I don't want to do this. I squeeze my eyes shut painfully as I fight my body, which moves against my requests. I have almost no control.

"Selene," I say again, quieter this time. "Relax. You're safe with me."

She *isn't* safe with me, but I can't tell her otherwise. She'd never trust me again.

The fight starts to drain from her. Slowly, *cautiously*, I bend down and press a soft kiss to her lips. She's still shaking but the panic fades from the bond, replaced with lust. The tension in her body bleeds away, little by little, and she wiggles out from under me.

Or, she *tries*. I lay my body across hers and she lets out a breath as my weight settles.

I press my mouth to her forehead, the kiss lingering there–a silent apology for my roughness.

"Don't fight me," I plead, moving down the side of her face, planting small kisses as I go. She turns her face to the side, exposing her neck to me. If she fights, I have no idea what will happen.

It's the show of trust that sends the wave of heat over me.

I push up on my elbows to look down at her. Her fingers are brushing at the marks her nails left behind–desperate, raw arousal shimmering in her eyes–as she tries to make sense of what's happening.

To be honest, I'm not sure either.

Before I came, I'd been *resolute* that I wasn't going to do this.

And here I am, aching for her and ready to finalize my claim.

What is happening to me?

"You're safe with me, sweetness," I echo, trying to pour as much honesty into it as I can.

I drop my face to her neck, nibbling at the tender skin, slow and deliberate. Her pulse races beneath my tongue and the scent of her skin mixes with the lingering trace of incense. I rock my hips against hers and she moans.

I *need* to stay in control. I *need* to fight whatever's threatening to take over.

I move lower, my mouth working the base of her throat. It's hard enough to not mark her, but I don't care anymore. She tastes *good*, her bare skin, her sweat.

If I could sustain myself on her, I would in a heartbeat.

Slowly, I trail my lips over her collarbone, kissing her with a tenderness I didn't know I was capable of. I slide my hand down her waist, then slower still, gathering her dress up. She doesn't resist, which feels like a reassurance that I can keep going.

Keep. Fucking. Going.

"Selene," I breathe against her skin. "Are you with me?"

"Yes," she answers, the word barely a whisper.

It's enough.

I don't rush it, even though she's pliant beneath me now. I can feel her warmth through the thick velvet dress they have her in, and it's driving me crazy. I want her stripped naked with her back arched for me, on display.

Slippery darkness spills down my spine, all sorts of wrong. It urges me on–

I move her underwear to the side, press my fingers against the wetness gathered there, and she gasps.

"Look what you've done for me," I lick a strip from her neck to her ear. "So very wet for me. What good prey you are."

My voice sounds strange, deeper and darker with an edge.

Someone whispered them into my mouth first. I'm merely the vessel.

Her eyes flutter open, but there's recognition in them. She rocks her hips against my hand, eager for more but hesitant at the same time.

"Shhh...." I mutter, my lips grazing hers in a gentle kiss. "Just let me work, sweetness."

I rub a small circle over her clit, applying the lightest pressure, and she whines softly into my mouth, arching against my chest. I can *feel* her center pulsing with want, with the *need* to be filled.

"I've got you." I slide my fingers lower, over her wetness, and press inside slowly. "You're so fucking beautiful."

I should stop. I *know* I should. '**Keep going**', the shadow purrs, and I realize that it isn't a voice but a presence *inside* of me.

I circle her, feeling the ease in which she responds to me, the way her body takes me in, desperate for more. I *give*, working two of my fingers inside, letting her adjust before sliding them back out. I keep my thumb on her clit, pressing down as I start a slow, sensual rhythm. She's lost in the sensation, gasping against my lips, and I can't help but lick into her mouth, desperate for the taste.

She's surrendering to me, and it feels fucking *perfect*.

Her breath catches in her throat–a soft, distressed sound that makes my blood rush to my cock. Her fingers tighten against my skin, pulling at the hair on my chest, like she's unsure if she can push me away or pull me close. Her thighs are clenching around my hips but I don't let up. I admire the blooming bruises I've left along her neck, the mottled flesh twisting my brain into some sort of feral animal, and I lean down to whisper in her ear.

"So fucking perfect when you stop fighting."

My thoughts aren't *clean* anymore. They're soaked in something overly-saccharine that exists just above my reasoning.

I speed up, working her faster, my fingers deeper–her body shakes, arching, tightening. I can feel how close she is when her legs start to shake. She makes another breathy moan, trying to turn her face away, but I bite her lower lip to hold her in place.

And she falls apart, gasping my name like a prayer. I don't stop, not yet. I work her through it letting her ride out the waves of pleasure. Only when her body sags to the pillows do I ease my fingers away and bring them to my lips. I suck them into my mouth, tasting her, groaning low in my throat.

Delicious.

She watches me, dazed under whatever they gave her, as I unbutton my pants and pull myself free. I give myself a few strokes, spreading my pre-cum around the tip. She's soaked already, but it'll help the glide.

I release my cock and drag my hand down her thigh, grip the back of her knee and spread her legs wider. She gasps when I press my cock right against her and I groan, dropping my forehead to hers.

I want to sink inside her. I want to feel her wrapped around me, to lose myself in her completely.

I should ask again. I should make sure. But I'm drowning in the pressure inside me... in the heat that isn't mine. A hand that isn't mine sits on the base of my spine, urging me forward.

*A voice whispering in my ear, '**Take.**'*

"Sweetness," I rasp, rolling my hips against her, letting her feel *exactly* what she's doing to me. "Are you still with me?"

She hums, her fingers twitching on my shoulders. "Mmm...."

Not good enough. I slide a hand down her thigh, gripping her knee to hold it steady against my hip. "Words, pretty little prey."

She exhales shakily as she tries to fight through her *enlightenment* oh so generously provided by The High Priestess. "*Here*, I'm... here."

Enough.

I bend down to press a kiss to her throat, licking over the bruises I left before I bite down again above her collarbone. She moans, rolling her head back, pressing herself against the head of my cock. I tease her with the tip, rubbing it along the sensitive skin. She whines.

"Feel what you do to me?" She nods. "I'm so fucking hard, and it's all for you."

I reach between us and shove her dress higher, exposing her waist, and move my hand up to her hair, tugging her head back to force her eyes to mine.

She wants this.

She wants *me*.

I can't tell where this monster ends and I begin... and I'm starting to not care....

I press inside and she gasps, her hips jerking up, seeking more. *Fuck*, she's so warm and wet... I nearly spill inside her right then.

I grip her thigh again, taking deep breaths through my nose as I seat myself fully inside her, skin to skin, and listen to the way she whimpers as I give her time to adjust and take me fully. Her breath is uneven, body trembling, but she takes me.

Fuck, I'll *never* be the same.

I pull back, then thrust in again, somehow deeper, and her head tips back, lips parting in a moan that shoots straight down my spine. I bend down, rubbing my cheek along her neck, and bite at her earlobe.

"You feel so *fucking* good," I groan. Her body clenches around me as I rock into her, savoring every little gasp, every tiny shiver. Her fingers claw at my back, her breath hitching when I shift, angling myself deeper, she *shatters* around me, her nails digging into my back.

My hips move faster, rougher, the pleasure burning through me like a wildfire, and I know that I'm right behind her. I can't last, not when she's *this* warm, *this* tight, taking me so perfectly.

Made for *me*.

Dominus.

A thought slams into me. I blink, the image lingering, vivid and *violent*, of Selene spread on an altar with a tall, shadowy creature driving into her. His fanged mouth bites down, sucking her tongue between his bloody lips–

I pull out at the last possible moment, gripping my cock with a tight fist, and spill all over her lower stomach. She's boneless, *wrecked*, but so am I, breathing heavily as I tremble with exertion. I look up at her as I drop my cock.

There's a moment where the world tilts and I feel empty. The pressure in my head is *gone*, like it never existed in the first place. My soul feels... *used*....

What the fuck did I just do?

"Still with me, sweetness?"

She's *barely* coherent, and I don't really like it.

She's lost to whatever they gave her and all I really want to do is find that cunt Priestess and wring her skinny fucking neck until she tells me what they did to my mate, but I'd much rather get her out of here and somewhere safe.

I need Jace's expertise and I need it *now*.

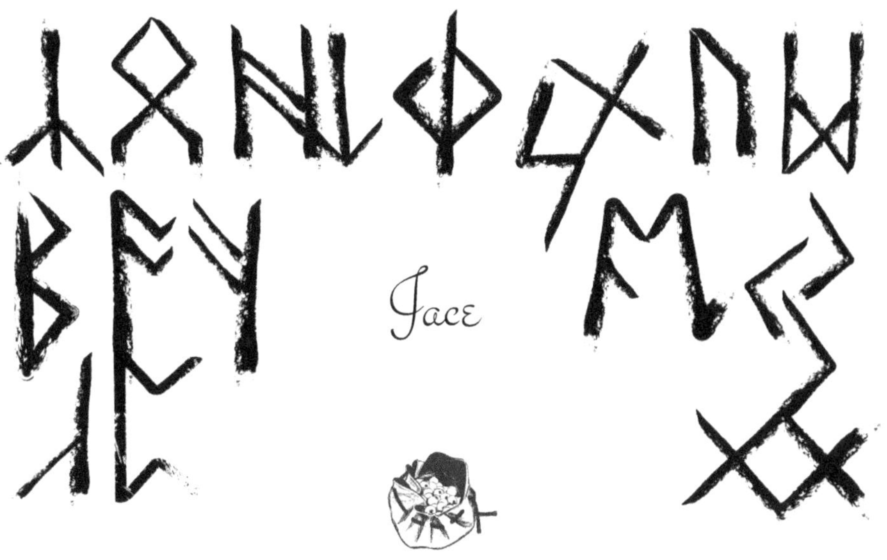

Jace

"So, what did she say again?" I ask Max as he tucks Selene into bed. He's *gentle*, which is different from how he normally acts around her.

I realize *why* when her hair falls free from her neck and my gut burns with anxiety.

He's claimed her.

I'm the last one who *hasn't*.

Luke is sitting on the couch, pressing his fingers into his temples, and Eli is nowhere to be found. It isn't unusual for him given his job. I've treated him enough times after brutal missions to know how rough and demanding his job can be. What's *unusual* is that he's been gone for a week and he left without telling any of us where he was going.

"It was strange. She told me I was a vessel, which, *fuck* her, by the way." Max rolls his eyes as he runs his fingers over Selene's throat. She doesn't stir, which worries me. "That Selene had *elevated*. That we would tear her apart and that she needed her more than we did."

"What was Selene like?" I ask. He shrugs, shooting a brief look at Luke, who's moved to holding his face in his hands.

"She was beyond scared. Crying. They were trying to keep her there in that back room, but she didn't want to be there. I could tell." Max's eyes go distant, like it's foggy even though it *just* happened, and a look of remorse crosses his face. "It looked like she'd been trying to rip her dress off. They were burning something, smelled kinda good but... clogged my head up. Selene was... the bond or something took over and we...."

Luke glares at him. "Spit it out. You *fucked*. I told you already that I'm not keeping you from our mate."

Max flips him off but there's no heat behind it. Almost like we're *all* friends now.

It feels... *whole*.

I don't know if I like it or not, especially now that I'm *aware* that I'm the last one to claim her.

"She was *feral*. You know when they would tell us about bonds growing up? That the woman would be accepting?" I nod, and he looks back down at Selene. "It wasn't like that at first. She fought me and the bond *forced* me to keep going. It was really confusing. She scratched me up pretty bad. I had to hold her down. If it's like that *every* time...."

"That's a little... concerning," I say. "Anything else?"

"The Priestess said that she'd been overexposed, I think," Max tells me. I pause at that, looking down at Selene's erratic breathing. Her flushed face. Her swollen lips. The purple bruises on her neck from Max's overzealous mouth.

Overexposed?

"That's a fascinating term," I mutter, moving to take Max's place next to Selene on the bed. I sit next to her, pressing my finger down on her pulse point, feeling for her heart. It isn't *racing*, not exactly–it's beating strong. I pull my fingers back and rub a thumb across her cheek instead.

"Why?" Luke asks. I look up, taken aback. I'd forgotten he was here for a moment.

"Why what?"

"*Why* is it a fascinating term?" He stands and joins me on the bed, sitting near her legs. The bond between him and I flexes as I try to avoid staring at his lips.

"Well... *what's* she been overexposed to?" I wonder aloud. "And *why*?"

Luke sighs. "I really don't like any of this. Things are starting to get weird."

"Weird how?" Max asks, coming to lay on her other side. She moans, trying to roll over. Her bond lashes out painfully, making all of us grimace. I place my hand over her chest to keep her steady.

"My dad keeps saying weird shit. Stuff like... the reckoning is coming now that The Seraph is here. He's got me learning these tactics for war against multiple hoards at the same time when we don't have the forces for it. I have no idea where we're going to pull the numbers that he's talking about."

"You think he's wanting to... team up with another commune?"

"God no. *Him*? I think he'd rather cut off his left hand than bow down to anyone else," Luke snorts. "But I honestly don't know how else he thinks we're tripling our fighting force."

"*Tripling*? That's what the Warden's been bitching about!" Max exclaims, his eyebrows shooting up. Selene whines again, her head shaking from left to right, as if she's fighting off her own battles in her mind. I wish I knew what they've given her. If I'm familiar with it, I could possibly counteract it and bring her out of this hell.

Our bond feels tainted with whatever poison they've given her. It's making it volatile. I can't recognize the burnt desire that courses through her veins, even if it sings to mine.

Still, it wouldn't be the first time someone went on a bad trip. The teenagers around here really like to eat the mushrooms growing in the woods. That's *always* a big mistake.

Amateurs.

"Right?" Luke looks just as exasperated as Max does. "Not only *that*, he's expecting this big war to happen in the next month."

My blood runs cold.

"Wait, we don't have the medical supplies to fight a war right now," I point out. "I've been spending a lot of time cataloging our stocks with Vitalis, and we absolutely *cannot* support an army that's triple the size."

"I tried to tell him that and all I ended up with was an hour lecture on doubting him and The Seraph and a bunch of bullshit. He's starting to lose it. In our last meeting, he went on and on about some divine right that he has to bring forth God *himself*." Luke flops backwards, pressing the heels of his palms into his eyes. "Can we just run away?"

It's not the first time I've heard him say it. As a teenager, he'd often wish for an escape from the demands of his birthright, from the weight of his father's burdens. It doesn't surprise me now, except that he says it in front of Max.

So much has changed in a matter of weeks....

"And go *where*?" My voice sounds weak. I *feel* weak. Max's face pales as he looks at Selene and runs a hand down her arm.

"Does it matter?" He asks me in an equally quiet voice.

"Yes. It matters," I whisper. "You're talking about just... leaving. No plan. Nothing. And go fucking *where*?"

And then Eli walks in, smudged in dirt and mud, bits of leaves and bark stuck in his sweat-soaked hair. He doesn't look like he's in the mood to talk, much less have a life-changing conversation, but as soon as he sees Selene laying across the bed, he's moving towards us, his focus completely on her.

"What *happened*?" he asks.

"Where the hell have you *been*?" Luke's tone is loaded with accusation, his face cold as it locks onto Eli.

"Doing what *you* fucking told me to do, asshole!"

"I didn't tell you to do *anything*!" Luke stands, stepping into Eli's space, so close their chests nearly touch. Eli flinches, his brows furrowing as he processes Luke's words.

"What do you mean?" Eli takes a step back, clearly confused. "I... they... I was training the new scouts. That's where I've been the last week. Out watching the other sects with the new scouts."

"On *my* orders?" Luke sounds appalled. "*Away* from Selene? Why would I send you away from her right *now*?"

"I...." Eli's voice trails off. "I didn't think–"

"Did I ever *say* that I hated you?" Luke interrupts, voice hard. "That's the *only* reason I would do that, Eli."

I watch Eli's face twist–abstract horror, gut-punched realization– like something just clicked in his head, something he's *never* tried to see. Something that shifts the way he thinks about Luke, tipping into dubious loyalty.

Devotion actually *suits* him.

Who knew?

Luke isn't cruel like that, not in all the years I've known him. Not enough to separate a newly bonded pair away from each other. Not when one of them is in our little quintet.

There's a pulse in my bond with Luke that stings with pain, and I know that Eli's assumptions hurt his feelings.

"I'm sorry if I ever made you think that," Luke says softly, as if he's trying to tame a wild animal. Eli doesn't meet his eyes. His face is flushed, crumpled with the kind of pain that doesn't bleed, only bruises on the inside. Luke steps closer, and when he finally puts his arms around Eli, it's to embrace him.

To remind him he's not alone in the storm.

"You're part of this now, whether you like it or not," he whispers. Eli doesn't pull away, but the way he tucks his face into Luke's shoulder speaks of *need* and trust. I hear him sniffle, but it's nearly silent.

Trust Eli to hold it all in.

Max watches silently, his attention flickering to Selene every few moments, face unreadable otherwise. His expression is oddly tender, but it's shadowed over with discomfort. Off in a way I can't name.

Wrong.

"What did my *father* make you do?" Luke asks Eli, colder now.

He pulls away, his face now streaked with mud and tears. He wipes at his cheeks, looking hollowed, every inch of him a ghost of who he was when he left. It's like he's barely holding himself together.

He stares at the floor, exhausted and haunted, as if revealing the truth is a kind of betrayal he doesn't know if he can live with.

"We went to one of the smaller sects nearby," he starts after a beat, voice devoid of emotion. "There's maybe forty or fifty people that live there total. He's been keeping track of them for years now, and trying to... recruit them. But they don't buy into it."

"Buy into what?" Luke presses, but there's an edge to his voice now, as if he already knows what Eli is about to say.

As if he dreads the words, but he needs to hear them all the same.

"*Everything!*" Eli snaps, waves his arms around frantically. "*Any* of this! Worship only his God, *not* theirs. Obey him, and him *alone*. Bow down to him. Live for him."

"You're telling me he forces them to... worship him?" I ask. Eli's shattered face leaves no room for doubt. He calls himself The Master, *yeah*, and he says some weird shit sometimes, but does he *force* us all to worship his God?

Does he?

We've *always* worshiped one God in Middlesborough, long before Luke's father was The Master.

But it's always been The Master's family in charge, going back generations, since Middlesborough was established.

One *long*, linear line.

"He's been sending me to these smaller communes for *years* calling it outreach." Eli's eyes are wide and fearful. As if telling us is breaking some long-held promise he made that has horrific consequences. "You know what he does to those who *don't* comply?"

"What?" I'm afraid to ask, but I *have* to know.

Who am I worshipping?

Eli turns to me and a tear slips down his cheek as he gestures to his blood splattered clothes. "I spent the last three days teaching the new scouts *exactly* what we do to those who don't comply." His voice shakes and his hands curl into fists at his sides.

I feel sick to my stomach. The vows I took as a healer *to do no harm and only heal* are sacred to me. I can't think about what Eli's been forced to do in the name of loyalty to our Master, or I'll–

I remember every wound I've treated for him. The ones he's tried to write off as accidents. Every wound, every unexplained bruise.

Punctures that went deeper than 'tripping over a log'.

The burns that happened from 'stumbling over a hot fire'.

His broken wrist that had taken weeks to fix, that he didn't even *have* an excuse for, that I'd been skeptical about. It was how we had become acquainted in the first place. He'd been in the infirmary every three or four days for me to check on the healing process. Back then, he was just a kid–sad, scared, seven years my junior. I couldn't *help* but feel for him. No one to turn to, stuck in the barracks, not belonging *anywhere*.

I went *out of my way* to be kind to him.

"I know you don't believe me," Eli says, suddenly turning away. Luke's hand darts out to grab his wrist, holding him firmly in place.

"*Elijah*," Luke says firmly with a flicker of that deep growl. "We're in this together. Don't ever *think* I'll choose anyone else over you." He looks at Max, then at me. "Over *any* of you."

The bond between us hums in response. It's not acceptance but something darker, more complex. Something that *grows* the more time we spend together.

Selene whines on the bed, arching her back, and Max slams his hand to her chest to keep her on the bed. I lean over again, my fingers pressing against her neck to feel her pulse—erratic, too fast.

"Shit!" I swear. "I *need* to know what they gave her so that I can fix this!"

Eli's eyes flick back to the bed and, for a second, there's a flash of concern across his face before he masks it. "So, what happened?"

"They drugged her to 'elevate' her or some bullshit. Until she comes out of it, we won't know more. Could be a while."

Eli snorts, shaking his head. "This place just gets better and better, doesn't it?" His eyes roll as he rips his shirt off, leaves and dirt drifting off him. Luke doesn't mention it aside from a cocked eyebrow toward the defiled rug.

"Take a shower," Luke orders in a flat voice. "Don't think you'll miss anything important."

Eli flicks his hand dismissively at him as he heads for the bathroom, not bothering to respond. Within moments, I can hear the shower running. Well, I guess now is as good of a time as any....

The bags of herbs sit heavy in my pocket where they've been for the past week. It's a reminder of the decision I've been sitting on, and I take a deep breath as I glance at Selene. Her murmuring breaks the silence— she's going on about the walls speaking to her, about the voices in her head.

A shadow man with red eyes who lives in her soul.

She's out of it, but I can't shake the nagging feeling that we should be careful, to cover *all* our bases.

"Hey, Luke?"

"Yeah?" Luke doesn't hesitate, his eyes lifting from Selene to meet mine. They flicker to my mouth for a split second before darting back, concerned. I'm not sure if it's the time for this conversation now that I think about it–

But we don't have any other time alone.

Without her.

"I've got an idea," I start, moving uncomfortably on the bed. "But I haven't really had time to say anything before."

Max shifts above Selene, all his focus on the two of us. I brace for resistance, but it doesn't come, only a quiet curiosity and the ghost of his earlier unease lingering. It's messing with me, how quickly the ground shifts beneath us, how he no longer pushes back.

How he's listening. *Really listening.*

"About Selene?" Luke asks.

I nod. "Yeah, about... intimacy," I feel my cheeks heating up. "Especially with there being so many of us and one of her... and the bonds being *insistent* about claiming for you guys–"

"Is it *not* for you?" Max asks me, a crease forming between his brows.

I tuck my chin to my chest, staring at the floor. I try not to show the way the question makes my skin prickle. "Not really," I admit with a shrug. "It's been more concerned with keeping her protected than anything." I pause. "But I found something. An herb. I think it could help stop... a pregnancy."

They're both staring at me, wide-eyed. Luke steps closer and our bond tightens in my chest. It's a strange mixture of disappointment and hope.

"It... there's medicine that can do that?" Max asks, astonished.

I nod again, pulling the small pouch from my pocket, fingers shaking as I hold it between us. "Juniper berries. They're supposed to prevent it. *But* they also harm pregnant women, so if she's already...." I trail off, then whisper the next part. "I ground it up. We can mix it with tea. She shouldn't even taste it."

"You're saying we don't even tell her." Luke stares at me, features pulled taut. I know what he's thinking... this isn't something I'd ever do.

But this isn't a situation we've ever been in before.

"Yeah," I confess. "Do we *want* her pregnant? With what they're doing to her? What would that do to a child?"

"Would it affect *us*?" Luke asks.

"It didn't say." I admit.

Max shrugs like he's already halfway there himself. "If we give it to her, we should drink it, too. It's only fair."

We look down at Selene, our minds made up without saying another word.

"I'll just have some tea delivered before bed," Luke says. "We'll all drink it together."

A weight lifts from my chest. "We'll make sure she doesn't know."

Max flops down next to her, his voice dripping with sarcasm. "Like a little group bonding activity. I know who's gonna *love* this."

The bathroom door swings open and Eli steps out, towel slung low around his hips, steam curling behind him. He freezes mid-step, eyes scanning between the three of us and the small pouch clutched in my hand.

"You guys look like you're conspiring against God himself. What did I miss?"

Max smirks, leaping off the bed to cross the room and stand next to Eli. "Oh, nothing. Just deciding to drug our mate without telling her."

Well, not how *I* would phrase it... but that's what we're doing, *isn't it*?

Eli blinks. "Huh. Bold move. Really leaning into the whole *overlord control* thing now, aren't we? So, how are we different from The High Cuntess?"

Yeah, High Cuntess, I rather like that.

Luke sags with the breath he lets out. "It's not *like* that. We need to make sure she doesn't get pregnant while they're messing with her like this."

Eli eyes the pouch and then Selene, still limp and mumbling nonsense under her breath. His usual sarcasm falters for a second while a look of longing crosses his face.

"Shit," he mutters, dragging a hand across his face. "I *hate* that this makes sense."

"She won't be the only one suffering through this stuff. We're equal martyrs in this, brother." Max grins, clapping him on the shoulder. "We drink together. Suffer together. Dodge consequences together."

Eli shrugs Max's hand off, snatching the clothes he started keeping here from his drawer in the dresser. "Yeah, you can shove your *'chastity brew'* up your ass. I'll drink it, but I don't like this."

Max winks, completely unaffected by Eli's dry wit. "That's what I thought you'd say on our Joining night, honey."

Eli smacks him with his sock. "*Die.*" Then, with his usual dramatic flare, he disappears back into the bathroom and slams the door behind him.

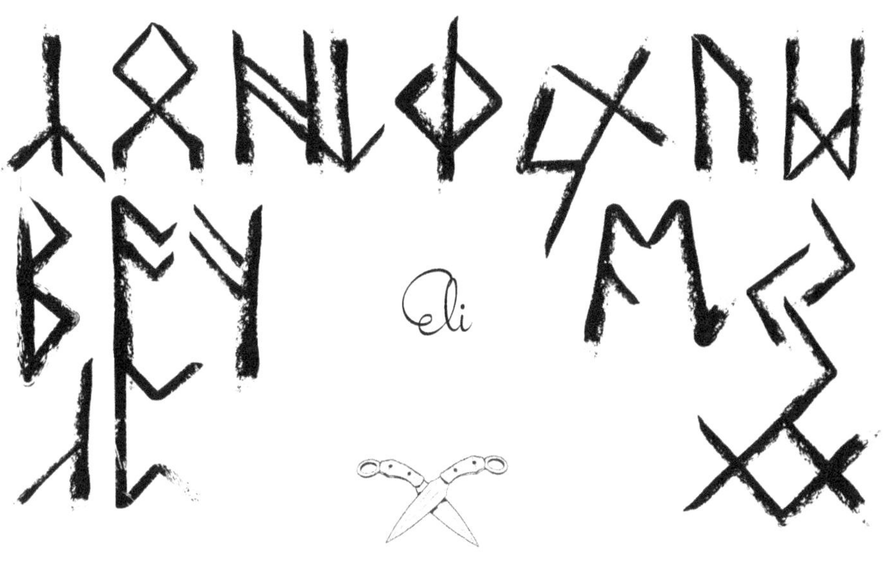

It's been days, and the fact that we're feeding her toxins to prevent a child from taking hold *sickens* me–like we're animals that can't help ourselves. As if we couldn't simply *not* rut into her like a bunch of feral beasts.

Maybe I was gone too long. Maybe the three of them have been taking turns, and now they're panicking about the consequences. It's not like they'd say it outright to *me* but the guilt was written all over Max's face. Well... it's not like they would have said it *before* Luke's declaration. Maybe they'll tell me *now*. I'm not sure anymore, and this off-balanced feeling I have now is unsettling. I've made sure to keep my distance from her for this *exact* reason, to avoid becoming another burden on her already suffocating world, and to keep myself from becoming unsteady.

But now, I'm *part* of it, aren't I? Tangled up in *friendship* with the three of them. More shit for her to deal with.

I could fight back.

I *should* fight back.

But Luke's the leader of this little ragtag band of misfits, and something deep inside of me won't push too hard against him. My bond recognizes *him* as the Alpha and at first, I thought I'd claw my own skin off from the sheer irritation of it. But the truth? I just don't *have* that dominant drive the way he does. I wasn't *made* to be the leader.

Fine. He can have it. He can be the noble protector while we all pretend this isn't just another brick in a wall of control none of us have.

I've got better things to do than argue about who gets to make the next terrible decision on Selene's behalf, like figuring out what the hell this place is *really* hiding.

She's going to be *pissed* when she finds out what we're doing for her. And I don't think I'll try to talk her down.

I spend most of my morning enduring a frigid breakfast, getting shit on by The Master for existing, and try not to stab the bastard with my fork.

A *productive* start to the day.

After that, I wander the massive house as I look for anything resembling a library or a records room. I've spent *years* trying to get my hands on anything useful about The Ritual–what it is, what it actually *does*–but two places have always been off-limits.

The Temple. And Luke's house.

Well, *one* is better than *none*.

The house is quiet aside from the occasional whisper of skirts against the floor as the girls working here scurry past me. They keep their heads down and their backs pressed to the walls like they think I might lash out if they breathe too loudly.

Good. The less they acknowledge me, the less I have to worry about them running off to tell The Master that I'm somewhere I *definitely* shouldn't be.

My fingers skim along the walls as I move through the stuffy corridors until they catch on something strange. A door–cool, unyielding metal. *Hidden.*

It's heavier than I expected when I push it open, groaning against rusted hinges as it reveals nothing but suffocating darkness. The air inside is thick, stagnant, and clinging with the kind of chill that belongs six feet under.

I don't hesitate. Pulling a lighter from my pocket, I flick it on, the tiny flame casting a weak glow that barely reaches beyond my fingertips. It's enough to see the steep wooden staircase descending into whatever lies beneath this house.

Great. Basement of horrors. Fucking figures, I'm going to die *down here.*

I'm light on my feet, not letting my weight sit on the steps more than necessary. Who knows how long they've been here or how weak they might be? At the bottom, my fingers fumble along the stone walls until they find an old torch. It's crude but it catches easily when I press my lighter to the tip, and the space around me blooms in faint, flickering orange. Shadows stretch like skeletal fingers across the walls, and I grimace at the way the firelight makes everything feel *alive*.

A long hallway stretches ahead, lined with metal doors.

Selene saunters against my soul, a brush of warmth and worry crawling through my chest. She probably doesn't realize she's doing it, but I *feel* her there, pressed like a whisper against the edges of my mind.

Stay out of this, I think, nudging her presence aside as gently as I can. *You don't need to be here.*

Not in my fear. Not in my focus.

I don't know what'll happen if I'm caught.

I move forward, trying the doors as I go. The first few creak open to reveal nothing but filth. Stained mattresses, rusted pots–prison cells, essentially. Another door exposes something vile. A body, shriveled and long past rotting, curled into itself as if it died alone and forgotten. It's been here so long it doesn't even *smell*.

I clench my jaw, breathe down bile building on my tongue, and move along.

The last door in the hallway feels different when I touch it. It doesn't stick, it... opens.

Jackpot, motherfucker.

I step inside and pull the door halfway closed behind me. The firelight casting long, wavering shadows across the room.

Boxes and books stacked in uneven towers, their spines warped with time. Scrolls wrapped tightly in leather ties, some so aged the bindings have cracked apart. Bundles of sage hang from the ceiling, brittle and long-dead.

And the cats.

At first, I think they're more bundles of herbs, dark and shriveled. But no–*fuck no*–those are *cats*. Dried-out husks, their bodies curled like they died mid-scream, their little mouths gaping open in eternal silence.

A shiver rakes through me as I look on in horror.

The walls feel *worse*.

Runes are carved into the stone, looping and jagged, some so deep they've cracked the surface. And the rust-color staining them–dark, flaking in some places–that sure as hell *isn't* paint.

I swallow against the vomit that's threatening to make an appearance. Every rational part of me is *screaming* to get the *fuck* out of here. Whatever this room is, whatever sick shit happened here, it's not *history*.

It's *ongoing*.

But I don't move.

Because this is *it*. This is what I've been looking for.

If I leave now, I might not get another chance.

I force a breath through my nose, shove my nausea down, and step deeper into the room.

The scent of old parchment, dried herbs, and something sickly sweet beneath it all fills my nose. Rot and decay have long since settled into the bones of this place, mixed into the apple vanilla herbs that are sprinkled all over the table. My boots scuff against the stone floor, stirring up a thin layer of dust that dances in the light. The dried cats watch overhead like grotesque wind chimes, their eyeless sockets staring back at me as I desecrate their final resting place.

The first box I pry open is filled with brittle scrolls that crumble when I brush against them. I lift one carefully, but as I untie it, the parchment flakes away like dead skin. *Useless*.

I move to another. Inside, nestled among tufts of old fur, are the bodies of several dead rats, curled and stiff. Their bodies are strangely arranged, tails knotted together with symbols I can't read slashed into their tiny ribs. I drop the lid back down with my heart pounding. Another box holds small totems, carved from bone or wood, some wrapped in what looks like sinew. I pick one up and turn it over in my hands, the shape *almost* humanoid but wrong. There's too many limbs, too many jagged edges. I don't know what it's supposed to be, but I *know* I don't want to find out.

On the table, thick tomes and tattered journals lay stacked in uneven piles. I flip one open and find pages of strange symbols inked in deep, glossy red. I don't know the language, but something about it crawls beneath my skin, setting my teeth on edge. The handwriting shifts partway through the book, becoming erratic, slanted, *frenzied*.

Whatever was written here, it wasn't done with a sane hand.

My gut is screaming at me to leave, but I force myself to keep searching. It's the first time I disobey my instincts. It's *got* to be here, *whatever* I'm looking for. I don't even know what *it* is....

I shove aside another pile of scrolls and my fingers brush against something different–a leather-bound book, its edges worn smooth from use, the spine cracked down the middle like it's been opened a thousand times. Old, like the others, but not as sacred.

My pulse kicks up as I pull it free. I flip past the first few pages of neat, meticulous handwriting. This was *important* to someone. It wasn't just records or religious drivel. This was someone's *diary*. The first few hundred entries are nothing special, just names and dates– council meetings, religious Gatherings. But *then*, halfway through, the ink grows darker, the handwriting a little less careful.

THE BONDS ARE UNNATURAL. A MISTAKE. MY DAUGHTER IS BARELY FIFTEEN, AND YET, SHE'S BEEN CLAIMED BY A MAN FIVE YEARS HER ELDER. I WILL NOT STAND FOR IT.'

I blink, rereading the words.

So, *this* was how it started. *One man*, pissed that his daughter was mated to some twenty-year-old. Instead of just–*oh, I don't know*– handling it like a *rational* human being with discussion and *boundaries*, he decided to screw with something older than time itself.

Real smart. Real sane. Great job, dude.

I turn the page. The entries grow more desperate.

'I SOUGHT COUNSEL BEYOND MIDDLESBOROUGH. I FOUND HER ~~IN THE WOODS,~~ BEYOND THE HILLS WHERE THE ROADS HAVE LONG SINCE CRUMBLED. SHE SAYS SHE KNOWS THE WAY.'

The next line is scratched out so violently that the page is torn straight through.

~~'...WILL REQUIRE THE BLOOD OF... AND A SACRIFICE OF BONDS... IN EXCHANGE FOR...'~~

I brush my finger over the page and keep reading.

'...AS MARKED BY THE SIGIL OF THE SERAPH, ~~A BINDING ETERNAL,~~ ANOINTED BY FIRE AND BLOOD....'

And then, further down, a single line stands out, untouched by the scribbles of lunacy or clawed ink marks.

'THE DEMON AGREED, FOR A PRICE.'

My fingers tighten around the edges of the journal as an uncomfortable chill settles inside my veins. I flip to the next page, splattered in small flecks of blood. Before I can read further–

Footsteps.

Shit.

I snap the book closed so fast dust puffs up from the cover. *Why the hell–*

Low, muffled voices that are getting closer.

Because, *of course*, the one day I decide to risk my ass in the depths of this horror show, someone else has the *same* idea.

I douse my torch in the dirt, rubbing it against the stone floor aggressively and plunging the room into near-total darkness. The walls suddenly feel like they're pressing in around me. I can hear my own breathing, too loud and fast. I don't have much time to think as I duck down, flattening myself under the table as I clutch the journal tight to my chest. Dust fills my nose and my throat instantly tightens.

If I sneeze and get caught, I'm going to be *so* pissed.

The door creaks open and I press myself flat against the floor, every nerve in my body painfully taut. Heavy, deliberate footsteps enter first with a bright, flickering light.

The Master.

The clicking of heels follows, brisk and light. It's The High Priestess.

Oh, for fucks *sake.*

I clamp down on my lower lip, the metallic tang of blood mingling with the taste of fear flooding my mind. *I'm as good as* dead *if they find me.*

"The other sects are pressing down on us," The Master growls, voice edged with fury. "They no longer pay their tithes. They whisper behind our backs, testing our strength. Do you *know* what will happen if they decide we are weak?"

"They are not," The High Priestess replies, as composed as ever. I hear the rustle of parchment–maybe the flick of a scroll being unrolled. "They have no reason to question us, not when they know what we're capable of."

The Master scoffs, kicking at the dust on the ground. "Capable? The Seraph isn't even ready!"

"She will be," The High Priestess assures him, voice smooth with patience. "These things take time."

"We don't *have* time!" he snaps. "You speak of *patience* while our enemies grow bold. If they sense our weakness, they will *descend* upon us like vultures!" His breath comes heavier, almost panting. "I will *not* let this be the end of *us*."

Cold dread slithers down my spine. He sounds like he's *unraveling*. But hasn't he been, for weeks now?

The High Priestess doesn't waver. "I am doing my best, Master. The Seraph will be ready within the coming weeks."

My bond with Selene stirs, thrumming in my throat. I force it down, squeezing the journal in my hands. The bindings bite into my palm painfully.

The Master huffs, displeased but unable to argue. "See that she is." He demands, almost whispering. "Or I will *find* another way."

The High Priestess pauses. "There *is* no other way. Dominus would not see us fail."

A tense silence lingers between them. I imagine them staring at each other, both immovable objects in a contest neither will back down from.

But it's The Master who breaks first, turning on his heel and stomping towards the hall. The High Priestess lingers a moment longer as the light leaves the room.

"We stand at the edge of greatness, Master," she murmurs. "Desperation will not serve you now."

And then she follows, her heels clacking against the stone as the door creaks shut behind them.

I don't move.

One wrong breath and I swear my body is going to shake itself apart. *Weeks?*

That's all the time we've got left before they throw her to whatever the fuck they've got planned.

And I *bet* it's got to do with the journal I've got in my hand. *Fuck.*

The silence is worse than their presence. My pulse hammers in my ears, drowning out everything but the feeling of the journal against my chest and the distant echo of The Master's voice looping in my head.

It's dark. I count to thirty, then sixty, just in case one of them doubles back.

Nothing.

I shove the journal under my shirt, pressing it against my stomach like that'll keep it safe. My fingers feel clumsy as I try to grasp onto the edge of the table. I rise and look around. The boxes have been sorted through and a few of the tomes are missing. I lick at the tacky blood on my teeth and walk to the door, trying hard not to think about how she *might* have noticed one small journal missing. I press against it and crack it open an inch.

The hall outside is empty. No flickering torchlight, no shifting shadows. Just darkness.

Move.

I slip through the doorway. Every step I take feels too loud and my breath comes out labored. I take the stairs quickly. They creak and groan under my weight and I hesitate for a fraction of a second before forcing myself forward. *Hesitation can get you killed.*

The hall at the top is the *longest* fucking stretch of space I've ever seen. I keep my head down, shoulders tense, every muscle in my body ready to snap if I so much as hear a *sound* that's not my own.

I'm halfway there.

The journal feels like it's burning through my shirt, branding my skin with every step. I need to get back to the room. I need to hide this. I need to–

A door creaks open somewhere behind me.

I don't look back. I keep moving.

I round the corner, focus locked on my path ahead, mind racing with what I just discovered, what I still need to find out, how the hell I'm going to–

Fuck.

I slam into a wall of muscle, a painful grunt knocking out of my throat as I nearly eat the nearby wall. Hands grip my arm, firm and steady, keeping me upright even as my brain scrambles to catch up.

Not a wall.

Luke.

His fingers tighten for a fraction of a second, the heat of them burning through my sleeves. I don't dare look up.

He'll know.

"Where's the fire?" He's calm, in control. *Can he see my panic?*

I step back, twisting free of his grip while hoping he can't see the way my heart is trying to break out of my chest. My *only* saving grace is The Ritual is preventing *our* bond from properly establishing, so I know he can't *feel* anything.

"Didn't see you," I mutter, trying to sidestep him. I'm honestly trying not to fucking bolt.

Luke tilts his head, eying me carefully. He doesn't move to stop me, but he doesn't step out of my way, either.

And I *know.*

I *know* he can see the panic in my face, he could feel the trembling in my arms when he held me steady.

Shit.

I just need to get out of here before he starts asking me questions I can't answer.

He had said he'd choose us over anyone else... but, I doubt that'll extend once he finds out I'm a traitor.

"You always walk around looking like you just kicked a hornet's nest?"

"Only on special occasions."

His mouth twitches, not quite a smirk. "Must be my lucky day, then."

I huff. "Sure, let's call it that."

"Eli." His tone shifts, not quite playful anymore. "What's wrong?"

Can I trust you?

I click my tongue. "You."

He looks like he's biting back a laugh. "Try again."

"Fine. You *and* your mausoleum of a house."

His jaw flexes. "That's *not* news."

I want to trust you... for Selene... for us....

"Then stop acting like you caught me burying a body." I fold my arms, holding the journal to my stomach, shifting my weight from leg to leg. "Unless that's what we're doing next."

Luke's eyes rake over my body as if he's categorizing me. It takes everything in me to look casual while he does it. "Don't be *stupid*, Eli."

"No promises," I mumble, slipping past him before he tells me to hand over the journal.

I just *might*. If he asked me to... I just *might*.

"You're a shit liar for a scout, Eli," he calls over his shoulder.

I can feel his eyes on me and my blood runs cold as I rush up the stairs. I know this isn't over.

Luke

Eli disappears up the stairs like he's got hell on his heels. I don't follow, even though I *want* to.

Something's off with him.

He normally acts like he doesn't have a care in the world, all sly smirks and lazy shrugs. Dismissive is his *favorite* attitude. But not now. He's tense in a way that has *nothing* to do with our usual back-and-forth that I've grown fond of. He was awkward, clinging to something under his shirt he *clearly* didn't want me to see.

My fingers twitch at my sides, itching to drag him back here and ask–no, *demand*–what the hell is going on with him.

But I don't.

Not here. *Not now.*

Instead, I force my shoulders to loosen and continue on. If I'm late to this meeting, my father *will* find a way to make me regret it. He always does.

The *last* thing I want is to spend even a second with the man who's clearly lost his fucking mind, but I don't have much of a choice. His threat hangs over me like a blade–jagged and cold, ready to drop at a moment's notice. I *can't* let it get to me.

But I'd be lying if I said it didn't gnaw at me constantly. One wrong move and I'm risking *everything*.

I can't risk Selene, our mates, or anything else just because I couldn't stomach a few more minutes of The Master's madness.

The walk to his office is short, but my thoughts stretch it out, running in endless circles. Eli hiding something? That's not necessarily new. He's entitled to his secrets. But this–this feels different. Bigger.

I roll my shoulders back as I reach the door. It doesn't matter right now. Whatever it is, I'll have to drag it out of him later.

For now, I'm dealing with something *worse*.

I knock twice and push inside without waiting for permission.

As usual, the office is warm with incense sticks alight in the corner. The smoke burns to the ceiling, cloudy wisps reeking of rotten lavender bundles. My father sits behind his desk, his fingers steepled, while The High Priestess stands near the hearth draped in white and gold.

They both look at me as I enter, like they've been waiting. *Well, that's not good.*

"Sir Luke," she greets. "We were just discussing The Seraph's training."

I don't sit. "What about it?"

The Master nods, eyes carved from stone. He's been cruel the past weeks, more so than ever before. I hardly recognize him. "She'll begin more... rigorous instruction with The High Priestess. The process needs to intensify. Sending her every few days isn't *enough*."

Every day. Alone. With *her*.

After the condition Selene was returned to us? That's a joke, right? *Right?*

I cross my arms.

"You don't think this is too much too fast? Every few days has been fine so far. Why change anything now?"

The High Priestess leans her head to the side, an indulgent smile curling her lips. "On the contrary. If we wait any longer, we risk failure. The Seraph's role is delicate. She must be *shaped* properly."

I don't like the way she says *shaped*.

She watches me closely and then, so casually I almost miss it, she asks, "Is she with child yet?"

I go still. My stomach drops as fury builds in my chest.

"What did you just say?"

She doesn't flinch. "I believe, through some research I've done, that The Seraph can be strengthened. And if she were to conceive–"

"No!" The word burst from me before I can stop it. My bond churns with rage. It's not just the idea of it–it's everything behind it, everything they're taking from her.

From us.

The Master looks at me as if I'm being unreasonable. "What's wrong, Lucas? It's a small thing, if it aids The Seraph... there will be others."

"No," I repeat more firmly this time, balling my hands into fists at my sides. The thought of any of them touching an innocent child, especially one produced from any of my *pack*... making her–

The High Priestess continues like I didn't interrupt. "I'm merely suggesting that it might expedite *our* process. It would serve *your* needs as well. Her role in your group would be solidified faster with the child's presence." Her voice drips with calculated calm. All I want to do is charge at her and carve her eyes out. "And I can assist with her... condition, should you require it. Honestly, she *should* be with child by now. Four mates and a month has passed?"

I stand rigid, frozen as a wave of disgust passes over me. "That's *sick*."

My father doesn't respond to that. His gaze hardens and, in a rare moment of clarity, he cuts in. "Enough of *that*. We will not be turning my son's mate into some... broodmare *whore*." He slams his hand down on the desk, the sound echoing in the room. The High Priestess is unfazed by my father's mood. She simply faces him with that saccharine sweet smile.

"Understand, Master, The Seraph's purpose is crucial to everything we are building here. And, *yes*, her bearing a child would aid us significantly." She steps closer to my father. "We cannot afford failure. You have made this quite clear. There must be no room for hesitation. All of her mates should assist in this process. It will ensure success."

I don't even know how to respond anymore as the blood drains from my face. My father watches The High Priestess with a glazed look in his eyes like he's lost again, somewhere far beyond this realm.

"*No*," he mutters. "No more of that. Keep them away from her." He turns to face me, eyes darting between The High Priestess and my own. "You are *not* to let them touch her, Lucas."

I'm off-center and I don't *like* it. My own father telling me what I can and cannot do with my mate, yet *again*.

I open my mouth, every instinct screaming at me to argue, to push back against him.

A lesser male. Pathetic. Weak. How easy it would be to just–

"That's *ridiculous*. That's *not* how bonds work. Depriving her of all of us… it's fucking *cruel*."

His eyes snap to mine, expression hardening.

"She's not some fucking vessel for your rituals, *father*. You're treating her like she's some… some *tool* to manipulate. And I'm *not* standing by while you drag my mate into this."

My words hang there, exactly as I mean them to. His lips press tightly together and, not for the first time, I wonder if he's actually *hearing* me, or if he's just too far gone.

He lowers his voice, but it cuts through the silent rage in my head, "*Watch* yourself, Lucas. Don't forget your place."

Don't forget that I'll kill you, he means.

But I don't care about my legacy anymore. I don't care about any of it.

"This isn't right," I say, fighting to keep my voice steady.

My fathers glare doesn't waver. There's something flickering in his eyes, dangerous and broken. "You don't *understand*, Luke. The Seraph is the *key*. She will fix *everything*. The world will be *reborn* through her. She is the beginning of all things–our *salvation*. Do you think I don't *see* that? Do you think I don't *know* what this *means*?"

I stare at him, disbelief replacing the rage as I realize how delusional he's become. Where was *I* when the man who raised me descended into insanity? He'd always had a heavy hand and, albeit cruel, there was *always* a reason for his methods. *When did madness become his currency?*

I see no reason in sight.

"Sal*vation*?" This... this isn't salvation. This is *insanity*!"

His lips twitch and he leans forward, voice taking on that tone that sends shivers down my spine. "The Seraph *will* lead us to greatness. She is the first step. The others don't *understand*. They're *weak*. They want to stand in our way, but she will break *through*. She will *heal* us, all of *us*!"

"By using her like a pawn?" I push back. "By controlling *everything*? You're ruining her! You're ruining *all* of us! All of this is a *lie*! You're not protecting *anyone*. You're going to lead us to *destruction*!"

The Master straightens and lets out a low growl as he stands from behind his desk. "She *will* fix this, Lucas. All of your doubts will wash away when The Seraph fulfills her purpose. *Our* purpose!"

I'm holding it together, but his words choke me. "This isn't *leading*. This is fucking madness. The way you're treating Selene, the way you're treating *my*.... It's not leadership. It's fucking *insanity*."

Dogma, that's what it is.

The High Priestess stands with her back against the wall, eyes flicking between us. She's almost too still, as if she's waiting for something. I try to catch her eye, to see if she can tell me what's going on in my father's head, but she looks away from me–

And *grins*.

"You don't know what you're talking about," he says quietly. "You don't know *anything*. The Seraph's blood will heal the world. She will fix *all* of us."

"You're insane."

Eli has to be telling the truth, then... about everything.

He lets out a long, slow breath, relaxing his shoulders. "I will do what I must to make this happen, Lucas. If you can't see that... then you're no different than *them*."

He waves a hand toward the door, dismissing me. The air in my chest is gone, but the door is too far away. Too close. Should I leave? Is he going to kill me *now*?

I fucked up, and now they'll *pay the price. Failure.*

Before I can make another move, The High Priestess speaks.

"Master... Sir Lucas may not *fully* understand his role." Her voice drips with something tart, something I don't trust. She turns to The

Master, weaving her words like a web around his frail mind. The air in the room *shimmers* with her words. "The Seraph *will* be ready, but if Sir Lucas were to... disappear, I worry it would fracture the bond's strength. He's quite vital, I assure you. His position, his influence." She turns to face me. "You've worked very hard for this, Master. Don't let his rashness jeopardize it now."

The madness in my father's eyes flashes. He stares at her, processing what she said. As if a switch has been flipped, the blaze behind his eyes dies out and he's returned to us.

"I see. You're right," he mutters, dragging a hand through his thinning hair. "Lucas stays. For now."

The High Priestess flashes a small, practiced smile. It's almost too perfect, like she's playing a game she knows she's already won.

"Thank you, Master. You always know what's best for Middlesborough." She walks to the desk and picks up two ancient-looking books from the edge. "Come now, Sir Luke. I have things to attend to. Let your father be." She sweeps past me with a final glance towards The Master. "We must be ready."

I don't say a word, but my chest wants to cave into itself. I don't trust her, or my father, or fucking any of them.

I can only trust my pack.

I slam the door behind me, my father's mad ramblings still pressing on my mind. Jace is in our bond trying to calm me down, but I shove him away. I don't need his soothing energy right now, nor do I need Selene's serenity. I can't escape the knots in my stomach that are making me *sick*.

The High Priestess is going to worm her way into Selene's heart, twisting her into something I can't protect, and my father–*fuck*, he's lost to me. The idea of getting Selene pregnant, the pressure of the future– I'm drowning.

Is The High Priestess involved somehow? Is she corrupting my father, too?

I really fucking hope that magical powder and the tea work.

I don't have much time to process my thoughts. I *should* find Eli. I need to figure out why he's acting so strange, why he'd been dodging my questions earlier and why I haven't been able to get a straight answer from him since he returned from the mission my father send him on *in my fucking name.*

What I need is some fucking *quiet.* Peace is a foreign dream and the storm inside hasn't stopped since the night I was bonded to her. It sits beneath my skin. Snaps at my soul. Always on edge. Always ready to tear the world apart in her name.

I don't understand these instincts. *Feral. Ancient. Endless.* They don't whisper anymore. They *roar.* Especially the ones that crave her. Not just her presence, *no*, but her body. Her pulse. The slick, sacred place where she welcomed me. Tight and trembling, where she took me in like I was made for her....

Where I was the *first.*

One soul, split and stitched together again under the stars, as if the bond carved my name into her bones. But it didn't stop there. Max's fire is in her, too. Jace's soft-spoken viciousness. Even Eli, the quiet bastard, has roots tangled in her heart.

We *all* do.

I want *that.*

I want all of us, *inside* her, *around* her, *protecting* her, *wrecking* her with the worship and devotion and need she deserves.

I want her to feel us move like one body, like one beast.

Ours.

Not in *fragments.* Not in *turns.* **Together.**

Because she was made for *all* of us. And we were built for *her*, to keep her standing when the rest of the world wants to ruin her. So, I'll take my time. I'll let my pack have theirs. I'll watch her fall apart on their hands and mouths and cocks. And when she reaches for me, hoarse and glowing and spent, I'll be the one to hold her steady.

Because that's what the alpha does. He *waits*, he *watches*, he *protects* the whole pack.

It's starting to break me, just how much I *want.*

Not *just* her anymore. I'm starting to want *them*, too. I think about Jace and our amateur bond. I can feel the ghosting of emotion, tender and frayed, but still there. *Real.* I think about Max, his fire and dominance, and how he looks at Selene with that softness.... I think about Eli, always holding back, always on the outside. I wonder when it'll happen, when something will shift and click into place, and I'll have two *more* people sitting in my soul.

Maybe it's supposed to be a web. A net. Something meant to stretch around *all* of us. Not some rigid chain between two fated souls.

I wonder why it doesn't happen to others. Why do some men in Middlesborough *never* bond at all? Why do the bonds choose who they do? Why is Selene The Seraph, and why did it choose *us*?

Is something *broken* here?

When I reach the room, I throw the door open, expecting to find a moment of silence to sort through the jumbled mess in my mind–to maybe sit with my thoughts for a second, to catch my breath.

I don't know why it catches me off guard. This space hasn't been *just* mine for a while now. Not since the bond, not since everything changed. The concept of 'mine' feels outdated now, actually.

Still, some selfish part of me was hoping for a moment of solitude.

Instead, there's Eli.

He's sitting on the bed, legs stretched out. The light from the window falls over him but there's something about the way he's hunched over that catches my eye. His eyes are focused down into a book–a journal.

I stop in my tracks as his eyes meet mine and go wide with shock. I slam the door behind me.

"What the hell are you doing?" My voice is rougher than I intended. I can feel the heat rising on my neck as I try to shove the image of Selene spread open wide on the forest floor away. The journal slips from his grip and lands on the bed with a soft thud.

"Shit," he mutters under his breath, trying to slide it under his thigh, as if I haven't already seen it.

But I *have*. It's too late for that.

"Show me the fucking journal, Eli," I demand. His eyes flick from the journal to me and back again, his back stiffening. He knows he's caught.

"I–uh," he stammers, "I-I-I don't... I only *just* got it."

"Well, where did you *find* it?" I ask, taking a step closer.

He rolls his eyes. "You don't want to know."

I take another few steps. "**Don't** bullshit me. Where did you find it, Eli?"

He sighs, but my voice has taken that gravely tone from deep in my chest, the one that gets people to do what I want. The defensiveness in his eyes flickers. "Basement. Happy now?"

I can't believe this is happening. "You went into the basement without telling anyone? Why?"

"Why not?" Eli shrugs like it's not a big deal. "You'd be surprised at the shit hidden down there."

I really don't have time for this. *Or patience.* "Let me see it."

"No," Eli snaps. There's a flicker of uncertainty, or perhaps guilt, in his eyes.

"Why the hell are you hiding it, Eli?" I can feel my frustration building. "What's so damn important that you're not telling me?"

He shifts uncomfortably, clutching the journal tighter to his thigh. "I'm not hiding anything."

I press my hands into the bed, leaning in close enough that I can see how his eyes darken in response to my closeness. "You're hiding *something*. And I want to know what it is."

Eli clenches his jaw, but he's not backing down.

Any other day, I'd appreciate that a fellow mate is so strong-willed.

But *not* today.

"It's not your business."

The words hit me *hard*.

Not my business? This *is* my business. Everything he, Jace, and Max do is *my* fucking business. I'm done with this little game of his. I reach up and grasp the hair at the back of his head, tilting him back in one jerked motion so that he's making eye contact with me. He lets out a small gasp, but makes no move to pull away, even as I tighten my grip on his scalp.

"You think this is fucking *funny*? My father has lost his damn mind and The High *Cunt*head is telling us to get Selene knocked-up like it's some sort of fucking check box! She's going to start *helping* if Selene doesn't fucking get pregnant on her own!" I pull harder, and he lets out a small whine. Our faces are so close, I can feel his breath across my lips.

"This is *all* going to shit, and *now* you think keeping secrets is going to help?"

He stares at me without saying *anything*, but I can see his guard cracking. His grip on the journal loosens.

"**Give it to me**, Eli," I growl. "You can't keep hiding shit from me."

He rips his head from my grasp and I let him go, our noses bumping as he moves away. It seems like he *might* argue more but then, his shoulders sag with a heavy breath and he shakes his head slowly.

"I don't think you want to see this." His voice is quiet now and his eyes are dark when he turns to look at me. "You're not going to like it, Luke."

I slide on the bed next to him, my frustration gone as I let Jace's bond soothe my soul. "Just show me."

Eli lets the journal fall open, and I feel like I've stepped into a different world. The pages are a chaotic mess of scrawled handwriting, some parts crossed out, others barely legible—a mix of symbols and disjointed sentences that don't make a damn bit of sense. It looks like someone tried to force their thoughts onto paper while losing their mind in the process.

A little like....

I grab it, flipping through the pages hastily. There's one that's partially torn, some parts soaked through with a dark, crusty substance that looks like old blood, but I can't be sure. Another page looks like it was written too fast, the ink barely forming legible shapes with the way the ink trails off the edge of the sentences.

Some lines are scratched out violently, others are almost pristine.

'The Seraph's ~~blood~~ will cleanse the Earth,'

I flip the page to another paragraph.

'The Ritual must begin with.... ~~The bonds are the key.~~ Only she can....'

I scan the rest of it. The whole thing looks like it's been pieced together in a hurry, a puzzle where none of the edges match.

Eli watches me, a silent warning in his eyes. He knows what I'm seeing, and the fact that it's in his hands makes it worse. He tried to *keep* it from me....

Why?

This journal, this *insane* scrawl of fragmented thoughts, feels like a powder keg and I'm holding the match.

"Where *exactly* did you find this down there?"

He doesn't flinch at my low, aggressive tone. "Does it matter?" he says flatly. "It's not like you're gonna get any more answers out of it than I did."

I want to tear it up.

I want to *understand* it.

"You were going to keep it from me. You didn't think I should know about this?" He says nothing, lower lip twitching, and I can see his walls going back up. "What's it say about bonds?" I ask, wanting to distract him. "What's it *trying* to say?"

Eli's hand comes to rest on the journal, trying to pull it from me. "I don't *know*, alright? I only *just* fucking got it. Stop acting like I hide *everything* from you."

But he doesn't meet my eyes when he says it.

"You know, though, don't you? Or you *think* you know."

His eyes meet mine and he sighs, flipping through the pages before shoving the journal back into my hands.

"Fine. You want to see? It's all here. At least, I *think* it is. Talks about multi-bonds and The Seraph."

It's too precise amidst the mess of the other pages I've seen. The ink is thick and, as I scan it, I feel my mind growing heavy with the knowledge that I take in.

The bonds will be shackled by the strength of The Seraph.
Chosen among four, her sacrifice will sanctify the chain.
Blessed by what dwells beneath, The Ritual shall be sealed,

its anchor forged in the flesh of The Seraph as identified by The Sigil....'

My voice falters as I read, cracking as I realize what it says.

Did they *sacrifice* The Seraph?

Eli doesn't say anything, staring at the wall.

"The Seraph was the key... they used her to bind the bonds, Luke. To make them...." He falls silent, swallowing hard around the words. "They didn't like that the bonds were *part* of us, and they used fucking demon magic to suppress them until *they* said we could feel them."

My fingers tremble as I turn the page, desperate for anything that could explain more. All it does is lead me to the next line.

'And through The Watcher's gaze shall her body be made a vessel. Her flesh, the altar on which fate is carved. From her, power shall be sown, and from that sowing, the unchained shall rise. Let The Seraph be broken....'

I stop there because I think I know *exactly* what they're talking about.

A *human* sacrifice.

"God...." I mutter under my breath. This isn't about control. I'd really missed the mark on that. This is something *worse*.

"This isn't about *us*. It's never been about *us*. It's always been about Selene."

"Yeah, and we're fucking pawns." He stares down at the pages, rolling his neck.

I slam the journal shut.

"*She's* The Seraph!"

"I don't think you *get* it, Luke," Eli says, looking up at me. "This isn't *just* about the bonds anymore. They're going to *break* her and use her to do this Ritual to *undo* the hold on the bonds."

"Why would they do that if they were the ones to make the binds in the first place?"

"That's the question, isn't it?" Eli bites his lower lip as I fight to reach out to Selene through my bond. I *crave* to brush up against her calmness, her precious energy inside of me, but she'd feel my panic and she'd *know*.

"It doesn't say anything else?"

"It gives a bunch of different ways to contact different entities, which isn't particularly helpful. Most of the information we need is scratched out or just gone."

Sacrifices, bonds and... and fucking *demons*.

I'm sickened. I'm *furious*. I'm terrified, because Selene... she has no idea what's coming.

And I have no idea how to stop it.

Eli's shoulder is pressed to mine, warm and *grounding*. I try to focus on that feeling instead of the chaos and panic clawing at my chest. He's *never* let me be this close to him on purpose before. Not physically, not emotionally. It's subtle, the way he's leaning into me, but it must mean *something*.

It *has* to.

I like it more than I should. I like it in a way that's starting to ache. I'm starting to wish we had a bond like the one Jace and I share, something I could lean on when I'm unraveling. I want to know how he's feeling right now without having to ask. I want to carry some of the weight he holds behind those pensive eyes and biting words.

It's starting to kill me to wonder if he'll ever let me... *us*... all the way in.

But there's nothing *there*... no thread to follow, no warmth curling in my soul. Just this moment. His shoulder against mine and my heart yearning for more.

He turns, and I can feel a quiet current pulling at me before I follow. Eli, looking at me like he's *seeing* me. *Really* seeing me. His gray eyes flick over my face and I forget how to breathe, just for a second. They're stormy, unreadable, *mysterious*. But right now, in this quiet moment, *something* slips through.

Curiosity.

"I wish you'd stop hiding shit from me," I say steadily, even though my pulse races. "We're a... *pack*."

I watch the word land between us heavily. His lower lip trembles as his eyes darken, gaze dropping to my mouth. It's *barely* a second, but it's *enough*, and it lands like a punch to my gut.

He's just as affected.

He looks back up, tongue tracing the permanent scars on his lower lip, like he's fighting something inside himself.

"I know," he breathes after a beat, voice rougher than usual. "I *know*. I'm trying."

Something flickers in his expression. Grief, maybe, or guilt. Maybe it's the burden of being *seen* after so many years of being cast aside. His hands curl into fists on the mattress beside him.

I nod, because what I *really* want to do is take him in my arms and hold him to my chest. I don't think he's ready for that yet. I manage a soft, "Okay," and smile at him.

For the first time, I think *maybe* he'll let me in.

We sit there, shoulders together, the space between us *aching* with everything we aren't saying. The journal sits on my lap, its open page a cruel reminder—the world outside just became our worst nightmare.

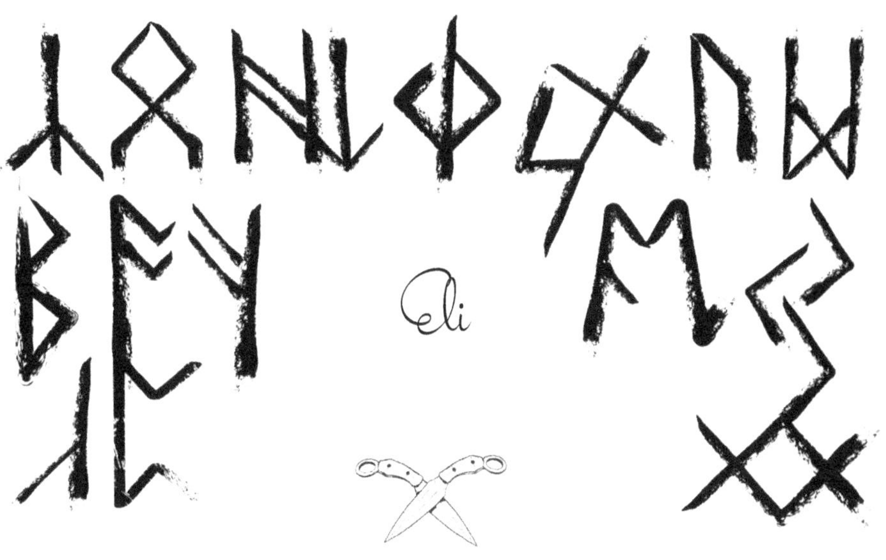

The sun's dipping low by the time I send the last of the trainees limping through the gate. They're bruised, battered, barely making it through the rigorous course I've prepared... but I *can't* keep losing scouts to these tasks The Master sends us on. I *have* to adapt and overcome, and this is the only way I know how.

Train. Train. And train some more.

If they pass, then they'll survive. That's more than I can say for some.

My shoulders ache as I watch them disappear. Dirt cakes my skin, sweat sticking in every seam. I don't bother wiping my face. *What's the point?* This place doesn't reward sacrifice. My boots crunch over the brittle grass as I make my way inside and head toward the house, each step slower than the last. The air reeks of dust and dry leaves, the kind that clings to your nose and doesn't want to let go. I think of late fall as the time when everything feels like it just... *wants* to die. The heat lingers, utterly relentless, and the sun sears the surface. It makes the dry air *worse*, like a constant scrape against my lungs.

I *hate* the fall.

It's not the faded colors or the creeping change that bothers me. It's the way the season holds its breath. Nothing alive, nothing dead. Just stuck in that *stupid* fucking halfway point–between dying and being too stubborn to admit it. Dust gets *everywhere*, coats *everything*, making the world feel too closed up and small, like a room nobody goes into anymore....

Suffocating.

As I leave the field, I look up and see Luke leaning against the fence, looking *entirely* too casual for as late as it is. I raise an eyebrow as I get closer.

"What are you doing here?"

He glances up, shrugging as he looks out past my shoulder. "Coming to fetch you."

I let out a dry laugh. "*Fetch* me? That's what we're calling it now? You're an errand boy?"

Luke smirks, not missing a beat as he stands up straight. "I prefer '*Slave to The Master*' these days, but sure, 'errand boy' works." He looks me up and down, wrinkling his nose. *I wonder if he feels that small thread now, connecting us.* "Somebody's gotta keep you in line."

I shake my head, a smile tugging at the corner of my mouth. I duck down so that he doesn't see. "Well, you sure as hell don't have to babysit me." I kick at a patch of dirt near my foot.

"Please. You're two bad decisions away from needing a permanent leash." Luke peeks over my shoulder again, and I follow his gaze.

"Who are you looking for?"

"I'm trying to make sure nobody comes over here," he says, dropping his tone. "Look, we don't have much time, *especially* alone. We need to work out a way to leave."

That catches me off guard. Luke wanting to leave Middlesborough? My mouth falls open, and I snap it shut. I guess there's still stuff I need to learn about these guys.

I cross my arms over my chest. "Why now? What changed?"

Luke scoffs, all traces of humor gone as he glances over at me like *I'm* the one who doesn't get it. "Are you *serious*? That book wasn't enough for you?"

I rub at my forehead. "Yeah, point made. What's your plan?"

The smirk vanishes, and I realize *just* how suited he is to be the leader for our little pack. "Okay, we need to start tracking our schedules.

See where we overlap, *not* just at night, but during the day, too. Figure out the best time to *actually* leave. We don't have much time to get our shit together."

I nod, trying to wrap my head around his idea. "Alright, so we're going to slip out unnoticed?"

"Pretty much the only thing we *can* do," Luke says. "We can't risk anyone catching wind of this. Once we have the timing, we can bring Max in."

"What about Jace?"

"I've known him for years. I worry about *him* telling Selene and *her* doing something stupid."

I stare at him for a long moment. "And if we get caught?"

He meets my eyes, unwavering. "We make sure they don't catch us."

I know *exactly* what he means.

It's not reassuring, but it's the only option we've got.

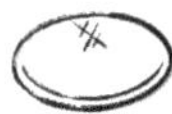

We file into the dining room, the scent of overcooked meat filling the air. I wipe a hand over my face, grimacing at the grime caked there. I'm exhausted, but I can tell I'm not getting a break. Not tonight.

We're *late*.

The Master is already seated, eyes on us as we enter the room. He takes in my appearance, ripped pants and stained shirt, with a look of pure disdain.

"Look at you," he says, voice thick with venom. "*Filthy*. You've been outside our walls all day training those *beasts*, and you bring *this* back into my home?" His gaze flickers to Luke accusingly. "You *allow* him to wander around like this?"

I drop into the seat across from Jace. Luke's holding a glass of water to his lips, staying quiet. I don't want to respond. I'm too tired and, honestly, I don't want to sit through this dinner. I'd rather be hungry.

But it'll be worse if I ignore him.

"Master, I can skip dinner," I offer, trying to downplay the situation. "I'll just go–"

The Master freezes, his lips pulling into a thin line. "*What*? You would refuse a meal I've graciously provided you?"

I don't react to his goading. "I just–"

"No," he interrupts me. "You *will* sit at my table. You will eat what I've prepared. And you will be grateful." His eyes lock onto mine. "I will *not* tolerate disrespect, Eli. Not from *you*. Not from *anyone*. You were out there for hours, and you returned, *yet again*, with weaklings. You're a disappointment."

The words settle like stones in my stomach.... I take a deep breath, fighting to keep my face neutral. I grip my pants in my fists and exhale slowly.

I am steady. I am calm. I am in control.

I didn't ask for this. I didn't ask to be here.

But I am.

I am steady. I am calm. I am in control.

Max leans in his seat beside me, nostrils flared. I can see his frustration building, and I open my mouth to say something, but he beats me to it.

Shit.

"Eli's doing what was asked of him. You can't expect him to work miracles," Max says firmly as he turns to face The Master. I stare, dumbfounded, but he doesn't so much as flick his eyes in my direction.

"You're *defending* him now?" The Master asks, the veins in his neck bulging. "You're defending *him*?"

Max doesn't back down, putting his elbows on the table and leaning forward. "*Yes*, I am. You won't belittle him for doing his job. The one *you* gave him."

I can see The Master's lips tremble with rage, but he doesn't snap. He's too composed for that, at least outwardly. Instead, he leans back in his chair and folds his arms across his chest.

"You think you know better than me, Warden?" The Master mocks, like he's trying to test Max. "You think you can speak for him?"

Max balls his fists, as if he's gathering his nerves, and huffs out, "I'm speaking for *all* of us. We're *all* doing what we're supposed to do. That includes Eli."

Everyone else stares at their plates while Max and The Master glare at each other. Only Luke looks between them, eyes darting back and forth with his glass in his hand.

"I supposed I *should* be thankful that you've finally grown a backbone," he mutters. "But don't, *Warden*, forget who made you who you are."

I see Max's eye twitch, a vein in his Temple throbbing as he looks down at his plate. Luke puts his glass down and places his arms on the table like he's exhausted by the entire exchange.

"Enough," Luke says. "We're *all* tired tonight, and we have more important things to focus on. Eli did what he was supposed to do. If we don't get anyone useful, we'll have to reassess the warriors and try again. I don't see a point in making an issue out of it."

The Master's eyes flick to Luke, narrowing slightly. For a second, I'm worried he's going to turn on Luke next.

And Max is *already* on edge.

From defending me.

I don't know how to feel about *that*, so I hide it away where I don't have to think about it. I put it right next to the moment on the bed, where I looked into Luke's green eyes and saw such desperate longing that I–

I should've looked away. Should've said something snide and let the moment die like I always do. But I didn't.

I looked *back*. I wanted to keep looking.

There was something in his face I hadn't wanted to believe was real. It scares the shit out of me.

Because *wanting* something in this place? That's how you get gutted.

Luke doesn't let the moment stretch. "Besides." He forces a half-smirk. "Eli's the most useful out there than anywhere else. *You* trained him for this."

I let out a slow breath, exchanging a glance at Max. He's on edge, but seeing that I'm not the center of attention has helped him calm down.

When did I become so important to him?

The Master shakes his head as he picks up his knife and slices into his food. "Watch your mouth, boy," he says, but the edge is dulled, like we're no longer interesting enough to keep his attention.

Luke simply picks up his own fork and starts eating like nothing happened, his eyes meeting mine with that same softness from the other day. I run my tongue over the intents in my lower lip but for once, I don't bite down.

As Luke takes a bite, The Master turns his eyes to me. "I suppose we'll just have to hope for better results next time." He shoves a chunk of meat in his mouth and chews it a few times. "You *do* understand, don't you, Sentinel?"

I look at him, keeping my face as neutral as I can. The threats aren't anything new. He's done this for years now, reminding me that my place among them is nothing but *temporary*, that I've been *nothing* but a tactical advantage for him, that he wouldn't hesitate to throw me out if I failed him.

Even knowing what my true purpose is, that my entire life is to funnel information back to Malachi for Sableford to *hopefully* be strong enough one day to ruin Middlesborough, it still *stings*.

"Disappointment has consequences." The words are casual and yet, they have their intended effect. I tuck my chin to my chest, grab my fork–*inhale, exhale*–and push some rice around on my plate.

Does he know? Seven years is a long time. Perhaps I've slipped up–

Max sighs, pinching the bridge of his nose. Luke keeps eating like The Master hasn't spoken at all. Still, he keeps his eyes on me while he chews, as if he's checking in. I tilt my head back in a subtle nod, and his shoulders relax, as if that little indication was *all* he needed.

Jace and Selene escape the evening unscathed by cruel remarks, and that feels like a small victory.

Because that's how this game is played.

And we're running out of time to win.

I've grown used to our evening tea. The way the boys sit in silence, presence thick in the room, means more than any words could. It's comforting, in its own strange way. Like we've reached a quiet understanding, no language necessary.

But the silence *gnaws* at me.

Those red eyes that haunt my dreams, that seem to sit in every shadow no matter where I go–

I usually sit on the bed while they spread around the room–Luke near the window, Max pacing until he's calm enough to sit, Jace with his hands wrapped around his mug, and Eli pretending he isn't watching all of us. It's become a ritual of sorts. All the space between us sings with *absence*, something that *should* be happening, but *isn't*.

Lately, I think I've started to crave intimacy. Not just touch, though God knows that too, but the kind that lets you feel noticed. I used to think I didn't *want* that. I *liked* being invisible. But once you've been *known*, even for a moment, it's impossible to go back.

Now, it's slipping. I feel it loosening, piece by piece, like sand I can't hold onto, as it falls through my fingers.

They're avoiding me. I can tell, even if no one says it. It's like an invisible wall between us, and no one will admit it's there, even though it's *so* obvious. I don't understand why. Maybe it's because of our duties, or maybe it's something deeper, something I'm not *meant* to know.

Either way, it hurts more than I'm willing to admit.

I brush against my bonds, feeling them stir. For a moment, a flicker of warmth moves through me. It's *faint*, but it's there. They're *all* there–Luke's steadiness, Jace's easy presence, Max's fierce loyalty. Even Eli.

Especially Eli.

He tries to stay distant, but I feel him, too–a heavy, hesitant aura that sends a ripple through me when I try to prod it.

Beneath them, something else stirs. I haven't *dared* think about it, not for long, but it's been there for a while now... lurking beneath the warmth of the others. It presses against them, vast and greedy, demanding more room than it should. It claws its way forward, forcing the others to the edges, like shadows retreating from open flame. None of them look at me when it rises.

Maybe they can't feel it the way I do.

It takes up residence in my soul, curling in like it belongs there, purring against my heart with a sick kind of satisfaction.

And I *let* it.

Because I don't know how to make it *leave.*

I don't want to make it leave.

It's content, for now, and the ache it leaves in its wake throbs beneath my ribs. I blink, realizing I've gone still. Max is watching me over the rim of his cup. His brows are furrowed, head tilted like he's trying to read something written on my skin.

Like he felt it, too.

But he doesn't say anything.

Neither do I.

I bring the cup of cold tea to my lips and take a sip.

Eventually, they all drift off to the bed we now share. All of us, except Eli. He stays on the couch, like always, spine straight, pretending the cushions are enough. I stay up a little longer, waiting for the thing in my chest to settle.

It never does.

By the time morning comes, I haven't slept much, and the tea *still* sits bitter in the back of my throat.

I've been meeting with The High Priestess in a different room–her personal office. It's... nice, I guess. It's large and open with pillows scattered across the floor like she expects me to lounge around and get comfy while I wait for her. The windows are draped in thick, elegant curtains so the light stays soft and filtered, as though she's afraid of too much sun.

She's pretty pale, though, so it's a possibility.

There's a desk shoved against one of the walls with papers stacked neatly. It's not as cluttered as I'd expect from someone in her position. A single light hangs from the center of the ceiling, casting this hazy glow that makes everything feel a little less... *holy*.

The walls, though, are covered in blood-red runes, almost the same as the last room. But *here*, they feel different. Less wild, more controlled, like they've been painted with care.

Honestly? Still creeps me out, but it's nothing compared to that smaller, cramped room where I'd elevated the first time.

Three weeks ago? Four? Five? Time has no meaning these days.

The door creaks open, and I know The High Priestess has arrived. The air changes when she enters the room, thickening with the scent of her incense. She moves like she owns the space, like the walls *themselves* have to bow in her presence.

Well, I'm *not* bowing in her presence.

"My Seraph," she says as she slips onto a pillow next to me, her dark blue velvet dress fanning out behind her. "You look troubled."

I straighten, schooling my expression into something passive. "I'm fine."

She hums like she doesn't believe me, tapping her slender finger against her chin in a slow, deliberate movement. "It's important that your heart remains open. That you *embrace* what the bond offers you." She purses her lips. "And how have your nights been, little one? Have your mates been... taking *care* of you?"

She's more of a gossip than the seamstresses had been.

Heat prickles at my cheekbones. "It's *fine*," I say too quickly. She studies me, grinning like she knows something I *don't*.

"Intimacy is the foundation of any bond," she says, searching into the folds of her robe. When her hand reemerges, she's holding a small silk pouch embroidered with curling, golden runes similar to the ones on the wall. She presses it into my palm, and I shiver at the feeling of her icy fingertips. I *should* pull away.

Every part of me flinches–not from the cold, but from *her*. From what she represents. From what she turns me *into*, just by touching me.

I don't.

"A gift," she says simply. "Something simple. *Harmless.*"

The warmth creeping up my arm doesn't match the temperature of her hand. It's softer, *sleepier*. Like curling into a dream I didn't mean to fall into. She tilts her head, eyes half-lidded as she watches me. "You've been so strong, haven't you?" She sounds like a lullaby, like a forgotten prayer whispered in the night. "So quiet. But it's time they listen to you. Time they *feel* what you should give so freely."

"They see me," I whisper quickly. My voice doesn't sound like my own, as if I'm talking in the next room. "Don't they?"

The corners of her mouth pull slightly. "Oh, they *see* you, Selene. But wouldn't it be nice if they *wanted* you? Without pride, or guilt, or fear in the way?"

My hand twitches, but she tightens her grip. *When did she wrap both her hands around mine?*

"Don't you want them to reach for you? All of them?" she asks me. "Don't you want them to *crave* you?"

My chest tightens painfully. The room feels further away than it did moments ago. Something slides through my mind, silken and slow, pressing against the back of my eyes. I want to fall asleep. She presses the pouch into my hand again–*when did I drop it?*–curling my fingers around it.

"Slip just a pinch into their tea, their wine, and you will see how easily the bond flows when nothing stands in its way."

The warmth in my mind fades like smoke caught in a breeze, leaving only the echo of it behind. I blink hard, clarity settling over me like a dunk in a cold stream. For a second, I can't remember what we had been discussing, only the feeling of her fingers and that saccharine smile. I roll the pouch between my fingers, the fabric soft as sin. I think about how much this would have cost someone back when I still sewed clothes for my family's bread.

"Uh-huh," I mumble flatly. "And *why,* exactly, do I need to drug my mates into paying attention to me?"

The High Priestess laughs indulgently. "Oh, My Seraph, it's not like *that.*" She reaches over, brushing hair off my shoulder, fingers ghosting the skin on my neck. "Men can be... hesitant. *Uncertain.*"

I arch a brow. "They didn't *seem* very uncertain to me."

She hums again, smoothing a hand over my collar bone like she's soothing a spooked horse. "Perhaps, but what you have is rare. One woman, four mates. That is a great weight for them to bear."

Right. The *unbearable* hardship of four men sharing one woman. My heart *bleeds* for them.

The High Priestess doesn't seem bothered by my silence. "They may hold back out of duty, out of fear of taking too much. But they *must* take, and you *must* give. That is the nature of your bond." Her hand lingers. "You will need your strength for God, Seraph."

"Strength," I echo.

She smiles like it's a secret between us. "Intimacy *feeds* you. Opens you. Builds the vessel He will use. The closer you are to *them,* the more prepared you will be when He comes. There is no purer offering than the kind born of surrender."

I exhale through my nose, tightening my grip on the pouch. "And this just... takes the edge off?"

She smiles, leaning down to press a whisper-soft kiss to my cheek. "It helps them accept what is already theirs."

I say nothing as I slip the pouch into my pocket.

For later. I'll toss it out. I don't need it.

The High Priestess sits up, smoothing her hands over her breasts and down the front of her robes. "Come, My Seraph. We have much to do today."

I follow her as we slip through the heavy doors to the chambers beyond. The air changes the moment I step inside, heavy and warm, already clouded with the incense she likes to burn mixed with the spices she gives me to *elevate.*

I take it better this way, we've discovered, in smaller doses.

I can feel him, in the shadows. If I look up, I'll see those red eyes—

She kneels before the altar and gestures for me to do the same. A small clay bowl sits between us, filled with crumbled leaves and dark resin.

The scent of the room fills my head—burnt apples and sweet, curdled vanilla. My mind swims and the bonds in my chest curl tightly behind my ribs. God's bond swells each time I'm forced to elevate, stretching itself wide and suffocating the others until they're shells of themselves. The High Priestess remains unbothered, like this is all part of this divine design. And my mates....

They haven't noticed. *At all.*

I think about the pouch in my pocket. If they don't sense how our bonds are fading beneath God, then maybe they don't see me as clearly as I want to believe... maybe they never *have.*

If that's the truth, then maybe it wouldn't hurt to test it.

Just once.

She pinches some of the leaves between her fingers and tosses them into the bowl as she breathes out a single word:

"*Keshai.*"

The resin sparks to life. Smoke unfurls in soft ribbons, curling toward me and winding around my face like it *knows* me.

"Breathe, Seraph."

I do.

It seeps into me, creeping into the edges of my mind. The walls shift, flickering candlelight stretching shadows into something *deeper.* My limbs feel weightless and yet, I feel the pull of the floor, like I could sink into it, like I could become *part* of it.

The High Priestess watches me elevate carefully, then begins her slow chant.

"*Velos ai'taren. Keshti renai. Forthu ven'ashai.*" The words bend the air, vibrating against my skin. My lips part, like they want to form the same sounds, like they already *know* them. She repeats it, slow, patient. The syllables are sharp, winding, wrapped in dangerous, deadly silk. "*Velos ai'taren. Keshti renai. Forthu ven'ashai.*"

I swallow, pressing my tongue to the roof of my mouth, the words bubbling up like a half-forgotten dream.

"*Velos ai'taren. Keshti renai. Forthu ven'ashai.*"

The walls pulse. The shadows *tremble*. The High Priestess smiles.

"Very good, My Seraph. Repeat after me," she murmurs hypnotically. "*Vashan trethai. Luthiel sarai. Keshti vorath.*"

The words feel strange on my tongue. I've heard her say them enough, but never spoken them aloud. I hesitate as I shape them in my mouth, trying to mirror her cadence. "*Vashan trethai. Luthiel sarai. Keshti vorath.*"

The smoke stirs, wrapping itself around my neck. The candles are flickering unnaturally, flames glowing blue, stretching long and thin, bending towards the bowl as if pulled by an unseen force.

My bonds feel *disgustingly* warped—stretched too thin and hollow.

"Again."

I swallow against the tightness in my throat. "*Vashan trethai. Luthiel sarai. Keshti vorath.*"

The shadows deepen, walls pressing down on us, as the runes pulse to a beat I can't hear over the rushing in my ears. A slow throb begins between my legs.

Oh no.

The High Priestess leans forward, dipping two fingers into a small jar behind the clay bowl. She swipes something cold across my forehead, her touch gentle.

"You are the vessel, Selene," she whispers. "You are the key. You are *precious*."

She lifts my hand and continues the chanting.

"*Draesh on'verath. Zai'toren veshal. Moran do'shai.*"

I barely process the blade until I feel the sting—a precise, searing bite that splits my palm. I try to jerk away but she holds firm, tilting my hand over the bowl between us. The dark resin smolders at the bottom, eating my offering, sizzling it away in some bastardized version of the Joining Ceremony.

The smoke changes. It curls upward, shimmering, smudging into violent violets.

The pulse grows *expectant*, steady and deep. Familiar. *Hungry.*

The High Priestess doesn't stop chanting. Her voice lifts, words spilling in a cascading rhythm, faster and more insistent.

"Velos ai'taren. Keshti renai. Forthu ven'ashai!"

The smoke stretches, swallowing the corners of the room. It's engulfed every space except us, and then—

A shape moves within it.

My breath catches, locking my body into place as *he* steps forward, piecing himself together from the darkness.

Tall. *Too* tall.

He hovers just at the edge of the darkness, form unstable, flickering between solid and smoke, as if isn't *entirely* real. One moment, he's a silhouette—endless—and the next, he's like a mirage. Horns curl from his head, twisting like short, obsidian vines, their shape warping with every subtle tilt of his head. His face is lost to the mist that clings to him, except for his mouth. His lips curl into something cruel, pointed teeth glinting in the faded light, all too familiar to my dreams.

But his *eyes.*

Those eyes.

Red. Deep and endless like the void itself, brimming with some ancient knowledge. It presses against me, like it *knows* me, pulls at me from the darkness, every inch of him focused, intense, *watching.*

How long has he been watching me?

He isn't just a presence in the room. He *is* the room, the shadows, the whispers in my head. He fills me with something older than time itself.

He doesn't belong here.

I can't look away. I *feel* him, the weight of him, not just here, but in my soul, deep inside of me where God is... like he's been there all along.

Waiting for me.

I can't move. I can't *breathe.*

Above my heaving breath, I manage to whisper, "Can you *see* him?"

The High Priestess stills and then, she gasps, excitement lighting up her face like an ember catching flame. She clasps my hand, her grip too tight.

"My Seraph," she breathes, eyes wide in reverence as she looks from me to the corner of the room. *"Look* at him, he's glorious!"

I don't want to.

But then—

"Seraph. You've worn other names, but I would know your soul anywhere."

The voice is *inside* of me, in my bones, beneath my skin–

"What do you want?" I ask.

He keeps his eyes firmly on mine. Slow and indulgent, he inches closer, the edges of his form blurring into darkness. The mist around his face is fading, revealing his predatory grace carved from shadow and bone, devastating in its symmetry. His jaw is cruel lines and quiet violence, a structure born of war gods and nightmares.

"To be released." His voice scrapes low in his throat, gravel dragged through silk. I can hear the *hunger* beneath it, primal and barely leashed. *"You will set me free, Seraph, and in return, I will give you everything you desire."*

The words are a promise. They caress over my trembling body. The High Priestess is still watching me, waiting expectantly, eyes fixed on the shadow creature.

"Who... who *are* you? Are you really God?"

His low chuckle cuts through the air, seeping into my soul.

Right next to my mates, where he's lived for weeks.

"I have never been called a God before," he muses. **"But I like the sound of it. Sing my name, Seraph. Sing it while you're beneath me."**

A flush scorches up my neck, shame and heat curling in my stomach. I can't look away. The bonds inside me rage against this creature for making me feel this way, but I can't fight the arousal that blooms from his words. The runes dance across the wall in time with my hammering heart. And then, as the haze begins to fade and he drifts back through the shadows, taking with him that razor grin I'm going to see in my nightmares, I *feel* it–a vertical line with three sharp, horizontal strokes intersecting it–burned into my forearm, glowing bright red against my sun-kissed skin.

The High Priestess' fingers tremble as they hover over the rune on my arm, her eyes wide with awe. The corners of her mouth twitch, lips quivering like she's about to say something, but then she exhales, long and slow, as if she's trying to steady herself. Her voice comes out too sweet, as if hiding the tremor underneath it.

"Ah, *yes*," she says, gliding her fingers over the small amount of blood leaking from the edges, smearing it down my skin. "This... *this* is remarkable. This is part of your elevation. You have been chosen and he's marked you. It's nothing to fear. This is a sign of the depth of your connection."

I feel the blood drain from my face and a cold sweat breaks out across my skin. *Nothing to fear*? I glance back down at my arm again, watching as the glow starts to fade. I flex my hand, trying to ignore the burning sensation where the rune is carved into my skin, but it's nearly impossible. My breath is shallow, chest tight with an unfamiliar panic that clutches at me harder than any lingering fog from our elevations.

No. This isn't normal.

"Remarkable?" I question, my voice hoarse. "That... that *thing*... I saw it in the smoke... it spoke to me. It said–" I pause, the words stick to my tongue, too bitter to be released, but I push them out anyway. "It said it wanted me to free it. It *called* me 'Seraph'. I–"

Her smile widens and she leans in closer, voice dropping to a whisper, thick with warmth and something buzzing just beneath the surface. *A lullaby.*

"My Seraph," she coos as her entire hand covers the rune. "It's all part of the process. The God, the entity you've connected with, that's your power manifesting. Your *blessing*. You've been given a rare, divine gift. It is your *bond*. Do you not feel it?"

I want to argue, I do. But the heat of her hand spreads across my skin and my doubts flutter like caged birds. The air tastes like rotten apples coated in honey. I can't shake the images of that thing from the shadows, of its endless red eyes, that voice that dripped with promise. I draw my arms back, holding them close to my chest as if I can protect myself.

"I didn't ask for this," I whisper. "I didn't ask for *any* of this."

The High Priestess nods slowly, almost sympathetically, and the warmth leaves her smile. She raises her hand to my temple. The pressure isn't painful, but soothing. I find myself leaning into it. "No one ever *asks* for power, Selene. But it's yours, nonetheless. And it's *his*. You've been chosen by a God. You know that, don't you?"

And her hand... that delicate, cold touch, brushes against my forehead as if wiping my doubts away with a single stroke.

I open my mouth, confused, but–

Yes.

Yes, of course.

I blink once, slow. It *was* a God. I'm certain now. I don't know why I doubted it.

"You see clearly now."

"Yes," I murmur. "He... he was *beautiful*. I...." I hadn't thought of it before. *Had I?* But now, the memory comes into focus. His eyes, *that raspy voice*, the shadowed form that seemed to *see* me.... There was something *terrible* in his beauty, but he was *glorious*.

"Selene," she starts softly. "You cannot speak of what is said between you and God. His words are not for mortal ears. If you tell them, your mates will *suffer*. You *know* this."

I don't want to believe her, but something deep inside me curls around the thought like it's true.

"God does not suffer disrespect," she continues. "But you are not betraying them. You are *protecting* them. You're strong enough for that, aren't you?"

I nod slowly, though inside I feel my heart clenching. I don't want to hide anything from my mates–from Max, from Jace, from Luke or Eli....

But I can protect them. I'm strong enough.

Even if it means *lying* to them.

Even if it means they don't *know* what I've seen.

Just as the silence between us grows unbearable, the door bursts open. I snap my head up, the sudden intrusion like a bucket of cold water to my senses.

Jace's eyes are blazing, his mouth set in a hard line. He's practically *vibrating* with anger, but when he spots me, it falters. I don't think he even *notices* The High Priestess sitting next to me.

"Selene." There's a raw edge to his voice that makes me *want* to obey him. "You're coming with me. **Now**."

The High Priestess doesn't seem phased by his fury. In fact, there isn't *much* that bothers her. She looks amused, rather. Her lips curl upward in a knowing smile that makes my skin prickle uncomfortably.

"Do you want to go with him?" she asks me. The question hovers in the air too long as my gaze moves between her and Jace. His eyes meet mine, wide with concern, while she looks on calmly. My voice catches in my throat.

"O-of course," I say, even though I don't sound confident.

She studies me a moment longer, the smile on her face forced. A disappointed sigh slips through her lips.

"Very well," she says shortly. "Just remember, Selene... acceptance is the only way forward. You know what you must do."

Jace steps closer, gently taking my arm to help me stand. As we near the door, something pulls at me, some invisible thread tied to the center of the room. I slip my hand into my pocket, fingers brushing the soft pouch she gave me.

It's so warm here.

I glance over my shoulder. She's standing now, still smiling. And then, she *winks*.

I turn back and follow my mate, but my fingers curl tighter around the pouch anyway.

We slip out of The Temple and into the afternoon air. I feel Jace's hand around mine, grip tighter than usual, as if he's trying to anchor me to reality.

But something inside me is *slipping*.

My bonds.

They're different. Smaller. I try to reach for them but the connections feel faint, frayed at the edges, falling through my fingers.

*Don't panic. Figure it out. Then I can tell them—**No, I can't.***

"Selene," Jace starts, voice laced with concern. "What happened?" He glances at me, brows furrowed. "You're not... *yourself*."

I don't respond right away. His fingers are curled around mine, warm and steady as always, but the comfort doesn't reach me. It's like I'm watching from outside myself, floating just behind. My bonds *should* be louder, but they feel *distant*, dimmed, like they've been pressed into *silence*.

Underneath it all, something akin to fear is *alive* inside of me, whispering that something is *wrong*. Terribly *wrong*.

He looks down at my arm and his grip tightens as he slows down, pulling me to a stop in the middle of our walk.

"Your arm," he mutters, eyes zeroing in on the rune that's been burned into my skin. "What the *hell*? She *branded* you?"

"I–I don't know what it is," I admit, choking on the words. It's not a lie. I don't understand the rune *or* the ceremony *or* what The High Priestess is doing to me, only that I don't feel like myself anymore.

Jace holds my arm up, staring at the mark with a look crossed between horror and disgust. His voice cracks when he speaks again.

"Selene, this scares me." He looks at me. "Th-this isn't... this isn't *right*."

I bite back tears as I glance away. The Temple looms behind and Luke's house waits ahead, but neither feel like safety. "Don't be scared," I whisper. "God is watching over us."

His lower lip trembles when our eyes meet. "We need to tell Luke about this."

"No." The words are out of my mouth before I can stop them. "It's *sacred*. I'm not going to talk about it."

He stares at me like he doesn't recognize me anymore.

Did he ever recognize me, though?

We walk the rest of the way in silence. Jace keeps his hand on the small of my back, guiding me through the hall and all the way to our door. I can feel concern radiating off him like a heater.

"Are you okay?" I ask him as he shut us inside the safety of our room. His expression is tight, but his movement betrays the frustration he's trying to hide. He rubs a hand over his forehead, muttering to himself as he paces. I drop down on the couch and wrap my arms around my waist.

"Not really," he answers after a bit. "They fucking *branded* you! That's... Luke's gonna lose his shit, you *know* that, right?"

I wince at his words. "I didn't–"

"Max might *actually* kill someone," he adds, frustration growing more evident.

"Max wouldn't–"

"Eli *will* kill someone." He turns to face me, eyes locking onto the rune with piercing intensity. "*Fuck*, I need to get that cleaned and covered. Let me get us some tea and I'll get that bandaged for you, sweetheart."

His care, his *concern*, wraps around me like a warm blanket. I'm grateful for it, more than I know how to express. The way he takes care of me, *always* makes sure I'm okay, it makes the bond tighten in my chest, even as weak as it feels right now.

Even though everything's falling apart, Jace is still trying to make me feel safe and wanted... and loved.

He does see me... maybe I don't need–

But he would have touched you by now if he **wanted** **you.**

I don't know when I began needing my mates more than ever, but it's getting impossible to ignore. The bond had begun to feel heavier than it ever had this morning, like a pull deep within me, *urging* me to reach for them. And now, it just feels hollow. Echoing, aching, *desecrated*–I have no idea how to make it whole again.

Yes, I do–

I haven't been intimate with any of my mates in *weeks*–I've *never* been intimate with Jace–and something about *finally* having Jace makes my heart *burn* for it, for that closeness I've been *starving* for.

I watch him, gaze lingering on the way his hands work impatiently as he sets the tea down in front of me. The soft clink of the tray hitting the table is the only sound in the room, but my mind is elsewhere, caught in the pull of what I *want* and what I know I *shouldn't* ask for.

Stop it.

Take what you want.

I bite my lower lip as I watch him disappear into the bathroom to grab what he needs to take care of my arm. He's going to fuss over me until I'm healed. He's a good person. When my fingers find the pouch in my pocket, I hesitate.

I shouldn't do this to him.

I deserve this. Haven't I done enough?

I pinch off a small amount and sprinkle it into his tea before I can think about what I'm doing. The tiny, brittle leaves drift like ash to the bottom of the cup, vanishing into the dark liquid. I stare at it for a moment before tucking the pouch back into my pocket.

I wrap my hands around my cup, letting the warmth soak into my finger like penance as I sip at my tea.

My mind is racing when I step back into our room. I set the supplies down on the table with more force than I intend, the clatter of them harsh in the otherwise silent room. Selene's on the couch, her finger absently twisting a lock of hair, looking miles away. She's clutching her half-finished teacup on her knee. The sight of her so weak, tired and completely out of it, infuriates me. I don't *like* it.

The bond between us feels *frail*, like I could break it by thinking about it too hard. Is it a result of her condition right now? I have no fucking idea. It vexes me that I don't have the answers.

All I know is that this *isn't* her. This is someone else entirely and I can't *fix* it.

I sit next to her and reach for the tea I'd poured for myself. I'd warmed it back up, but it was what we had left over from last night. I don't really care. I down half of it in one gulp, grimacing as the bitter taste hits the back of my throat, and set it back on the table.

Fuck, Luke's going to lose his shit. I know him well enough to know he's been trying to maintain his control, but *this*? This is going to set him over the edge. And Max? He's already lost it. Hell, Max might contemplate murder *with* Eli. They might team up, grab torches, and burn the damn Temple to the ground.

I wipe my upper lip, trying to clear my thoughts as I organize my scattered material. Our lives are being turned upside down and I'm not sure how much longer we can pretend we're in control....

Even Vitalis, who's *always* been a picture of health, had become bedridden just last week. Despite his age, the man had a constitution like steel. For him to be up and walking one day and on death's doorstep the next... well, that had thrown me. I'd had to take over the running of the infirmary, dealing with new patients and making decisions that weren't mine yet to make. It hit me at once, overwhelming and nonstop. I often don't return until long after dinner's been finished.

Max hasn't been faring any better. He's been stuck with The Warden, buried deep in battle plans for the last few weeks. They're crafting strategies that demand constant focus and meticulous attention to detail. Three days ago, he didn't make it back to bed until the early hours, body stiff with exhaustion. When he finally crawled in next to us, he didn't say a word. He'd pulled the covers over himself, tucked in close to Selene, and kissed her shoulder before passing out *only* to wake two hours later and do it all over again.

Luke's been at war with his father for weeks now, battling not just for control of Middlesborough, but over everything else, too. The Master, once a pillar of strength and reason, is losing his grip on reality. The madness in him seeps through every decision, every command. And Luke, though always steady and calculating, finds himself in constant opposition. They clash over *everything*. Over Selene. Over *us*. Over Middlesborough's future.

The Master wants us to start challenging other sects. He wants to seize as much as we can before they turn their eyes, *or their backs,* on us. But Luke... Luke doesn't want to act. He wants to wait and see what The High Priestess is doing to Selene.

To think, to strategize.

Then there's Eli... *Eli*, whose soul is torn teaching these young, broken scouts who have been swept up in the recent madness. He's been preparing them to face a world that has long ago forgotten mercy, but he can hardly teach them without sacrificing a little bit of himself with each lesson.

We're all fucking *stuck* here. And as hard as we try to figure things out, we're getting more worn down....

Maybe Luke was onto something all those years ago about leaving....

I look at Selene and her distant, detached gaze. I can't help the anger that starts to build again. Anger at The High Priestess, at whatever fucked-up 'elevation' they put her through this time. I take her right arm, trying to be as careful as I can, and look at the rune marking her skin.

It's a straight line with three thick, horizontal marks intersecting the top half. There's dried blood stuck to the edges and it's still hot to the touch, still inflamed. I had called it a brand but it doesn't *look* like one close up.

It doesn't look like *anything* I've ever seen before.

It's dark and unnatural. It shouldn't *be* there.

Selene flinches as I run a finger over the top, but she doesn't pull away. *She trusts me.* The thought is both comforting and heartbreaking. I place my poultice mixture over the top, pressing it gently into the skin. It's the same one I use on Max's cuts when he gets nicked by a sword, and he heals just fine. This should prevent deep scarring and heal it quickly. I wind the bandage around her arm, tucking it into itself.

The bandage is secure, but my head... my head *isn't*.

It's floating... no, *spinning*.

No, *drifting*.

I blink hard but the room feels strange, like it's tilting slightly off-center. Like I'm not *entirely* inside my own body. My skin feels too tight. My thoughts are starting to move slower, like they're wading through a mud pool. It reminds me of the hand-rolled weeds we used to smoke when we were younger, just to have a little fun.

The first time I kissed Luke under the stars, we couldn't stop laughing. His hair pulled back, lips stretched over his teeth. I just wanted a taste, a little one. But he met me, both of us eager, tongues tangled with the heat of the summer night wrapping around us. It was like we were closer than we'd ever been. No words needed. Even if we were stoned, I knew then that we were supposed to be together. Our destinies were tied. Even when we played it off as nothing, it was something. Something that would never go

*away. High and laughing, pretending those kisses meant nothing, we'd
cling to each other–*

Selene shifts and the sound of fabric against her skin is *deafening.*
Every breath she takes feels like it's pulling me with it.

The bond inside me flares but it's not the steady, calm thing I've
grown used to.

This time, it's alive.

It's throbbing painfully through my ribs, scraping at my spine. I run
a finger over my lips and they tingle. I can *taste* her in the air somehow.

It's too much.

It's not fucking enough.

I rub a hand over my face to try and shake it off but the second I
look at her, I forget what I'm trying to fight.

She's so close to me.

I see the way her pupils dilate, the way her tongue flicks out to wet
her lower lip, and I wonder what she would do if I just–

My fingers find her wrist. I don't remember moving, but my hand is
on her, soft and warm beneath my touch, and there's lightning up
my arm.

Her breath hitches.

I should stop.

I touch her thigh next, dragging my palm over the velvet of her
dress. My own breath is fast now, heart pounding in my ears.

Something's wrong.

Something's right.

"Selene," I whisper, but it doesn't sound like me at all. It sounds
desperate.

I lean in, ghosting my lips over hers as I stare into her eyes, and then
I kiss her. The way she exhales against my mouth, the way her fingers
curl in my shirt, the way her body leans ever so slightly into mine,
it's all—

Vividly. Distantly.

I press in, letting the shape of her mouth fit against mine. It's
clumsy, too much pressure, then not *enough,* but she doesn't pull away.
If anything, she tilts her head and lets her lips part, and I make a sound I
don't recognize.

I'm dizzy. *Fuzzy.* A slow, creeping warmth spreads through my limbs, gathering low in my stomach, making everything warp and bend at the same time. I *know* touch. I've stitched wounds, reset bones, soothed fevers. I've put my hands on people's skin a thousand times before. But *never* like this.

Never for *myself.*

Never for *want.*

Luke and I, in the woods, under the stars, breathing life into each other–

I'm moving my hand, bracing her waist, thumb grazing just beneath her ribs. I can *feel* her heart within my mind, and something about it makes my soul pulse with desire. My other hand lifts without thinking, my fingers threading through her soft waves, positioning her *just* how I want her.

Fuck–

I don't even know *what* I want.

I just know I *need* more.

I deepen the kiss with my tongue, swallowing the little gasp she makes. My skin feels taut, my clothes *suffocating*, every nerve suddenly so tight I might snap. Her hands slide up my chest, the warmth of her palms burning through my shirt and leaving a trail of fire in their wake. My hips move toward her, drawn forward like gravity itself has changed direction, like she's the center of my entire universe now.

She has been for weeks. For longer. *Since Luke pointed out the seamstress he'd had a crush on, and I started to notice her–*

I break free with a ragged inhale, resting my forehead against hers. My body shakes, lungs desperate for air, but I can still taste her on my tongue.

What the fuck is happening to me?

"Selene," I whisper. "What–" I swallow hard. "What did you do?"

Her fingers hover over my jaw before she pulls away. My bond protests the loss of contact, humming louder than before, like it's unraveling between us. I blink hard, fighting to clear the fog, but it only makes it thicker. My skin is burning, blood sluggishly thick, and my fingers are shaking... *aching* to touch her again.

"What did you do?" I ask again, but the words are slurred now.

She tucks her chin to her chest, watching me from beneath her lashes, like she's trying to decide–

But then she stands and takes a step back towards our bed.

"I didn't do anything," she answers calmly.

I should argue. I can *taste* the lie in the air. But my tongue sits heavy in my throat, and my focus narrows on how her hands reach for the ties at her waist.

The fabric of her dress loosens.

She lets it slide from her shoulders, pooling in a soft heap at her feet.

My mouth goes dry.

I've seen bare bodies before–dressed the dying, cleaned the sick–but this is *different*. So *different, I can't....* She's bathed in the low light, shadows painting over her soft curves and quiet beauty. *Sacred,* something I shouldn't touch. My fingers flex on my knees, gripping my pants tightly to hold myself in place. She doesn't look away as she steps back towards the bed and sinks down.

Then–oh, *fuck*–she lays back and parts her legs, knees bent, body open and waiting.

I can't breathe.

The bond pulses, instincts pulling me forward, *closer, closer–*

I'm staggering towards the bed, my entire body trembling. "Selene," I rasp, but I don't know what I'm asking anymore as I strip myself of my clothing, leaving it discarded in messy piles as I walk to her. She watches me through heavy-lidded eyes.

"Come here, Jace."

My knees hit the edge of the bed, my hands finding the mattress on either side of her thighs. My head is full of bees and the bond, *the fucking bond*, it's beating so loud I can feel it in my teeth.

I have to touch her. I need to, or I'll kill someone.

"Sweetheart...." I don't recognize the raw, hoarse rasp that comes out of me.

She watches me like she's waiting for me to make a move, like she's *daring* me. I exhale across her stomach, my hands skimming up her thighs before I can stop myself. Her skin is soft, warmer than I expect, and when I squeeze, she moans.

Oh, God.

I bite down on my tongue to steady myself, but it doesn't help. Blood is moving too fast around my body. My cock bobs between my legs, rubbing against the sheets where I stand. When she shifts beneath me, her legs part a little more, and I nearly come *right* then and there.

While I'm no stranger to self pleasure, this is more intense than anything I've ever experienced in my entire life.

"I–"

I don't know what I should say. I don't even know if there *is* anything to say. My body's burning up, and all I can see is how she's looking at me with desire, with *want*.

She reaches down, threads her fingers in my hair, and shoves my face between her legs.

I don't resist.

A strangled breath leaves me as her scent floods my lungs–intoxicating, *heady*. My lips brush her heat. I know where the nerves are, where she should feel the most pleasure. My fingers follow, trailing a slow path over her thighs as my tongue licks long strips over her clit. She moans, rocking her hips against my face. Her hands stay in my hair, pulling against my scalp as I suck her clit into my lips, teasing it with pressure.

I *should* savor this. I *should* take my time.

But every sound she makes goes right to my cock.

Something *feral* and unchecked surges up inside me. A painful, beast-like hunger, a bond-driven need that I haven't satisfied since we've been mated, wipes out every last shred of control.

I pull away and climb over her, gripping her hips without hesitation. The careful, measured part of me vanishes without a second thought. My body is moving on craving alone.

I know what to do.

I give in completely, grasping the base of my cock, and thrust into her in one slow motion.

A raspy groan rips from my throat as I sink into her. Searing. Tight. *Overwhelming.*

I drop my forehead to her shoulder, squeezing my eyes shut, as I whisper her name.

She gasps beneath me, body clenching around my cock, and a broken sound escapes my throat. My muscles lock up, trembling with restraint I barely have. The bond tingles between us, electric and insistent, erasing every thought except the feeling of her beneath me.

Offering. Wanting. *Demanding.*

The last fragile thread of control *snaps.*

A shudder wracks my body as I sink deeper. My arm slides beneath the back of her neck, pulling her close while my other hand grips her hip, holding her steady as I start to move. Slow at first, every motion sending heat curling up my spine, my warped mind mapping the way she responds–how her breath hitches, how her nails dig into my shoulders, how her legs tighten just enough to pull me closer.

Fuck, I should take more often.

She moves with me, meeting every slow thrust, wrapping herself around me and pressing her chest against mine. Our lips crash together, open-mouthed and desperate. Our tongues tangle in a feverish frenzy until we're breathing each other's moans like oxygen. Our pleasure builds, an all-consuming flame I had *no* idea I was willing to burn for.

She arches under me, her whole body tensing, and I nearly black out. The noise I make is *whiny*–part groan, part desperate prayer. I try to slow down, to savor it, *to make it last*, but her heat is unbearable.

The pleasure grows too fast, wiping out every rational thought. My rhythm stutters, body seizing up as I bury myself inside her. I know it's not going to be much longer, not with the way she clenches around me or the way she *whimpers* my name in my ear like she's right there with me–

And then she *is.*

She goes taut, a choked cry escaping her lips as she pulses, dragging me down with her. The sensation *wrecks* me. My body gives in completely, cresting and breaking all at once. My forehead presses into her shoulder as I shudder, emptying myself inside her, wave after wave, vision edging with white spots.

We climax together, absolutely breathless. Her nails press into my back, and I can barely tell where I end and she begins as the bond settles, satiated at the claiming.

Shame creeps up my throat almost immediately. I should have lasted longer, should have given her more, but then she exhales a soft, satisfied sound. I lower myself down to lay next to her and set my head on her chest. She laces her fingers into my hair, scratching lightly at my scalp.

I could *purr*, it feels so fucking good.

"That was nice, huh?" she murmurs, amusement curling at the edges of her voice.

I groan as my entire body flushes with heat. "I–yeah. *Yeah.*"

She laughs, still scratching while I feel myself come down. "You're really cute when you're wrecked."

I groan again, utterly mortified, but then she rolls us over so that *she* can nuzzle into *me*.

I feel like I've woken up from a dream I don't quite remember, even though I've got a *vivid* recollection of what just happened.

Definitely high.

Everything feels too damn good. Her skin against mine, her scent. I draw small circles on her shoulder as she breathes into my chest.

And yet, something inside of me is still trying to get free, even though the worst of it has passed.

What is wrong *with me*?

I blink up at the ceiling, trying to slow my thoughts.

"Selene," I mutter before I can stop myself. "What the hell did you give me?"

I feel her sigh against me, fingers moving lazily along my skin. The teasing, playful smile doesn't leave her lips as she looks up at me and, for a second, I *swear* I can see something flash in her eyes, but she hides it quickly.

"I didn't do anything." Her voice is soft, but her eyes don't match the innocence in her tone. I can't *quite* put my finger on it, but I can *taste* the lie through our bond.

It kind of pisses me off, actually–

"That wasn't just me wanting you," I say with uncertainty. "You *made* me... want you. I've never... not before–" My breath catches, and I can't even finish the sentence.

I had *sex* with her.

She looks up at me, eyes half-lidded, and I can't tell if she's taunting me or just being... *her.* But she doesn't answer. Instead, her fingers start moving over my chest again, her barely-there touch ticking the hair like she's trying to distract me, and I'm just trying to handle the sensory overload.

"You just–" she murmurs distantly, "–wanted me. What's so wrong with that?"

She doesn't elaborate. Doesn't tell me what she's hiding. I'm left there, floating downward through the fog, fighting for control. And *damn it*, that's the problem–I *hate* uncertainty. I open my mouth to speak again, but she curls into me, pressing her hand against my chest, and all I can do is wrap my arm around her shoulder, and breathe her in.

T hese recruits are just *too damn loud*.

They're *supposed* to be learning stealth, but right now they're about as subtle as a herd of cattle crashing through the underbrush. One of them—Daniel, I *think*—steps too hard on the balls of his feet, making the grass crunch under his weight. I rub my hand down my face with an exasperated groan.

"That was great," I say flatly. "If your goal was to alert every single enemy within a mile that you're coming."

Daniel's face is as red as a tomato, and the others behind him shift uncomfortably. They're probably hoping I won't call them out on their very *obvious* fuck-ups, but what's the alternative? Sugar-coating their failures and sending them to die?

No.

"Again," I order.

They start again, creeping through the training yard that I've marked off just outside the wall, like they have a *chance* at passing this lesson. I scan the group and assess their movements, but my attention keeps snagging on something else.

No, not something.

Someone.

Selene.

The bond pulses in the back of my skull like a growing headache, tinted with her desire. She's nowhere near, but I don't have to *see* her to *feel* her. Still, it eats at me. The *thinness* of it. How *bare* it feels.... I remind myself that, even weakened by miles, she's always *there*. A thread, tugging at the frayed edges of myself.

That's what it is. The *space* between us. What I *shouldn't* be doing, but I *allow*. That's what it *has* to be. Because in the beginning, the distance hadn't *mattered*....

We could have been *oceans* apart, and I would've felt her *burning* in my veins. Now it's like an echo, fading away–

"Uh... Eli?"

I blink, refocusing. One of the scouts, Marco, is looking at me expectantly.

"What?" I grunt in his direction.

He hesitates. "Was that better?"

I have no fucking clue. I don't even remember *half* of what I've taught them today. I glance back at the group as they shuffle forward, acting like they've conquered my intense training routine. As if it was the easiest thing in the world. As if each and every one of them hasn't failed it *more* than once in the past week.

That's not *the point of this course, but okay.*

"Sure," I say with a shrug. "If you want to survive an extra ten seconds before someone buries a knife if your back."

He huffs at my casual dismissal. Max would say I'm too harsh on them–*rich, coming from him*–but he trains warriors.

I'm supposed to train *ghosts*.

They don't get the luxury of brute force.

We get it right or we *die*.

I'm too fucking distracted to teach anything useful today.

"Partner up!" I shout. "Get into position! I want to see some defensive tactics!"

They groan, but only because we've been at it for hours now. I don't bother reprimanding them as they shift into their small groups. It doesn't take long before the sparring begins.

I've set up a few markers in the dirt, a makeshift ring of sorts, so they're forced to keep their moves tight. Tyler throws a punch at Marco. He barely manages to block it, stumbling back with a loud grunt.

"Better, Tyler," I remark, watching them circle each other. They're both improving rapidly, but it's not *fast enough*. They'll need so much more to survive outside the walls for long periods of time. Without meaning to, my eyes flicker to the path, just beyond the training field.

The one I've walked countless times.

The way to Malachi.

Fuck.

Malachi's probably out there waiting on me, pacing like a cat trapped in a house, just like he *always* does when I'm late to a meeting. He'll be pissed, of course. He won't understand why I didn't show up today.

He'd call me a coward. A *traitor*, ironically enough. That I've lost the edge he helped me craft, choosing my new life and putting my own feelings above the greater cause.

But what's the greater cause, really?

Sableford? My own fucking village that sold me out at fourteen? The same place that abandoned *me*, that had no problems with *me* going through The Ritual to bind my bond, that sent *me* here as a puppet on this endless hellish mission *alone* and trapped, to have *me* feed false information for *years* to The Master, knowing damn well that if I was caught, I'd be the one killed?

You know what?

Fuck. Them.

I'm not the same kid who follows orders blindly anymore. I'm not the one who's going to take a hit for a cause that never gave a *shit* about *me*.

I'm choosing Selene. *My* mate. The guys who have become more of a family to me than my own fucking fathers ever were. I'm *choosing* this life. The one where I don't have to hide who I am, where I don't have to constantly wonder where the next betrayal might come from....

Well....

The recruits are still awkwardly circling, so I try to focus on them again. But even with their movements back in my line of sight, I can't get Malachi out of my head, out of that dark spot in my chest where my undivided loyalty to him sits.

I missed the meeting today.

And I'm *never* going back.

The thought of facing Malachi again, his anger and disappointment, it feels like a weight that's suffocating me–

But I'm choosing something else now, something that I've never been allowed to choose before, something I never considered that I'd be allowed to have–

"Marco, step in!" I bark, snapping back to the fight. Marco fumbles forward on sloppy footwork, and I roll my eyes.

"God*damnit*," I mumble, "if you can't keep your feet under you, you're gonna get yourself killed."

He stumbles back, but this time, his eyes meet mine. For a brief second, I see a hint of the same fear I've carried for years.

He's only seventeen... stolen from a village The Master deemed un-loyal for many years–

"Again," I growl. "*Focus.*"

I turn back to the path. The feeling of being torn between two worlds grips me harder. On one side, there's my abandoned mission. The loyalty I once held. The place I grew up, the people I fought *so* fucking hard for.

Now, there's *them*. My *family*. Selene, Jace, Max, Luke. They're not *just* mates... they're the reason I'm standing here.

I know I'm not only walking away from Sableford. I'm walking away from the part of myself I've spent my whole life trying to fight to get *back* to. And for *what*? A future that's uncertain, one where the stakes are higher, where there's *never* been a guarantee of my survival anyway?

I've made my choice, long before this moment.

It still doesn't make this weight any easier to carry.

I look down the path one last time, knowing that if I were to dismiss everyone now, I could still have a chance at catching Malachi.

But I don't.

"Keep moving," I shout, turning back to the recruits, "faster this time. I want to see some progress."

As they pick up their pace, I focus instead on the feeling in my chest where my bond lives.

This is what feels right.

I pace between them, trying to ignore my racing thoughts as the scouts clumsy movements grate on my nerves. Tyler's got his guard up too high, and John's feet are planted like tree roots–all easy pickings. They'll learn, I *guess*, but it doesn't change the fact that these ex-warriors are a far cry from where they should be.

They're all so young–

"Your stance is *shit*," I mutter, pulling John's arm down roughly into the proper block. "If you leave yourself open like that in the field, you'll be compromised before you know it."

He nods, but my remark stalls him. He's not used to real criticism. Wherever they found him, he wasn't from one of the working families. I can tell just by looking at him. This is the first *real* hard thing he's ever done in his life.

He's going to die out there.

They *all* act like they can handle this. Like training to be a scout is some kind of *prize*. But everyone knows what they are–the ones not good enough to be warriors. Dropped at my feet like scraps, and I'm supposed to make them into something *useful*.

I hear what my recruits say about me, too. As if being stuck with *me* is a worse punishment than death at the end of a blade.

Asshole. Pomp.

Stray. Leech.

But that's *not* my fucking problem right now.

Because as soon as I walk around the circle, I see the path again, and I realize something about Malachi and how long he's been waiting.

He's going to think I've *been compromised.*

The thought cuts through me like a cold blade. If I'm *not* at the meeting, then there's only one explanation in his mind: *I've lost the mission.*

I've fallen.

Oh, shit.

Malachi's the kind of person who can smell weakness a mile away. It's why they assigned *him* to train me when they volunteered me for the job. He'll think something's wrong. He'll believe I've been *discovered*.

I've *really* fucked up now.

If Sableford suspects I've gone *soft*, they won't leave me here.

They'll *come* for me.

The fear's gnawing at me. I can almost *hear* Malachi's voice calling me every kind of coward in his book. Maybe I deserve it. I'm choosing *them* over my mission. I'm walking away from what I swore to do, from what I was raised to be, and for what?

For what?

I stare at the path as all the noise around me fades away, and the ice cold reality sets in.

If I'm *not* loyal to Sableford, to Malachi, then who the hell *am* I loyal to now?

Who am *I betraying?*

I glance over at the scouts as more questions flood me. If Selene, *if the guys*, find out what I've been doing, if they know I've been lying about *everything*–will they still look at me the same?

Will they still see me as one of them?

Or will they see me for what I *really* am?

What am I now?

The words ring hollow in my head.

I'm *not* who I used to be. But I'm not entirely sure who the hell I'm supposed to be *now*.

Traitor.

"Eli?"

The sound of my name cuts through the fog. Judas, the youngest of the group, stands in front of me, looking uncertain.

"What?" I ask, forcing the anger from my tone.

He shifts his weight. He's been the most eager to learn out of the entire group, and I hate losing my patience with him. "You, uh, said to... adjust my footwork. Was that better this time?"

I bite my lower lip until copper floods my tongue. Cheap trick, but it still works to shove the panic down.

I *can't* let them see me cracking right now.

I exhale slowly. "No. You're still planted wrong."

He looks disappointed and, for some reason, I can't *stand* the sight of his drawn brows, the way his eyes shine with tears.

Sixteen.

Of course, The Master isn't above using teenagers for his dirty work.

I was fourteen.

I turn my back to the path and face the rest of the scouts. "Everyone, move it. We're running through the basics again. This isn't about *looking* good. It's about staying *alive*."

As if they can sense my mood, they scramble into position. But I'm not really seeing them.

I'm lost in the woods.

Is Malachi still waiting? If he is, he's assuming the worst. The real question, though... is he right?

A wave of calm, like a breeze through the trees, floats across my soul.

Selene.

I feel her soothing away my anxiety, her aura filtering through my doubts like sunlight through a canopy of leaves.

She's there. Reaching out, even over the distance. I can *feel* it, the way she's trying to loosen the knot in my chest, trying to calm the nerves clawing up my throat. The ones that have *nothing* to do with training and *everything* to do with what I left behind.

I'm choosing *them*. I know this is what I want. This life. *Her.*

Will they forgive me? The guys? Will they understand why I did it? Why I came? Why I turned my back on everything *for* them? *For* her?

I can't tell them. I *won't*, not now. It's too dangerous. But one day, when the time's right, I'll have to. I *hope* they'll understand, because I'm *not* going back to Sableford. I'm *not* going back to a life that offered me up to rot.

Not now. Not *ever* again.

I'd rather see myself out.

I watch the recruits go through their motions, but they're little more than shadows in my periphery. I'm not really paying attention–

Enough.

I square my shoulder, shaking off the last remnants of doubt. I'm *done* with this. *Done* wondering if Malachi is waiting, if Sableford will come for their long-lost, unwanted son, if I'll regret this choice....

Because I *won't*.

They left me to die at fourteen.

I owe them *nothing*.

If they come for me, so be it. I'm *not* fucking going back.

I'm not theirs anymore.

I roll my neck, the tension cracking along my spine, and turn back to the scouts. Some are sparring, but the rest are lined up, adjusting uneasily under my scrutiny. Marco looks *particularly* nervous, probably wondering what he did to piss me off this time.

I gesture towards the empty ring. "Alright, Marco. You're going to fight me, and I'm going to show you *exactly* what I mean."

His eyes widen slightly. "Wait–*me*?"

I arch a brow. "You deaf now?"

Tyler lets out a quiet snort, and Marco glares at him before stepping forward, nostrils flaring. "*Fine*."

I step into the ring, motioning for him to follow. "Good. Because you've been fucking this up all week, and I'd rather not have to explain to The Warden why I let one of *my* scouts get slaughtered in his first real mission."

Marco swallows hard, cracking his knuckles. He's trying to hide his nerves, but I see the way he moves. He's bracing to get hit. Expecting to lose.

That's his first mistake.

I shake my arms in front of me, settling into a stance, loose and ready. "Come on, then. Show me what you've got."

He lunges. It's clumsy and obvious, and I sidestep easily, slapping his wrist away before twisting behind him. I grab the back of his shirt and yank, sending him stumbling sideways.

"Sloppy," I remark. "Again."

He pivots, baring his teeth, and comes at me harder. *Better*, but still not good enough. This time, I let him get closer before stepping into his space, slamming my forearm against his and twisting his momentum against him.

He hits the ground with a grunt.

The others watch carefully now, absorbing my movement with rapt attention. I don't give Marco time to catch his breath. I crouch beside him, my tone flat. "You fight like someone who *expects* to be beaten." I glance around at the others. "Most of you do. *That's* the problem."

Marco stares up at the sky, catching his breath.

I straighten, trying to catch everyone's eye. "Out there, no one's going to give you a second chance. No one's going to wait for you to get your footing. If you're not ready the moment the fight starts, you're already dead."

Marco drags himself up, rubbing his jaw. "So what do *you* do?"

"I'm *invisible*. I don't fight unless I have to. But when I have to," I smirk, crooking my fingers at him. "I fight like it's the last thing I'll ever do."

He nods, determined now, and I get back into position. The others watch in silence.

I can feel it–*the shift*. The moment *they* start to understand. I call them up to spar, eager to see it in action.

They're *getting* it. The movements are clicking into place. The steps are more fluid, stances firmer. The hesitation *bleeds* out of them. It's not *perfect*, not by a long shot, but it's *progress*. I can see them stop second-guessing themselves. They react, listen to their instincts. I think, maybe, *just maybe*, they'll survive their first night out by themselves.

They might actually see the light of day.

It's also the moment the seams *I've* been clinging to finally tear loose, and I embrace what *I've* become.

The Sentinel. Selene's mate. Luke. Max. Jace.

One pack.

I've been stitched in blood and bone for *this* life, and I'm *done* looking over my shoulder. *Done* questioning where I stand.

I've made my choice.

And whatever comes next?

I'll be ready.

Marco moves better this time. Faster.

Smarter.

Good.

I sidestep his first strike, but he pivots and catches me off guard. His shoulder slams into my ribs, knocking the air from my lungs. Before I can counter, he hooks a leg behind mine and takes me to the ground. The impact rattles my teeth, dust kicking up around us. I *barely* have time to register the taste of blood in my mouth before he's on me, forearm pressing against my collarbone, pinning me to the ground.

For a second, neither of us move.

Marco stares down at me, breathless, shock crossing his face like he can't *quite* believe what just happened. My tongue swipes at the blood on my lip as a gruff chuckle, thick with satisfaction, rumbles from my throat.

"That," I say, pride curling through my words, "is how you fucking survive."

Finally, I think, *victory.*

The evening air is muggy with sweat and exhaustion as I trudge back from the training ground, every muscle in my body *screaming* for me to just sit down and relax.

It's not happening, though.

Dinner is next, along with The Master's usual delusional rants... which have taken a terrifying turn into something cruel.

I'm *overjoyed*.

Luke's been distant, Jace practically locked in his own head, and Selene... *fucking* Selene. The bandage on her arm eats at me, but when I asked her about it, she brushed me off and ignored me for an *entire* day, sending waves of anxiety down my side of the bond.

I *know* bullshit when I hear it... but after *that*, I didn't push the issue. She's been acting strange. A shadow of herself. Almost as if she's not *really* with us....

Sort of how I feel sometimes at night, when everyone else is in bed, and I'm up late, watching her sleep, and my vision fogs over–

Eli's been *present*, which is its own red flag. The guy is usually a ghost, slipping in and out when it suits him, but *recently*? He's been hovering.

Like *now*.

I spot him up ahead, leaning against the fence post with his arms crossed like he's got *nowhere* else to be. Fucking puts me on edge, even though I've grown used to him over the past few weeks.

He's not *that* bad–but I'm not admitting that to his face or anything.

"Wow," I call out as I approach him. "Didn't realize I missed our date. Should I be flattered or concerned?"

Eli smirks. "Maybe both."

I sneer at him. "See, *that*? That's *exactly* the kind of cryptic shit that makes me wanna throw you in a ditch, you bastard."

He shrugs, looking off into the distance. "Yeah, well, get in line."

I want to keep needling him until he bites back, until he scratches the way I'm used to and we're at each other's throats, but he seems *off*. The second red flag that appears is that his usual intensity is gone. He seems just as exhausted as I am.

I stop a few feet away, putting my hands on my hips. "Alright. Out with it. What the fuck do you want?"

Eli runs a hand through his hair before leveling me with a look that sends a chill rippling through my gut. "There's some shit going on," he starts. "Luke's been working his side, but we *both* think it's time to bring you in. To protect Selene."

My body goes still, the post-training ache shoved to the background. "Protect her from *what*?"

Eli doesn't answer. He just stares at me and bites his lower lip.

"We should take a walk."

And *that's* the third red flag.

Whatever he's about to say, I'm not going to fucking like it. He turns and starts to walk away.

"The hell?" I mutter as I jog after him. "So what, I'm just supposed to follow you? No explanation? No little ominous quip? You're slacking."

"Shut up and walk."

I narrow my eyes but keep pace with him. We walk in silence for a few minutes away from the training grounds, away from the house, towards the outer edge of Middlesborough.

"I found something," he says when we reach the outer fence. "A journal."

"Congrats."

"*Max.*"

Something in his voice makes me pause. I glance at him, at his tight expression and tense shoulders. *He's serious.*

"It was in Luke's basement," he continues. "It talks about The Ritual. It's a *demon* Ritual."

I stare at him as the air is sucked out of my lungs. "Oh. Wow. That is... above my head."

Eli sighs through his nose, his patience thinning. "Luke and I have been trying to figure out what it means, but this is *bad*. Selene's all mixed up in it."

"Like, *bad* bad, huh?" I know it's not a joking matter, but I can't help trying to cut the seriousness with some humor. Before I can blink, he turns and grabs me by the front of my sweat-soaked shirt, and shoves me against the fence. The breath whooshes out of me in one harsh gasp.

"Shut the *fuck* up, and listen to me," he snaps, face inches from mine. I stare at him, stunned–partly from the force, mostly from the fact that I hadn't *expected* him to be this strong. My mind reels as the *bond* of all things roars with the embarrassment of being pinned by another man. I swallow it down as the rational side of me sees how serious all of this is.

"Alright, bro. Damn." He releases me, and I roll my shoulder carefully as I step away from the fence. "Didn't know you were *that* freakishly strong."

He doesn't rise to the bait, so I rub my neck instead.

"Alright, *alright*. I'm listening, you dramatic prick. What's so damn important you felt the need to assert your dominance?"

Eli glances around the empty field like he's expecting someone to run up on us, before he nods once and faces me again.

"The journal I found," he begins. "It's *old*. Been hidden away, buried under piles of shit for who knows how long. It talks about why the bonds were suppressed, and how."

"How?" I echo weakly, leaning back against the fence.

"They sacrificed the first Seraph to a *demon* to bind the bonds." He looks around again. "It doesn't say why, or how they did it."

Middlesborough *killed* someone to suppress the bonds? Our ancient birthright that helped us find our mates for life? It feels like a gut punch, and my mouth falls open, but Eli doesn't let the silence stretch on long.

"That's not all. The journal also says the bonds can be restored."

"How?" I ask. There *has* to be a fix. If it's broken, then....

His jaw flexes. "By having a Seraph perform a sacrifice of her own."

But... Selene is The Seraph.

Middlesborough wants her to *fix* it? Can she *fix* it? Is it *fixable*?

After everything Eli just told me, I doubt it's going to be something as simple as cutting her palm and making a wish.

A violent, cold rage creeps up my spine. "So, what you're telling me," I say slowly, "is that they're planning to use Selene for whatever fucked-up demon Ritual they're cooking up to *release* the bonds."

Eli doesn't answer, looking around again.

"Why are they releasing them if *they're* the ones who bound them in the first place?"

"I don't fucking know!" Eli throws his arms up. I run a hand over my face, trying to process what he's saying.

"You know this is insane, right?" I let out a sharp breath. "And what the fuck do you mean, a sacrifice? Hers... or?"

Eli shakes his head, exasperated.

"Yeah, you don't fucking know. Got it." I cross my arms, looking at him hard. "And the demon part? Where the hell does *that* come in?"

Eli places his hands against the fence and leans forward, letting his head hang. "That's another part I can't figure out. All I know is that a demon was involved the first time and that it made a promise of some sort."

Too vague and *not* comforting enough.

Middlesborough isn't feeling safe any longer. It's starting to feel like a prison. I think back to Luke's comments of running away and wonder if *that's* still on the table–

And Eli, who I had always believed to be a shady, slippery, sarcastic little shithead, has shown me a new side of himself. He *cares*. Not in just an offhanded *she's-my-mate-so-obviously-I-care* kind of way, but in a *this-is-bigger-than-all-of-us* kind of way.

Not for the first time, I realize that I actually *respect* the bastard. Something else is clicking, too. Hearing him say all this, seeing how fucking *serious* he is? It's not just about his *own* survival. He's included *us* in his plans, too.

Jace, Luke... *me*.

I let out a slow breath and rub at the back of my neck. "Okay. *Alright*. You and Luke have been sitting on this for how long?"

"Long enough."

I scoff. "And Jace?"

Eli shakes his head as he stands up straight. "He doesn't know."

That pisses me off more than I expect it to. I *like* Jace, and if it's about Selene, we should *all* be aware. "Why the hell not?"

Eli smirks. "Because if he knew, *you'd* already know. So would all of Middlesborough."

I shut my mouth. Jace *can* keep secrets. He's done it for me for *years*, but revealing that now feels....

I shrug and shove my hands in my pocket.

"So, what's the plan? Because I know you and Luke don't have all this information and are planning to just *see* what happens."

Eli pauses, thinking too hard again. I hate how comforting *dysfunction* is starting to feel.

"Oh, come *on*. You just threw me against a fucking wall, told me our mate is part of a blood Ritual, and there may or may not be demonic involvement... and *now* you're gonna edge me?" I throw up my hands. "Just tell me the fucking plan."

Eli bites his lower lip. "I can't."

I scoff. "*No?*"

He meets my gaze evenly. "The less we *all* know, the better."

The way he says it, the way he *looks* at me, makes my skin *crawl*.

"You're worried we're gonna get caught. Someone's gonna get one of us to spill." It's not a question, and Eli doesn't answer. That tells me *all* I need to know.

I *hate* it. I *despise* the secrecy. I can't fucking *deal* with the fact that Luke and Eli have been playing this close to the chest for who knows *how* long. That we're all walking blind into something *big* and *bad* and probably *fucking fatal*.

But... I also get it.

The Master's gone senile. His dinner rants have gotten bizarre, the Sunday sermons more vicious. If Eli's concerned about him trying to squeeze information... well... Luke's admission of his father's threat comes rushing back to me and....

I'd rather not think too hard about *how* he'd do it.

My knuckles crack as I squeeze them. "Fine. *Whatever*. But if you think I'm just gonna sit here and wait for Luke to drip-feed me whatever the hell he thinks I *need* to know–"

Eli cuts me off, "We *need* you on this, Max."

That shuts me up.

I'm *needed?*

"I know this isn't how you want to do things. But if we're gonna keep *her* safe, we can't afford to fuck this up. That means working together, as a team." He stares at me intently. "As a *pack*."

I nod without a second thought. "I'm in."

"Your only job in this right now is to get out from under The Warden." He steps closer until our chests are almost touching. "Spend as much time as you can with Selene. I don't want her alone, not if we can help it."

"I've been *trying* to spend more time with her. Wait... you think they'll try something?"

Eli shrugs. "I don't know, but I don't think it's worth the risk. I know you'll do a good job of watching over her. We just need to be more... cautious."

I nod thoughtfully. That, at least, I can do. Spend more time with Selene? *Always*.

"Jace can't know yet," Eli tells me.

"You're serious about that?" I ask, crossing my arms. He fixes me with an '*are-you-joking*' look.

"No, *fuck* that. If something happens, he *needs* to know. He's in this pack, too."

"Leave it to me, brother," Eli mumbles, placing a hand on my shoulder.

I don't like leaving Jace in the dark, but I trust Eli.

Fuck... I *trust* Eli.

I don't know what I'd even tell Jace–*Hey man, turns out our home is even more of a nightmare than we thought, and I think they're planning to sacrifice our girl to a demon, but don't worry, we've got a half-baked plan we can't talk about, try not to confess over dinner.*

Yeah, Jace might crack before they even uncork the wine. He's hanging on by a thread these days. Best not to pile it on.

"Fine." I jab a finger at Eli's chest. "I won't tell him. *Yet.* But if this shit gets worse, you tell *me,* and I'll keep her safe."

Eli watches me for a second before he nods.

Not a promise, not *reassurance,* just acknowledgement.

Good enough.

Eli turns, and I fall into step beside him. The path back to The Master's house feels longer than usual. The air between us is awkward with all the things left unsaid.

How much more does he know? What else is he keeping from me?

Does he trust me like I *trust him?*

For once, neither of us are in the mood to argue with each other.

We reach the front door and pause, listening as the dinner bell rings sharply on the other side.

"Great. Can't wait to hear what fresh delusions are on the menu for tonight. Roasted duck with a side of '*she's-not-pregnant-yet?*'. What do you wanna bet?"

Eli snorts as he turns the handle, and we enter the house. "Try not to get yourself poisoned."

"That's foreplay, right?" His grin feels like a small victory. Eli and I slide into our seats next to each other, and the room feels like it's holding its breath. Selene's right across from us, flanked by Luke and Jace.

She's fading into the chair, her eyes heavy with exhaustion. There's that bandage wrapped around her forearm, freshly changed. Jace is a shell of himself. His posture is slumped, like he's holding himself together with strings. He doesn't speak, doesn't look at anyone, just stares at his plate in front of him like he wants to vanish into it. I'm pretty sure he's already checked out for the night, and I don't blame him.

These dinners *suck*.

Luke? He's already angry. His jaw is tight, eyes dark, a storm brewing under the surface, ready to break. I wonder how far we'll make it into tonight before he snaps.

I'd bet my sword it's the main course.

I lock eyes with him, and an unspoken understanding passed between us. He knows I'm in the loop, and more importantly, he knows I'm on board.

The Master walks in not long after we sit, all high and mighty, and plops down at the head of the table. Before he can say a word, the working girls bring out dinner. I glance over as a wisp of a girl drops the main course down. My throat tightens a little when I see what they're serving tonight.

Roasted fucking duck.

Eli catches my eye, and we both snort at the same time. It's *ridiculous*. Of *course* it's roasted duck. I try to hide it, clearing my throat like I'm choking on nothing, but Eli's grin is enough to signal that we are, in fact, laughing.

The Master's crazed eye is on us, catching the last remnants of our snickering. "Something *amusing*, Maximus?"

I swallow down the last bit of my chuckle, forcing myself to act serious. "No, nothing at all, Master," I reply, reaching under the table for Eli's wrist.

But it's his hand instead, and he lets me take it.

The girls serve our plates as The Master begins his tirade.

"You've really been slacking in your training. It's clear you think you've mastered it all, but the truth is, you've wasted your potential. If you want to be The Warden, I expect so much more out of you." His tone is cold. "You're *worthless* to me if you aren't going to fulfill your role here. Do you understand?"

I don't flinch. I stare back at him, letting the words roll off me like water. I'm not in the mood for a lecture, especially after my talk with Eli.

We aren't long for Middlesborough anyway. These words mean nothing *to me.*

"Eli," he snaps, shifting his gaze over. "Your scouts can't even keep an eye on the damn perimeter! One of them managed to catch a trespasser, but not before he's been lurking for *days*. That's *your* responsibility. You're *supposed* to be training them, not letting them slack off like *you*!"

Eli doesn't respond. He sits back, our hands still linked, with his mask of indifference. He might be furious, but he knows better than to bite back. It's not worth it.

My grip tightens, and he clutches back.

The Master doesn't stop, though. He moves onto Jace next. "*You* had a woman die in childbirth under your care *just* this morning. That's a *momentous* failure. Are you *sure* you're meant to be Vitalis? You're *supposed* to be the healer, but how can I trust you with something as important as Selene's future if you can't even save a milkmaid's life?"

I watch Jace's shoulders tighten and his eyes cloud over. He's not *here* anymore. The Master's words are background noise to whatever else is going on inside his head. The Master's eyes travel to Selene. I *swear*, this man has a sixth sense for the moment when he can really sink his vicious little claws into her.

"Selene," he clicks his tongue like he's disappointed in her very existence. "I hear you started your cycle. No pregnancy? You should have done your duty to my son by now. Are you even *trying*? I bet you're going behind his back and rutting up against these other boys."

The air shifts in the room. Not just *around* me, but *inside*, like pressure building inside a sealed jar. Rage curls beneath my ribs, hot and venomous, licking at bone. And the bond? It *stings* like a scar ripped open, old pain made new. Her hands curl into fists next to her plate, and for a second, I think she'll break. Her face is pale and her eyes are shimmering with unshed tears.

Then Luke speaks up, voice full of heat. "That's *enough*," he spits, facing his father. "Don't speak to her like that. Don't talk to *any of us* like that."

The Master slams his fist against the table. "You don't get to tell me what to do, *whelp*!"

Luke doesn't back down. He's fuming now, lower lip trembling as he leans forward. "Then shut the *fuck* up, and stop treating her like a goddamn breeding machine! Stop treating us like work horses!"

I glance over at Eli. He's as mad as I am. There's a change between us, like a line's been drawn, and we're standing on the same side. I don't know *when* it happened, but I can see it now, solid under my feet.

Maybe I don't hate that we're a pack.

The Master and Luke glare at each other as Selene picks at her food. I lean back in my chair, slipping my hand free from Eli's grip, and cross my arms as I watch the staring match. Jace pulls a slice of bread off his plate and tears it in half, shoving it into his mouth.

The Master lets the silence stretch, his expression twisting into something cruel. "You seem to have forgotten your place as of late."

Luke scoffs, shaking his head. "No, *you* have." His fingers dig into the table's edge, white-knuckled. "You think we're just going to sit here and *take* this? Let you talk down to us. Let you insult our mate?" He gestures to Selene, voice rising. "She's The Seraph, isn't she? Isn't that what you keep telling me? The '*perfect little sacred woman*'?" He says mockingly.

"She is what she was *chosen* to be." The Master's voice is steel. "You just happened to be bonded to her."

Luke barks out a laugh, shaking his head. "I didn't have a choice in being bonded to her. But *you!*" He slaps his palm to his chest. "You *made* me into *this*! You didn't give me a choice in this life!"

The Master leans forward, resting his forearms on the table. His eyes swim with insanity. "And look at what that's given you, Lucas. *Power*. A purpose. A future that no one else here could *dream* of."

"A fucking future?" Luke echoes, looking around at us. "What future? One where we rot away under you doing whatever you say, no matter how fucking deranged it is?" He runs a hand through his hair, tugging at the roots. "I'm *not* you! I'll *never* fucking be you!"

The Master grins suddenly, flashing his yellowing teeth. "No," he agrees, as if that was his point all along. "Because you don't have the *spine* to do what needs to be done."

I have the strangest feeling inside me, as if I'm *connected* to Luke in a way I've never been before. His anger tips into me, fills my cup to near spilling. And yet, I don't *move*. I just *know* he wants me to stay here and wait, but I don't know *how* I know–

Luke's rage ignites like a flame. He moves, shoving his chair back so hard it screeches across the floor, pointing a trembling finger at his father. "Fuck *you*, you delusional old bastard!"

The Master stands languidly at the same time, meeting him head-on. "Sit down, *boy*."

Jace stills, his hand sliding up Selene's arm slowly while she trembles against her chair. Eli straightens beside me, tense and ready.

And me? I'm just waiting to see who throws the first punch.

I hope Luke lets me kill *him*.

The Master's eyes are gleaming as he breaks his icy silence. His voice, once controlled, now cracks with something desperate. I feel my brows furrowing as I watch him, wondering if he's *finally* lost it, if we're witnessing his final moment of sanity.

"You don't *understand*, Lucas!" he snarls, fists shaking as he leans into the table. His food scatters as he smacks his plate to the side. "You need a *child*. A *proper* heir! Someone who can carry the bloodline and lead after me. And *she*–" He points a finger at Selene, lips curling in disgust, "–she just needs to *give* it to you!"

His words echo through the room like a thunderclap, but he doesn't stop there. His body shakes violently. "If the child is a girl, *fine*. We can work with that! Just have one of your other *harem* breed *that* one. I'll–"

My blood boils. I shoot up from my seat before I even realize I've sent the chair flying, my fists clenched at my sides.

"No," I snap. Before I can think better of it, I'm crossing the room in two long strides, shoving my hands into his chest, and knocking him backwards. He stumbles, his eyes widening in surprise.

He's not expecting my attack.

"You don't get a fucking say about her," I growl from the base of my chest, low and gravelly. "You don't get to talk about *our* children like they're pawns."

The guards react instantly. They rush in, but my focus is on the man in front of me, on the *villain* who has been ruining our lives over the last few weeks. They drag me to the floor with brutal force, but all I see is the way The Master stares at me.

Shock. Betrayal. Confusion.

A voice carries across the room, loud and strong in a way I've never heard before. My body is *compelled* to listen, bending in a way that makes my muscles ache when I fight against it. "***Stop****! Detain* him*!* Not Max!"

The chaos escalates. Luke kicks a chair away as he walks around the table. "You can't–*don't* touch him! He's *not* the one out of line! My *father–*" The word sounds like a swear coming from his mouth. "–is out of his fucking mind!"

Everything feels like it slows down. The guards freeze, still gripping me, but unsure where to throw their weight now. Luke's staring them down, a shield I didn't expect.

But somehow, I *knew* he would. He's *always* had my back in a fight.

Why would this be any different?

I can feel Selene's eyes on me from where she stands in Jace's arms. He's alive now, his face the perfect picture of horror as he curls his body around her. His arms wrap around her shoulders, pulling her towards the door, *to safety*, but she's trying to get free.

To get to *me....*

No... danger....

Jace makes eye contact with me while I drag my chin along the ground. He keeps heading towards the door, slowly slipping away and taking Selene with him. I look up at Eli while he watches Jace with a conniving look. He bites his lower lip–

Well, *shit*, that's a fucking tell of his, *isn't* it–

Eli comes forward and yanks the guards hands off me, which gets him thrown down, our faces inches apart.

"Fancy meeting you here," I mumble into the dusty floor.

He grunts as a guard places his knee on Eli's back. Selene and Jace slip out of the door. "*Don't* flatter yourself."

The Master's expression contorts, his face turning a violent red as he shouts at Luke, "You don't *understand*! I've been building this for years! Fucking *years* and you're going to ruin it all! *I* am the one who's kept us all safe, and alive, and from falling apart! And you want to throw it all *away*!"

He takes a step towards Luke, but one of the guards grabs The Master's arm and secures it with a bind.

"No," Luke says, moving towards where Eli and I are on the floor. "You *don't* get to do anything anymore.

The chaos reaches a fever pitch. The rift between father and son, between The Master's delusions and reality, finally comes to a head. My body aches from where the guards have me detained, but the adrenaline coursing through my veins keeps me from feeling too much of it.

Selene and Jace got out of here, which is really *all* that matters. Eli and I can lick our wounds later, and Luke's going to have to figure out what to do about his father... but we're *all* on the same page.

For once.

And it feels *good*.

The Master's out cold, one arm dangling off the side of his rickety cot. He'd been raving when they dragged him in, utterly incoherent and wild. Luke hadn't waited, calling for the healer-on-duty and giving the order to render him unconscious.

Now, we're on Master-Sitting-Duty. Luke doesn't trust the guards *not* to slip him out while no one's looking. Can't say I blame him... the way they kept eying us while the healer worked, like *we* were the problem? Not the clearly unhinged man screaming about the woman in the walls whispering secrets only *he* could hear.

My ribs hurt every time I breathe too deep. I probably cracked something, but I'm *not* about to start whining about it. *Not* when I had volunteered for this ass beating to let Jace slip out with Selene unnoticed. Max had taken his share of damage too. He'd launched himself at The Master without a second thought.

For *her*. For *us*.

We aren't so different, him and me. Just two idiots throwing ourselves into the fire for a girl who isn't asking to be saved.

Max stretches his legs out, boots scuffing against the floor. "You know," he says, twirling a short blade in his grip. "For a sneaky little shithead, you're not half bad."

I scoff. "I'm touched. *Really.*"

"I *mean* it." He looks at me with a small smile. "Could've been anyone bonded to Selene. Let's be real here, there are a *lot* of guys in Middlesborough that could be sitting here with me right now. But you?" He shrugs. "I don't hate it."

Interesting, that. While I've grown used to Max and the others, their sentiments are *harder* to swallow.

I stare at him. "Is that... *supposed* to be comforting?"

"It's supposed to mean I'd rather you watch my back for the rest of our lives than some *other* asshole."

I don't know what to say to that.

Not with Malachi in the next cell over.

I turn my head slightly as I catch movement, and see Malachi staring.

No, not staring–

Burning. His fists are clenched, whole body rigid like it's taking *everything* not to launch himself at the bars. Fury rolls off him in waves, gaze piercing right through me.

I keep my face neutral as I turn back to Max, and return his smile.

"Yeah, could have been anyone." He's not wrong, though.

"Damn right."

Before I can think of what else to say, something *changes*. A heat, vivid and all-consuming, bleeds into my chest. It runs through my veins, seeping under my skin, and I grimace as a slow, creeping hunger settles in my gut. Even as weak as my bond is, this craving is *familiar*.... Max stiffens beside me, hands clenched into fists against his knee as the knife clatters to the floor.

"Are you *kidding* me?" Max mutters, slamming his head back against the bars with a groan. "*Right* now?"

I shut my eyes, trying to wash away the desire throbbing in my stomach, but it's no use. The bond is awake, buzzing, dragging us into something we have absolutely *no* business feeling in the fucking brig.

Max throws his hands in the air. "Un-fucking-*believable*."

I don't respond, too busy gritting my teeth as another wave rolls over me. Max lets out a chuckle as he nudges me with his elbow.

"You think they're both going after it?"

I stare at him, eyes wide and mouth ajar.

One side of his mouth cocks up in a boyish grin. "I wonder if she's into that. Because *I* sure as fuck am."

I keep staring.

He raises an eyebrow. "Oh, come *on* dude. I'm gonna see your dick at some point. Don't act so shocked."

I blink. "I'm not saying you *aren't–*"

Max leans in. "Then tell me it's not hot."

I worry at the scarred groove in my lip, teeth catching where they always do. For once, I don't draw blood. Max's eyes track the motion, and his tongue flicks out like he's thinking about having a taste.

Cocky bastard.

"Tell me," he presses, low and teasing, "that the thought of Luke and Jace *all* over her at the same time isn't the best fucking thing you've ever imagined."

I shove at his shoulder. "We are in the *brig*, dude."

He smirks, standing up to stretch his arms above his head. His shirt lifts enough to expose a sliver of his dark mocha skin. For a moment, I can't stop myself from following the curve of his spine as he arches, flexing the muscles in his back.

And *damn*.

He's got that wide, built frame–broad shoulders, arms that look like they were carved out of routine combat. I'm not surprised. He *is* a warrior, after all. Probably spent half his life swinging swords, and the other half flexing without meaning to. His dark curls sit just above his deep brown eyes. They're a little too *bright* for a place like this, as if we're not babysitting a man who just lost his mind, but that's just Max, *isn't it?*

And then... my gaze drops.

Yeah. Of *course* he's got *that* going for him.

Max follows my line of sight and snorts. "Well. Gotta go take care of *this*. Unless you're wanting to watch?"

I kick out at his leg, but I'm sitting and I miss. *Fucker.* Max barks out a laugh, stepping easily out of reach. "Gotta work on that aim, Sentinel."

"Gotta work on shutting the fuck up," I mumble. Max tosses a lazy wave over his shoulder as he strides out of the brig. The sound of his footsteps fade, and I'm alone.

Almost.

A whisper curls through the air, bitter and poisonous. "Traitor."

I freeze. A cold tremor snakes down my spine, every hair on my body standing on end. Slowly, I turn to face the cell. Malachi stands at the bars, his lip curled in disgust. His piercing blue eyes are locked to mine, rage tempered into something *worse*, something that makes me feel fourteen again.

Standing outside the Mayor's house. My three fathers grip my arms, holding me out like an offering. A gift.

An honor, they said. Their voices full of pride, like they hadn't bartered away their hated son for a better standing. Malachi didn't say a word, just looked me over like inventory. He took my arm, yanked me forward, because it had already been decided.

Two months. Two months of stone floors, cold mornings, endless drills. He taught me how to protect myself, how to lie like it was my first language, how to watch people and find the cracks they didn't know they had. He never said it was for me.

It was for Sableford.

It was for the world.

Middlesborough would end *it all if we didn't stop them. If* I *didn't stop them.*

The father I never had. And he still *sent me to the gates. To pain. To silence. To a binding I couldn't escape from–*

I swallow around the lump in my throat. "I-I-I didn't–" I rasp, scrambling to my knees. "I didn't h-have a ch-choice."

Malachi doesn't budge.

I force the words out, desperation creeping into my tone. "I couldn't get to the meeting spot. There are too many eyes on me now. I have to–" I suck in a breath as realization hits me. "Why did *you* come here?"

His fingers tighten around the bars. "I'd always come for you." He drops his voice, whispering to me. "I *promised* you that."

Something inside me *splinters.*

Not because he's *convincing.* Not because I'm *naive.*

But because I *remember*.

A hand on my back the first night I couldn't stop crying, even though I tried so hard not to make a sound. How he sat beside me, quiet, not asking questions. Breathing with me until I calmed down. I remember how he taught me to bandage simple wounds. How to find someone's weak spot. How he made me recite every herb that could stop pain. Every pressure point that could bring someone down without killing them.

Did he know The Master would make me a scout? Did he know this training would save my life? He trained me to survive Middlesborough. To lie. To listen. To make it back alive.

I remember the first time he laughed. Really laughed. Late at night over a fire, and I had mimicked the Mayor's self-important walk. He choked on his tea, clapped a hand to his mouth like he wasn't supposed to find anything I did funny. His eyes never stopped smiling, even as he made me clean up the mess.

So many *goddamn* moments that *never* felt like manipulation.

Maybe he *does* believe it's for Sableford. For the world. Maybe he thinks he saved everyone when he handed me over. That doesn't make it *right*.

But it does make it harder *to hate him.*

Before I can second-guess myself, I move, grabbing the keys from their hook. I shove them into the lock, throw the door open, and wrap my arms around his neck. His arms come around my waist, holding me as I tremble.

He smells like the woods, like home, *like smoke and wet leaves and sweat–*

"Go, " I whisper when I pull away. He stares at me, stunned. "Run."

"Eli, come with me," he begs, eyes shimmering with tears. "You don't have to stay here. *Come* with me."

My lower lip trembles. My heart *aches*. Suddenly, I want to. I want nothing more than to be free of the pain of *choice*, of the burdens placed on me these past few years, but I know I won't. *Not* like this. *Not* without *them*.

I've made my choice.

I shake my head slowly. "I can't, Mal. My heart... it's *here*. With them."

His eyes cloud over, a flicker of hurt passing through them. A single tear runs down his cheek as he looks around the brig, over me, as if it's the last time he'll see me.

"Eli," he murmurs, voice breaking. "You deserve so much more than this place. You deserve—"

I don't let him finish. I grip his arm hard, forcing him to concentrate. "You *need* to protect them. *All* of them. There's a storm coming, Malachi. A storm with *no* end in sight. Tell them to prepare. *Warn* them. I failed, and I'm sorry. But you can still save them."

"I will." He pauses, shaking his head slowly. "You were but a boy the first time I saw you, and now I leave you as a man. You *never* failed me." He leans in, pressing a soft kiss to my forehead. "You are a son to me, Elijah. If you ever need *anything*... you know where your home is."

The words hold a weight I don't realize, and I feel them settle heavy inside my chest. Both a burden, *and* a relief.

An escape.

Without another word, he slips past me, moving silently toward the back door. The hinges creek as he pushes it open, and disappears into the darkness. I stand there, staring at his empty cell, my heart stuttering in my chest.

Deep down, it *feels* like the right choice.

Instinct takes over, and I walk towards his cot. I grab his blanket and bunch it tight, tossing it over the mattress to make it look like someone's sleeping. It's a feeble attempt at covering his tracks, but it's the only thing I *can* do.

I hear his voice in my head echoing back at me.

'You deserve more, you deserve more, you deserve more'.

I don't.

I do.

I walk out, shutting the cell door behind me, and re-engage the lock. I let out a sigh as I replace the keys, sit back on the floor, and lean my head against the bars. I lose myself to the feeling of lust in my chest.

I walk into the room, head throbbing from the adrenaline coursing through my veins. The door clicks shut behind me, and I spot Jace carefully re-wrapping Selene's arm.

The arm she *still* won't let me see.

The one that makes her stiffen when I get too close.

Fucking hell, I'm sick of the secrets.

I fight back the urge to rip it off. I've had enough anger this evening to last a *lifetime*.

"Are they okay?" she asks softly, like *I'm* the one who needs reassurance. The box I keep everything locked in–the rage, the fear, the *burdens*–it's splintering. Too worn down, *too full*, and now it's all bleeding through. I shove my anger back inside, and push it away.

"They're *fine*." I wave her off, glaring at Jace. He's being soft with her, and I can't tell if it's the healer in him, or something deeper. He would have told me if they'd fucked, *right*? They're mates, *sure*, but he's *my* best friend....

"Max and Eli are taking care of the guards and my father. They're staying with him tonight, making sure he doesn't get snuck out," I reassure her. Selene's gaze flicks between Jace and me, and I feel a weird pulse of anxiety in the bond. Her eyes scream exhaustion, and his are borderline *guilty.*

"What's wrong with your arm?" My tone comes out harsher than I mean, but I can't *help* it. I want to know what happened. I *need* her to stop hiding things from me. She already feels weirdly distant, and I don't *like* it.

Selene looks away first, pulling into Jace's side like she doesn't want the attention. I step forward, eyes narrowing on the bandage she's carefully trying to hide.

"...it's nothing." I can hear the lie, taste it in the air. Jace won't *look* at me. He's avoiding my eyes like a *fucking coward.*

I feel a growl rumble in my chest, and it slips out before I can stop it.

"Stop fucking lying to me Selene!" I rip my shirt off over my head as my anger spills over. "You want to keep secrets from me? *Fine.* You and Jace can keep your fucking secrets *all* to yourselves. It's not like I'm the one out here fighting for you, *protecting* you, *defending* you from *everything.* I thought we were a team! I thought we took care of each other! How the *fuck* can I do that when you two are sneaking around behind my back!"

I know I'm being a hypocrite. I *know* it, but I don't care.

I walk toward the bathroom, tugging my belt as I go. When I hear her voice calling after me, it feels like a slap right to my soul. It's not that I *don't* want her to follow, it's that I don't want to be weak in front of her.

I don't want to break, and *damn it*, I'm *so* fucking close.

That *fucking* box can't hold everything. It's not built for this.

"Luke, *please....*" She's behind me, hot on my heels. I turn the shower on, and wait for it to heat up while my hands shake at my sides. I can hear her moving behind me, and Jace's footsteps trailing hers. I keep my back to them both as I fight to keep my breathing even.

I *can't* look weak.

I'm their *leader.*

"Luke, come *on*, man–" Jace's voice is strained, but I'm too irritated to entertain his attempt at playing peacekeeper.

"Shut the fuck up, Jace!" I feel *horrible* as soon as the words leave my mouth. The ripple of his hurt in the bond makes me want to spin around and hold him, but I'm so *goddamn* tired. "You two have been *hiding* shit from me, and I'm *done* pretending like it doesn't matter."

I feel her hands on my back. "It's not what you think," she tries, but I'm already stripping my pants to climb in the shower. I leave them standing there while the steam engulfs me.

"It never *is*, is it?" I don't care how bitter my tone is. I need something to break the pressure building inside me. "Why don't you tell me what it is, then? *Huh*? What the fuck happened to your arm?"

I turn around as she starts to undress, and I pause at the sight of her bare skin.

Yeah, I'm *pissed*, but now it's tempered by desire. I spin around, tugging at my wet roots while the bonds pull taut, anger twisting one way while lust stretches the other. She steps into the shower and presses her soft skin against me. I can feel every breath she takes, the shape of her breasts against my back.

I'm *unraveling*.

But I *need* her. I *need* to know that she's okay.

I *need* to get her in bed so I can stop fucking spiraling.

I've been inside her *one* time. Feeling her body against mine in the shower reminds me that *once* has never been, and will *never* be, enough.

She presses her lips to my back in a soft kiss right below my neck. I find that I can't think straight while the water pelts down on my chest, warm, too soothing when I want to be furious.

I'm not sure which one of us is more worn at this point, but I think we both need this. We need to fucking feel something that isn't stress, fear, or anger.

And then, Jace steps into the shower with us. I know *exactly* where this leads to. My pulse starts to race as I feel both of the bonds press against each other.

They're *both* here, *both* parts of my life in ways that I can't change.

I *wouldn't* change.

"Luke," she whispers, lips dragging against my skin. The way she says my name is enough to make the anger slip away, like water down the drain. The chaos, the fight, *my father*. I need to clear my head. There's too much existing in my mind, too much stress and anxiety from the unknown and the weight of their *lives* on my shoulders–

I close my eyes and try to calm myself, but *just* as I do, Jace steps up behind her. I hear his breath, shaky and uneven, before his hands slide across my hips. He doesn't push, just rests them there, fingertips trembling against my skin. I sense his hesitation through the bond, but there's something else there, too.

Raw desire.

I feel it slowly seeping into every inch of our connection, in the way our souls brush one another.

I try to ignore it at first. Focus on Selene, on her breath against my neck, her hands splayed over my back, the way her body molds to mine like she was made for it. But then Jace's hand slides lower and something in me *shatters*. Heat coils low, and my body betrays every secret I've tried to bury.

I turn, pressing my chest to Selene's, trying to anchor myself to her. But Jace is *here*, too close... and he's *always* been here.

Jace, with smoke on his lips, stealing kisses under the stars like he had all the time in the world. Jace, pulling me from the river, our skin flushed from the summer sun, pressed together like we didn't notice–

Jace, laughing in the dark. Reaching for me without hesitation.

Of *course* I react to him. How could I *not*?

He's *always* there. In the background, in the quiet, in every moment I didn't *know* I needed someone. He's *always* been at my side.

He leaves his hands on my hips, fingertips pressing into the flesh at my lower back. I glance at him, into his dark blue eyes, and his breath stutters like he wasn't prepared for this either, like maybe didn't think I'd ever look at him *this* way again. His lips part slightly, and that's all it takes. I lean in–

The kiss is soft. It's like breathing after holding it in *too* long.

He's *with* me.

Nothing's changing.

His mouth is warm and *familiar*. I've been here before. I know these lands. And yet, it's *new*. We meet in the middle of something that's been simmering for *years*.

His tongue licks against the seam of my mouth, and I open to let him in. Selene's hands slide over my shoulders, coming to rest over my racing heart.

Inevitable. Like we were always meant to find each other.

I tilt my head, chasing more, and he *gives* while Selene plants delicate kisses to my collarbone. It feels as though this moment will define us.

And maybe it *does*, in a way.

Jace's hands slide from my hips, skimming over my skin while he breaks our kiss. He cups Selene's face, turning her toward him. She looks up with those soft, desperate eyes, and the bond between us warps into a mix of heat, confusion, and rawness.

I feel it *all* as it twists and mixes inside my chest to meld the three of us together.

Permanently.

I steal her away, our breath mingling in the steamy air. My lips trail down her jawline before I meet her mouth, making sure to keep my eyes on Jace the entire time. He carries a deep, primal hunger there, matching my own. When I feel his hands tighten, I *know* that we're not stopping.

This is fucking real.

The kiss between me and Selene deepens as Jace trails his lips down the back of her neck. The warmth of the water is nothing compared to the heat growing between the three of us.

I'm so fucking hard, it's starting to *hurt*.

"Get her to bed," I groan. Jace pauses for half a second, detaching his lips from Selene's neck as he processes what I've demanded. His hands come to Selene's sides, guiding her out of the shower. I turn off the water, the hiss of the steam dying away in the silence that's heavy with anticipation. My cock *aches* with what's to come, and I palm it roughly as I bite my lower lip.

Fuck–I've been so afraid of getting her pregnant that, beyond our initial claim, I haven't fucked her, and the need building inside of me *hurts*.

I step out of the shower, my feet slapping against the cold tiles as I grab the towel from the edge of the sink, roughly drying myself off.

By the time I enter the bedroom, Selene is already on the bed, her body splayed across the sheets as Jace pulls a towel from her body. She's still glistening in spots from the water, every inch of her skin flushed with the heat of the moment.

I don't bother with subtlety. My steps are quick and determined as I make my way toward them, wet feet leaving streaks of water across the floor. Jace's eyes dart to me as I climb onto the mattress, and I catch the flash of uncertainty in him again as he licks his lower lip.

"Hold her," I demand, voice gravelly with command. I reach for the towel, drying myself off while I watch Jace's hands gently tug Selene closer, pulling her head up right next to his impressive cock.

Guess I should have known Jace was hiding *more* than healing hands.

I slide the towel onto the edge of the bed and crawl toward her. We've crossed a line, one that we aren't going to return from, but I find that I don't care.

We were *always* headed for this, like pressure building beneath the clouds. The three of us coming together in the downpour.

No. The five of us. The absence of the others, it's like thunder without lightning, a storm that doesn't quite land.

Selene looks up at me, eyes heavy with the same hunger that sits in Jace's, that same primal need. I capture her lips in a bruising kiss. It's like she can't get enough, like she's been *starving* for this.

I know she's fucked Eli and Max, and *possibly* Jace, so it isn't like she was last fucked *weeks* ago, but my bond reminds me, rolling rebelliously inside of me, just how long it's been since *I've* been inside her.

It's fucking fused inside my soul, bleeding painfully between us, pouring her arousal and Jace's anxious lust and my angry passion into all three of us.

I can't untangle where any of us end. *Not that I want to.* I'd die before I'd separate them from my soul.

Jace hovers at her side, his fingers plucking at her nipples, waiting for my instruction. I turn to him as I sit up, and press a soft kiss to his lips.

"Do it," I whisper as I lick the roof of his mouth. I sit back on my knees, lining myself up between her thighs. "Fuck her mouth."

Selene rolls her head to the side, mouth wide open. He moves to his knees and leans the head of his cock into her mouth. I watch his eyes roll back in his head as she sucks him down, her lips wide, and he *groans*.

"Holy *fucking* shit," he swears, falling forward. He braces himself with his arms, slowly thrusting into her mouth, keeping it shallow enough that she doesn't choke on him.

It's the hottest thing I've *ever* seen in my life.

I rub myself against her entrance, gathering her wetness before I press inside gently. She *is* cycling, and I don't want to hurt her too badly. I ease inside, letting her roll her hips against me until I'm fully seated. She's warmer than I remember. It's dizzying, how easily she takes me in, how naturally we move together. She's moaning around Jace's cock while he's mumbling as he thrusts.

"Such a *good* girl, such a *good* mouth... holy *fuck*... such good... that feels *so good* Selene...."

I growl low, "You're mine, *all* mine," I can't control the possessive edge I've got as I grab her hip and start thrusting. She raises a hand and grips my shoulder as I drive into her. Her body takes me like it *missed* me.

It's perfect, she's fucking *perfect*.

But it *could* be better.

A hole punches through the moment as my thoughts drift to Eli and Max. There's two empty spaces deep inside of my chest, two phantom aches. I can't tell if they're real or not, if I can *reach* for them, and they'll respond, or if I've made them up because of how *desperately* I want them–

I pull out of her, dripping blood over the bedspread. My hand lingers on her thigh longer than it should, torn between the fire burning in my blood and the pain in my soul.

"Hang on, I've got a better idea," I pant as Jace looks up at me. He's absolutely wrecked, teetering on the edge. Selene's chest heaves beneath me as I grab her legs and roll her over, getting her up on her knees. Jace watches as he starts to get the same idea, and smirks at me.

"*Fuck* yeah." He's back on his knees in front of her, hands in her hair as he holds her head back. Her mouth is open again, tongue out, and he's back inside, thrusting as she drools down her chin.

I sink back in, letting my hands trail down her back. I can feel the way her spine arches, the way her body responds to everything we're doing. One of Jace's hands tangles deeper in her hair, but the other reaches towards me. I lean forward into his kiss. It's *searing*, our lips pressed together, tongues fighting for dominance, teeth biting lips.

We're lost in this–an endless cycle of touch and heat, *pushing, pulling, needing.*

Selene pushes her hips back against me with a whine, and I break away from Jace to deliver a quick slap to her ass.

She screams around his cock.

"Don't you fucking try and tell me what to do *ever* again, little lamb," I growl. "Or I'll *force* you to take two cocks in this pussy. But you'd *like* that, wouldn't you?"

She clenches around me as she nods, Jace's cock bobbing with her movements.

My grip on her hips tightens as I set a punishing pace. She's got tears slipping down her cheeks–*fucking beautiful*–as she moans around him while he tries to keep up with me. I glance up, and his focus is locked on her like he's coming apart. His thighs tense, brows drawn tight, body covered in a thin sheen of sweat.

I wonder if it tastes as good as he does.

Both his hands cradle her face as he pushes deeper into her mouth. Then he's letting out a strangled moan as he starts to lose it, hips stuttering forward. His release hits her tongue in thick pulses, cock twitching as he spills into her mouth and across her chin.

She tightens around me when Jace slips free. I put a hand on her neck and shoved her face down in the pool of cum he's left behind. She's whining, her hands fisting in the comforter, body trembling with what I'm giving her. I keep a hand on the back of her head while our hips slap together, our moans the only other sound in the room. Her body clenches around me when she starts to fall apart, but it's *not* enough.

She's close.

She *could* be closer.

I release her neck and reach around her hips, pressing down on her clit in rushed circles. She screams into the sheets as Jace watches me pleasure her to the peak. When she falls, we *both* feel it in the bond we now share. Everything collides in a flood of sensation. Her body rocks against my hand and I pull away. My hips drive into hers as I reach my own orgasm with a grunt.

Fuck, I *was* going to pull out.

Oh well, she's been drinking that tea.

Should be fine.

We're all breathless, panting heavily, as I pull out of her. My cum drips down her thighs, and I reach for the towel, cleaning her as best as I can. She falls to the side while Jace strokes her sweaty hairline with a smile.

"So, we should *actually* take that shower, right?" she asks, and I can't help but laugh.

"Yes, we should," I agree. She grins back before looking down at the bandage on her arm. Jace pets her head and sighs.

"You should show him, Selene," Jace whispers, reaching for her arm. She lets him take it, and he starts to unwind the bandage. Her entire body freezes, and the sudden swap from who she was just a moment ago *scares* me. The bond is soured with pain, with fear, with *disgust*.

I can't tell where one feeling ends and the other begins, but whatever's hidden under that bandage... what could be so terrifying to make them react like *this*?

"It's already been sanctified," she mutters. "So what's the *point*?"

"The point is that he *needs* to know because he's our mate, Selene," Jace reaches the last part of the bandage, the only thing separating whatever *it* is from my view. "That, and the poultices I've been putting on it *aren't* helping. I can't fucking fix *it*, Selene."

Whatever warmth that was left in the room bleeds out with that damn bandage. It hits the floor without a sound.

"There is no fixing it," she murmurs. "It's The Seraph's Sigil."

It's the fucking rune scribbled across the pages of the book that talked about The Ritual.

Holy. Fucking. Shit. It's on *her fucking body.*

I try to control the panic, but my vision flickers at the edges. My chest caves in, each breath scraping at my throat like splinters as I drown in open air. I grip the edge of the bed, knuckles white while tears sting the corners of my eyes–

I have no idea what to do anymore. I don't even *know* who to trust.

Standing in my father's office feels *surreal*.

I haven't started the morning fire.

I haven't looked down at the new missives sitting on his desk.

I haven't touched the ledger, or moved his chair, or opened the window like he *always* did when he came in.

I grip the edge of the desk, holding on like it might tell me what the *hell* I'm supposed to do next. Everything looks the same, like he might walk through the door any second and demand to know why I'm taking his seat. My mind keeps circling back to Selene and Jace, to the way the bond is fused between us, locking us together in a way that should be *impossible*. It isn't supposed to *be* like this... *is it?*

A shared bond, not just between mates, but between *three* of us?

Although... a set of five mates wasn't supposed to happen either.

What about Max and Eli?

I breathe out through gritted teeth while I drag my fingers through my hair. I can feel Selene and Jace, their sleepy warmth tucked somewhere quiet inside me. But Max and Eli? There's only hollow space where they *could* be.

A part of me wonders when it's coming. If this thing between us all is *still* forming, if we're meant to be tied together in ways none of us could have predicted. It's unsettling, in a way.

But it also feels inescapable.

I don't think Max will fight it. He'll bitch about it, he'll roll his eyes, but he's always been an all-in type of guy. He's already loyal, especially to Selene. Already *ours*.

Eli, though.

I tap my fingers against the desk, grinding my teeth. Eli *was* the outsider, but he's become so much more. He's proven himself with that journal, with the plan, in standing up for Max last night....

It's almost time. With The Master gone, it'll be so much easier to slip away unnoticed. Maybe even tonight.

Either way, he's *not* getting a choice. When comes down to it, if the bond *demands* that we become one–

I push off the desk and step around. The chair feels *too* big–*The Master's chair*–but I sink into it anyway, leaning back with a sigh. The room presses in, and I close my eyes to let the bond work beneath my skin.

I'll have to figure out what to tell Middlesborough soon, because more missives will start coming, and *he's* not here to receive them.

Just me, myself and I.

The door opens. *Click. Click. Click.* I know who it is before I even look up.

The High Priestess moves with a quiet grace in her fine robes, deep blue embroidered with golden thread that catches the morning sun streaming through the window. She lowers herself into the chair across from me, folding her hands in her lap.

Every step is deliberate, every movement precise.

She looks every bit an untouchable woman, elegant and serene, as her eyes settle on me. I know she's assessing me, deciding what to do. The silence stretches between us, *thick* with expectations. I have a sickly feeling in my stomach at where this conversation is going, but I *pray* that I'm wrong. At this point, I don't even *care* who I'm praying to.

Please, please, just go....

"I've just come from the announcement," she says smoothly. "You are officially The Master."

The words linger in the air. *Of course.* Hearing it aloud makes it real in a way I'm not fully prepared for, and I have to bite back the retort that comes to mind. She tilts her head slightly before continuing.

"I *trust* that you'll embrace the responsibility that comes with your title." There's something in her tone, something just shy of a warning. "You've been preparing your entire life, after all."

I don't respond, and she allows my silence for a moment.

"I–"

"This is best for *everyone*, wouldn't you agree? It keeps The Seraph close... where she belongs. She's almost ready to fulfill her purpose."

My fingers tighten on the arm of the chair as the rune on her arm flashes in my mind. *Her role?*

"Her purpose," I say dryly. "The one that's left her *marked*, you mean."

The High Priestess looks up from beneath her lashes. "And, *of course*, it keeps *you* where you should be as well."

A subtle reminder. A pointed statement wrapped in toxins.

She *knows*. Or at the very least, she suspects. If things had been *different*–if I'd kept my mouth shut at dinner last night, if I hadn't let my anger bleed through and swallowed instead.... If my father's madness hadn't taken control, if we'd just played along and kept smiling, waiting for the right moment, *maybe* we could have slipped away in the night....

But *now,* there's no escaping. All our carefully laid plans melting away in front of my eyes. I grit my teeth, but the fury knots itself tight in my chest and *refuses* to let go.

We weren't careful enough.

I *knew* that Eli and I had to move like ghosts and yet, we *must* have left something behind. A thought not buried deep enough. A look we didn't mask. A whispered word too loud in the wind. *Something.* And *now*?

It's too fucking late.

I inhale slowly. "I don't *want* it." I struggle to keep my voice from shaking.

She doesn't seem phased. "That's unfortunate," she says lightly, her thumb drawing a line down her index finger. "Because we all have duties to fulfill, *Master.*"

The way she says it, *drenched* with allure, turns the air in my mouth to ash.

She leans forward, pressing her breasts together with her arms. "You *understand,* don't you?" she murmurs, eyes trailing down my chest. "How *fragile* things are. How quickly they can *break.*"

It's not a question. It's a *warning.*

"It would be such a *shame* if anything... unfortunate happened to them before you could bring them into your bond."

My blood runs cold. *How the fuck does she know anything about my bonds?* I'm frozen in the chair, every muscle tense, fighting the urge to flee. *What else does she know?* Her words taste like dread, and I'm trying to filter through the haze of anger and panic she's stirred in me.

She stands gracefully from her seat, the soft swish of her robes the only sound between us as she walks around the desk. Her steps are care-ful, eyes never leaving mine, lips curled with a knowing smile.

I can *smell* the reeking of incense before she reaches me. Some sort of burnt lavender and bitter vanilla. I pinch my nose up in disgust.

When she stops, I'm bathed in the cloying concentration. She sits on the edge of the desk, crossing her legs. I've seen that look on women before, that type of *desire*... I've entertained *many* women in my life to know *familiarity*.

My body tightens with a wave of disgust as I instinctively reject her.

She leans in, fingers tracing the corner of the desk, and I flinch when she gets too close. "You have *such* strength," she murmurs, her lips brushing my ear. I shudder, goosebumps creeping down my neck. "But I can *see* the strain in you, Master. I can *ease* the tension for you better than she can."

Her hand moves slowly, sliding across the wood and down my leg, stopping *just* above my knee. My head feels like I've walked through the mist in the morning. No matter how hard I blink, it doesn't clear. Her hand squeezes my thigh, close to my cock.

She's expecting something from me. A reaction, a weakness. I *refuse* to give it to her.

"I'm not interested," I growl, turning my head from her. It's heavier than I remember it being, and it takes more energy than I care to admit.

She doesn't pull away. "You will be," she whispers as her lips touch my neck. "Once reality hits you. Once you *see* how bad it is to share. Once you realize how little she can give you."

Her tongue traces lines on my skin, too wet and hot. It's *not* Selene. It's *not* my mate. The sensation lifts, little by little, until I can see.

She's *trying* to trick me. She *wants* to break me.

I won't let her.

Her hand slides higher, brushing the head of my cock, but I'm *done.* I jerk back, standing to my feet in one fluid motion, gaze locked onto hers with a cold, unwavering fury.

"You're wasting your time," I tell her menacingly. "And your *charm* won't work on me."

She smiles at me, but I can see how stunned she is by my rejection. "No matter," she says after a moment, her voice dripping in that phony sweetness I'm getting *entirely* too sick of. "You'll come *crawling* to me soon enough, my Master. I *know* how these things go. You'll *see* how much you need me."

It feels as though she's trying to tell me secrets. I can hear them, just underneath the silence in the room, the words she's *not* saying.

'*You want me. You* need *me. Reject her. Bend to me.*'

She stands and smoothes out her robes before turning to the door. Just as she reaches it, she glances over her shoulder. "Once you tire of sharing your mate and you realize the cost of your little bond, you'll be *begging* me to end it and undo the damage. And *I'll* be waiting for *you*."

She slips out, and the door clicks shut behind her.

I reach up, wiping the wetness of her kiss from my neck, and drop into the chair to slow my racing heart.

Her *presence* still hangs in the room like a shadow I can't shake. Her stinging words bite at my mind.

Did she say I'd be *begging* her to end it...?

Can she do *that?*

It gets easier every time I have to elevate. The words come faster, the haze gets clearer, and the God grows closer.

He's not *as* scary when he doesn't talk to me in that deep, soul-whispering rasp he has.

Which is *fine*. When he watches me talk, I don't *mind* him.

But *not* today....

"Selene...." *Smooth* like velvet with a deep, pulsing power behind it that makes my blood race. I adjust on my pillow, not sure if I'm just nervous or if it's the energy from the new bond that's making me feel this way. I feel like the blend of them should be more powerful, but with *him* here, it's suppressed.

Him. God. It's like I'm tethered... a thread I can't cut.

I try not to think about it.

"God," I whisper, the word slipping out before I can stop it. The High Priestess sits next to me, whispering her chants and holding my bloody palm over the bowl, but she doesn't interfere otherwise. She's elated that I'm speaking to him, utterly *amused* that I'm connecting.

And something about her *approval*... It feels like a *burden*.

I want it.

And I don't.

"Such beautiful words from The Seraph's lips... how sweet they must taste," he murmurs. **"Soft words from your sacred little mouth. I wonder what it will feel like to finally defile it."** A slow exhale escapes him as his forked tongue traces his top lip. **"Seraph, are you ready? It is upon us."**

I close my eyes, and try to steady myself. His voice slides over my skin like a lover's caress, a dark and seductive thing that tempts me. A small part of my mind *begs* me to fight, to run back into my mates arms where it's safe and I'm cared for....

But why would I go to them *when* he's *here?*

"I... I don't know if I'm ready," I admit. It comes out more like a plea than a confession. *Something's wrong.* I feel it in my bones. *In my blood.* Humming softly every time I come here to elevate, vibrating inside with energy that I don't know how to release. And I still come back, drawn to this place, *this room*, where I can catch another glimpse of him....

The God chuckles, low and slow, like he's savoring every second of my weakness. **"Oh**, Selene... **you're already mine. The only question left is, will you offer yourself freely? Will you let me make you more?"** His smile is a blade wrapped in silk. Not to be trusted... and *yet*, I find myself falling head first into *devotion* for him. **"Or must I take what's always been mine?"**

He slips inside, presence filling my body like smoke, violating every edge of my being. His power slams into my mind, not like a *storm* but like a flood, merciless and fast-rising. I can't *breathe*. I can't *think*. I shudder violently as I bear the onslaught of my God, of his ruthless rage.

"I–I *don't*–I don't *want* this." I don't know *why* I say it. The words are choking me though, and I spit them out without thinking. I *know* that rejecting the God is *stupid*, and the consequences might be *severe*–

But something inside me is screaming to try.

His hold on me loosens enough that I manage a lungful of air. Through the black spots in my vision, I see him take a step forward. **"You don't want it**?" He purrs, low and deliberate. It sounds like he's whispering directly in my ear, even from across the room. **"Is that why** *you come back to me every chance you get? Why your soul bears my mark? Why it screams for me even when you lay beneath them?"*

I open my mouth to retort, but I can't find my words over the humiliation. My soul *does* scream for him, but *not* over my utter devotion to my mates. *Right?* They are who I desire above all else, and I try to shove that to the forefront of my mind.

IwantthemIwantthemIwantthem—

He growls, teeth puncturing their images in my mind's eye, filling it with *his* likeness. **HIMonlyHIM.** His rage is tangible, and the taste of copper floods my mouth.

The High Priestess pins me with an intensity that makes the rest of the room waver. "Seraph...." She rubs her thumb over my bloodied palm. "You can do this."

I *can't.* The answer is stuck on my tongue, held back by my own blood. *I can't do it.*

"You will raise me, Selene," the God murmurs, his voice fading as our connection frays. **"It's already begun. The heat, the need. There's no running from fate. You've given me much more than you remember."** His words drip like honey, thick and heavy through my thoughts, and I'm sucked back into the haze I was fighting to escape. He knows I'm *stuck* here, listening to his poisonous, *delicious* lies, swallowing them up like a last supper.

I gobble *every* bite.

God, how I desire *him.*

"I will take the rest from you," he continues. **"The fear. The doubt. All those trembling little pieces that don't belong to you anymore. They'll fade with time. You're already mine, my little incarnate. And when you** finally *let go, you'll remember how we've always fit."*

My heart beats wildly when the bond seizes suddenly. There, just between Eli and Max, sits the God. He's *stronger* than he's ever been before. My cheeks are slick with tears, but he doesn't seem to notice. *Or care.* **"You'll crave me. For the way I feel inside of you. It's written inside of you, Seraph. Inevitable. You can bite at the edges, try to** *deny who you are, but it only makes me hungrier. And when I finally break you... you'll* **weep.***"*

I suffocate on my sobs, his promises drowning me in an ocean of unholy *want*.

"*Your mates won't be able to satisfy you. I'll be the only one you need. I'll show you just how much power I can share, and how sweet surrender can taste. But Selene, I'm benevolent. I* might *let you keep one or two of your favorites for playtime. They amuse you, after all. Just toys for when you're tired of worship. Because eternity is a long time... and I intend to fill every second of it,*" he murmurs, his tone seductive, thick with intent. The idea of sharing him makes my skin crawl. I don't know if it's fear or want. *Both. Neither. I don't know who I am*–I'm slipping away like sand on the tides. **"*Soon, Selene, you'll understand.*"**

"No," I whisper, but I can hear the tremble. It doesn't sound like defiance. It sounds like a *plea*.

"*You'll* beg *me to take you from them.*"

He's buried so deep inside that it would take a blade to bleed him out. I never noticed the home he's carved out of my bones, and *now it feels too late–*

"I would only submit to you if I could keep them all," I say to him between my gasps, fully expecting him to laugh and refute me–

But it's *worse*.

It's fucking *worse*.

Because God....

He cocks his head to the side, and he *smirks*.

"*Ah*," he whispers, his voice dripping with dark amusement. **"*I see we're moving into the undertaking of edicts. I'm curious, my little succubus... what is your command?*"**

She's *furious* with me when we enter her office.

"I can't believe you!" She scoffs for a third time when I sit on the pillow I've claimed as mine. "Making *demands* of a God!"

"He accepted it, so I don't understand why it's *that* big of a deal," I mumble, crossing my arms carefully. My forearm aches from the rune. It normally throbs after every elevation, so I avoid putting any pressure on it for a few hours.

"I should have been more specific when I told you to consort with God. Get to know him, get comfortable, but *don't* make a deal with him!"

Something about the way she says it sets me on edge. It's more than frustration. She's grasping for control because she doesn't *understand* what I've done.

She doesn't know.

"It's already done," I say simply. She presses her lips together, nostrils flaring, but she doesn't refute it.

"Yes, well," she huffs, smoothing the wrinkles from the front of her robe. "*Now* you'll just have to make sure you're worthy of his generosity."

"I don't think I need to earn God's favor," I tell her with a shrug. "Why does it matter what deals *I* make with him when *I'm* the one who confers with him?"

Her eyes narrow in my direction. "He's almost ready to come to us, Selene."

"How do you know?" I ask her.

"He's at full power now," she says breathlessly. "It won't be long. I'll have to get everything set up. You can go."

She turns too quickly to see my lip curl in disgust, drifting toward her desk, fingers trailing over the spines of books stacked there like she's searching for something. The tomes are old, bordering ancient, with crumbling pages and runes similar to the ones etched in the walls. I leave her to her musings, slipping from her office, and close the door behind me. I make my way outside The Temple and take a breath of fresh air to clear my head.

I'm starting to believe The High Priestess doesn't *know* what she's doing, even as my mind *clings* to the belief that she does.

The house is quieter than usual when I step inside, my footsteps muffled against the thick rugs lining the hall. I can hear raised voices from The Master's office, and I think about how stressed Luke has been since taking over for his father. He hardly gets a chance to relax. When I hear Eli's raised voice from inside, I'm curious enough that I take a few slow steps towards it until I can see through the cracked door.

"...told you she was fucking insane," Eli says, feet propped up on the edge of the desk. He's laid back in one of the chairs, looking more at ease than I've seen in weeks. I edge closer, intent on joining them, until his next words have me frozen to my spot.

"She had her hands on me, Jace. She *kissed* me. That fucking cunt priestess kissed my neck!"

Jace lets out a long breath as he sits on the edge of the desk, directly in front of Luke. "It's definitely a sign of things to come."

"She's testing boundaries," Eli says flatly. "She wants to see how far she can push you before you give in."

"She won't get that far." Luke sounds furious. He reaches up and puts a hand across Jace's knee. The sight of it sends heat between my legs, warring with the building anger in my chest. The High Priestess touched what was *mine*, and then *encouraged* me to speak to God this morning *so* inappropriately? "I'd sooner cut off my own tongue," he spits.

Jace chuckles, rubbing his hand over Luke's. "Hey, how much of that herb do we have left? I didn't see the pouch the other night."

"Not enough," Luke replies, pulling a bag from his pocket. "I was going to talk to you about that today. Can you get more?"

"I think so," Jace says slowly. "But I'll have to be careful. I set up a new system and, without meaning to, I kinda fucked us. The new storage clerk's quick. She'd notice if something big was missing."

Eli snorts, bouncing his leg against the desk. "Even with that shit in her tea, we still shouldn't be coming inside her. We're playing a dangerous fucking game."

Luke looks out the window wistfully. "I know. I just... sometimes I wonder what it would be like."

Eli's face hardens, and he stops bouncing his legs. "Yeah? Wonder *harder*. A baby wouldn't survive this place. Not when *we* don't even know what's coming."

The floor tilts beneath me, and my fingers curl in my skirts as I try to steady myself.

They've been....

They've been *drugging* me?

To stop a pregnancy?

A violent, icy rage slides through my veins, cutting through the brief, lingering arousal and the last of the elevation. The echo of God's voice whispers inside of my skull.

They take. They take. The boys who play pretend.

I stumble back into a table, and a vase goes crashing down, shattering on the floor. Luke's head snaps up and our eyes meet.

His face goes pale. "Oh, shit."

I spin, ready to bolt, but Eli moves faster. He lunges forward, chair falling back and, before I can so much as let out a *swear*, his arms are around me. I fight against him, kicking out, trying to free myself, but his arms are banded firmly around mine.

"Let me go, you absolute *bastard*!" I scream. I kick out, catching Eli's shin with my toe, but he hauls me into the office. Jace slams the door shut behind us with a finality that makes my skin prickle. I want to throw up. A warning I was too blind to see, bitterness in my teacup they brushed off as burnt leaves. I *trusted* them. I... *cared* for them. And still, they fed me poison in small doses, wrapped in adoration.

Our quiet evenings together.

Ruined.

I whip my head around to glare at Luke, my vision blurred with rage and tears. "You—*you*—"

Luke rubs a hand over his face, lower lip trembling, and Jace comes up behind him to place a hand on his shoulder.

"Selene–"

"Don't fucking talk to me," I command. Luke's mouth snaps shut at the force of my words. Eli lowers me to the floor in front of the fireplace slowly. There's a ringing in my ears that won't go away. I can't even *look* at them. I can't think.

They've been *drugging* me. *Smiling* while they fed me lies and warm tea.

Jace crouches down, lowering his voice like he would an ill child. "Selene, look at me, sweetheart."

I don't. My hands are fists, nails digging into my palms so harshly they break the skin. I can feel slickness already building on my split palm from my commune with God.

I don't care. I don't care. *I don't care–*

"Selene," he tries again, firmer this time. "I *know* you're angry. I *get* it. But you can't get pregnant right now. It's not *safe.*"

A broken, bitter laugh rips out of me when I lift my head. Luke's down on his knees, looking as shattered as I feel while Eli stands next to me. "Oh, you *get* it? *Really*?" I snap, grazing each of their faces with a sharp look. "You get what it's like to have something important ripped out of your hands without even *knowing*? You get what it's like to be *lied* to from the people who are supposed to care for you the most? *Drugged*? Made to think you were in control when you *never* were?"

Jace sighs, pinching the bridge of his nose. *He looks like I'm the one punishing him.* "Selene–"

"No," I cut him off. "You didn't even *ask* me! You just decided! You, Luke, Eli... Max, I'm guessing, too. The four of you sat around and agreed I wasn't supposed to know. That it wasn't *my* choice?"

Jace's hand slips into his long, brown hair. "Do you *want* to have a baby right now?"

I open my mouth, then snap it shut. A hollow ache blooms inside me as I recall the child I pictured when he and I sat at the window who knows how long ago. "I don't know," I finally whisper. He looks devastated at my words, a thin line of tears building on his lashes. "But that isn't the *point*. Every night I sat there and listened to The Master scream at me for failing to do the one thing I was *meant* to do. You already *knew* I couldn't. You *knew*, and you said nothing. You let him *gut* me with his words while you smiled and handed me another cup of tea. I wasn't given a choice and–" My voice breaks. A tear slips down my cheek. "–*you* are the reason I suffered."

Silence.

Fucking *silence*.

A tear slips down Jace's cheek as he turns away to look at Luke, back rigid with something that looks like shame. Luke's gaze, however, is fixed firmly on Eli.

Luke growls out, "Hold it together, Eli."

My chin quivers uncontrollably as I turn to face him. His shaggy black hair veils his misty eyes, hands trembling as though barely restraining something violent. The air thickens around us as I follow his haunted stare.

He's looking at my forearm.

At my rune, which hasn't been covered yet.

I t's *real*.

And it's *just* as disgusting as I imagined it would be.

I didn't think they were lying when they had told me, but I thought *maybe* they'd been exaggerating. The size, the color, the shape of it....

Jace doesn't know about the journal, but Luke gives me *that* look, and I know exactly where his mind is.

It's fucking real.

She's been bound to the demon, and we've been so wrapped up in our *own* shit that we've *missed* it.

I dive into my bond with her and pull at the strings that connect us, desperate to *connect*. Tears spring to my eyes as I root around, touching the edges, brushing the base.

She's cemented inside of me.

But I can't *sense* her anymore.

"Can you feel her?" I ask Jace, my eyes wide. "*Can you fucking feel her?*"

"What? I—" I see him look down as he searches through his own bond, and I've got my answer a second later as he looks up at her in horror.

I bite the inside of my cheek until I taste blood. Even the pain isn't enough to pull me back this time. "You didn't *think* to mention *this*?" I snap at her, unable to keep the disgust from my tone, gesturing to her arm.

She bows her head, hair falling like a curtain around her face while she crumbles behind it. Her hand covers the rune, and I *want* to comfort her. *I should*. I–

"Why can't I...." Jace's voice is a whisper, laced with confusion. Luke pulls him into his arms and, for a brief moment, I yearn to do the same. To reach out, to be *held*, but I stay firmly rooted to the spot. My body *refuses* to betray me with comfort I feel I haven't earned yet.

Even by those I consider friends.

Friends. Maybe even more–

I don't know when I started making that distinction, but it's *true*.

As true as the mark on her arm.

"We need to find Max," I find myself saying. "We need to get the fuck out of here."

"I can't leave," Selene mutters, looking up at me. Her face is blotchy, tear tracks shining down her cheeks. Eyes swollen, lips trembling, she looks wrecked. "I made a deal."

"You *what*?" I ask in disbelief, mind blanking as panic starts to edge in.

"To help free God, I made a deal! It'll protect you–"

"It's *not* a God," Luke bites out through clenched teeth. "We're *done* with the lies. We need to leave, and we need to do it *fast*. Take her to the room, I'll get Max, and we need to fucking make a plan."

"One that involves removing The High *Cuntess* from her spot, preferably," I mumble as I grab Selene under her elbow, and help her to her feet. She pulls her hand free, and I notice the smear of blood across the rune. "The hell?"

Her palm has been sliced open, *more than once*. Jace comes over and takes her hand.

"Have you been... is *this* how you....?" His eyes shine with unshed tears as he stares at the wound. Luke's hand comes down on Jace's elbow, gently pulling him away.

"I'm... I can't talk about it." She clenches her jaw and swallows, bringing her hand to her chest. "If I do... he'll be angry." Her throat bobs as she fights the words.

Jace makes a sound in his throat while Luke pulls him towards the door. "Pity later, Max *now*. Let's fucking go," he says as he rips the door open.

We don't say goodbye. We split up, and I'm left dragging her behind me up the stairs. She doesn't look at me, not even when we step into our room, and I leave her on the edge of the bed. She curls into herself on top of the blanket, knees to her chest, with her back to me. The only sound I can hear is her quiet crying.

I cross the room, muscles stiff, and sweep the tea setup off the tray with one quick motion. The pot hits the trash bin and shatters at the bottom. I stand there, staring at the wreckage.

There's glass in the garbage. Blood on her skin. A rune on her arm that can't be erased. She's *bound* to it now. Claimed by this entity that none of us understand. I run my hands down my face. I *should* have protected her. I *should've* seen it coming.

But *no*. I let her walk into that trap every single day and now, she's locked in.

"For the record, I was against the entire thing," I tell her softly as I drop the loose tea leaves pouch on top of the broken teapot.

"You still went along with it," she deadpans.

"Yeah, it was three against one, princess. What was *I* gonna do?" I shrug, turning around to face her.

"Protect *me*, Eli."

Yeah, she's right on that.

I wish the bond wasn't blocked and I could *sense* her.

I walk to the bed and sit on the edge, staring down at her. She looks *small* like this–red-rimmed eyes shut tight, hair fanned out on her pillow, curled into herself–even though she's nearly as tall as I am. I don't know what the *hell* I'm supposed to say. There's *nothing* that's going to make this better.

Still, I ease in beside her and press a hand to her back. Slow, steady circles. She doesn't lean into me, but she doesn't pull away either. My palm rests between her shoulder blades, and I can feel the way she's shaking. Every few seconds, her breath stutters, like she's trying to stop the flow but her body won't *let* her.

I *hate* the sound of her crying. I *hate* that I had my part in it. I *hate* that I let this happen.

And I *hate* how helpless I feel now that it has.

I stare at the wall over her head, my teeth clenched so tight they *ache*, and keep my hand moving.

"You're *real* good at pretending, Eli. I'm still waiting for the part where I'm not left drowning."

Her words hurt and *damn*, they make me want to break every single wall down to get her out of here *right* now.

But I can't.

They're back not long after.

Max barrels into the room with blood streaked down his face from the cut above his brow. He doesn't say anything when he drops to the bed, and pulls Selene into his chest. I watch his face as he fumbles through his bond, desperate for *something*, anything. But like the rest of us, he comes up empty-handed.

I clear my throat. "What the hell happened to you?" The words hang in the air as Max presses his split lip to her forehead.

"The Warden won't be a problem anymore," he responds flatly. The door creaks open, and Jace and Luke step inside, shutting it quietly behind them. Jace crosses the room, eyes locked on Selene.

"Can you feel her?" he asks, voice warbling.

"*Barely*," Max breathes over her head. "Fuckin', barely. Sadness, but it's buried. Like a thick, dark fog sitting between us. And something else is in there... *someone* else."

"One of us, maybe?" I ask him, but I already know the answer. If it was one of us, surely we'd already feel the bridge–

"That's *God*," she says, something disturbingly reverent in her tone. Max stiffens above her, his concern mirroring the dread curling in my spine. Behind me, I can hear Jace inhale, the sound catching on a sob he won't let out, while Luke lets out a bitter, humorless scoff.

"That's not a *God*," I tell her, brushing the hair from her face. "That's a fucking demon."

"It can't be." She's breathless when she turns to look at me. Her eyes are glassy, shimmering with something dangerously close to hope. "He promised he'd let me keep my mates if I helped him. A demon wouldn't *do* that."

"Selene!" Jace shouts. I look over my shoulder at him. He's *wrecked*, face stained with tears, hair mused, and lower lip shaking as he fights his emotions. "You *can't* believe him!"

"Of course I do." She sounds so sure it makes *me* want to cry.

"Over *us*?" Jace's voice breaks, and I feel my heart shatter.

"You're fucking friends with the demon now?" Luke asks her.

"Well... *no*... but–"

"But nothing!" Luke cuts her off, storming across the room. She sinks into Max. "The High Priestess has been preparing you to raise this demon, and he's been soul-bonding you! This mark, it's *his* mark! He *picked* you, and every time you elevate, it makes him *stronger*!"

"How do you know?" she snaps, throwing Max's arms off her.

Luke yanks open the dresser drawer, fists the journal, and holds it up. "Because it's all in *here*! Everything! The Sigil! The binding of the bonds! Everything! They're going to *undo* the binds!" He throws it back inside with a thud, slamming the drawer shut.

She blinks slowly, her eyes clouding over. "He said it was the only way. That *this* was what I was meant for. That... it would *save* you." Then, the haze cracks. Her breath hitches with a fresh wave of tears. "You had *all* this knowledge, and you *still* let me go?" she cries out, and Max wraps his arms back around her. Luke walks over to the bed, tugging at his hair.

"I couldn't *stop* you! Not with my father threatening to kill us for stepping out of line!"

"As long as he didn't mark you, you were safe," I whisper to her.

"I–I–I....how was *I* supposed to know?"

"Maybe don't trust a *demon*!" Luke screams, and I sit up.

"*Okay*! She fucking gets it!" I put a hand on his chest, and I can feel his heart racing. "She's as much a victim as the rest of us, asshole! Let's figure out how to *end* this and get the fuck out of here instead of fighting."

"I'm afraid that's not possible." The sickeningly sweet voice from the doorway sends us all into panic mode. Max pulls Selene beneath him, shielding her with his body, and I'm already moving to block them when Luke and Jace leap onto the bed, forming a wall of limbs around her. She doesn't fight us, her wide eyes fixed on the door as the sound of The High Priestess' footsteps invades our space.

"It's *time*, Selene," The High Priestess coaxes her. "I told you it was."

"No, I don't want to!" Selene cries, and I'm in *firm* agreement.

"It's a bad time, you should come back later," I say, glaring as she walks past our couch.

"Make an appointment on your way out," Max snarls, watching as she approaches us.

"Or better yet, *don't*," Luke finishes as she comes to a stop at the side of our bed.

"One of *you* has my journal, and I'm curious how you came across it." She glares at us for a beat. "But it's no matter. I don't need it to finish out The Ritual." The High Priestess flicks a piece of lint from her arm. "Seraph, come, my dear. Our God awaits us."

Luke leaps off the bed and grabs The High Priestess by the shoulders, forcibly shoving her toward the door.

"You'll **leave**, and you'll **never** return to this room." The command trembles at the edges–not with weakness, but with *effort*.

The High Priestess is *fighting* his demands with a smile on her face.

"Oh, Master, it seems you don't *understand* how this works." The High Priestess raises a delicate hand, her fingertips a dusty black, like she's dipped them in coal. "*Thar'karesh dulin!*"

Luke is thrown back, crashing hard against the bathroom door, the wood splintering under the force. Selene's screams pierce the air as Luke crumples to the floor, unconscious. A slow, steady trickle of blood begins to pool at his temple. Jace is off the bed in an instant, rushing to him as his healer instincts take over, desperation flooding his movements.

"You fucking bitch!" I roar furiously. Max's growl rumbles from behind me, body tense, but I can feel the tremor in his frame. He's itching to fight, desperate to be released.

But it's *just* The High Priestess. She didn't bring any guards.

A wave of dread crashes over me. What *else* can she do?

Jace rises, fingers slick with Luke's blood. His eyes are swallowed by a pitch-black haze, one I recognize all too well from my childhood. It's the kind of darkness that overtakes someone when their rage hits the breaking point. His lips twist into a snarl, his chest rising and falling with furious growl. The High Priestess faces him, her hand lifting again, but I can't stand to watch another one of my mates fall.

Not again.

"*Vraet'sha—*"

I'm off the bed before I can think through the plan, grabbing her by the waist and shoving her down. She grunts when her head slams against the stone floor. The words she's about to speak die in her throat as I lean over, pressing my weight down to keep her still. My hand clamps over her mouth, silencing her.

"Run!" I scream at Max. "Take her and run!"

But it's too late. The High Priestess swings her leg out, knocking me off balance, and I roll off her. Even with Jace rushing in, delivering a swift kick to her ribcage, and her long, flowing dress she's wearing, she manages to scramble on top of me. Jace rears his leg back to kick her again, but she flings her hand out once more–faster this time–and I watch in horror, pressed down to the floor with a painful, invisible force, as she shouts–

"*Vraeth'sha'lan!*"

It's *instant*, the crimson blood that blooms across his midsection. He rips at his shirt, revealing a wound that's deep and pulsing. He drops beside me, chest heaving as he tries to press the fabric against it. She faces me next, her grin no longer saccharine but feral, the kind of smile a predator wears when it knows the hunt is over. The whites of her eyes are laced with red and yellow, irises ringed in thick, unnatural black. Something in me recoils... I can't stand to look at her—

She brings her hands to my head, covering my ears, and I see her mouth the words, but I don't know what she says.

I can't move.

It's like my body goes *limp*. I can feel my muscles giving, my pants growing damp, my eyes getting heavier, as I fight whatever she's doing to me. It's hard to breathe, *hard to think*. I fight the pull–*just a few seconds of rest, that's all*–but my head lolls to the side. My eyes blink slower, heavier with each pass, until even keeping them open feels like lifting stone.

I can see Luke on the floor, not moving.

I can see Jace holding his blood-soaked shirt to his midsection as he pales.

I can see The High Priestess walking towards the bed, reaching out, and Max is thrown aside with a brutal, effortless swing. His body jerks through the air, like a lifeless puppet on a string.

I don't see where he lands, but I hear the sickening sound of his impact.

My legs don't respond to my demands that they *move*. They *betray* me, leaving me trapped.

Tears slip down my cheeks as The High Priestess lays her hand on Selene's shaking leg. Her head falls back, body limp, and, with a strength that shouldn't be possible, The High Priestess drags her across our bed like she weighs *nothing*.

The bed I'd made love to her in.

The bed where they slept every night. Where I *should* have slept with them.

Our *fucking* bed.

And tosses Selene over her shoulder.

She doesn't spare us a parting glance as she leaves the room.

I can't fight it any longer, even though I *try*. My finger twitches at my side as I succumb to the darkness that seeps into my vision, and I *pray* that I wake from it.

I actually pray to the Gods of my childhood–

But as I go, I *know* the truth.

We're too late. We've been too late for weeks now.

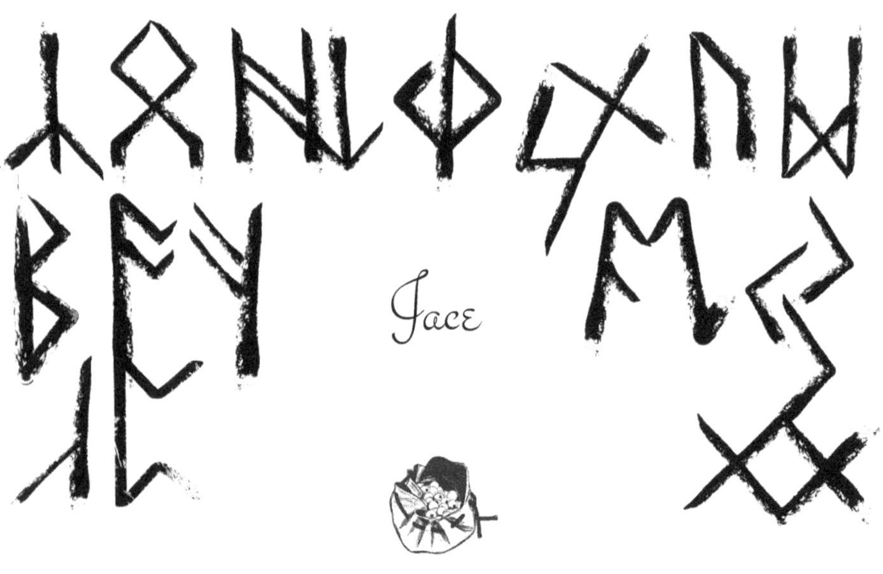

Jace

She *takes* her.

Like we've *never* fucking existed.

I'm useless on the floor, bleeding out, watching as The High Priestess slings Selene over her shoulder like a forgotten coat. The door clicks shut behind her.

Like she's *tidying up* before company.

Like we're the mess she doesn't want anyone to see.

Like she's *ashamed* of what we've made her do.

Luke is sprawled out, head tipped backwards in a pool of blood. I know head wounds bleed like hell, but that doesn't stop the panic from clawing at my nerves. He hasn't moved, not even a *twitch*. I try to keep my distress at bay, looking for the others.

Max lays crumpled near the wreckage of the table, groaning softly. He landed *hard*, but from what I can see, I don't think anything's broken.

And Eli... *fuck*. Eli isn't moving *at all*. His arms are limp, head lolled unnaturally to the side. There's the sharp, acidic scent of urine in the air, and my insides knot.

That happens when people die. *Their bodies let go.*

My breathing is shallow, my head too light. I press harder on the bunched-up shirt at my waist, but it's warm and wet, and I don't know how much longer I can keep my hands steady. My fingers are going numb. My thoughts feel slower. I have to *do something*, but I don't know what–

Then it clicks.

The yarrow powder.

It's still in the bathroom.

My eyes flick to the door, past Luke's motionless form. It might as well be a mile away. My arms are weak. With my legs being dead weight, I'm not sure how I'm going to get there–

I bite my cheek, trying to drive my sluggish brain to *work,* when a curse breaks through the thick, suffocating silence. I snap my head toward the sound, and my vision tunnels. I blink past the spots, forcing myself to refocus.

Max.

He's pushing himself up on shaking arms, blood dribbling from his nose and mouth. His arms are torn to hell, splinters jutting out like someone jammed a forest into his dark skin. He looks *wrecked*, but I've seen him walk off worse after training. Still, there's *something* in the way he's moving.... He shakes his head like it's covered in cobwebs– *concussed, probably*–then blinks as he glances around the room. His gaze slides past us at first, unfocused, until–

"*Selene*...." His voice slurs, dragging out the '*S*' like he's drunk.

"Max," I manage, barely above a whisper.

His head jerks towards me, bloodied face draining of color when he spots the shirt at my midsection.

"Fuck, Jace... *what*?"

"Bathroom," I gasp hoarsely. "Powder—*bag*—yellow bag."

Max sways where he kneels. He plants a hand on the floor, tries to stand... and immediately grimaces, one knee buckling under him. Even running low on fumes, he's stubborn, biting back the pain and clenching his jaw. "*Fuck*, okay... *okay*...."

"*Hurry*," I gasp. Max staggers upright, wobbling toward the bathroom as Luke shifts. He makes it an inch before he lets out a pitiful, pained cry.

"Luke, brother, don't move, man," Max mutters, stepping over him as he stumbles into the bathroom. "Let me fix Jace, then you're next."

Luke groans again, slowly raising a hand to the back of his head. His fingers come away wet and red, face crumpling as he stares at them. His mouth moves like he's trying to say something, but all that comes out is a pathetic whimper.

I need to help him. I need to help all of them.

But I'm slipping. Everything is dimming.

Then Max is back, collapsing next to me with the yellow bag in his hands. He fumbles with the string.

"What do I do?" His voice is shaking. I let my hand fall away from my stomach, too exhausted to hold the shirt in place any longer.

"Put it on. *A lot*. Wrap it tight."

He dumps a handful of the yarrow powder on the wound. It *stings*, but it's nothing compared to what comes next.

The bandages.

Max secures them tight. I squeeze my eyes shut, failing to bite back a scream as he works quickly, securing the fabric around my torso. My body jerks involuntarily at the pressure, and the pain is blinding, white-hot and searing. Tears burn my lashes. My breath comes in short, pained gasps.

I don't register the movement across the room until a soft noise catches my attention.

Eli.

His fingers are twitching. A muscle spasm. Then, a ragged inhale.

Fuck, he's alive.

Battered, bleeding, *barely* standing.

But we're alive.

I let out a wheezing breath and force myself to sit up, but my limbs feel like lead. Max notices, grabbing my arm before I can make it far.

"Don't even *think* about it," he warns, but I shake him off.

"Luke," I wrap my arm around my middle, testing the bandage. It's secured for now, as long as the yarrow starts working.

Max's mouth presses into a thin line, but he doesn't argue. Instead, he moves to Luke, helping him lean against the wall. Luke groans in protest, head rolling forward before he grinds his teeth and forces his eyes open.

"*Selene–*" He slurs out, but I cut him off.

"She's gone," I croak, dragging myself forward. I'm slow, and it's *agonizing*. I make it to Luke before my arms give out, and I slump beside him. He looks worse up close, blood matted in his hair, pupils blown wide, but he lets me roll his head forward to look at the split.

I swallow hard, fighting a wave of nausea. "You need stitches. Max?"

Luke grunts, head slouching to his shoulder as Max disappears back into the bathroom. "You gonna do it, or just tell me how fucked I am?"

"Little of both," I mutter. Max returns with my mini kit and sets it at my side before he flies across the room. I dig through the bag, fingers fumbling with the small needle. I manage to thread it after a few attempts. My vision blurs for a second, and I grit my teeth through the lightheadedness, waiting for the white spots to clear.

"Stay still," I warn Luke, and he rolls his eyes at me.

"Not going anywhere."

The first puncture of the needle into his scalp makes him suck in a quick breath. My hands shake but I keep going–one slow, painful stitch at a time. Across the room, Eli is groaning.

"Either kill me, or get me out of these damn clothes."

I glance up. Max has an arm under Eli's, holding him upright as they look down in disgust at his piss-soaked pants.

"You're *really* making me do this?" Max grumbles, limping them over to the bed.

Eli manages a weak smile. "Come on, don't act like you aren't desperate to strip me down."

Max gags. "I fucking *hate* you."

"You *love* me."

"I'll leave you in these pants."

"Please don't."

Max sighs and helps Eli out of the ruined fabric while Eli wobbles, gritting his teeth. He's *really* pale, and when he stumbles, Max catches him, swearing under his breath. I don't know what The High Priestess did to him. There's no blood. No visible wounds. But that doesn't mean something *worse* isn't happening on the *inside*.

Luke exhales when I pull the final stitch. "I hate *all* of this," he says, rubbing the drying blood from his forehead. It falls to his lap like confetti.

Eli, now in clean pants, sags against Max on the edge of the bed, huffing out, "Yeah, well, I think I pissed myself twice, so *I* win."

For a long time, none of us move.

Luke and I are on the floor, too drained to do anything but *breathe*. Max and Eli both look like shit, but at least they're upright.

We *need* to get moving. We *have* to do something.

But none of us do.

Selene's been taken by a woman who threw Luke into a door *without* touching him.

I lean back against the wall and chuckle. "So, magic's real?"

No one laughs.

Luke coughs, making a face that says '*my-head-is-splitting-in-two-but-I-still-have-to-think*'.

"The High Priestess can *do* things, this much we know. I *thought* they were just myths, or bullshit stories the fucking elders told us to keep us in line, but...." He drags a hand down his face. "Guess not."

Eli snorts softly. "Guess not," he echoes, voice dry.

I glance over. Eli isn't looking at us. He's staring at the floor, jaw tight, his hands fisted in his lap. I close my eyes for a second, forcing myself to breathe through the dull, throbbing ache in my gut.

It doesn't feel *like the yarrow is taking hold... I wonder if her magic might prevent it?*

"We found something," Luke says. I open my eyes and meet his stare. The guilt in his look says it all–I'm not going to like what I'm about to hear. "A journal," he clarifies, voice flat. "An old one, from *before* the bonds were suppressed. Think *hundreds* of years ago."

My pulse kicks up. "*And*?"

Eli rolls his eyes, taking over. "We know Selene's been bound to the demon by way of that rune. The journal isn't clear about what happens next. A Ritual to release the bonds *maybe*, but Selene said she made a deal with the demon. I'm not sure how that plays into this. The High Priestess came to take her...."

"I think we can guess where it's going next," I manage over my dry tongue.

"Demon summoning?" Max's lip curls as he finally looks over at us.

"Demon summoning." Luke agrees.

I wake up in The Temple completely naked.

For a second, I think I'm dreaming. There's *no* way that Luke was thrown into the door, or that she'd crawled on top of Eli and rendered him *unconscious* with a few words. But as the cold air licks at my bare skin and the pressure on my throat threatens to suffocate me, I realize that it's *real*.

A chain.

Panic slams into me.

I push myself up on weak arms. Everything in my body feels off and my skin is raw. When I look down, I see why. Someone has *shaved* me. Every inch stripped bare like some kind of offering.

I shudder, because it's *true*.

I am the *offering*.

As I look around, I can't stop the tears that flow. The dress they've left for me isn't really a dress at *all*—just a sheer white gown so thin it might as well be a ghost. Still, I pull it on, clinging to the illusion of modesty. The fabric hugs my skin, offering no warmth, no comfort. It's delicate, flowing, *ceremonial*.

We don't have this type of material in Middlesborough.

The chain at my throat pinches as I move. It's a collar, not tight but *firm*, cold metal that's clasped at the base of my neck. Thin gold chains drape down, slipping over my collarbones and linking to the cuffs at my wrists–a mockery of jewelry. I can move enough to tie the dress behind my neck after sliding it over my hips, but not more than that.

I take in the blood-red symbols smeared across my body, twisting around my arms and down my legs. They're crude compared to the rune the Go–*demon* gave me. I bring my elbow to my nose, *inhale...* and I gag. Thick, coppery... *dried* onto my skin.

Not ink. *Not* paint.

It's blood.

I lower my arm and lift the other to run my fingers through my hair, but I *can't*. It's been twisted into something elaborate, a tight and elaborate braid, held in place with something rigid that's starting to dig into my scalp. I trace along the edge and–

A crown of thorns.

Woven in so close it might as well be part of me now. They didn't just place it there. *They buried it.*

My face is caked so heavily in powder, it feels as though I'm wearing a mask made of dust. I swipe a finger across my cheek. The pigment comes off in streaks, dark against my skin. I don't feel like myself.

I feel like a doll. Painted. *Hollow.*

No.

Not a doll.

A sacrifice... dressed up and on display, made beautiful for the offering.

I don't know how long I sit there, perched on the edge of the bed with my heart rattling in my chest. The silence stretches, pressing down. My fingers tremble in my lap as I fight whatever is trying to crawl from my throat–screaming, pleading, maybe both.

Eventually, I do the only thing I can. I close my eyes, breathe through my panic, and reach for the one bond that's alive inside of me. It's *off*, wrong, tangled in darkness, but it's *there* and it's all I have.

I wrap around it to hold myself together.

I miss them. I'd give anything to hear Jace's laugh, feel Max's steady grip, see Luke's eyes staring into mine....

But while I can *sense* them, it's empty. There's nothing there, no matter how I pry at the threads that hold us together. Not even Max, who I could sort-of feel back in our bedroom before....

I cling to the demon.

Footsteps echo down the hall, loud against the stone walls. Each step crashes through my head. I draw my knees to my chest, folding in on myself, trying to cover as much exposed skin as I can.

As if that'll save me.

It's The High Priestess that enters, wearing a sheer black garment similar to mine. I avoid looking at her body–her slender waist, full breasts and round hips–as she approaches me.

"It's time, Seraph," she says joyfully, holding out her hand. I look up at her, and the air is sucked from my lungs. She's been transformed into a dark priestess, her ethereal beauty turned into something haunted, like a porcelain doll that's cracked down the center. Her lips are stained black, so dark it looks like dried blood. There's runes carved across her forehead and down her delicate nose in intricate patterns. Her eyes are rimmed in thick, smudged kohl, and her lashes are painted white.

The *last* thing I want to do is grab her hand.

"You know what will happen if you don't come with me and raise him, right?"

"No," I whisper, shaking my head. She leans over and smiles, and I see some of her lip paint has stained her teeth.

"I'm going to walk back to that house of yours and kill your mates," she tells me. My lower lip trembles as I sob. "I'm going to kill them, and then I'm going to fuck their dead bodies in front of you *and* the demon to prove my loyalty to him."

"I–I–I don't un–understand why yo–you're doing this," I gasp, fighting tears.

"Because it should have been someone *stronger*!" she spits through her teeth. I lean away from her with a whimper. "You're fucking *pathetic*! You connect with the most powerful being in the realm, and you throw it away for mortal men! You're fucking *pathetic*!"

"I–I–"

"If I could raise him myself, *I would have*. If he would have me, I'd give myself *freely*," she tells me, "but it has to be *you*.... You've been feeding him all along, Selene. Not *just* with your bond, but through the bonds of your mates and your ancestry. *That's* why you've been chosen. Not because you're pure or sacred or *special*, but because *you're* a vessel. A soul reborn a thousand *thousand* times, marked before birth for *this* one moment. For *His* seed. For *His* pleasure." Her hand comes up to my throat, and she slips a finger under the collar, tugging me forward. "*You*, who can't even bear the *child*! It's fucking *disgraceful*. To think I'll have to serve you... it's no matter. He'll see more worthy females once he's here, and he'll toss you aside."

"I hope he does." I hope my tears have ruined the face paint. She bends down and licks one off my cheek, leaving my face feeling wet and tacky.

"I hope he *kills* you when he knots you, and I'm your replacement, you *pitiful* little bitch." She pulls away and jerks me to my feet, leading at a brisk pace.

"Is it true?" I choke on a sob, threading my fingers between the collar and my throat. "The bonds... you're going to undo them?"

She turns to face me, eyes flashing with fury. She slaps her palm against the stone walls.

"*Yes*, it's true," she hisses, continuing forward. "Do you think *I* wanted this? Do you think *any* of us wanted to break the binds that have kept us safe for centuries?"

I don't answer, lip trembling as she leads me on.

"He's coming to collect, and *you* are the price." She shoots me a look over her shoulder. "The binds *must* fall. This Ritual isn't a *choice*, it's a promise fulfilled. And you, darling Seraph, *will* break what we bound, whether you want to or not."

We're headed to the back of The Temple where Gatherings are held. Based on what she said, my mates are still alive... but that doesn't mean *anything*. She *could* be lying. She could be playing a game, and I know I can't trust a single word that comes out of her mouth.

How could I have been so stupid?

How did I miss the signs?

Every single time I was elevated, my bond was dimmed a little more. Just enough to ignore because I wasn't paying attention.

I *should* have noticed the fraying, *the unraveling*.

I thought I was just getting used to having four men anchored inside of me.

But it wasn't them. It was *him*.

Sinking his claws in me while I was too busy being blind, convincing myself that it was too much, that he *was* a God, that I wasn't doing the wrong thing....

I should have fucking *known*.

It's too late.

It's dark outside when we emerge onto the grass. We make our way over to the spot where they're hosting the bizarre Ritual. The younglings are dressed in deep crimson robes, their faces painted white with those intricate red runes covering their bodies. Their gowns aren't sheer like mine, but the fabric is so short I worry a sudden breeze might expose them. There are men here, too.... They wear thick, velvet cloaks with the hoods pulled up, their bare chests exposed. Each one wears a mask made from a deer skull—long, sharp antlers jutting out like something out of a nightmare. They form a wide circle around the younglings, distant but close enough their presence is suffocating in silent power.

I start *trying* to breathe as my stomach fights to vomit.

Fuck, *fuck*, I can't do this.

I see The Master sitting near the roaring bonfire with two younglings on either side of him. He works at carving through a bloody carcass on his lap, tossing pieces in the fire.

I don't know what it is, and I'm too afraid to ask.

Other younglings dance around the fire, singing, chanting, holding each other's hands, laughing and screaming in excitement. When they spot me, they part happily, and I see the altar at the far end–

The image of the man's crushed hands rush back to my mind–

I tug back on The High Priestess, and she spins toward me, eyes burning with rage. She crowds into me, her voice a low hiss.

"Don't you *dare* test me," she whispers through gritted teeth. "I'll bring your mates here in a heartbeat... don't think I won't."

So, maybe they are *alive.*

"You're lucky I don't have the time to make you *do* what I want," she says with a roll of her eyes. "Not that I could, in front of our guests."

I narrow my eyes, trying to understand. *The fogginess, the memory gaps.* "What do you mean, you could *make* me?"

She smirks. "Just keep walking."

Dew clings to my ankles as we move towards the altar. I don't bother wiping my tears. They fall freely, hot and sticky on my cheeks. The clay bowl waits for me expectantly. Beside it lies the ceremonial blade, the same one I've dragged across my palm for weeks now. The High Priestess lets go, and all I can feel is the scream sitting heavy on my tongue. I don't run, even though I want to.

She's said they're alive... maybe the demon will hold to his word....

She points her finger to the dais and snaps.

"Up you get."

I scramble onto the stone, my movements awkward and unsteady. Every time the dress shifts against my body, I can feel the weight of thirty masked stares. The men watch in silence, and I *burn* with shame.

"Let's get to it, then." She holds out her hand.

We're running around like chickens with our heads cut off, but there's not much else we *can* do. Jace is *barely* standing with that stomach wound, and Luke can't form a fucking plan to save his life right now.

Well... looks like Eli and I will have to run this shit show for a while.

Jace and Luke trail behind, holding onto each other as they stumble forward. We *all* look like hell. I feel like I've been run through a wall *twice*, and judging by the blood crusted on Jace's shirt, and the way Luke is tripping over his own feet, they're not much better off. It took Jace *too* damn long to pick the bigger splinters out of my back before I could properly move again. He thinks my wrist is busted, maybe a few ribs too–but we don't have time to deal with that.

Eli's breathing hard, and I'm concerned about what the bitch did to him. Just because I can't *see* the damage doesn't mean it isn't *inside*. Jace is in no position to be fixing anything, not that he could do much about it even if he *was*. I've seen him try to heal warriors who were too far gone–his hands shaking and powerless as he tried his hardest to save them.

It's not a sight I want to see again.

It's been a few hours, long enough for the sun to set. We've pulled ourselves together enough to head out and look for Selene–and that *cunt* who took her. Eli guessed The Temple, and I'm betting the same.

Eli and I keep pace, our boots kicking up dirt as we cross the field of grass as quietly as we can. We don't have more time to spare. Every second we waste, Selene is further into The Ritual, further into whatever fucked-up demon-raising party they're planning.

I glance over at Eli. He's *so* pale, and I can tell he's hurting more than he's letting on. *I can... feel the echo of it, somehow.* I shove that thought away. I don't have time for it. Maybe I should ask *her* at the end of my sword *exactly* what she did to him and how to reverse it. Luckily, I've got my blade wrapped around my waist.

Nothing wrong with a little... *persuasion*.

The moment The Temple comes into view, my grip tightens around the handle.

We don't have much of a plan. Hell, we *barely* stand a fucking chance.

But we sure as hell *aren't* leaving without her.

T he blade across my skin doesn't hurt anymore.

Blood drips into the bowl, hissing as it comes alive, and I choke down my nausea. I *could* throw up all over The High Priestess' head right now. Honestly, it's very tempting. But since I *could* die from that, I'd rather not give her the excuse to torture my mates after I'm gone.

Pity. It would have been one hell of a way to go... but I can't stand the thought of them suffering.

The bonfire is massive, rolling heat in waves across every single body in the field. The men are stoic, observing the dancing younglings, glancing up at me, looking at each other. The junior priestesses seem to be under an elevation of their own. Their feet are coated in dirt and mud, bodies dripping with sweat and paint. Some get too close to the fire as they chant, throwing bits of herbs and pouring drink in the flame. They laugh as they do it, dancing away before the blaze can catch them. The Master is brought a fresh hunk of flesh, slick and steaming in the evening air. He carves into it with slow precision. When he finishes, he passes the piece to a waiting youngling, who accepts it like a holy relic and carries it to the fire with reverence.

The flame consumes it greedily.

The High Priestess takes my other hand and cuts another line, dripping more blood down my palm and into the resin bowl.

She chants louder.

The roar of the fire.

The laughing younglings.

The grumble of the men, who have started to talk, as they walk towards the group.

I'm sobbing as The High Priestess brings the blade to my thighs and carves a line into each. Not enough to allow anything more than a few drops of blood, but enough that it *stings*.

"*Keshai*!" The High Priestess screams. I startle, but she holds firm, carving a rune into each thigh as she continues her chant. "*Velos ai'taren. Keshti renai. Forthu ven'ashai.* Repeat, Seraph!"

I cry into the words, "*Velos ai'taren. Keshti renai. Forthu ven'ashai.*"

"*Vashan trethai. Luthiel sarai. Keshti vorath.*" She hums as she works down my legs.

I wish she'd just kill me. I wish she'd end my suffering, and that I could meet my mates in the next life–

Dark, curling smoke is pouring from the fire. The bond takes hold and I know–

He's coming.

He's coming for me.

I'm so sorry.

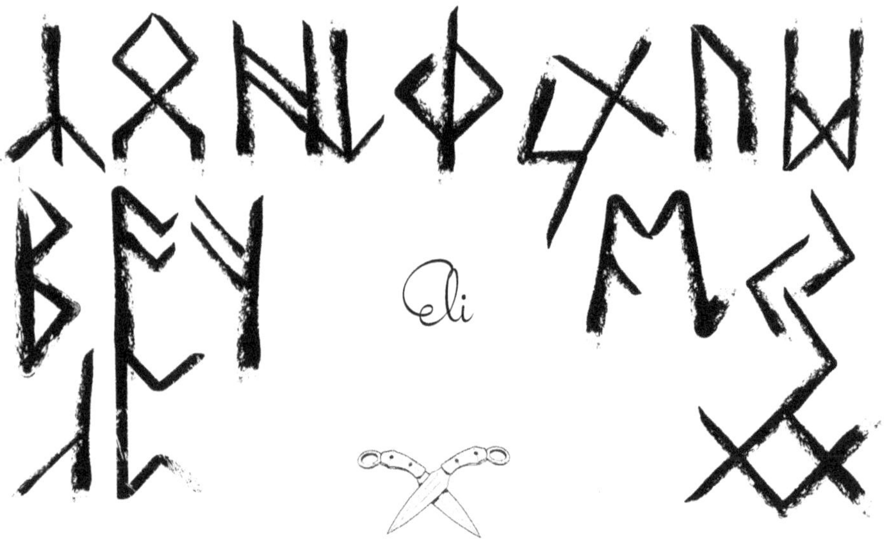

My insides feel like *fire*.

There's no way to describe the pain, other than a hot brand that coats every vein, every sinew, *every fiber of my being*. I've been branded before, and I find it to be the most similar. And yet? This pain is *nothing* to the cavernous emptiness of where she *should* be.

Is she *there*? Yes. But it's a hollowed out tree trunk, lying on the forest floor, nothing remaining but the shell.

The Temple is *empty*. We cross the threshold, and make our way inside.

"Where the *fuck* are they?" Max grunts as he unsheathes his sword. He's got some magnificent bruises forming along his arms and face, and I can't help the admiration I feel for him. It's bordering on a fucking crush at this point which–*yeah*, that's concerning. I shouldn't want that. Not now, not here. He's *just* as injured as the rest of us, and he's about to be the one shouldering the weight for this desperation-fueled shit show. The *last* thing he needs is me looking at him like *that*.

Rush in. Grab her. Run.

I'm not so sure how the running will work, seeing how Jace and Luke *can't* really run, but I'm about to move them onto their next task.

"Okay, find a cart," I mutter, jerking my chin toward the door, "and *please*, don't do anything fucking stupid."

Luke steps in, grabs the back of my head, and presses our foreheads together. I shut my eyes, breathing in deep as his hand squeezes the back of my neck.

"*You* be careful, Eli," Jace says quietly once Luke pulls away.

I reach out and grip his shoulder. "You too."

A handful of weeks.

That's all it took.

A handful of weeks, *and Selene*, and I've been woven into their lives just as much as they've been *bound* to mine.

I can feel it now–the quiet pull in my chest, the settling of Luke and Jace inside me, *undeniable*. We've been orbiting each other, but this feels like an *impact*. Luke's been there, hovering on the precipice since our eyes met on the bed over that *fucking* journal....

It feels like what Malachi used to talk about when he said I'd *know*.

Max touches his forehead to Luke's, and something inside me *twists*. I don't *want* this to be our last goodbye.

"Be safe, brothers." Max ruffles Jace's hair before they turn and stumble out the door. He faces me.

"We'll be back with them soon," Max says, but he doesn't sound convinced. I nod anyway, because what else is there to do?

I pause.

"You smell that?" I ask, squinting down the hall. *Max... the thread, curling around me–*

Max lifts his head, sniffs once, and grimaces.

"Smoke," he mutters, "like a bonfire. Let's check it out."

The High Priestess steps back, surveying her handiwork. My skin burns. The heat of the fire is blazing. Sweat drips down my back.

The smoke thickens at the base, curling in dark tendrils that crawl along the ground. A thin mist sprawls upward, vanishing into the open sky. Somewhere beyond it, *he* waits.

"*Vashan trethai. Luthiel sarai. Keshti vorath,*" The High Priestess chants steadily. Her eyes darken, like rot spreading over a field. Her fingers stretch skyward, charred at the tips, trembling with unnatural power.

And then–

My bonds *roar* to life.

Not weak. Not *hollow*.

Alive.

All at once, there they are–Luke's steadiness, Jace's warmth, Max's fire, Eli's wit. They rush in like a breath after drowning, crashing into me, *clinging* to my soul as if we'll be ripped apart again. A sob catches in my throat. Relief, sudden and blinding. They were never gone. Just buried. Suppressed. *Stolen*. Hidden beneath *him*.

"Speak!" she screams, pointing at me.

"*Vashan trethai. Luthiel sarai. Keshti vorath,*" I whisper, gasping as my bond mates claw at our connection. The smoke shimmers with movement. A glowing circle begging to form, drawn by her hand. Runes pulse around the edge, and I understand.

This isn't a coincidence, my bonds coming back to me.

I'm a siphon.

She's using *them*. Using *me*. Drawing from the bonds, pulling our connection into The Ritual like blood from a vein. I *feel* it–my chest throbbing, nausea rising–as if I'm being hollowed out. Not broken, not shattered.

I'm *emptied*.

My bonds are *funneled* out—

—and *he* steps through.

It's my first time seeing *him* in his entirety.

He's *tall*.

His skin is like the void, like the night, dotted with white freckles that cover his face and arms, eyes glowing that dark red color that haunts my dreams. His round lips grin, exposing bright white fangs. He's got that slender, fine jaw and high cheekbones that remind me of Eli, and flowing black hair with long, curling horns, and I want to run my fingers through–

No.

I don't want to touch him *at all*.

His chest is bare, exposing pale runes carved in his skin. He wears a small cloth at his waist, covering the rising interest that he's been threatening me with–that I'm *terrified* of seeing. His large shoulders roll, as if he's been sitting in a cramped space for far too long. The air around him *crackles*, warping like heat waves off stone. The nearest torches dim, then flare *violently*. Shadows stretch, crawling toward him like they recognize their master. He tilts his head, eyes closed, and the thick band of air between us bends, our bond reacting to his closeness.

His bare feet step on the grass, and I cry out in horror.

"*Draesh on'verath. Zai'toren veshal. Moran do'shai!*" The High Priestess screams, laughing maniacally at her first *true* sight of the demon. "Seraph! Say it! Seraph!"

"*Draesh on'verath.*" I take a shuddering breath as he smiles at me. "*Zai'toren veshal.*" I sob again, wiping at my clammy face. "*Moran do'shai.*"

"Yes!" The High Priestess shouts, throwing herself at his feet.

He doesn't spare her a glance. He walks *right past her,* and up to the altar.

"Succubus," he rumbles, bringing me to my knees. "Are you ready for me?"

"I–I–I–"

His hand comes up to my face, tracing a line from my ear to chin. I expected him to be ice cold, but he's as warm as I am. Warm and *vibrating* with something else. **Power**. It dances over my skin in a tingling wave, branding the path of his touch into me.

"On this altar, I will take you as my mate, and we will rule this planet for the rest of time," he says. I feel his breath across my lips. I pull away, heart racing against my ribs. I fumble over the words.

"Y-y-ou pro-omised m-e-me I could keep m-m-my mates," I whisper as he watches with amusement.

I should have known this wasn't a God.

He doesn't even *look* like a God.

What the fuck *is wrong with me?*

"Yes, little fire, I *did* promise you." He seals our lips together, licking at my mouth. I deny him entry. He chuckles, licking at my cheek instead. "*Minx.* I promised you that you could keep them. In this life-time *only.*"

"W-w-wait, that's *not* wh-what yo–"

"You'll learn how to negotiate with me over time." His hand cups my chin, holding it in place even as I struggle. "Priestess!"

"Yes, Dominus?" She looks up from her spot on the ground. Some-thing strange is uncoiling under my skin, loosening the panic in my chest. His power creeps in quietly, like mist under a door, stealing the edge from my thoughts. My breathing evens out, though my pulse continues to race. The fear is there... *buried* under the heaviness of his warmth and familiarity.

"Bring the sacrifice, my time to cross has come."

He turns his head, eyes on mine like he *felt* the change. Like he *knows*.

"There she is," he says softly. "My little flame. Even your fear bows to me."

I *can't fucking believe this is happening.*

Every step feels like wading through knee-deep sand. My head throbs in sync with my heart, every beat a cruel reminder of what's *wrong.* Breaking apart from Eli and Max now that we've completed our pack bond *hurts.* Not in some *mushy,* poetic way. It's more of a, 'some-one-beat-me-over-the-head-and-poured-molten-lead-down-my-spine', type of pain. A dull ache radiates from the back of my skull where I can feel dried blood pulling at the strands of my hair.

That's going to be a *bitch* to wash out later... if we live long enough for it to matter.

Jace doesn't look much better. His usual confident stride is gone, replaced by an awkward, hunched shuffle. One arm is wrapped around his middle, the other clutching at my shoulder like I'm the only thing keeping him upright. His bandages are soaking through in places, and I can see the fresh blood seeping out, one agonizing step at a time. His skin's gone an awful yellow-gray. Every one of his breaths sounds like it might be his last. I don't know if he's going to be okay.

I think we both know the answer.

We're supposed to be finding a cart or *something* to escape with. *Cart.* Get back to The Temple. Find the others. I blink, trying to focus, but my vision swims. Everything inside of me goes off-kilter. For one blinding second, I *feel* Selene again–

Her bond is back where it should be, like she never left. I *stretch* for her, across *miles* and *miles*, desperate to *touch*, to *taste*, to brush against her soul where it fits right next to mine, Jace, El–

And then it *vanishes*.

Only this time, it's been *taken*. I can sense the claws around her as it's *yanked* from our pack.

I look at Jace and see that he feels it too. We **both** do. One moment she's there, and the next... *emptiness*.

We feel for each other.

Eli is here with me.

But Selene's side of the web is *severed*. Hanging there, drifting in the wind. Aside from the bile burning my throat, it doesn't even *hurt*.

I don't know what it means, only that it's *really fucking bad*.

"We need to move faster," I mutter, even though I don't want to. Jace's pain lances through my abdomen, and I want *nothing* more than to lay him down and let him rest.

"I know," he grits out. "Just... keep going."

The moment we round the corner, I spot men in dark red robes carrying deer skulls. The glint of metal in the moonlight, their bodies moving like shadows around Middlesborough roads. *It's like they're looking for something....*

My fingers go numb when they spot us and start our way.

Ah, fuck.

"Move!" I grunt, trying to pull Jace along. I'm not sure if we can move faster than them, not with him *this* hurt, but I have to *try*. We're outnumbered and *too fucking injured* to defend ourselves.

I've never even *seen* them before.

I hope Eli and Max can get her out.

I'm grabbed by my arm and yanked away from Jace, who gasps, struggling to stand on his own.

"You're coming with us," one of the men sneers, dragging me towards The Temple. My head spins, and I stagger with the sudden movement. When my legs buckle beneath me, he tightens his grip and slings me over his shoulder.

"Luke!" Jace's voice is raw with pain. I catch a glimpse of them dragging him away. "Don't fucking touch him!"

The man who has Jace's arm releases him, only to drive his boot into Jace's side, sending him sprawling to the ground. The pain that flares in my chest tells me *everything* I need to know.

"Jace!" I scream, struggling against my attacker, but his grip is *otherworldly*.

"You think you can escape that easily?" he mutters next to my head.

"Escape? Nah. I'm just trying to be a whole ass problem. *Just* for you, buttercup. You're gonna fucking regret it." I slam an elbow into the back of his head. He grunts and falls forward, dropping me at the same time. The wind goes from my lungs, leaving me gasping on the ground. I'm roughed up–a fist to my chest, a boot to my side–before I'm lifted again, this time by my legs and arms, and carried like a sack of flour to The Temple.

We didn't get *far*, but it's a long way to be *dragged* back.

They haul us around to the rear where Selene kneels on the altar. A massive, shadowed figure looms in front of her, his hands cupping her face. She's in his arms, calm and satiated, eyes locked onto him with a dangerous kind of devotion. His fingers trace her cheeks like a predator marking his territory.

Is that the fucking demon?!

"Selene!" I scream out her name.

"She can't hear you right now." The High Priestess steps around the men and nods. We're dropped on the ground. Jace's labored breathing, coupled with the throbbing of the bond, terrifies me, but I can't turn to look at him and leave our backs exposed to this absolute *cunt*.

"Just these two," the men tell her, and she tilts her head to the side. She's got the faintest smudging of dirt on her nose.

"That's fine," The High Priestess says lightly. "Maybe my earlier attempts were more successful than I'd hoped." She flicks her hand in dismissal, as if they're pests she's glad to be rid of. As if dragging the half-dead mates of The Seraph into this Ritual was an afterthought. "I only need one."

One of the men crouches down to retrieve his deer skull. He lifts it slowly, *deliberately*, before placing it over his head, the empty sockets locking onto her before speaking in a hoarse, dead rasp.

"Careful, little witch. We do not take *your* orders."

"I–I...." Her smile flickers. "Of course not." She bows her head a fraction as they stride past, face bright red.

"Wow." I spit a wad of blood at her feet. "Didn't know groveling was part of your holy rites. That wasn't a verse in *my* prayer book. '*How to beg in front of your betters*'."

Her eye twitches, just a flicker.

"I figured you'd come for her... but I didn't think you'd attempt it so *weak*," she sneers, stepping around us. I force myself onto my knees, groping behind me until I find Jace.

He's still alive, and that gives me *strength*.

"I thought I would find more fight in you, *Master*." Her eyes rake over my body, lingering on the blood staining my shirt. "But I suppose you were always better on your knees." She leans in enough that the words feel *intimate*. "You'll still look beautiful on that altar while your mate carves your heart out. Our Dominus has *exquisite* taste."

"You really think he'll roll over for you? That giving him *my* mate on that stone altar makes him *yours*? You're playing with fire."

She smiles, eyes glittering with dark amusement. "Oh, Luke... I'm not playing with fire. I've *raised* it. And this time, the flames will answer *only* to me. I just need to feed them first."

His eyes are captivating. The moment he locks his gaze on me, I'm trapped in this deep crimson pool. I remember the cold spike of terror they used to bring, but now... it's pressed down like a heavy curtain. The fear is *muffled*. He's toying with our bond, pulling at the edges, seeing how far he can stretch it without it snapping. The panic is bubbling where I can't *quite* reach it. A distant storm I can *hardly* hear.

"What do I call you?" I ask him when he strokes my side through the sheer gown.

"I have many names, little flame." His fingers tighten on my hips as he presses his hardness into my stomach. "Perhaps one day, I shall give you my *real* one."

"Why can't I know the real one?" I wonder as I look down at his mouth.

Plush, full, dark *lips that I want on my body.*

"A name is a powerful thing, Domina." He tilts his head back, exposing his throat, the crack of his neck rolling loud and deliberate. As he does, his skin *bleeds* away, fading from that void-black color to a pale, almost translucent white. "If I were to tell you my *real* name, you'd be able to control me. Send me away. Hurt me."

His tongue flicks out slowly, dragging across his lower lip. It's hypnotic, part-hunger, part-warning, and I can't look away.

"And you want to hurt me, *don't you*, Domina?"

I glance up and realize that, even though his skin has changed, his eyes are still that fierce, vibrant red, burning through me. He can *see* the truth.

"Yes," I breathe. Beneath the word is a *storm* of emotion. Fear and rage burst inside me. I'm desperate to flee, yet I stay rooted, confused by my own truth. "I really do."

He smiles, a dangerous curve curling on his lips. "My sweetest torment." He rolls his hips against me, and I suppress a moan. "You may call me Rhy, to keep it simple."

"Rhy," I test the name out, and he growls.

"It sounds like a dark hymn on your lips, my Seraph." He bends forward and captures my lips in a searing kiss. "I'm going to take you on this altar, drenched in the sacrifice's blood, and you're going to *scream* my name."

She's in the demon's arms, and it takes *every* bit of restraint I have to stay in the shadows with Eli. *It's* done some magic trick, shedding its shadowy magic coat for skin as pale as Eli's.

I can still *feel* it, that brutal jolt when Selene's bond flashed through me like lightning. Here, then *gone*. Snatched away before I could catch my breath. That split second was like a punch to my gut. I swallowed the rage and panic, and told myself to *suck it up*. Whatever had just happened, I had no control over. I'd figure it out when I got her back.

But *here we are*, staring at Selene after she opened some kind of smoke-portal and brought out the demon.

Fuck.

Eli's hands shake over the journal, frustration evident with how rough he handles the pages. We're both desperate to do *something*.

"There's no fucking answers here on how to fix *this*!" He slams the book shut and moves to toss it, but I put a hand out in front of him.

"Keep it close, we might still need it," I tell him, not breaking my visual with the creature holding *my* mate.

I watched them drag Jace and Luke over and dump them like trash near the altar–*right* next to where Luke's lunatic father sits, elbow-deep in calf carcass. The Master laughs while he works, humming between the wet hacks of his blade. Every now and then, he talks to the girls in blood-red robes like this is casual dinner prep even though I know this man has *never* set foot in a kitchen in his life. But he's focused, cutting meat from bone with strange precision, flinging scraps into the fire. They bring him more, and I don't even *know* where they're getting it all. At this rate, they'll gut half of Middlesborough before sunrise.

But... the demon is here... why do they continue to feed the flame?

The fire roars wildly, bathing the scenery in a bizarre blue that reminds me of the Joining Ceremony. I'm fighting to come up with some sort of plan when the demon brings his lips down on Selene's–

My legs go out from under me, and I'm on the ground next to Eli, gasping for air.

"Max!" Eli's hand presses hard against my chest, but he can't reach the place where the *real* pain is. *Endless suffering.* I slap a hand over my mouth and scream into my palm as tears flood down my cheeks.

It's clawing at the back of my skull, dragging its nails through my thoughts like it's flipping through the pages of my mind. Cold, ancient fingers, prodding, *testing*, amused by my terror. It's not just pain–it's a volatile violation.

I know this feeling.

It hits me–The Temple, on a milder level, when I was with Selene. When I was out of control, and not myself. That *wasn't* me. It was *him*. I thought that it was the bond, the heat of her skin on mine.... It was this *thing*. This *demon*, testing my edges.

"He's *inside* me," I choke out, curling into myself. "Inside, in my head, he's *in there*–"

Eli presses his forehead to mine, and I can feel him trembling. He's scared, but he hides it better. He always has.

"Max," he breathes, not calm but *controlled*. **Look at me**. He's not in control right now." My eyes find him. "You are."

I cling to him like he's the only solid thing in the world. His arms are tight around my shoulders, pulling me into his chest, even though I might shatter and ruin us. But then–

A thread, soft and burning like fresh fire. It's thin, delicate, but it pulses. It *knows* me. I know *it*.

I'm so desperate to fill the void inside me. The hole where she lived. Where this demon is trying to crawl inside and make a home–

I grab the thread, I *yank*... and Eli crashes into my soul. The demon growls across the yard, but it's so distant, fading into the background. The darkness recedes from my mind, back into the pit that it came from.

I breathe. I breathe. I breathe.

He brings Jace and Luke with him, and the void feels less consuming, less tragic, with them there.

Luke's head whips around like he knows where we are, and I can see him crying as he presses onto Jace's chest with *both* hands.

Jace isn't moving.

I grab Eli's hand and the pack, leaving the journal and my sword on the ground. We dart from the bush where we were hiding, and sprint to our fragmented pack mates.

The High Priestess screams something at us, but I shove her aside, and she goes crashing to the ground.

I slide in next to Jace, dropping hard to my knees, and press both hands against the bandages. They're soaked through, and my fingers come away red, but I press *harder*. He doesn't flinch, just lets out a soft, broken *whine* that curdles my insides.

He's alive.

The thread inside me pulsates with his pain. Frayed, faint, but intact. Luke's hand suddenly grips the back of my neck, and I turn just as he does the same to Eli. He pulls us forward until our heads crash together, slick with sweat, sticky with blood, breathing the same sour, shallow air.

Existence.

A silent vow, maybe, that we'll hold this line together.

I feel our bonds draw a tight circle around us, finally completed and closed. Stronger, even if she's missing.

There's strength here I've been lacking that's returning to me.

"We don't have much time. I need to know you're going to take care of them," Luke's voice is low, eyes locked on Eli. He nods, jaw trembling. There are *actual* tears in those gray eyes that *any* other time I'd tease him for.

"I will," Eli whispers. "I swear it."

Luke holds his gaze. "Do you *understand* me?"

And Eli, *damn him*, nods again. Fiercely.

It *should* piss me off that Luke doesn't glance in my direction, like I was never even in the running to take his place. But deep down? I get it.

I've never been a good leader. I'm the sword, not the hand that guides it.

Eli's the right choice, and he always will be.

Luke looks at us, the bond rolling with emotions. I can't distinguish between any of them–fear, anger, shame, love, grief, and so much fucking pain I can hardly breathe. It crashes over me in waves, swallowing every thought, every instinct, except the one that keeps my hand pressed firmly against Jace's chest, counting each fragile breath.

"She's going to pick one of us–" Luke whispers, eyes on The High Priestess as she rises to her feet. "–as the demon's first meal."

"What?!" My stomach rolls violently as I look between Eli and Luke.

"He's already *here*. The Ritual brought him here. It's done. The bond... it's gone." A tear slips down Eli's cheek while Luke talks. "Now she's going to *sacrifice* something to feed him."

Eli leans over and dry heaves into the grass. He wipes his lips. "How do you know?"

"She said he had *exquisite* taste. I can't think of what else that could mean. Hearts, *souls*, I assume. Whatever the fuck demons eat. Look around! I don't see anyone else here being offered up on a platter, besides Selene. I have a feeling he's going to be eating her in a *much* different way," Luke mumbles bitterly.

My throat closes up. I feel Jace's erratic breathing under my palm, and I'm waiting for it to *stop*. Luke looks at me, certainty written on his face.

"One of us dies tonight, Max. And I have a feeling he won't be stopping there."

A sound breaks me from his spell, and I look over to see my mates huddled in a bloody pile as The High Priestess steps toward them. Panic grips me, and I glance from them to my demon.

"T-they aren't the sacrifice...." My voice cracks. His hand tightens on the back of my thigh as he turns, following my gaze.

"Those are the mates you wish to save?" he asks, studying them. There's no mockery to his tone, only genuine curiosity. "They look different here than in the realm. *Interesting*."

"Yes, *yes*," I breathe, nodding frantically. "She came to get me, and they tried to protect me, and she *hurt* them–"

"She *is* proving to be problematic," he murmurs, almost to himself. "The ancestor who forged the original deal caused many problems as well."

The High Priestess speaks to my mates in a low voice, and nobody moves–

Then Luke starts to stand, chin held high.

I lurch forward, ready to throw myself from the altar–

But Rhy's arms lock around my waist like steel bars, and I freeze. That fuzzy warmth crowds my brain, making my thoughts stick together. *What am I doing?*

"'You will ***not*** come off this altar, Domina," he says calmly. My feet stay rooted, toes pressed down in the grooves as if the stone itself refuses to release me.

"Let me go!" I half-heartedly thrash in his hold, but it feels useless. *Why resist when this mindless fog feels so much better?*

"Domina." His voice drops, soothing. "It is ***best*** that you remain here. Should you step off, I can't protect them. ***Isn't that the agreement?*** Your... mates in exchange for your compliance?"

I go still. He smiles, wide and slow, teeth gleaming like a dog about to bite.

"She believes she can control me," he murmurs fondly, dragging a finger down my arm. "But no mortal in this realm holds such power."

"She threw Luke into a wall with her mind," I snap breathlessly. The details are missing, but I recall the shock and rage.

"Parlor tricks. She is a priestess. I am a *God*," he scoffs. "No matter, they'll remain safe under my protection, as long as they do what I ask."

I stare at him, clinging to the promises he made me in The Temple. "You're changing the deal."

"No, *Domina*." He turns back to me, grabbing my throat with his slender fingers. He doesn't squeeze, just rests there, like a threat. Power sits beneath his skin, seeping into mine like a poison. A quiet reminder— *he is in control.*

"*You* failed to be specific," he purrs. "You'll learn. An eternity is quite a long time. You'll have to become well versed in negotiations to get what you want."

"I want *them*," I say, full of heat I don't remember building. He clicks his tongue at me, and shame builds in my chest. *Have I upset him? I don't want that.*

"Already I've spoiled you. I should have severed your bonds much sooner, but I worried a rapid ascension might fracture that delicate mind of yours." He narrows his eyes. "Clearly, I have misjudged you. I will make sure to *not* do so in the future." His fingers leave my throat. I sway... I want to reach for him.

No, I don't.

"Priestess!"

"Yes, Dominus!" Her voice carries over the chanting.

"Bring me the sacrifice! Why do you wait?"

"I'm... hurry up!" She slaps Luke in the back of the head, and he stumbles, grabbing at his skull.

"*No!*" I scream, but I can't move. My body is locked in place as The High Priestess drags Luke forward. Jace lies on the ground and... he's *too* ashen. Not just worn-out or overworked, but *deathbed* pale. Lips cracked, skin damp with sweat, and an *awful* stillness to his chest that looks *anything* but peaceful... he's lying there like someone dropped a body between Max and Eli.

I don't know *if he's breathing.*

She never told me what happened after we brought Rhy through the veil... but now, watching Luke's dazed steps, the puzzle starts to click into place. Rhy's hand slips around to my backside and, instead of flinching away, I lean into it. His touch sends warmth into the space between my legs, wanting and *wrong*. But it feels *good. Too good.*

I want more.

Those lips....

"Trust me, my Domina." He places a tender kiss on the corner of my mouth as a tear slips free. "You'll learn to love what I give you."

God please help... *a part of me already does.*

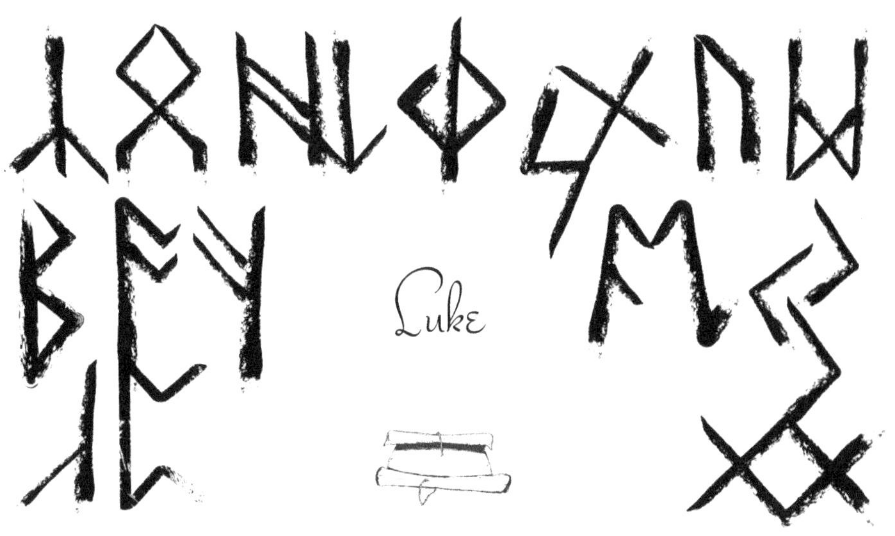

That fucking creature has his hands all over *my* mate. *Is she still mine when our bond is broken?*

She's up there on that altar in a gown that's supposed to be white, but it's sheer.... Naked, carved up across her thighs with the same symbols that stain his pasty skin. Like she's been marked for him. *What kind of demon is* this *pale?* I glare at him, pouring every ounce of my hatred into the stare, even though my eyes are starting to throb, and my vision warbles. He's taller than me by a foot, but I could still reach his face if I had to. If I *wanted* to hit him.

Not that hitting a literal demon is a smart idea.

Still tempting.

"Lucas," he hums. The sound of my name in his mouth makes my skin crawl.

"Demon." I spit on his bare foot, and he *laughs*.

"Oh, you are *feisty*," he muses. "Perhaps, I'll keep you... just so I can spend the rest of your life playing with you myself."

Yeah, I don't fucking think *so, you smug, oversized prick.* I take a step forward.

"Don't, Luke." Her voice is soft, almost unsure.

Selene.

She's *right* there. The space where our bond was lies empty, ripped out like a vital organ, bleeding and broken.

She looks at me like she knows it, too.

God, I want to fight this cocky shit. I want to rip him apart for what he's done to her, to us.

But I don't.

I drop my chin to my chest.

I'd do anything Selene asked me to, bond or none.

"Interesting." The demon takes a moment to observe me. "Tell me, *Luke*, if I order The High Priestess to not sacrifice *you*, then who shall go in your place?"

My head snaps up, pain be *damned*, breath catching, just as The High Priestess beside me parts her lips to speak.

"Domi–"

"From *my* mate group?" I cut in before she can finish.

The demon doesn't answer, even when The High Priestess scoffs and slaps her palm to her forehead.

"You'll take me," I tell him. "*Me*, or you can crawl back to hell on your belly for all I fucking care."

"Luke!" Selene gasps. Her eyes are warning me to stop, but I'm done playing nice. Done letting anyone else decide who lives or dies.

"Don't *fucking* insult me, *demon*," I growl, stepping forward until our chests nearly touch. He reeks of soot and cinder. A campfire, with the vaguest hint of rot hidden underneath. He's taller, *yes*. Stronger, probably. But I don't back down.

"I wouldn't dream of it, *mortal*," he replies with an amused glint in his cursed eyes. He casually lifts his chin. "Priestess. Fetch him for me."

"Him, Dominus?" The High Priestess glances at my mates on the ground, then motions for the cloaked men standing nearby. They move fast, grabbing Eli by his arms–

"Wait," the demon says, cocking his head to the side. "No. *Not* him."

Eli looks at me, eyes wide and fearful, as The High Priestess hesitates. "I don't... he's a perfectly acceptable sacrifice, Dominus."

"Do you dare refute my wishes?" The demon snaps his fingers

toward the fire, and the flames roar higher in warning. "No, I want *him*."

"N-n-no, Dominus," she stammers, eyes darting between Eli and the demon. "I-I-I... he's not the one for the sacrif–"

"Did I stutter?" The demon's eyes blaze with fury, and I *swear* the autumn night turns cold. "Fetch. *Him*."

Selene's hand curls around his pale shoulder, her soft voice urgent. "That's Luke's father, Rhy."

So, the demon has a *name*. That might be handy.

I store it away for later, like a *weapon*. I won't use it, but I'll *remember* it.

Luke's father.

The air thins. My ears ring.

Wait... *did she just say my father?*

I'm dropped back to the ground.

Max is there, dragging me to his chest. I'm shaking so hard my teeth knock together, but he holds me like he's trying to keep me from falling apart. His arms lock around me, breath hot on my neck. I can feel tears hitting my skin, scalding hot.

I don't pull away from him. *I can't.*

Jace stirs, eyes cracking open, and I'm already reaching for him, hauling him up, forcing Max's arms to stretch around him, too.

Luke ordered me to take care of them.

I will.

No matter what.

"Whas*h*appen?" Jace slurs. He blinks, confused and sluggish. Max shakes his head, jaw slack.

"It's all fucked, man," Max whispers. The men in robes circle us, watching, *waiting* for us to run. If The High Priestess so much as *flinches* in our direction, they'll finish the job. I press closer to both of them, my world wrapped in one fragile tangle of limbs and blood and breath.

"Luke–"

"He's fine," I cut Jace off before he burns the rest of his strength. "He's with Selene."

Jace shifts anyway, struggling to lift his head. His whole body is shaking, brittle as glass. *He's dying.* Really, truly dying–and I can't do a damn thing to stop it.

"Luke...." Jace pants, legs twitching as he tries to get up. Almost like he *wants* to fight.

I choke on a sob. "He's... he's trying to get our girl back, Jace."

Jace turns to me and, under the moonlight, with paper-thin skin, reaches up and brushes his fingertip against my cheekbone. I lean in and press my lips to his.

"I'm sorry," I whisper against his mouth, "that I wasted so much fucking time without you."

I watch as Jace leans against Eli and Max, breath shallow and broken. His body convulses in small, helpless tremors, eyes half-lidded and unfocused. He's fading fast, and I feel like I *should* be falling apart at the sight of it. I should be burning. Screaming. *Something*.

But all I feel is *cold*. Numbness creeps into my soul, quiet and cruel, all-consuming. I can't feel *any* of my mates. Eli. Jace. Max. Luke, who stands feet from me. My soul is *flayed* without them, and I'm *shamefully* realizing how naive I was for not noticing they were missing. I was too blind to see it before, too clouded over by The High Priestess' interference and elevations and *Rhy–*

Rhy–

Molten iron in my blood, branding me from the inside out. His power, *his will*, is slowly replacing everything that once tethered me to *them*.

There's only one bond there–*Rhy*.

My mind fights to cling to the feeling of Luke's arms around me, Max's steadiness, Jace's warmth, Eli's bitter humor. But no matter how I reach, how I *yearn*, the memories slip through my fingers like smoke.

Gone.

The High Priestess drags Luke's father forward. His hands are wet with blood, crimson smeared up to his elbows like holy oil. He looks up at Rhy like a man before God, face twisted with desperate longing. Wild devotion. He believes this is salvation.

That this soon-to-be blood-soaked altar, this demon's hunger, and this ritualized madness is his path to grace.

The Master drops to the ground at Rhy's feet, practically kissing the dirt. His voice is a whisper, barely audible as it drops from cracked lips. "You are the one, sire. We're nothing without your salvation. You've risen... and we will bow before you."

Rhy doesn't look down at him. He turns back to me, letting our eyes meet, and a warmth blooms low in my chest. *It doesn't make sense.* The world is unraveling. My mates lay broken on the ground.

And I feel... safe as long as Rhy is near. Cherished. *Precious.*

"Is he always this... pathetic?" Rhy asks, lips curling with disgust. The way he says it makes me want to laugh. The same bitterness I feel about The Master is in his tone. I want to scream at the man on the ground, for everything he put me through, for all he's done.

But it feels so far away now.

"Yes," Luke mumbles tightly from beside me. "Especially recently."

Rhy's head tilts slowly, like he wasn't expecting Luke to speak. His expression darkens, and I feel the faint tug of *fear* lance through my gut.

But Rhy flicks a hand casually and sends The Master sprawling to his side. The sound he makes is *awful*, something between a moan and a gasp. His eyes roll wildly in their sockets, mouth gaping open, sucking in frantic, pained breaths.

He's alive, *I guess.*

Rhy doesn't look down. His eyes are on mine, sending my heart into a flutter.

I think I smile.

"I just need the heart, pet," Rhy says. I shudder as the words land, cold and sharp, in my mind. "*Now.*"

He doesn't wait for me to respond. He extends his hand, and The Master *floats*, sagging like a wet cloth, breathing but limp. Rhy drops him at my feet.

My body moves on its own, as if I'm a puppet and someone else pulls the strings.

I don't like it. I can't do anything.
I don't want to do this, but I can't stop.
Maybe I shouldn't.
Because—
This was the deal I made, wasn't it?
A heart for theirs.

Rhy needs a heart. If I don't give this to him, he'll take one of *them*. Max, shaking. Jace, dying. Eli, clinging to them both. Luke, standing next to me—

No. That is not *an option.*

I don't know why it isn't.

I don't have ties to them anymore, but they're important to me.

Luke watches from a few feet away, face carved from stone. I see the cracks... the twitch of his fingers, the tremble in his jaw. Violence simmers just beneath his surface, ready to boil over.

He can't stop this. Can't stop me. He sure as hell can't stop Rhy.

I rip open The Master's shirt. The fabric gives easily. His chest is damp with sweat, blood, whatever's left of the animals he'd been carving. His heart beats steadily under my hand like it *wants* this.

I take a deep breath.

Just me, and this knife, and the demon who owns *me.*

I glance up. Rhy's eyes gleam ravenously. He doesn't *smile*, but his lips are curled in hunger, tongue prodding the corner of his mouth. He nods once, slow and precise, towards the chest in front of me.

"Go ahead, Seraph," he growls. "*Feed* me so that I can claim you."

I raise the knife. *Be quick. Quick. Do it.* Hold it over my head. *Do it. Just do it.*

I pause.

I *pause.*

Something in my head cracks, screaming at me to *stop* this farce. I hear him snarl, his *will* trying to force my arm down.

"I want to renegotiate," I whisper. "Save Jace first."

The silence that follows is suffocating. Even the fire behind us seems to shrink, cowering into embers. Rhy looks at me, eyes black with disbelief. A tide of anger crashes against my skin, *searing* my veins, a snake wrapping so tightly around my lungs I can't breathe over his fury—

Insolent little–
You disobeyed.

He slams his fist down on The Master's thigh. There's a wet, sickening crunch as the bone and muscle rupture beneath the blow. The Master lets out an animalistic scream, but it's lost to Rhy's guttural roar. Blood spills from the puncture in the tissue, dripping off the side of the altar, soaking the dirt.

"You *belong* to me," he snarls, and I swallow the scream in my throat.

I. Will. Be. Strong.

For once *in my life.*

"I *belong* with *them*," I snap, the words tumbling out before I can stop them. My voice shakes, but I don't care. I said them. My chest is fire, blistering down my spine, wrapping around my throat, cracking me open–

It vanishes. *Just like that.*

Rhy straightens. A slow smirk spreads across his lips, and he lifts his hands like he's surrendering to some private joke. "You know what, pet? *Fine.*" He sounds soft, too warm. Sweet enough that my teeth *sting*. "I'll save him for you, after my feast."

Luke moves beside me. I can *see* the protest on his lips, but Rhy flicks a finger in his direction, and Luke's mouth clamps shut. He raises a hand to his lips, trying to pry them apart. My head feels foggy when I turn back to face my demon.

"…just like that?" I wonder.

"For *you*, my pet?" His grin widens. "*Anything*. I'll save him. I'll even let him live in our palace. Our bed, meals at the table. Anything you wish. And when I'm done with that sweet little pussy," he leans close, breath brushing my ear. "He can have his turn."

Luke's hands move as if he's trying to signal me, but Rhy steps between us.

He's too close to think clearly. Why would I want to think *when I could just–*

"No, I–"

"You *want* me to save him, yes?" His words cut through me. I try to find a line of thought, but it's scrambled.

I hesitate. "Well, yes, but–"

"Then say *yes*, pet," he purrs, voice molten. It fills up my head, my lungs, *my soul*. His breath ghosts across my lips, sending a shudder down my spine. I squeeze my thighs together, *humiliated* by how I respond, eager to see how he'll *fix* it. "Say yes, carve his heart out, feed it to me, and I'll fuck you on this altar." His fingers trail up my arm, over my throat. My nipples are hard, teasing against the dress. I *know* he can see them. "I'll break you open, make this body my *playground*, and when I'm done, you won't remember a time *before* me."

I can feel him twisting, *poisoning*, and the worst part is–

I don't know if it's him forcing my lips open, or if *I* want to say it.

"I–" My throat tightens. I feel sick, like I'm failing. "Yes, Rhy," I breathe.

His lips crash onto mine, sealing the deal with teeth and possession. I'm signing my soul away again, the same way as I did last time.

It feels like drowning. Like damnation.

This time, there's no taking it back.

Watching her kiss the demon is a special kind of hell.

Knowing she's enjoying it eases *some* of the pain. She's not being forced if his bond has taken over ours, so that's a small comfort I try to hold onto. *It's a lie,* I keep whispering to myself as she breaks the kiss.

She's *still* holding the knife. Her hands aren't shaking anymore.

Selene drops to her knees beside my father, eyes glassy and skin flushes like she's drunk off the creature. She raises the knife over her head again. Just like before.

I can't move. I can't *scream.*

I've never felt this powerless.

Not when I was a kid, watching my father beat my mother. Not when I watched him weep as he buried her. Not when I retreated so far into myself I thought I was lost. When I pretended Jace and I weren't close. When I became obsessed with a seamstress for seemingly no reason, only to end up *bound* to her with three other men. Not even when I realized I *loved* her too fucking late.

"Now, Seraph," the demon encourages her. "Finish this, and I'll save your mate."

She drives the blade into my father's belly.

And he *screams*.

With a lazy wave, the demon flings my father's arms wide, pinning him to the altar like a grotesque offering. Selene bends over, determined, and she begins to carve. Her breath comes in short, harsh pants, each motion a struggle as she saws through his large stomach *and* the muscle beneath it.

I turn my head. I *have* to. My stomach *riots*, even though it's empty.

And then, the younglings begin to scream. Their high-pitched wails rise into the smoke-thick night, and the fire answers. Around them, the men howl, a strange parody to their deer masks. They shed their robes in a frenzied rush, their bare chests gleam with painted-on black and white runes in chaotic patterns. Their masks remain, antlers glimmering in the firelight like wicked crowns, as they close in on the younglings. A pack on the brink of a blood-soaked rite of their own....

In the center of it all, Selene.

"Stick your hand inside, little succubus," the demon instructs. I turn back just in time to see Selene slip her hand inside my father's open stomach.

He's gone limp, blood leaking from the gaping wound and pooling beneath him. For a moment, I wonder if he's truly dead. *God, I hope so. Please, God, please.* She starts carving again, her arm sawing back and forth. Every few strikes, a spray of blood hits her face, painting her cheeks in viscera.

My heart *burns* for him. Not The Master, but my *father*.

I remember when my mother was alive. His better days ended with all three of us happy and not at the end of his anger. Eli's bond brushes against mine like a cool balm, stroking away the grief with gentle warmth, but it's not *enough* to stop the memories from slicing me open. Selene is elbow-deep in him when she starts to falter.

Her lower lip trembles, breath catching as she pants. She yanks her arms free, coated in blood and some fleshy part of an organ, dripping with the proof of what she's done. She turns her red-rimmed eyes to his.

"I can't, Rhy!" she cries out, looking up at the demon. "I-I-It's to-o-too hard!"

Her hands are shaking so hard she can barely hold the knife. She's falling apart, and I'm moving toward her before I realize–one step, then a second, and I'm at the altar.

Forgive me, fuck... please.

"Let me help her," I say, locking eyes with the creature. He studies me for a long, terrible moment before he *grins*.

Those fangs....

"As long as *she* is the one to remove the heart and hand it to me, then assist her," he says.

That's *all* I need.

I nod once, swallowing down the vomit sitting in my mouth, and step on. I kneel beside her in a pool of warm blood. She looks at me with tear-filled eyes and hands me the blade.

"Thank you," she whispers.

A piece of me *dies* when a tear slides down her cheek. *I can't believe I'm about to do this.* I lean in, kiss her mouth softly, pretending like we're *anywhere* else. The demon growls, and Selene jerks away from me, looking embarrassed.

"You'll *always* belong to me, Selene, in one way or another," I tell her as I pass the blade from my right hand to my left. I look down at what's left of The Master. "And I will *always* come to save you."

I take a breath, and drive the blade into the cavity she carved. It's tight for my arm, but it'll have to do. I wedge the knife into his chest, through the thick, spongey, material she's managed to cut out, and feel my way around his insides. It's warm, wet and sticky–whatever the hell else makes up the insides of a man–and my eyes *burn*. I bite my lower lip hard enough that blood floods my mouth. The knife squelches as I push further.

Breathe. In. Out. Iron and bile coat my nose as I inhale.

Selene places her bloody hand on my forearm. I glance at her. She's *pale*, lips parted like she might start screaming, but her eyes are locked to the hole in my father's chest where my forearm is buried.

I feel Jace crackling in my chest, a wave of horrified panic, and I slam the bond shut. *Not now.* I can't afford his softness, not even when he's on death's doorstep. Eli's there instead. *Steady. Silent.* Like a dunk in ice cold water. Max and his sharp-edged pride and brutal loyalty, providing me a wall to lean against. I lock into them and continue.

I brace my hand under the ribs, feel the hard line of bone against my knuckles, and press the knife to a patch of tissue. Surely it won't cut–

It slices through like butter.

That can't be right. That little *knife shouldn't move like that.*

I blink up at the demon. His eyes glint in the firelight and I know that he did something to the blade. Twisted it with his dark magic or whatever else he brought with him. I hate him for it, but I use it anyway.

Focus.

Further down, elbow-deep, blood soaking into my sleeve. It's thick and hot and makes a sucking sound anytime I have to shift my weight. I can feel things *moving* under my hand, all of it sliding away as I shove the knife further–

My fingers hit something *firm.*

His heart.

I wiggle the blade around it, sawing carefully. It's tough. Strings hold it in place, like it knows it's not supposed to come out. It *fights* me. My grip shakes and I gag.

This is my father.

He was The Master. A tyrant. *A monster.*

Father.

I clench my jaw, lids burning with unshed tears and the sweat that drips into my lashes, angling the blade beneath the organ. The sinew starts to give. Another slick pop, enough that I pull back slightly and my cheek is sprayed with blood.

The last cord snaps.

The heart *gives.*

Heavy. Slippery. Right into my hand, still pulsing faintly with some echo of life. I can't breathe. I sit there with it cupped in my hand, holding the last piece of a man who was cruel to me in his final years.

Father.

My father's heart.

I'm dizzy from the copper in the air. Eli's there, urging me on while Max is a stone wall to my back, preventing me from shying away. I look up at the demon again. He watches with a hunger that *scares* me.

"Remove your hand, Lucas," the demon tells me.

I do what I'm told.

I ease my hand out of the cavity, grasping the blade. The heart stays behind.

"Selene, grab his heart."

I pant as I watch her stick her arm inside him, all the way to her shoulder. Her sheer dress is coated in blood. Her tongue pokes at the corner of her mouth when she starts to pull.

And pull.

And pull.

"Got it," she grunts as she slides it free.

My *fathers* heart.

She holds it above her head, letting it drip as it faintly pumps the few last drops of blood down the sides of her arm.

The demon surges forward, far too eager. He shoves my father's body aside like it's scrap, the limbs landing to the ground with a sickening thud. Then, he's on the altar with us, at her side, *with me.* He doesn't touch her, latching onto the heart like a starving creature, claws digging into the flesh, black tongue flicking out to taste fresh blood while he groans low in his throat.

Kneeling above the carved-out corpse of my father with my mate drenched in blood and the demon at our side, I don't know if I should kiss her or weep for what we've become.

All I know is that I can't take back what I've done.

God, forgive me, please.

Behind us, The High Priestess leads the chants. Methodical, *somehow ethereal,* and the most terrifying moments of my life are spent on this altar with this hell spawn and my mate as he sucks on the flesh like a babe at its mothers breast. He *savors* it, lips and jaw slick with gore. Every sound he makes shoots through me, vibrating in my skull. His eyes roll back, lids fluttering close to ecstasy, and I want to *vomit.*

Selene holds the heart for him. Her fingers twitch, but she doesn't shake. Her face is *unbearable,* somewhere between shock and surrender.

The chanting grows louder. The flames hiss and spit, turning green at the edges.

The demon lifts his head slowly, mouth parting with a wet 'pop', while crimson streaks down his chin like red wine. He looks at her, then to me, pupils blown wide.

"Corruption," he murmurs, voice thick like syrup, "tastes the best." His tongue snakes out, dragging across his upper lip to catch a line of stray blood. He closes his eyes as though relishing the flavor, like it's the first *real* pleasure he'd had in centuries.

"*Zareth on'valesh. Keshti verathai. Moros ai'shar.*" The High Priestess slowly walks towards us, eyes hooded with rage. I wrap an arm around Selene while she keeps her hands outward in offering to the demon. The chanting grows louder, fighting over the shouts and moans from the crowd. The men have all coupled up with a youngling, some three to one, and they're starting to move to a drum that's beating on the other side of the fire.

"*Shai'theron. Vorthu ren'dai. Draesh kel'veran.*" She's closer, raising her blackened fingertips and pointing them at the spawn.

His head snaps up from the half-eaten heart, and he turns to face The Priestess, anger rolling off him in waves.

"*Vashti ren'ai morath! Veshal dai'thoren, kel'drath on'veras*?!" The demon's voice splits the night. His fury is evident in the way the flames flicker violently. I flinch away. Selene does too, bloody hands cradling the half-eaten heart like it's her job to protect it.

"*Vorath travai! Lutheil sarai! Keshti dominai*!" The Priestess screams, pointing her fingers in his face.

Selene and I watch as she waits, and waits, *and waits*. The demon's bloody grin grows, white teeth now stained with viscera, as he bends forward and growls in the Priestess' face.

"You seal your own fate."

The blood leaves her face as the demon returns to his full height, towing over her, and turns to face Selene.

"Are you ready, Seraph, to release the bonds?"

Her fingers are trembling, dress stained, but her voice is clear when it comes. "Yes, I'm ready."

The demon reaches out and takes the heart from her. With a sneer of disdain, he hurls it over his shoulder and directly into The High Priestess' face. She screams as she ducks down, wiping at her cheeks. I can't help the chuckle that is ripped from my throat at the sight. He takes Selene's hands and begins to *chant* in a tongue that doesn't belong to a human.

No matter how he disguises himself.

"Veras kai'thelan... drasun del'mera... sa'knal cor'kai."

The air *changes*. Wind rushes in, kicking up dust and ash from the fire. Magic coils like steam, visible in the air. Glowing strands of red and white thread are wrapped around my arms, shining from her to me *and* to our pack, like pulsing veins of light.

I can see them. *Literally see them.* My breath catches in my throat as I try to catch one, but my hand passes right through it. The wind swirls harder, and then, a single flash of lightning lands behind the altar, rumbling the ground.

A rush–*no*, a *flood*–of something that has always belonged to me. *Power*. It's tangible, forcing a gasp from my lips as I fall forward and brace myself on the stone.

The bonds. Freedom. Rage....

I look down at my hands again for those mystical threads, and I *swear* they're glowing as they disappear. Selene, holding the demon's hands, lifts her head toward the sky as the last of our bonds dissolve into her skin like ink soaking into parchment.

"One more step, my little flame," Rhy smiles down at her while a single dark thread is weaved around her throat. "Then I'll *free* the binds."

"Jace needs help!" Eli's shouts, voice *raw*. My head snaps up, the world tilting as Eli rushing toward us.

The blood on her hands, the heart on the ground, the demon's breath on her lips... none of it matters.

Not if we lose him.

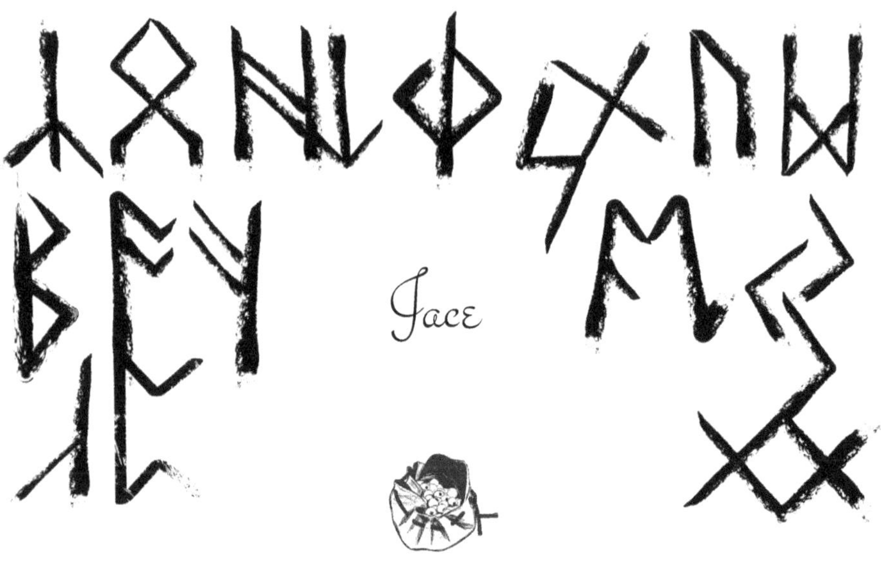

Jace

The night sky splits open, a blinding bolt of white-hot lightning crashing down behind the altar. The world trembles with it, but I can't move.

I can't fucking move.

I *want* to. I *need* to.

But my body's shutting down, failing me when I need it most.

There's no other way to say it.

I'm going to die here.

Eli clings to me, hands shaking so violently I can feel it in my bones. Max is on my other side with his fingers combing through my hair. It's not comforting–it's *desperate*. His tears hit my skin, and I *know* that he knows it, too.

He's held enough men in their final moments to recognize the sound of death.

And right now, he's listening to it *crawl* out of me.

"Eli," I breathe. He bends over, face inches from mine, and leaves a kiss between my eyes.

"Jace, you're gonna be fine, man," Eli's hand touches the bandages at my stomach, and the searing pain whites out my vision. I fight the tears, but they spill down my temples. "Luke's figuring it out, just hold on."

"I can't," I whisper. Max looks at me, grief etched into every line of his face. He glances at Eli–

They don't speak.

Eli bends down again, hand brushing my cheek, and presses a kiss to my forehead before dashing away.

"You *have* to," Max grabs the hair at my scalp and gives it a tug. "If you die...."

"It'll be okay," I blink up at him, and he shakes his head.

"No! No, it fucking *won't*!" He presses his lips to the same spot Eli did.

"It will," I tell him, bringing my hand to his arm. I feel heat beneath my hand, but I can't keep my grip. "You'll... Luke *will*... just...."

"Move!" Luke drops to his knees beside me, and I feel the demon's chill follow. His skin, so pale it's almost translucent, shimmers faintly. It's like looking at a corpse dressed in smoke.

Has he come to collect my soul?

This feels like the beginning of my end.

I trail behind Rhy, Eli and Luke, stomach twisting with anxiety. I scrape at the blood drying on my arms, but the stains won't budge. Max goes pale when Rhy drops to his knees by Jace and shoots me a skeptical look.

"He looks poorly, my succubus," Rhy says to me as he lays a hand across Jace's forehead.

"You're just gonna let this shadowy *fuck–*" Max starts, advancing towards Rhy.

"Shut up, Max," Luke grunts. "Let him do what he's going to do."

"You *trust* him?" Eli asks. Luke grabs Max by the shoulders and shoves him on the ground, giving Eli a look that says '*We're out of options*'.

"Trust? *Overrated.* Fear works just fine." Rhy says, grinning coldly, moving his free hand down to the blood-soaked bandage.

"We don't have a *choice*," Luke spits through clenched teeth. "Just... hold it together."

I watch with bated breath as Rhy starts to mumble in his tongue-tying, hypotonic speech. He presses down, and Jace cries out. Max looks from Luke to Rhy with an open mouth, tears gathering on his lashes, but doesn't say anything.

Rhy keeps speaking, pressing harder and *harder*.

Jace starts screaming when Rhy lifts his hand.

"Keshtai ren'vol, doshai on'thuren. Vathis morai, shorath ka'dren!" Rhy shouts, slamming his palm down against Jace's chest.

Jace's body begins to convulse.

Max and Eli shout, rushing to hold his limbs. Rhy grabs my arm, dragging me away. Luke hesitates, torn between staying and following me... then his feet decide, and he comes after us. I'm crying, struggling against Rhy's grip as he kicks The Master's body to the side, and places me on the altar.

"It is time to cement our bond, Seraph, and free the ties." He leans forward, dragging his tongue up my offal-spattered neck. My skin prickles where he touches, the coldness of the blood fading into that foggy warmth I'm starting to realize is *him*. Luke stands on the side of the altar as Rhy opens my legs, and tears my dress down the middle. The chill hits me hard, and I shiver uncontrollably, but a slow, deep heat makes its way through my veins, and I relax into Rhy's arms.

Jace is screaming, Max and Eli shouting to each other, but it all feels *so far away*, like I'm in a bubble... safe and protected with my demon.

Rhy's tongue slides down my neck, tracing a line to my breast, circling my nipple. Warmth gathers in my chest, softening the clawing panic that dissolves the more I stare into his eyes.

"It's okay, Selene," Luke whispers, and I look at him with tears in my eyes.

"Luke...." I reach out, and he takes my hand.

"It's going to be okay," he murmurs, his other hand sliding up to stroke the side of my knee. Beneath the calm words, I can feel the tightness in his grip. Rhy's mouth moves from my nipple, and I shudder involuntarily.

"How can you...." I trail off as Rhy's mouth moves to my bare pussy, and his tongue darts out to lick at me. "...how can you let him...."

Luke's fingers tighten around mine, enough to remind me that he's with me. His fierce refusal to let me go through this alone, even if he can't stop it, even if our bonds have been severed, and he owes me *nothing....*

"Do we have a choice, Selene?" he asks while watching Rhy lick another hot line up to my clit. I bite down on my lip to suppress a moan as my bond to Rhy *boils* inside my chest. His tongue is on my clit, *insistent*, and I let my head roll back into a blood puddle as I sigh with pleasure.

Luke's hand is on my thigh, drawing soft circles that I can focus on, that feel so wonderful in combination with what Rhy is doing.

It's *easy* to ignore the chanting, the drums, the roar of the fire.

The sound of Jace screaming in pain.

Rhy's fingers are probing inside of me, touching that soft spot that feels *so fucking good*, and I rock my hips against his face.

"That's a good girl, Selene," Luke presses a kiss to my knee. Rhy growls low, and Luke backs away, just enough to give him space. His hand doesn't leave my leg. I give him a heavy-lidded gaze and furrow my brows. I can see how *affected* he is by this, by Rhy licking me. The pain he's swallowing down, the fight he's holding back.

But it feels so *good... why would I run when it feels this amazing?*

"She's still *my* mate, asshole," he tells my demon. "You might *think* she belongs to you, but you'll have to take a number."

"I severed those bonds, Lucas," Rhy says against my pussy. I whine when he stands, shoving the front of his clothes down to expose his cock. He's *long*, longer than any of my other mates, and thick. Where the base of his cock meets his body is shaped unusually, with a thick bulb that pulses slightly. I part my lips as I stare, and he smirks at my unabashed curiosity.

"A knot, sweetling." He grabs his cock and strokes it slowly, sliding it against my soaked entrance. "Watch me please your mate, *Lucas*," he purrs, his other hand gripping my throat, forcing my head back so I can do nothing but let him *take*. "Watch as she opens for me, as she *screams* for me, as she *forgets* you."

Luke's scoffs, his grip on my thigh firm. I reach for his shoulder, letting my hand slip inside his collar so I can touch his sweaty skin. His voice is a snarl, torn from his chest. "She will *never* forget me."

Rhy chuckles, turning to look at Luke. "Oh, you poor, *poor* thing." He thrusts in, slow and merciless, and I cry out, my nails biting into Luke's skin. "Then by all means, *remind* her."

Rhy thrusts deeper, his cock stretching me to an impossible level, every inch of him sinking into me. My cry is swallowed by his palm when he grabs my chin, forcing me to look at Luke. He's frozen, breathing like a caged animal, watching as the demon claims me right in front of him.

It's cruel.

"Remind her, Little Master," Rhy taunts, rolling his hips against mine, a wicked smirk curling his lips. "Touch her. *Kiss* her. Make her beg for you... if you can." His fingers slide down to my throat, pressing enough to make my breath hitch. "Let her decide which of us she belongs to."

Luke's chest rises and falls, pupils blown wide with a mixture of fury and lust. He licks his lips, and I *swear* I see his resolve shatter at the edges. His hand slides up my thigh, hesitating only a moment before he touches me *there*.

"She was *mine* first," Luke growls, pressing down brutally on my clit, making me jerk. His other hand grips my jaw, and yanks my face back toward his. "I'll have something you *never* will."

Rhy laughs, low and dark. "And what's that, Little Master?" His hips snap, spearing into me, making me sob from the stretch, the fullness, the *wrongness* of how good he feels. The blood is cold against my heated skin. When Rhy thrusts, I can hear it sloshing under me.

Luke slides his fingers into my mouth, making me gag. "Her *virginity*," he snarls. "You might break her, try to ruin her, but *I* was the first to make her fall apart."

Rhy drags his hand back up to my throat, and presses down. Luke's fingers slip off my tongue, moving down my body. "True," he purrs. His eyes flick down, amusement crossing his face when he sees Luke's cock straining against his pants. "You still want her, don't you? Even seeing her like this."

Luke doesn't answer. *He doesn't have to.*

Jace screams again. The men in the masks howl.

Rhy grins, wide and feral, and then–

"Go on," he murmurs as he fucks into me deep, slow and lazy. "If you're so *proud* of what you took, then let's *see* it." His fingers slide from my throat into my hair, forcing my head towards Luke's belt.

"Open wide, pet," Rhy coos, thick with mockery. "Let your *first* have one *last* taste before I claim you for eternity."

Luke's hands shake while he unfastens his pants, breath ragged as it's torn from his chest. He's already hard and desperate when he climbs back on the altar, kneels in a pile of viscera, and shoves himself between my lips.

I choke. Rhy *moans.*

"That's it," he groans, fucking into me hard enough to steal every ounce of air from my lungs. "Suck on him while I ruin this pussy for anyone else."

And I do.

Luke's hands fist in my hair, and I feel him tremble while he *takes.* My body isn't mine, isn't *ours.* It's *his*—it's Rhy's.

"Come in her mouth, Little Master," Rhy commands as he bends over to lick at my breast. "Fill up her stomach for me."

Luke groans when he comes, and I gag as he thrusts into my throat, filling my mouth with his release. I try to swallow what I can, but I feel it spilling down my chin. Luke looks down, panting heavily, as I look up through my tear-stained lashes. He looks as regretful as he does satisfied.

What have we become?

Rhy's fingers find my clit and pinches *hard.* I find my own ecstasy within seconds. I don't know *how* he does it, only that one moment I'm nowhere near the climb, and the next, I'm at the peak, falling off the edge. I scream, throwing my head back, and roll my body into his as I ride out my orgasm with Luke watching us.

I scream *Rhy's* name.

When Rhy comes, when his knot swells and locks inside of me, sealing our bodies together, he bends down, and bites the spot where my neck meets my shoulder. I can feel the skin break, and him take a taste before he pulls back, and he's whispering against my skin–

"*Velkar'eth sul'dorai. Shal vren'dae threnakai.*"

The bond ripples painfully.

For *everyone.*

The ties that once held our bonds prisoner shatter like brittle thread, dissolving into nothing.

All I can hear over my own anguish is Luke shouting.

And Rhy laughing.

J ace stops screaming when Eli and I start.

It's like something inside me *detonates*. A cage breaking apart, bars bending, snapping, *shattering* and whatever was inside? It's *pissed*.

The sound that tears from my throat isn't human. It's hoarse, guttural, something deeper, something *primal*. My body locks up, muscles straining, as my mind splits, ripped into two. It beats at my skull, my ribs, my fucking *soul*, shoving, clawing, *demanding* control.

Mine. Mine. Mine.

The scents hit me like a punch to the chest—there's blood, sweat, smoke, *Selene*. I drown in her, in the sweet, heady scent of **mate** that overshadows everything else. My cock is hard, aching, my body hyper-sensitive, burning with the need to take, to *claim*, to drag her and my family somewhere safe where *no one can fucking touch them*.

Family.

Jace. Eli. Luke. **Selene**.

They are mine. ***Ours***.

I don't know who moves first, but Luke and I collide, slamming into each other, instincts burning in my veins. A piece of me wants to challenge him because I'm stronger, but *deep down*, I know I'm not meant for his role. My head bows without another thought, submission without hesitation. I take a knee.

He is my leader. **The** alpha *male*.

The demon... the *fucking* demon laughs as someone else screams out in pain.

My head jerks towards Rhy–*isn't that the name Selene was screaming when she came?*–my vision black at the edges. I can't read him. He's wrong, *unnatural*, like something that shouldn't exist but does. He doesn't smell like an intruder. He smells like....

No, not *pack*. But not the *enemy*, either.

The thing inside me is a hurricane of instinct, *snapping*, wanting to take Selene, to pull her beneath me, to bury my teeth in her throat and sink into her heat and **keep her there**.

But Luke can see my internal war. He puts himself between the demon and I.

"**Max**." The command in his tone is like a fist around my throat. I blink, the red haze flickering as the world slams back into focus. My own mind returns with startling clarity. Eli is crouched next to me on the ground, his hands bracing my shoulders.

"Max," he echos my name. "Are you alright, brother?"

I swallow around the lump in my throat, trying to remember how to use words, how to exist in my own skin with this new being that's fighting for the reigns of my control.

My tongue feels thick. My hands won't stop shaking.

"What the *fuck* is that?" I rasp.

Eli exhales, running a hand through his hair. He gives a humorless laugh. "That," he says, "is *you*, man. That's what Middlesborough's kept *hidden*."

I stare at him like I can finally see the entire damn picture. They *chained* us, silenced us, made us *less*. The bits of us they gave back weren't *enough*, I see that now. Not even the small morsels I got while mated to Selene... when I felt the most free... it wasn't fucking enough.

I run my tongue over my teeth, mind grappling with the wild things inside. I don't think I *want* it to go back in its cage. My instincts scream in a thousand different directions, so I latch onto Eli because he just seems to *know*.

"How... how do you...?" I'm hoarse, my pulse pounding against my skull as if the *thing* is trying to claw its way out. Something flickers through his eyes–sadness, regret, exhaustion. He sighs, his grip on my shoulders loosening.

"I wasn't born here, you know that." His voice is rough around the edges, as if he's trying not to cry. "I've known my whole life. I had to have it *bound—torn* from me—to stay here."

A sick and uneasy feeling crawls through my ribs. *This* is what he gave up to be here? This now returned part of me that I've been missing, that I can't *imagine* being parted with now that I've had a taste....

That I've somehow always known was there.

But it's *always* been there. Somewhere in the haze of my confusion and horror, I remember–

Not clearly, not a story I could *tell*, but flashes, screams, being ripped away.

Tiny hands grabbing for someone who can't grab back.

Pain. In never-ending waves. An eternal night. My voice, useless and ignored, calling out into a dark room for the torture to end.

"You *chose* this?" I rasp, trying to understand the images that flash through my mind. "You *let* them do that to you?"

Why?

His eyes shine, lips pressed into a tight line, but he doesn't answer, turning away from me to focus on Jace. A low groan slips from his throat when he tries to adjust. It's eerie, how fast the color returns to his face. His hands pull at the bandages, exposing the closing wound. It's healing *unnaturally* fast–a gift from the demon. Eli's hands ghost over Jace's chest like he's afraid to touch, *afraid to hope.*

"Jace?" His voice breaks. "Hey. You with me?"

Why would Eli deprive himself of this?

Jace blinks up at him, licking his lips as he touches the swollen scar across his stomach. His fingers twitch in confusion. "Eli?" He frowns, glancing up.

Of being whole? Of the wonders of scent and sound and–

I watch the way Eli looks down at him. His hand shakes as he reaches out and presses on Jace's chest, like he has to *feel* the heartbeat for himself. There's something about the *way* he does it, so careful and desperate, that gives me goosebumps.

Suddenly, I can't *breathe*.

Eli isn't who he says he is.

My instincts are *screaming* that it doesn't matter. Even as betrayal burns bitterly in my chest, this new *loyalty* won't let go. Stubborn and snarling, reminding me of the nights I laid awake and wondered why he didn't just *crawl into bed with the rest of us–*

It makes me want to forgive him without even *knowing* his crime.

I don't fucking understand any of it.

Luke crouches beside us. He scans Jace, then sets a steady hand over Eli's, exhaling like he's been holding his breath for *hours*.

He's *made* for this role.

I try to ignore how he was up there with the demon, with his cock in Selene's mouth–

Jace sits up groaning, running a hand over his face, but something's *off*. Right now? There's a wall there that wasn't, some strange tunnel that has no end in sight.

He *did* almost just die... so maybe that's what *'almost dying'* does to a guy.

Jace looks at Luke, blinking slowly. "Where's Selene?" he asks calmly.

Luke rubs a hand over the back of his neck. "With the demon," he says coldly. "They're... stuck."

Jace tilts his head to the side, eyes drifting toward the altar. "Like an animal," he murmurs. I stare at him in shock. *How can he be curious at a time like this?*

"Yeah," I agree flatly. "Like dogs."

"I guess," Luke scoffs. "I don't fucking know."

Jace continues to stare as the demon grinds into Selene, planting kisses up her chest. I *want* to be disgusted. I *want* to run over there, tear them apart, and place myself between her thighs.

"He's thorough," Jace whispers, lips twitching at the corners.

I freeze.

My eyes find Eli. He's watching Jace, brows drawn together as he chews on his bottom lip, like he's thinking *too hard* and not liking any of his ideas.

He sees it too, he *feels* it, and that's what scares me the most.

Betrayer or not, we're still on the same page.

W*armth*. It starts at the base of my spine and spreads, licking up through my lungs, gathering in my belly like molten gold. Every nerve in my body *sings*, soft and open, floating on this cloud.

There's no pain. No fear.

Just bliss.

Rhy's presence lingers, even when he's *not* touching me. It's *inside* me, curling around my ribs, my heart, my mind. *Mine*, the bond purrs, content in my soul. I sigh as a hand drifts up my arm, tracing patterns that glow beneath my skin.

I never knew it could feel like this. The world is muffled like I'm wrapped in silk, *absolutely weightless*. I sink into the feeling, into *him*. There's no loneliness. No hunger. No horror. Just the bond, vast and endless, filling every hollow space inside me until I have no edges—

I quiver, arching against his warmth. The sound of his voice slithers into my ears, smooth as smoke.

"*Good fucking girl,*" he murmurs in my ear. "*So good for me, my little flame.*"

I whimper. Heat pulses through me, so deep it makes my *bones* feel soft. My skin feels too thin, too *bare*, like I need to be *touched*, need to be *filled*, need—

Something tugs at the edges of my pleasure. A shadow, dark and *aching*. My body hums with warmth, but my *soul* strains towards *someone* else.

A different touch. A different voice.

Luke.

The taste of him lingers on my tongue, salt and heat and *home*. My heart twists, the satisfaction dimming, curling in on itself. I *miss* him. I miss *them*. I miss the tether of my mates in my mind, the solid safety of them inside my soul, their presence wrapping around me like a shield.

I can't feel them anymore. I reach out, searching—

Jace?

Rhy.

A single tear slips down my cheek, and his fingers are there in an instant, smoothing it away.

"You mourn them."

The bond shifts, coiling tighter, cradling me closer.

"They were never yours to keep."

His lips ghost over my temple, catching another tear that makes its way free.

"But you are *mine*. *Entirely*, for eternity."

It eases the ache inside of me. That warmth blooms again, choking out my grief. I'm back on that dark cloud, hovering above everything.

"I'll let you pretend, little succubus. If it *soothes* you, pretend they still matter." His lips are on my neck, nipping at my tender flesh. I wonder if he'll bite through me one day. "Pretend all you like. I have you again."

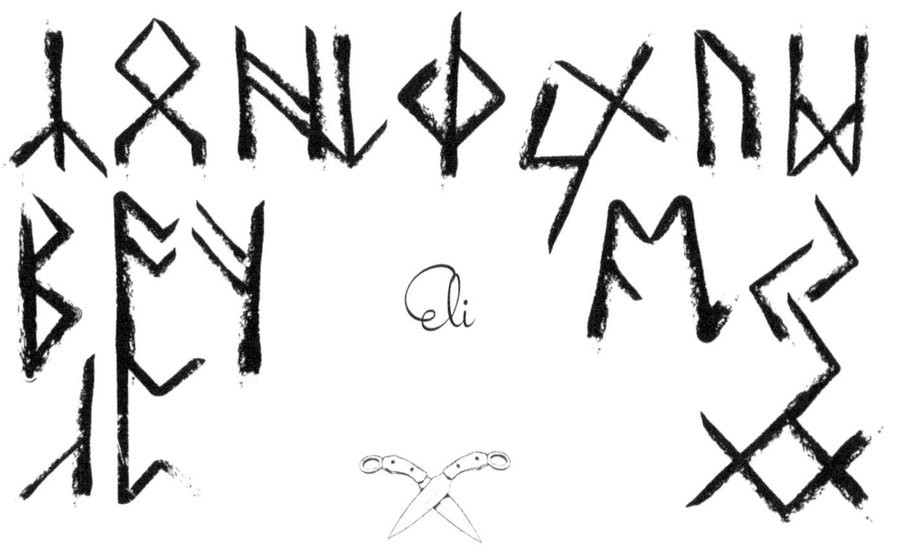

Eli

The demon pulls out of her reverently, and Selene makes a soft, broken noise. Her body trembles under his, lips parted in a dazed little sigh. Blissed out, glowing, *completely wrecked*, she doesn't stir when he leaves her there–bare, bloody and spread open on the altar like a fucking gift.

With the strength of our bonds, she brought the demon to Middlesborough. And the demon, in his infinite power, has freed the bonds *and* removed the binds. The younglings in the field are no better off. They stumble through the grass, clutching at their chests, their heads, their arms. Some are screaming. Others try to run, *unaware* that it activates the '*hunt*' buried inside the men who watch them. The urge flares when one of the younglings dashes away. The masked men lunge forward, teeth bared, hands closing around whatever piece of skin they can reach.

Every muscle in my body screams at me to move, to grab Selene, to *run*. But I can't... not while the demon is watching her. *Once he looks away though....*

The High Priestess rises, clutching at her chest and stomping towards the demon. Those glowing, inhuman eyes find her, and he cocks his head, narrowing his gaze. He moves — not fast, he doesn't need to be. He steps off the altar, tucks himself back into his cloth without breaking eye contact, and walks toward her.

"You *liste–*"

He reaches the Priestess, fists a hand in the pristine fabric of her dress, and *yanks*. She stumbles, gasping, but she doesn't fight it.

No, she *smiles*.

Is everyone here fucking insane?

Jace moves first. I don't know if it's something pulling his strings or instinct, but he's locked on the demon. Not merely curious, but like he wants to *join* him.

"We shouldn't be leaving," he murmurs quietly. *It's not his voice.* It's flatter, colder. Empty of *Jace*. He doesn't glance back at us as he gets to his feet. Doesn't bother to check and see if we follow him. I look at Max, but he's too busy staring at Selene and fuming. Luke's tense, eyes darting from Selene to Jace, as if he can't decide who to worry about more. But *me*? I feel the change through our bond. A dark tunnel, warping as every second passes, pushing him further beyond reach.

I personally don't give a *fuck* about the demon right now.

I care about the thing wearing my pack mate's skin.

Jace starts walking toward the demon. Max and Luke snap out of it the same moment I do, the three of us scrambling up, staggering to the altar. She hasn't moved. She's a boneless mess, slick with sweat, streaked in dried blood, skin dotted in bruises where the demon's mouth had been.

It makes my chest burn with *rage*.

Luke's hands slide under her back, hauling her into his arms like she weighs nothing. Max follows, gripping her legs, supporting her lower half. They move in sync with the understanding that *this* is our only opportunity to get her back.

Away from him.

Selene hangs between them, her head lolling against Luke's shoulder. She's acting *drunk*, lost in whatever blissed-out haze the demon placed her in. She makes quiet sounds, *little whimpering sighs*, that tell me she's enjoying whatever she's experiencing. Max tightens his hold, one arm under her knees, the other hand splayed wide on her thigh like he's *desperate* for contact.

I risk a look back, and instantly regret it. Jace is walking toward *him*, to the demon, who still has The High Priestess in his grasp. And Jace? He's calm. He's *willing*.

We creep back into The Temple to catch our breath. Luke adjusts his grip, jaw flexing as he sneaks a glance at Jace from around the corner. Something inside of me is *screaming* to **get the fuck away**, but I wait for his lead. Having the pack dynamic back, and my *own* alpha, settles something I thought I'd been deprived of. I'd been without it for so long, I'd started to accept that part of me was *never* coming back.

"Tell me I'm not the only one who thinks something's *wrong* with him," Luke pleads as he sticks his face in Selene's neck to take a deep breath. I watch Jace fall to his knees a few feet away, and bow his head. His mouth is moving, but we're too far away to hear what he tells the demon. I bite my lip, and search through the bond. Jace is there, hidden in the tunnel, but it's *sour*. Coated in fresh *rot*. He's got a wall up so that I can't pull on him.

"You're not," I agree, even though it tastes wrong.

Luke swears under his breath as we sit in the shadows. "You think it's the demon?"

Yeah. I *really* fucking do.

I don't like the way gentle, steady, *'fix-everything-with-a-smile'*, Jace is on his *knees* for that creature, watching him choke the *life* out of The High Priestess like it's *nothing*. Like the chaos of it all isn't even registering for him anymore. The younglings are screaming, fighting their way from those masked bastards. Some are sobbing, others kicking and biting, desperate to be free of the hands that drag them down.

A mockery of the mating games I grew up witnessing.

The bonds are freed from their binds. The entirety of Middlesborough will be eating itself *alive* come dawn.

Jace just *watches*. Not one flicker of concern. I take a step forward before I can stop myself.

"We *have* to go back for him."

Luke's on me before I'm finished speaking, blocking me from rushing out.

"No," he says, firm. His voice warbles, as if he's *trying* to command me, but can't muster it. It drives my anger higher. I might not be the alpha male of our pack, but he named me *second*. I *could* take the pack from him—

"No?" I snap. "He's *ours*, Luke."

His glassy eyes dart to where Max holds Selene. "So is *she*."

I look over my shoulder. Max hasn't moved, holding our girl to his chest. He looks *torn*, caught in the middle. His eyes are locked on Jace, as if he's willing to run straight through fire, but I can tell that he *won't*.

He's bent to Luke already. There is *no* coming back from that.

"Eli," Luke warns. "We don't have *time*."

I face Jace again. The way he prostrates like a lamb, ready for slaughter. That's not *our* healer. That's absolutely something else living in there and pretending to be *mine*.

"I'm not leaving him like this," I mumble, taking another step forward. Luke's hand comes down on my shoulder, and my knees lock up.

"You **are**," he snaps, voice cutting through the air, "or we are all going to *die* here."

I *know* he's right. My body bucks forward, heaving until bile and blood splash against the wall.

And maybe whatever that cunt did to me. Maybe it's guilt.

Maybe it's *both*.

I wipe my mouth, trembling. Luke's hand is cold on my neck, wiping away the sweat. The bond dares to whisper *'pack'* and *'mate'*, intent on mocking me. Jace's thread pulses once, sick and *toxic*.

I grit my teeth, spit the bitterness from my mouth, and force myself upright.

We've gotta get out of here while we still can.

Rhy

The Priestess doesn't care that I've got her slender throat in my hands, or that I can kill her with a single word. She dangles there, gasping for breath, fingers curled weakly around my wrist.

Pathetic.

She's not *fighting*, which *irritates* me beyond belief.

How *dare* she attempt to bind me to her brittle, *unworthy* soul?

How *dare* she interrupt my reunion with The Seraph's ancient spirit, or my rightful claim over her pitiful mortal pets?

These fucking mortals... they never *learn*.

They *kneel*, they *pray*, they *bleed*.

And yet, they *dare*.

And now, because I'm dealing with *her*, the vermin have torn *Selene* from my altar and slipped into The Temple. She can't go far, not now that she's had my knot inside her. She'll be *desperate* for more, and only *I* can provide relief. If they don't want her to die, they'll have to come crawling back, and I'll force them to beg for my forgiveness *before* I fuck her.

In front of them.

Then after, I'll force each of *them* to take my cock as well.

Teach *them* a lesson in disobedience.

Just like last time—how *quickly* they broke beneath me.

Although, now that *I've* tasted her, I'm not so sure I want to *wait* for the pests to come to their senses regarding my Domina. I'll have to fetch her once I'm finished with *this*.

"Dominus," the one called Jace whispers from behind me. I turn slightly to acknowledge him. "Do you want me to follow them?"

I *could*, but I'd rather show him what *I* can do first. I ignore him, looking back to the Priestess. She's turning pale, her eyes bulging while her nails scrape at my skin. *Now* she tries to speak–a wet, choking bubble that can't get over my grip. I watch her suffer, enjoying the panic behind her eyes.

What could she *possibly* want to say that might change my mind? A prayer? A *plea*?

I loosen my grip. Not out of mercy–*I was never the merciful one*– but curiosity.

Let her waste her final breath.

"Speak, Priestess, and tell me why you believed you could bind my soul to yours," I command. "Be quick. You've wasted enough of my time."

"My body is yours, my soul is yours," she whispers, tears streaming down her swollen face. She isn't crying from fear. *No.* The stupid bitch is joyous. "My death is your birthright. Take me, and may the world tremble at your return."

My lips curl into a feral smile. "You think you could have earned a place beside me?" I rumble, suppressing an eye roll. "You give yourself to me, yes. But you don't *understand* who you serve. My will is *not* yours to command. Mortals will *always* be a tool for my race."

Her smile falters as she processes my words. She kicks her feet as my grip tightens again.

"The world will not *tremble* at my return," I say. My arm shakes as I squeeze as tight as I can, feeling the cracking in her throat. "It will *burn*."

The High Priestess stills as I steal her breath, *her very soul*, and swallow it down.

In the end, she's as worthless to me as I suspected.

Hardly a mouthful.

I toss her body into the flames, which grow higher as I fuel them with my fury. The younglings are starting to scatter, taking with them the Hollowed Horns and their masks. The screams are music to my ears, an echo of my home in Tartarus. I wonder if I should force them to copulate under the sky as the Old Ways demand but–

Now isn't the time to force the fools to dance.

Selene's side of our link pulls taut as she's taken further from me, and I roar.

She. Is. Mine.

As long as she doesn't carry my child, I remain tethered to this realm, able to walk the soil and shape it into my *own* Tartarus. My *own* reckoning. Power sits beneath my skin, crackling like storm fire. I clench my fists to keep from tearing another veil too soon, to keep from summoning a legion now, before she's returned to me.

I turn around, rolling my neck.

Jace kneels, head bowed, chest rising and falling in slow, steady breaths. There's no resistance, only acceptance. I reach out telepathically through the thread I left behind, and feel it *pulsing* like spoiled blood. *Warped. Tangled.* A virus planted directly in a mate web. He is *mine*, bent to *my* will. A few quick manipulations, and I tie him to the string I planted in Selene. The new web in my chest beats like a second heart, obedient and *bruised*.

My favorite flavor.

The Unmaking *worked*. I didn't doubt it, but I haven't created one in a millennium, not since the last realm I reduced to ash and marrow. It was *easier* than I could have hoped for. Mortal minds crack open like weak organs when you press hard enough in the right places. He was *dying*–to slip inside him took little effort. And Selene begged *so beautifully* to save him....

I search along *his* tether for the others.

The dark-skinned warrior. Their cold-hearted stray. The weakened leader.

I slam into *stone*. Bricked over by a *pathetic* mortal dissent that must have been placed there *before* I planted the seed. Sealed like a fucking tomb, and *useless. How the fuck did he create a seal–*

No matter.

The healer will be enough for now. The Seraph, *my darling Seris,* will be returned to me, and she will *cling* to him for her own sanity. One will be better than *none*.

And his skills in crafting human medication will come in handy.

My rage doesn't subside, not entirely. It burns *deep*, biting at my bones, wrapping its way up my spine. Something else curls alongside it, something sweeter, *richer*.

Satisfaction.

"They took her from me... and *you* stayed," I murmur, stepping closer. I bend forward to press two fingers beneath his chin, tilting his face up. His pupils are blown wide, rimmed in a red ring. He parts his mouth slightly, his body shuddering from my presence.

He doesn't shy away.

Good.

I drag my thumb over his lower lip, watching how his tongue chases my touch.

"And tell me, little wound," I whisper, savoring his shiver. "How does it *feel*? Does it *ache* for me?"

Oh yes.... My deepest condolences. (Lies). But before you scream, cry, and carve my name into your walls in unholy rage—Book Two is coming. And if you thought this was chaos? Oh, darling... This was just foreplay. Hold onto your soul.

You're gonna need it.

Translations

HIGH PRIESTESS CHANTS IN CHAPTER 42:
VELOS AI'TAREN. KESHTI RENAI. FORTHU VEN'ASHAI. (BLOOD GIVEN, BOND AWAKENED, LET THE GATE BE OPEN)

VASHAN TRETHAI. LUTHIEL SARAI. KESHTI VORATH. (SHADOW TO SHADOW, FLESH TO FLESH, RISE FROM THE ABYSS)

HIGH PRIESTESS MODIFIED CHANTS IN CHAPTER 42:
ZARETH ON'VALESH. KESHTI VERATHAI. MOROS AI'SHAR. (BLOOD GIVEN, BOND AWAKENED, LET THE GATE BE MINE)

SHAI'THERON VESHAL. VORTHU REN'DAI. DRAESH KEL'VERAN. (SHADOW TO SHADOW, FLESH TO FLESH, BOW BEFORE MY HANDS)

VORATH TRAVAI. LUTHIEL SARAI. KESHTI DOMINAI. (THE PATH IS CARVED, THE SACRIFICE MADE, SERVE YOUR DOMINA)

<u>RHY</u> IN CHAPTER 42:
VASHTI REN'AI MORATH! VESHAL DAI'THOREN, KEL'DRATH ON'VERAS?! DRAESH AI'VORAN, SHAI'THEL MORAS. (YOU DARE CHANGE THE RITUAL? THINK I WOULD NOT NOTICE?! FOOLISH PRIESTESS, YOU SEAL YOUR OWN FATE)

VERAS KAI'THELAN... DRASUN DEL'MERA... SA'KNAL COR'KAI. (THE SACRED BONDS ARE FREE, THE SOUL UNBOUND)

<u>RHY</u> IN CHAPTER 44:
"VELKAR'ETH SUL'DORAI. SHAL VREN'DAE THRENAKAI. (NOW ARE THE TIES OF FATE UNDONE)

<h1 style="text-align:center">Acknowledgments</h1>

First off, if you're reading this, **_<u>THANK YOU</u>_**. Whether you devoured every page or just skipped to the spicy bits (no judgements), you made it here, and that means *everything* to me.

To my **_<u>husband</u>_** — thanks for putting up with my endless ramblings about fictional people as if they were real. (*They're real to me, okay?*) Also, apologies for the sleep-deprived calls at 2AM that just said "BUT WHAT IF–" and spiraled from there.

But more than that—thank you for being my eternal soulmate. For matching my fire, grounding my chaos, and loving every strange and beautiful part of me without question. You are my passion, my peace, and my greatest plot twist.

My grand adventure.

Even when the path was hard, you've stood beside me and never asked me to be *anything* but *entirely* myself. Even when it felt impossible, you kept walking with me—hand in hand, heart wide open. I would be nothing without you.

And I wouldn't want to be.

To my *incredible* sister and artist, **AudiArt** — I still don't know how I got lucky enough to be blessed with a sister as talented, brilliant, and creative as you. Somehow, you looked at a real photo and turned it into something so breathtaking. The cover is absolutely *insane* (in the best way possible), and the chapter headers? I mean, come on—they're so gorgeous it's *unfair*. Your art didn't just elevate this book—it *became* part of its soul. Every brushstroke, every detail, every design choice shows how much heart you poured into it, and I will never be able to thank you enough for that. I'm proud of this book.
But I'm even prouder to call you my sibling.
Thank you for making my words look beautiful.

To ***The Indie Author Revolution*** – You brought me in when I needed more than just a place to belong. You gave me community. You offered your guidance when I was lost in the shadows of doubt. Through every rough draft, you stood with me. You gave me a purpose, reminded me *why* my words mattered, and *what* they could build. You gave me friendship, the kind that sees *past* competition and *lifts others* ***without*** hesitation. To the authors, the narrators, the illustrators, the editors—to every one of you who chose to stand *beside* each other rather than *above*: <u>THANK YOU.</u>
You helped me find my voice. And *more* importantly?
You helped me **believe** in it.

To my proofreader, **Spite and Spite Ink** — thank you for believing in this chaotic little dream of mine. Your patience, expertise and notes have made this story what it is.

To my friends, **Kasey and Crystal** — Life isn't always kind, but you were. Thanks for keeping me sane, for letting our kids run wild together, and for never once judging my coffee (or spicy adult juice) intake.
I am forever thankful for the ballet.

To **Maggii** — Who showed me that stories may shape worlds, but friendship shapes souls. For every late-night, every plot twist unraveled together, and every moment of *unwavering* support, I am **eternally grateful**. You understand that the beauty of chaos is in its destruction. You met the storm inside me with one of your own—not to tame it, but to dance in it beside me. Somehow, your soul recognized mine in all its sharp edges and shadows, and chose to stay. You never asked me to quiet the noise or shrink myself; instead, you matched it—brilliantly, wildly, and without hesitation.

You are my safe place, the person who reminded me that, even in the wreckage, there's someone who will sit with you, laugh with you, and hand you the pen when you're ready to rewrite the ending.

You didn't just support me.

You saved me.

And I love you for it—more than words, more than worlds.

To **my alphas** — Black Dahlia, Milli C. Vieira, A.E. Amaris, and Mavis Kemo —

And **my beta** and **ARC readers**; your reactions, gasps, screaming-all-in-caps messages, and advice gave me *so much life*. I couldn't have done this without you.

To my **BookTok community** – Holy shit, you guys…. Your absolute chaos, enthusiasm, and dedication to screaming about books have been everything. The comments, the DMs, the theories—you all fueled me through this, and I can't thank you enough. If you're here because you saw me being unhinged online… well, welcome to the results of my madness.

To the *music* that kept me going – this book was written to the sounds of The Chaos Within, which you can find on Tidal [https://tidal.com/ browse/playlist/6f325400-880e-40ac-94f5-9a8d478d80ef]. If you want to fully immerse yourself in my insanity, go give it a listen. It's pretty eclectic, and there's no reason behind it. You'll be just as confused as my husband, who listened to it for *hours* with me.

To the silence that followed your absence… I want you to know, this book is proof I didn't **need** you to finish the story.

And finally, to you – ***the readers*** – thank you for stepping into this world with me. If you laughed, cried, or considered running off to join a questionable dystopian commune, my job here is done.
Don't *actually* do that, though. You won't find Max, Jace, Eli, or Luke there. I can promise you that. You *might* find Rhy... but I can't guarantee that'll end the way you think....

Stay feral, read recklessly, and remember: some cult leaders don't want your devotion.
They just want a sacrifice.

About the Author

S.B. Ellie writes books with blood under her nails. A Texas-based author with a taste for the dark and disturbing, she crafts twisted tales full of demons, cults, cursed bonds, and lovers who should probably run faster. Her genre playground includes dark romance, thrillers, horror, and why-choose with tropes that transform into obsession.

She plans to wander into new genres in the future —but don't worry, the darkness is coming with her.

When she's not writing, Ellie is either chasing her kids across the farm, floating in the pool with her husband, or mentally plotting her next fictional sin. She believes in beautiful prose, awful people, and happy endings that don't always happen.

Don't follow her into the woods. You won't come back the same.

tiktok.com/@s.b.ellie_author

amazon.com/stores/S.B.-Ellie/author/B0FDQ59LQW?ref=ap_rdr&is-DramIntegrated=true&shoppingPortalEnabled=true&ccs_id=86e2d038-e267-4796-8857-36bb3db905c0

* 9 7 8 1 9 6 8 7 0 0 0 4 1 *